BLINDED BY LOVE

"Oh, sweet, silent one, you do have a way of getting into a man's blood. Suppose I told you that because of that one night with you, I am able to find a glimmer of happiness?" Tag murmured.

Tag felt hot tears fall on his hand, and he crushed her in his arms while he kissed the tears away. "Do not be sad for me, little one. Just give me a few more hours of forgetfulness. One can ask for no more than that."

Alexandria felt his hand brush against her cheek. "Because I cannot see you in the darkness, I will have to be content with the sense of touch." He outlined her face with his hands. "You have a beautifully shaped face—your hair is curly, and you wear it shorter than most women. Your mouth is full and made for a man's kiss." He proceeded to demonstrate by brushing her mouth with his and then crushing his lips to hers. Moving forward, Alexandria felt as if her body were being absorbed into his. A deep longing filtered through her body, like a slow-burning flame. She could now feel the urgency in him as his lips moved across her face, touching her closed eyelids, whispering against her ear, and then dipping down to nuzzle her neck. She could hear his labored breathing and knew he wanted her, and Alexandria knew that his desire would only be matched by her own!

Savage Spring

CONSTANCE O'BANYON

ZEBRA BOOKS
KENSINGTON PUBLISHING CORP.

ZEBRA BOOKS

are published by

Kensington Publishing Corp.
475 Park Avenue South
New York, NY 10016

First printing: December 1985

Printed in the United States of America

Dedication

For the father confesser of my childhood, my brother, Robert Hoyle, and for the redhead in my life, Larry Henderson.

The Winds of Change

*The winds of time began to blow, they sweep across
the land.*
*The time has come to find his way, for he is now a
man.*
*Although the past still pulls at him, he yearns for his
release,*
But he must go and face a man before he is at peace.
*To leave the land he loves so well, to seek the great
unknown —*
*The time is now, he must be brave, for he will walk
alone.*

Constance O'Banyon

Chapter One

Philadelphia, October 1847

Claudia Landon floated from group to group chattering happily. She had become famous for giving the most elaborate parties in all Philadelphia, and she was in her element when playing hostess.

Her laughter bubbled out when she was caught from behind, by a gentleman whose wife had not attended the party tonight. Sam Boyer had been pursuing Claudia for some weeks now, and when he planted a kiss on the nape of her neck she shivered with delight. Realizing others were watching, she tapped her overamorous guest playfully on the shoulder with her fan.

"Sam, what will the others thinks?" she asked in a throaty voice, giving him her most beguiling smile.

"Meet me later," he whispered near her ear.

Claudia only smiled at him before she walked over to a group of ladies who had their heads together gossiping.

"Are you having fun?" she inquired of the ladies, playing the perfect hostess. She knew the old crows would like nothing better than to see her fall on her face. They came to her parties only because everyone who was anyone came. She endured them because they brought respectability to these affairs.

"Claudia, my dear, what a lovely gown you have on. You must tell me who your dressmaker is so I can give her my patronage," one of the women said.

"I would be happy to give you her name; she lives in Paris, you know. As you are aware, I go to Paris each spring to have a new wardrobe made up."

The woman's eyes narrowed jealously. "Tell me, my dear, how does your husband feel about your going out of the country? I understand he is an invalid. Why is it that we never see him?"

"Yes, poor dear Howard had a stroke some years past that left him partially paralyzed. His speech is garbled, and he never sees visitors."

"You are to be commended for taking such good care of him. I understand that you also look after the large shipping business. Surely, that can be a trial for a woman?"

"I have no choice, Mrs. Hammond. Someone has to do the job. You know how hard it is to get honest workers. If I didn't keep my finger on the pulse of the business, they would rob me blind."

"I understand that the business doesn't really belong to you or your husband. It is rumored that everything belongs to distant relatives, and you and your husband are merely the custodians," Mrs. Hammond said.

Claudia watched as the women's eyes gleamed with obvious satisfaction. Mrs. Hammond had found and hit Claudia's one vulnerable spot. "One should not listen to rumors, Mrs. Hammond," Claudia said, moving away. The fun had suddenly gone out of the party for her. All she wanted was for everyone to just go home.

When the last guest had departed, Claudia made her way upstairs. She stopped before her husband's bedroom door and opened it quietly. She tiptoed to his bed thinking he was asleep, then saw that his eyes were open staring at the portrait that hung over his fireplace. She had hung the portrait of the James family in Howard's room, thinking to irritate him, but his eyes were always glued to it, and it was beginning to irritate *her* instead. She followed his eyes and knew he would be staring at Joanna James.

"You just can't get her out of your mind, can you, Howard? How does it feel to look at her day after day and know you can never have her? How does it feel to know that she preferred her Indian lover to you?"

Howard turned red in the face, and Claudia felt she might have pushed him too far. Above all, she had to keep Howard alive. Only through him was she able to control the Jameses' empire. Should he die, she would be out in the cold. She smiled to herself at how people called her the devoted wife looking after an invalid husband. What they didn't know was that she was tied to Howard for the rest of her life. They also didn't know that at night many of her lovers came up the backstairs and made their way to her bedroom. She had learned to be discreet, since she didn't want any scandal to touch her life.

"You are not to upset yourself, Howard. We must take the best of care of you." She leaned forward and placed a kiss on his forehead, and his angry eyes showed his distaste.

"Poor Howard, you do so hate being married to me, don't you? Don't I take such good care of you? Don't I see that Cook prepares your favorite meals? Don't I allow that portrait of Joanna to hang in your room so you can just stare at her all day?"

Howard closed his eyes, cursing the sickness that had made him an invalid. He wished for strength so he could strangle the life out of Claudia. Yes, he was grateful for the portrait—it was the one thing that kept him alive. He had to stay alive long enough to see Joanna and Tag return so they could take care of Claudia. Claudia hated Joanna and Tag—Howard knew she feared that one day they would come back to Philadelphia and she would have to face them. Once he had schemed and planned, trying to steal the James fortune from them, but now he wanted only to see them get it back.

Claudia tucked the covers about Howard's neck and walked over to the lamp that burned below the portrait. She would have blown it out, but Howard showed his disapproval with a guttural grunt. She shrugged her shoulders and walked toward the door.

"If you want to spend your nights and days staring at Joanna, far be it from me to complain. After all, you have so few pleasures in life now. Didn't I leave Joanna's room just as she left it—as you asked me to? Don't I look the other way when you have Barlow carry you into that damned room so you can feel close to her?" Claudia smiled as she moved across the room. "Goodnight, Howard. I hope you will sleep well."

After Claudia had gone, Howard's eyes returned to the portrait of beautiful Joanna. If ever a man was

12

obsessed by anyone, he was obsessed by Joanna. In his mind he would talk to the picture, and in his mind she would answer him back. Each day would bring new hope that Tag and Joanna would return to claim what belonged to them. Howard knew they would come sooner or later, and his only hope was that he would be alive to witness their return.

Howard thought of the past when he had driven Joanna and Tag away from their home. Even then he had been obsessed by Joanna's loveliness. If only he hadn't tried to make impossible demands on her and Tag at the time, perhaps they never would have left.

What good did it do to dwell on past mistakes, he wondered, knowing it wouldn't change anything.

Howard Landon was now a sick old man with nothing to keep him company but his memories. His eyes became heavy, and he closed them, wishing he could have just one night's restful sleep. He had nothing to live for, except the hope that Joanna and Tag would return to Philadelphia.

He felt a chill move over his body and shivered. "Come soon, Tag and Joanna," he whispered. "Come home before I die, so I can make up to you for the past."

The old man slipped off into an unrestful sleep. His dreams were haunted by the girl in the portrait.

When Claudia reached her bedroom, she sank down into a chair, leaned her head back, and closed her eyes. For some reason she didn't find the parties fun anymore. She was becoming discontented with her life. Why couldn't she be happy when she had everything she had ever wanted: money, power, and many friends.

13

Standing up, she removed her gown and tossed it onto the foot of the bed. She knew why she wasn't happy. None of this belonged to her—it all belonged to Joanna and Taggart James.

Sitting down on the foot of the bed, she removed her stockings and shoes and dropped them to the floor. Sometimes the hatred that burned in her heart for Joanna and Tag seemed like the only real thing in her life. Claudia smiled to herself—soon she would be free of Joanna and Tag for good. She had already found the means to send them both to their deaths. She was waiting for word from the three men whom she had sent to rid her of her two most hated enemies.

She lay back on her bed and smiled to herself. How wonderful her life would be when she no longer had to fear Joanna and Tag.

Hearing a fumbling at the door, Claudia sat up and watched as Sam Boyer entered the room. "Why, Sam, what are you doing here?" she purred.

"You knew I would come," he said, advancing toward her.

"What about your wife?" she asked, as he stood above her allowing his eyes to roam over her body.

"My wife is gone and you are here," he told her, lowering his body on top of hers.

As Sam Boyer found her lips, Claudia closed her eyes. For a time she could find forgetfulness in Sam's arms. For now she could forget about Joanna and Tag.

Blackfoot Territory

Taggart James sat beside the Milk River, absent-mindedly skipping stones across the smooth surface.

14

It was a cold October morning, and he could see huge chunks of ice floating down the river. Raising his eyes, he looked toward the distant mountains, which were snow-covered and had the appearance of a huge, impregnable fortress. Those mountains seemed to divide and protect the Blackfoot Territory from the rest of the world.

He sighed inwardly as his eyes moved to the dense forest where he knew the snow would still be very deep. The countryside had the appearance of a winter wonderland, and his heart was filled with the majesty and beauty of it all.

Lately, however, there had been a restlessness within Tag, and while he tried to ignore the feeling, it gnawed at his insides day and night.

Tag stood up, revealing the fact that he was very tall. The morning sunlight reflected off his golden shoulder-length hair, which was encircled with a wide leather headband. His face was deeply tanned, emphasizing his deep blue eyes, which were framed with long, dark eyelashes. His face was ruggedly handsome—there were dimples in his cheeks that would make themselves known whenever he smiled or frowned. The buckskin shirt Tag wore fit snugly across his broad shoulders, and his buckskin trousers shaped his long, muscular legs. He wore fur-skinned moccasins that were laced to the calves of his legs.

Tag seemed to have no control of his thoughts as his mind began to drift back in time. He remembered his life as a boy, and the wonderful adventure he had shared with his family when they had first moved to Philadelphia from England. He remembered vividly

15

when his mother had died of the lung sickness and his father had been killed in the far-off Oregon Country. He could still feel the same helplessness he had felt when he and his sister, Joanna, had been left at the mercy of their Uncle Howard, who was a cruel and bitter man. Tag could still see Howard Landon's face so clearly in his mind that sometimes he had a strong urge to return to Philadelphia and face the man who had robbed him of his birthright.

Tag's father, Russell James, had left Tag and Joanna a considerable fortune. There was the huge shipbuilding factory in Philadelphia, not to mention the export business, with a fleet of ships that sailed all over the world. But Uncle Howard now controlled the James empire, and Tag could feel his hatred for the man like an ache deep inside him. In truth, Howard Landon wasn't even really Tag's uncle. He had married Tag's Aunt Margaret, who was now dead.

Tag knew is uncle had no legal hold on the James estate, and he wondered why he didn't return to Philadelphia to face Howard Landon and assume his rightful place as head of the James empire.

Nine years had passed since Taggart had first come to live with the Blood Blackfoot tribe. After the wagon train he and his sister, Joanna, had been traveling with had been attacked by hostile Indians, Windhawk's tribe had given him and Joanna a home.

Joanna had married Windhawk, the legendary chief of the Blackfoot, and had found great happiness with him. Windhawk and Joanna now had a son and a daughter, and Joanna was content to stay with her husband, feeling no ties pulling her back to the white world.

Tag thought of his wife, Morning Song, who was the lovely sister of Windhawk. They were expecting a child. Though he loved Morning Song, there was something that kept tugging at him, drawing him back to the past. Inside his heart, there burned a strong bitterness and hatred toward the man who had robbed him and Joanna of their birthright. Although he tried to push his troubled thoughts aside, still, he yearned for revenge against his Uncle Howard. He knew deep in his heart that the time would come when he would have to face Howard Landon—and that one of them must die!

Inside Tag there raged a war, and he tried hard to put his troubled thoughts aside. But no matter how he tried, the past still pulled at him, and he couldn't seem to find the peace of mind he yearned for. Not even in the arms of the woman he loved could he block out the desire for revenge that burned in his heart. He knew he was torn between his loyalty for Morning Song and his need to right an old wrong.

Gazing downriver, Tag caught a glimpse of a magnificent stag bending its head to drink from the icy waters. Tag was suddenly overcome with the beauty and serenity of this land. How could he leave everything he loved to return to a world to which he no longer belonged? Here in this land where the Blackfoot dwelled, Tag had found love and a certain amount of contentment. He watched as the stag lifted its head and tested the wind. No, he thought, he wouldn't go to Philadelphia . . . his life was here now. He was married to Morning Song. How could he leave her when she was expecting his child at any time? Let

Howard Landon keep the James empire—Tag doubted it would bring the man happiness.

Tag watched the stag as it bounded up the hill, feeling a closeness with the animal. He, too, was a part of this land. The white world in which he had been born had no hold on him. Here, in the Blackfoot lands, he had found what most men search for all their lives without finding. He had love and peace of mind—except at those times when he couldn't control his thoughts and they drifted to his Uncle Howard.

Hearing footsteps behind him, Tag smiled to himself. His Indian training had allowed him to tell the difference in the way people walked. He could tell that the soft moccasin steps approaching him were those of a woman, and he knew it would be Morning Song.

"What kept you, my love? I have been waiting for you," he said, turning around and opening his arms to her.

Tag watched as Morning Song smiled at him. He drew in his breath as he looked into her dark eyes. Never had he met a girl who had her soft, gentle beauty. There was almost an aura about her as if she almost didn't belong to this world. Her ebony hair was worn loose and spilled down her back. Her features were soft and delicate, and her dark eyes were shining with love for him. Morning Song barely came to his shoulder. Small in stature, she carried herself straight and tall. His heart warmed at the smile she gave him.

She threw herself into his outstretched arms and beamed up at him. "I love you, my husband." She laid her soft cheek against his rough one, reveling in his strength when he swung her into his arms.

18

"Always love me, Morning Song." His voice was deep, and he tightened his arms about her. "Never stop loving me!"

She reached up and framed his handsome face with her hands. Sometimes it was still hard for Morning Song to believe that this young golden god loved her and that she was his wife. "Oh, Tag, I love you more than life itself. To stop loving you, I would have to die."

He gave her a heart-warming smile. "Why do you never call me by my Indian name, Morning Song?" he asked, kissing her on the cheek.

She laced her hands through his golden hair. "To the rest of the tribe, you are Night Falcon—but to me, you will always be my Tag."

He laughed heartily and set her on her feet. "You and Joanna will always keep me in my place by reminding me who I am, will you not?"

Morning Song smiled mischievously. "As long as your place is beside me."

Tag allowed his eyes to roam over Morning Song. Her doeskin gown was fringed and beaded with blue beads and green porcupine quills. The fullness of the gown hid the fact that she was carrying his child. Tag reached for her and clasped her tightly against him, feeling the roundness of her stomach. Turning her around, he molded her backside against him and lightly caressed her swollen stomach.

"I am getting anxious for the child to be born. It will be a new and exciting experience to be a father," he told her tenderly.

"You will not have long to wait, my husband. My mother says the child will be delivered before the new

19

moon," Morning Song told him.

"In that case, we had better see that you do not overwork. I want you to start taking better care of yourself. I will see that Joanna and your mother help you."

"Please do not say anything to them. Already my mother and your sister treat me as an invalid. I am very strong and can take care of my duties to you and our tipi without help. I like doing things for you, my husband."

His laughter was deep as he took her arm and led her back to the village. As always, his laughter was infectious, and Morning Song felt her heart growing lighter. Tag had filled her life with laughter and happiness. She knew no one could possibly be as happy as she was.

By the time they reached the village, it had begun to snow. Tag lifted Morning Song into his arms and carried her into their tipi. Once inside, he laid her down and dropped down beside her. Morning Song shivered with feelings of delight as his hand trailed down her neck and across her breasts to rest on her stomach. She saw desire fan to life in the depths of his blue eyes and felt an answering longing within herself.

"Hurry and have our child, Morning Song. I want to make love to you."

She touched a strand of his hair. "I, too, want this. You will not have to wait too much longer, my husband."

Tag pulled away from her, knowing he must put his desire aside before it raged out of control. Morning Song was too near her delivery date for him to make love to her.

"Perhaps I should take another wife to satisfy the fire that burns within me," he said teasingly. Tag watched the pain dance fleetingly across Morning Song's face, and was immediately sorry that his teasing had hurt her.

"It is your right to take another wife if you so desire," she whispered through trembling lips.

Tag tilted her face up to him, and a tear dropped onto his hand. "My sweet Morning Song—I will never have any need for another wife—I was but jesting. I shall live to be an old man without ever having loved any woman but you. Have we not loved each other since we were children?"

Morning Song nodded, unable to speak for a moment. "I would not object if you were to enforce your right in taking another wife," she said with effort.

He smiled. "I think no one would want to be a wife to me. If I took another, all she would ever do would be the cooking and cleaning while I lay on the mat with you."

Morning Song laughed delightedly. "I was not telling the truth when I said I wouldn't mind, Tag. I do not like the thought of your touching another woman."

Tag leaned forward and captured her lips with his. A warmth and contentment spread throughout his body. When Morning Song was in his arms, he could forgot about the restlessness for a time.

Morning Song turned her head and kissed his cheek. "Tag, I know of this feeling inside you that will not give you peace. I feel this part of you that cries out to the white world. If it is your wish to go and face this

21

thing that causes your unrest, I will understand. Go and settle this thing between you and your uncle. I will wait for you to return."

Tag pulled her tightly against him. He had not been aware that Morning Song sensed his troubled thoughts. He should have known he could hide nothing from her.

"I will never leave you. One day I will come to terms with what my uncle did to me and Joanna. Bear with me until that day, Morning Song."

"Tag, you have never told me what your uncle did to you and Joanna. I have never asked because I thought if you wanted to talk about it, you would come to me."

"It is not that I was trying to keep anything from you, Morning Song. I did not want to trouble you with my problems, and I never wanted the ugliness to touch my life with you."

"Do you not know by now that your troubles are my troubles, Tag? Share this thing with me so you will not have to carry it alone."

He sat up and looked toward the tipi opening. "It is not a pretty story, Morning Song."

"More the reason you should not carry it alone," she said, laying her head in his lap and clasping his hand in hers.

He looked down at her, and Morning Song could see the pain in the depth of his blue eyes. "Yes, perhaps if I share it with you, it will help." His eyes took on a faraway look as if he were remembering.

"Morning Song, Joanna and I were born in a place called England. It is a very long way from here . . . across the big waters."

"I know about England—Joanna showed me a

picture in one of your books. The United States once belonged to England."

"Yes, that is right," Tag said, smiling at how well Joanna had taught Morning Song her history. Joanna had also taught her to read and write, an accomplishment of which his little wife was very proud.

"Joanna and I sailed to America with our mother and father when we were but children. My father was a successful shipbuilder, and he had moved his headquarters to this country," Tag said, slipping from the Blackfoot language into English without even realizing it.

"For a time, we were happy, even though my father was hardly ever home, as his business took him all over the world. When I was but twelve, my mother died. Her death came at a time when my father was away. Little did Joanna and I know at that time that our father would soon be dead also and our fate would be in the hands of our unscrupulous Uncle Howard."

"What does unscrupulous mean, Tag?"

"It means a man who has no qualms about what is right and wrong. My uncle wanted my family's fortune. You see, my father was a very wealthy man, and as his heir, I would inherit all that had belonged to him."

"I know that your uncle once captured Joanna and tried to take her back to the white world, but Windhawk saved her."

"Yes, that's right. Uncle Howard would do anything to get his hands on me and Joanna. You see, he cannot have what, by rights, belongs to me. He can only be in charge of the estate until I return to reclaim it."

Morning Song's eyes seemed to cloud over. "If you went back, you would live in one of the grand houses that Joanna showed me in a picture book. I can see why you are often troubled."

"That isn't what troubles me, Morning Song. It's the fact that my uncle stole from me and Joanna. That is very hard for me to accept. At times, I feel this anger inside that such a man is living in my home." Unconsciously, his hand drifted down to rest against Morning Song's swollen stomach. "By robbing me of my birthright, my uncle has also stolen our child's birthright."

Morning Song laid her face against his hand. "I am so sorry that this thing was done to you and Joanna. It is not right for a man to steal from another. It is very bad that such a man should not be punished."

He smiled down at her. "Feel no sadness for me, Morning Song. I am happy here with you. I would not want to give up my life with you to return to the white world."

Morning Song was wise enough to look into her husband's heart. She knew she had made him happy, but there were times, like now, that he seemed to be pulled in two directions. She knew if it were not for her, Tag would return to reclaim what belonged to him. She also knew Tag would never be completely happy until this thing with his uncle was settled, and it saddened her greatly.

"I know that you and Joanna were traveling on a wagon train when my brother, Windhawk, first saw you," she said, trying to distract Tag's troubled thoughts. "My brother told me he loved Joanna from that first day."

"Yes, your brother and my sister have the perfect marriage. Each loves the other above all else. It warms my heart just to be near them. My sister has been able to put the past behind her, while I have not."

Tears gathered in Morning Song's doelike eyes. "If only I had the power in me, I would erase all your unhappiness, my husband. If I thought it would make you happy, I would release you from our marriage so you would be free to return to the white world."

Tag drew in a shuddering breath and held her close to him. "You are my happiness, Morning Song. Never say this to me again," he said, lapsing back into the Blackfoot language.

Morning Song's tears were wet against Tag's face, and he knew that he couldn't be happy without her. He had never known anyone with her goodness. She was the only totally unselfish person he had ever known. Her kindness to others was well known throughout the Blackfoot tribe.

"Do not let what I told you make you sad, Morning Song. Life is not always fair, but one can always have a certain amount of control over his destiny. My destiny is here with you and our unborn child. Never doubt that I love you, and that this is where I want to be."

His lips covered hers, and Morning Song put all the love she felt for him into her kiss. This was a man like no other. He was so well respected in the Blood Blackfoot tribe that it was rumored he would one day be war chief—a title that went to only the strongest and bravest warriors . . . never before had it gone to a

25

white man. But Tag had proven himself to be worthy of the Blackfoot, and if he had an enemy among the fierce warriors, Morning Song was unaware of it.

Morning Song could not help but wish that Tag would find the same happiness and serenity that his sister, Joanna, had. Joanna never seemed to think about the past. She was happy and contented as Windhawk's wife. The love that she and Windhawk shared was so beautiful that it seemed to reach out to those around them, drawing them into its circle.

Closing her eyes, she wished with all her heart that the child she was carrying would bring Tag the peace he sought. She was wise beyond her young years, and she realized that she could only occupy a part of Tag's heart.

Morning Song knew deep in her heart that one day Tag would have to return to the white world to find peace within himself. Perhaps when he left she would lose him, and he would never want to return. But until that time, she would love him and take what love he gave to her. She knew that she loved Tag more than he loved her, although she doubted that Tag was aware of that fact.

Tag smiled down at her, and she felt her heart melt. Oh, yes, she could hold him for now . . . but not forever.

Chapter Two

Joanna smiled to herself when her son, Little Hawk, came rushing into the lodge with his dark eyes shining brightly. He was a small replica of his father and such a joy to her. Little hawk grabbed her about the waist and giggled up into her face. "I love you, Mother," he said, as his eyes danced with mischief.

"I love you, too, but I would love you even more if your face were clean. What have you been doing to get so muddy?" she wanted to know. Joanna pushed a dark strand of hair out of his face, and finding a clean spot on his cheek, kissed him soundly.

Little Hawk laughed and darted out of the lodge, returning to whatever children's game he had been playing.

Joanna pushed her red-gold hair back from her face and smiled at Windhawk's mother, Sun woman. "That grandson of yours always seems to be getting into trouble. I think Windhawk is too indulgent with him at times."

"He is the son and the grandson of chiefs," Sun Woman said with pride. "It is good for a child to be active—it means he will grow up to be a strong warrior."

27

"I suppose. But he does seem to get into trouble more often than most boys his age."

"I know you are referring to his jumping into the river two moons ago. There was no harm done, and he did prove to the others that he could stay under the icy water longer than they could."

"I have trouble finding as much pride in that accomplishment as you and Windhawk do, my mother. Little Hawk could easily have drowned."

Sun Woman laughed. "But he did not. Instead, he proved himself to be very brave and fearless at the age of only five winters."

Sun Woman noticed that her lovely daughter-in-law was frowning, and she knew Joanna was finding many of the ways in which the Blackfoot raised their children difficult to accept. "Let him go, my daughter. Allow him to run free with the other children. Coddle the new baby, but allow Little Hawk to find his own way."

Joanna sighed. "I will . . . I know I have a tendency to overprotect him, but give me time to accept the Blackfoot ways. They are very different from the way I was brought up, my mother."

Joanna walked over to the cradle and smiled down at her baby daughter, Sky Dancer, who was but two months old. "I believe it will be much easier to raise a daughter than it is a son, my mother."

"It is so Joanna. I myself find great joy in my granddaughter. She will be a comfort to me in my old age. Perhaps Morning Song will have a daughter also."

"You are not old, my mother. I myself cannot keep

28

up with you."

Sun woman stared at Joanna, who looked strangely out of place in the Indian lodge. She lent an elegance to the simple doeskin gown she wore. Sun Woman had watched her son, Windhawk, change from a man who sought happiness but was unable to find it to a truly happy man when he had taken Joanna as his wife. Windhawk was a loving husband and father because of this white woman whom the Blackfoot called Flaming Hair. Joanna was looked up to and revered by the women of the tribe, not only as the wife of the chief, but because she commanded and deserved their respect. No one could say that Joanna was unworthy of their chief.

Joanna handed Sun Woman a warm drink of broth and sat down beside her. "It will not be very long until Tag and Morning Song's baby will be born, my mother. I look forward to the birth."

Sun Woman nodded. "I will have three grandchildren before the full moon has passed. Both of my children are happy with their lives. What more can a woman ask for when she reaches my age?"

Joanna patted the older woman's hand. She loved Sun Woman and was proud that her love was returned. "Tag is so anxious for the child to be born. I believe he will be a very good father."

"This is so. I have not before spoken to you of the pride I have in your brother. He has made my daughter happy. You will know when Sky Dancer grows into a woman, that to see her happy will be a great joy to you."

Joanna smiled slightly. In the Blackfoot tribe, a

29

woman was forbidden to speak directly to her son-in-law. Therefore, Sun Woman had never told Tag how much she admired him. "You know my brother would be glad if he could hear these words from you, my mother. Since he cannot, I will speak them for you."

Sun Woman squeezed Joanna's hand. "I have two daughters and two sons. Although you and Tag are not children of my body, I love you as much as the two children who were born to me."

Before Joanna could answer, the lodge flap was thrown aside and Windhawk entered, carrying his son by the seat of his leather britches. Little Hawk giggled delightedly as his tall father plopped him down in his grandmother's lap.

"Do you know where I found your grandson?" he asked his mother.

"How would I know? Do I look like a shaman that I can read minds?" Sun Woman replied, laughing.

"You might not be so pleased with him if I told you that I found him climbing up the lodgepole in your tipi, and he fell off and broke some pottery," Windhawk said dryly and without humor.

"Was he hurt?" Sun Woman asked, examining her grandson for cuts.

"He is not hurt, but you will have to replace some of your pottery," Windhawk replied, casting his son a displeased glance.

"I care nothing for that . . . pottery can always be replaced. Little Hawk is no more mischievous than you were as a boy, Windhawk," the doting grandmother said, hugging her grandson to her tightly in her arms.

30

Joanna gave Windhawk a look of exasperation, and his eyes softened when they rested on her face. Taking her hand, he raised her up to stand beside him and rested his face against hers.

"Do you think our daughter will be such a trial when she grows older?" she asked, pressing her face against Windhawk's buckskin shirt.

His laughter was soft against her ear. "Let us hope so," Windhawk replied. "Let us wish that it will be so. I would like to think she will have the same strong spirit as her brother possesses."

Joanna felt Windhawk touch his mouth against her ear, and tiny shivers ran up and down her spine. Again he laughed softly, knowing how easily he could arouse her.

"I can see that the two of you want to be alone," Sun Woman said, smiling. Taking her grandson by the hand, she led him outside.

"Now see what you have done, Windhawk," Joanna scolded, moving away from him. "You have made your mother leave. Can you not control these urges of yours until we are alone?" she said in exasperation.

He lifted her into his arms and gave her a mind-destroying smile. "I am never in control when I am near you, Flaming Hair. For that matter, I have not been in control since the day I first met you."

Joanna rubbed her cheek against his face. "My dearest, love, I do not think any woman can control the powerful chief of the Blackfoot."

"You do, Joanna. If you but knew the power you wield over me, it would allow you to take unfair

31

advantage of this great love I feel for you. I would do anything to see you happy, for in your happiness, I find joy."

She arched an eyebrow. "Who would take advantage of whom?" she asked laughingly.

Windhawk looked deeply into her violet-colored eyes and realized Joanna would never know how she held his very life in her tiny hands. She could only guess at the deep love he had for her. Perhaps it was better that way, he thought. His hands moved across her face to trace the outline of her mouth. When he dipped his dark head to taste her lips, her mouth opened to receive his kiss.

Joanna's body became soft and yielding in his arms as she became lost in the feelings his kiss evoked. Remembering that Tag and Morning Song were coming for the evening meal, she broke the kiss off and pushed against Windhawk. Looking into his dark eyes, she smiled.

"Have I ever told you that you are the handsomest man I have ever known, my husband?"

His dark eyes flashed to life with a warmth that reached out to Joanna, heating her with its intensity. "If you continue to say things like that to me, you may find yourself on the mat," he challenged.

Joanna knew from past experience that Windhawk made no idle threat. "Put me down, Windhawk. I must see to the meal. Besides, Sky Dancer needs to be fed, and Tag and Morning Song will be here shortly."

Windhawk placed her gently to her feet. "I can wait until tonight, Joanna," he told her with a teasing light in his dark eyes.

32

She allowed her eyes to travel up the long, lean line of his body to rest on his handsome face. "You eyes are bold my husband—they promise more than your words," she said, arching a delicate eyebrow.

Windhawk reached out and wound a red-gold curl around his finger, then brought it up to his lips. "I will go and tell my mother it is safe for her to return," he said, chuckling to himself.

Joanna watched her husband walk away, loving the way he carried himself so tall and proud. "Stop by Farley's tipi and tell him he is welcome to come tonight if he wishes," she called after him.

Joanna went to the cook-fire and turned the deer roast that was cooking there. She smiled to herself, thinking how much Farley loved to be included in the family gatherings. The old trapper, Farley, was especially dear to her. There was a time when Windhawk had allowed him to live in the village only because she wanted Farley to be near her. The old man was now accepted by everyone, and Joanna was glad. She loved that dear old man, and he brightened up her life with his colorful speech and wise sayings.

Tonight Joanna would have those about her whom she loved most in the world, and that made her extremely happy. She hummed softly to herself as she bent over Sky Dancer's cradle and lifted the baby into her arms. Joanna looked into the blue eyes of the child, thinking her life was perfect. There was nothing more she wanted out of life, except the happiness of those she loved.

It was snowing outside the big lodge where the chief

33

of the Blackfoot and his family resided, but it was warm and cheerful on the inside. The lodge was unlike any other in the village, since Joanna had brought many of the white man's comforts into it. There were bearskin rugs on the floor, and a brass bed, which was covered with luxurious furs. Brass kettles and pots hung from one of the lodgepoles, and Windhawk's weapons hung from the others. There was a feeling of warmth and togetherness among the people who sat upon the bearskin rugs after enjoying a good meal.

Tag studied the faces of everyone present. There was Morning Song, his wife, whose face glowed with happiness. With her, he had become a man. She was the only woman he had ever taken to his body, and the only one he had ever wanted. On their wedding night, their love had been so beautiful and innocent because it had been the first time for them both. Morning Song had been his wife for two years now, and soon she would make him a father.

His eyes then traveled to Sun Woman, his mother-in-law. She was somewhere in her fifties and still a very attractive woman. Her family was her whole life, and she was always doing special little things for those she loved. He remembered the time she had made him a buckskin shirt and trimmed it with dyed porcupine quills. Her joy had been apparent when he had shown his pleasure over the gift. Althought she was forbidden by Blackfoot custom to speak directly to him as her son-in-law, she showed her love for him in the way her eyes would light up when she smiled at her.

His eyes moved to the small bed at the back of the

34

lodge where his nephew, Little Hawk, now slept, then to the cradle where Joanna's newborn daughter lay. He was delighted with his niece and nephew and looked forward to the time when his own child would be born.

His eyes next went to Windhawk. There wasn't a man living whom Tag respected and admired as much as the chief of the Blood Blackfoot. Windhawk had been his guide and his teacher ever since he had first come to the Blackfoot village to live. Tag watched as Windhawk's dark eyes went to his sister, Joanna, and caressed her face. One had but to look at Windhawk to know that he loved her deeply.

Last of all, Tag looked at his sister. Joanna had always been there for him. She had been his strength as a child, and he thought she still might be. He remembered how she had always made him read his books and do his lessons when he was a boy. She had badgered him into learning all he could. She had versed him in the ways of being a gentleman, telling him he would one day return to Philadelphia to claim what, by rights, belonged to him. Joanna had been wrong—he would never return to Phildelphia. His life was here with Morning Song.

He felt Joanna's eyes on him, and he smiled at her. His love for Morning Song was deep, but nothing could touch the closeness he felt for his sister. They had been through so many heartaches and trouble together, but they had come through them with very few scars—at least, not the kind of scars that showed.

Joanna could feel Tag's restlessness. It seemed to grow stronger each day. The thing that she feared

35

most was beginning to happen. He was starting to remember how their Uncle Howard had forced them to flee from their own home, and she knew he had come to resent the past. His old life was beginning to beckon him. She knew he would never leave Morning Song to return to Philadelphia, and he couldn't take her with him, because she would never be accepted by the white race. This thing would eat at him until he faced it once and for all. Joanna wished he could just put it out of his mind and be content with the way things had worked out, but that would never happen. She feared that before this thing could be brought to a conclusion, she and Morning Song might both lose Tag.

Tag realized by the look that Joanna gave him that she knew about his thoughts and was aware of his restlessness. He had never been able to hide anything from her when he had been a boy, and even though he was now a man, she could still see into his soul.

Standing up, he walked out into the night. Pulling his warm blanket about him, he watched as the snowflakes drifted lazily earthward. He could hear the sound of laughter coming from the other tipis and began to feel lonely. Where did he belong?

Would he ever find peace within himself? he wondered. Would this feeling of unrest ever release him from its grip? It was with him day and night now, and he wanted to rid himself of its dominance.

He felt, rather than heard, Morning Song next to him. She slipped her hand into his, and they both watched as the snow covered the ground. Tag smiled down into her lovely face, trying to mask his thoughts

36

from her, but he knew by the sadness in her eyes that he hadn't succeeded entirely.

"I love you, Morning Song. I always will."

"Come, let us go home," she said, taking his hand.

Tag turned and looked at the outline of the tall mountains that separated him from the white world he had once known. Somewhere beyond those mountains was a man living in Tag and Joanna's home—the food he ate and the clothes he wore were all bought with the James's money.

Tag knew that after his Aunt Margaret had died Howard Landon had remarried. The woman who was now his wife was none other than Claudia Maxwell, who had always hated Joanna. It bothered him too, that Joanna's old enemy was living in their home.

Drawing in his breath, he tried to push his thoughts aside. "Come, we will tell the family goodnight," he said, leading Morning Song back into Windhawk's lodge.

Chapter Three

The Chinook wind was blowing across the land, bringing with it the warm, dry air from the nearby mountainside. The snow had melted into slush, and although there were dark clouds on the horizon Tag didn't think it would snow today. Morning Song had been begging Tag to take her for a ride, and he thought this would be a good day since the weather was pleasant.

Tag had learned from experience that the weather could turn cold without any warning, and he didn't want Morning Song to be exposed to a sudden norther. He decided it would be best to return to the village by early afternoon.

Tag noticed that Morning Song was having trouble mounting her horse because of her advanced stage of pregnancy. He lifted her up and placed her on the padded saddle, then tucked a blanket about her to keep her warm.

"Today we will not ride far from the village, Morning Song. It is too near the time for the baby to be born, and I would not want to be the one to deliver the child," he teased her lightly.

"Please, Tag, could we not ride to the foot of the

mountains? It has been so long since I have been away from the village," she pleaded.

He had never been able to deny her anything, so he gave in easily. "Only if you walk the horse, Morning Song. It will be much too dangerous for you to run the animal," he cautioned like a fretful mother.

Morning Song nodded her agreement. The sun was shining as the two of them rode away from the village, and they both felt carefree and light-hearted. Morning Song had packed some dried meat and berry-cakes, and she hoped she could convince Tag to stay away from the village until nightfall. Soon she would have a baby to look after, and while she looked forward to having Tag's child, she knew their life would change. She would no longer be able to go with him anytime she wanted, since she would be nursing the baby.

When they crossed the river, Tag pointed out a white-tailed deer to Morning Song. They both halted their horses to watch the doe and her fawn drink from the Milk River.

Today Tag's mind was clear. He could see happiness reflected in Morning Song's dark eyes, and it gladdened his heart. How could he ever have allowed his unrest to come between them? He could be happy the rest of his life in making Morning Song happy. What he had found here among the Blackfoot tribe was a good life, and he didn't want his bitterness to spoil any part of it. He thought of his unborn baby and realized he had everything a man could ask for. No longer would he allow the past to tug at him. Let his uncle have all he had stolen from him. Most probably it wouldn't ever bring the man true happiness.

Tag realized that his uncle would always be watching and waiting for him to return. He could imagine him unable to sleep at night, wondering if he and Joanna would one day appear and show him up for the thief he was. Tag would have to find his revenge in knowing he was causing his uncle many sleepless nights.

They rode until midmorning before they reached the foot of the mountains. Tag lifted Morning Song from her horse and held her in his arms.

"Smile and make me happy," he told her.

She laughed delightedly as he made a silly face for her. Setting her on her feet, he held her against him. "I want always to see a smile on your pretty face, Morning Song. If it is in my power, I will see that you have much to laugh about."

"Have you no more regrets, my husband?"

"I have no more regrets, my wife." The baby chose that moment to kick, and Tag felt the movement. "That is our baby telling you that its father will always make the sun shine for its mother."

Morning Song looked up into Tag's face. "Will you mind if this baby is a girl?"

"No, I will not mind."

"My mother says she can tell by the way I am carrying it low, that it will be a girl. I was afraid you would want a son first."

"I will want it even if it is a girl, but I have one request. She had better have your pretty face and dark hair."

"I want her to have your eyes, Tag. Would she not be beautiful if she had your eyes?"

At that moment a shot rang out, and Tag turned to

look over his shoulder, thinking it would be a hunter beyond the valley. He knew Windhawk would not be pleased if the white man had encroached on Blackfoot lands.

Turning back to Morning Song, he started to take her arm with the intention of pulling her behind a rock formation until he could find out who had fired the shot. He watched in bewilderment as Morning Song seemed to be gasping for breath. Slowly she crumpled to her knees, and that was when Tag saw the dark red stain on the front of her gown!

"My God, Morning Song, you have been shot!" he yelled. Picking her up in his arms, he carried her behind the rocks and held her.

Small whimpering sounds were coming from her throat when she tried to speak. "Don't talk," he urged, trying to stem the flow of blood with his hand. In a flash Tag knew that Morning Song was going to die. Tears of grief washed down his face as he watched her lifeblood spill onto a patch of snow, turning it a bright scarlet.

"N . . . no, Tag, do . . . not weep . . . for me. The baby! Save my baby!"

Tag laid his hand on her stomach and could feel the contractions that were tightening her stomach muscles. He could see that the bullet wound was high enough that it had not hit the child. Tag was fighting to put his grief aside to help his wife deliver their baby.

"The baby is fine, Morning Song. Try not to talk . . . save your strength."

She reached out her hand and touched his face. "I . . . must talk, Tag. Do . . . not grieve for me . . . go

41

back to the white . . . world and reclaim . . . what belongs to you."

Tag realized it was an effort for her to talk. He tried to hide his grief from her, but he could tell from her her eyes that she knew she was dying.

"P . . . promise me that you will go back, Tag . . . Promise me!"

"I will go back, my dearest love. I promise."

"The . . . baby comes, my husband. Give her to . . . Joanna, she will love . . ."

At that moment a pain ripped through Morning Song's body, and Tag didn't know if it was from the bullet wound or from the birth of the child. He watched Morning Star twist as if she were bearing down hard. He wanted to help her, but he didn't know what to do.

Morning Song gripped his hand so tightly he could feel her nails digging into his skin. He wanted to scream out at the injustice of it all. Someone would pay for what they had done to her! Why would someone want to hurt sweet, gentle Morning Song who had never harmed anyone? His thoughts were wild in his grief, but he had no time to think, because another pain shot through Morning Song's body.

"Tag, you will have . . . to help, the . . . baby . . . comes," she whispered.

He raised her gown and saw that the head of the baby had already appeared. Tears were blinding him so badly that everything was a blur. Taking the small head in his hands, he guided it as it was expelled from Morning Song's body. Knowing the child could die from exposure, he quickly removed his coat and wrapped the baby in it. Holding the child upward, he heard it take its first breath. The cries from the newborn baby seemed to echo through the mountains and reverberate down into the valley.

"T . . . Tag, you must cut the cord and bind it tightly so the baby will not bleed to death . . . do it quickly!" Morning Song whispered urgently since she knew her strength was waning.

Tag was in a daze as he ripped his shirt from his body and cut a strip with his knife. He then cut the cord that attached the baby to its mother and bound it tightly. When that had been accomplished, he laid the baby down and turned all his attention to Morning Song. Lifting her gently in his arms, he cradled her to him.

"I love you, Morning Song—don't leave me," he cried as deep sobs tore from his lips.

"Tag, I am so cold . . . hold me," Morning Song whispered weakly. She looked upon the grief-stricken face of the man she loved, wishing she could bring him comfort.

"I will hold you forever, my love. I won't allow you to die!"

"Tag . . . I . . . love . . . yo . . . ."

Tag felt Morning Song go limp in his arms, and he knew she was dead. An agonizing animal cry arose from his throat as he cried out in his grief, "God, don't take Morning Song! I cannot bear to live without her!"

Looking down into her face, which was still beautiful even in death, he cradled Morning Song to him while hot tears washed down his cheeks.

Tag was never to know how long he sat there rocking Morning Song in his arms. He couldn't accept her death—it had come too suddenly! One moment she was happy and laughing, and the next she had been mortally wounded.

Tag was unaware that the baby had ceased crying and the weather was growing colder. Dark clouds had passed over the sun, and it had begun to snow lightly.

Tag was brought back to the present by the sound of approaching riders. He could tell by the sound of their shod horses that it was two white men. Gently laying Morning Song down, he closed her eyes and picked up the baby, laying it beside her. He knew these two white men would be Morning Song's murderers, and he intended to see that they paid for taking her life!

Touching Morning Song's face softly, Tag picked up his knife and quickly moved to the side of the rock, waiting until he could see the intruders come into view. He saw them when they emerged from the trees not more than fifty yards away. He could tell by the looks of them that they were buffalo hunters, and his lip curled into a snarl. Even if they had accidentally shot Morning Song, they would still pay with their lives. His eyes glazed with hatred as he patiently waited for them to ride closer.

It didn't take long for the two men to discover Tag's and Morning Song's horses. They halted their mounts, and their voices carried to Tag.

"Where you 'spect they got off to, Gibbs? I know I shot me the girl," one of them said.

"You weren't suppose to kill the girl, Walter. Mrs. Landon said she wanted Taggart James dead; she didn't say nothing about killing anyone else," one of the men said, looking about for some sign of his prey.

"Ain't I a good shot? You know ifen I took aim, I

44

got a steady eye and often as not hit what I was aiming at," his companion answered as he also searched for some sign of Taggart James.

"Well, you sure missed what you was aiming at this time," his partner grumbled.

"Look at that blood there on the snow. I bet the Indian gal is dead, or ifen she ain't, she soon will be."

"You're crazy to have killed the Injun. Unless I miss my guess she were a Blackfoot, and ifen that's the case, we'll have a hell of a time getting out of these hills alive, Gibbs."

"What the hell—a dead Injun don't carry no tales. After we find Taggart James and do away with him, who's gonna be alive to tell who killed the girl, Walter?"

Tag's eyes glazed over with hatred. These men had been sent to kill him by Claudia and most probably his Uncle Howard. There had been no reason for them to kill Morning Song! Leaping over the rock, he propelled himself into the air and knocked the man called Gibbs off his horse. Before the startled Gibbs could react, Tag drove his knife into his chest several times to make sure he was dead.

Not pausing to think, he stood up and faced the man who was called Walter. By now, however, Walter had recovered from the shock of seeing his partner killed and swung his rifle around, aiming it at Tag.

"I got me a present for you, Taggart James, and it comes from someone that wants you dead real bad," Walter said, looking into cold blue eyes that stared back at him unafraid. Walter felt a shiver slide down his spine, and he knew if he didn't kill this man quickly, he would be as dead as Gibbs was.

Tag leaped toward Walter and Walter squeezed the trigger on his rifle. The bullet ripped through Tag's shoulder and knocked him to the ground. Tag didn't feel the pain as much as the sudden weakness that seemed to overwhelm his strength. Trying to get up, he fell to his knees and then onto the ground. He tried to gather the strength to rise again, but his head was spinning, and he knew he was about to lose consciousness. He wanted to kill the man who had deliberately and wantonly murdered his beloved Morning Song.

Tag shook his head, trying to clear it, and staggered to his feet. He saw that the man was aiming his rifle at him, ready to fire a second time. He didn't mind dying; after all, Morning Song was dead and it was only right that he join her, but he wished he had the strength to end the life of the man who had killed his wife. He was so weak that it was an effort to stay on his feet. He could do no more than wait for the impact and the second bullet to hit him.

The shot never came! An arrow whizzed through the air and the man fell from his horse, dead. The arrow had pierced his heart, and he died before he even hit the ground.

Windhawk threw down his bow and urged his horse swiftly forward. He jumped from his mount before it came to a halt and knelt down beside Tag. Raising Tag's head onto his lap, he looked at him, puzzled, wondering how such a thing could have happened.

"Are you badly hurt, Tag?"

"Not me . . . Morning Song!" Tag said, just before losing consciousness.

Windhawk heard the cry of a baby coming from behind the huge boulder and got slowly to his feet with a feeling of dread. He motioned for his friend, Gray Fox, to take care of Tag while he circled around the rock with his knife drawn. The moment he saw his sister, he knew she was dead. Dropping down on his knees, he touched her cold face. Tears of grief filled his dark eyes as he picked Morning Song's newborn baby up in his arms and held it closely to him. How could such a thing happen? he wondered wildly. Morning Song had never harmed anyone. Why should she be dead?

It was a sad procession that entered the Blackfoot village a short time later. Windhawk carried his dead sister across his lap, while one of his warriors held the baby, and Gray Fox carried Tag across his horse.

The people gathered around them and sounds of unbelieving grief echoed through the village. Above it all was heard the cry of a tiny newborn infant.

Morning Song had been well loved by her people, and there was a heavy sadness that hung over the Blackfoot village like a dark cloud.

The sad task of informing Joanna and his mother fell to Windhawk.

As evening fell, the campfires burned brightly, and the death chants could be heard echoing across the valley.

Chapter Four

The scaffold had been built and Morning Song's body had been placed upon it so that the people of the Blackfoot village could gather around to mourn the death of their beloved princess. The mourners showed their sorrow openly, for Morning Song's passing had left a deep void in many hearts. The sounds of grief could be heard all throughout the dismal day and on into the dark night.

Joanna sat beside her brother, holding his hand, and calling on all her strength to get through this horrible nightmare. She couldn't believe that sweet, gentle Morning Song was dead and that Tag had been gravely wounded. Tag hadn't regained consciousness since Windhawk had brought him home, so no one knew what had happened. All Windhawk could tell her was that two white men were responsible for the tragedy.

The bullet had been removed from Tag's chest, and Joanna had cleansed the wound. Now there was nothing to do but wait and pray that he would recover.

A small cry came from the cradle where Joanna had placed Tag and Morning Song's baby. Standing up, she walked over to the baby and lifted it into her arms.

Tears fell on the child's face as Joanna hugged the tiny body to her. So much had happened, and the child had all but been forgotten. Joanna didn't even know if the baby was a boy or a girl. Laying the child down, she dressed it in clean, warm clothing and discovered that Tag was the father of a daughter.

Brokenhearted sobs wracked Joanna's body as she unfastened her doeskin dress and began to feed the baby. The child nursed hungrily, and Joanna's heart went out to her poor motherless niece.

"Do not fret, little one," she said, touching the soft, downy black hair on the baby's head. "I will love you as your mother would have. You will be as my own daughter."

Joanna hadn't heard Windhawk enter, and when he knelt down beside her she saw the tears in his dark eyes. Reaching out to him, she brushed a tear away from his cheek.

"Oh, my dearest love," she cried, "my heart is breaking for you."

Windhawk leaned his face against hers. "Help me get through this, Joanna. Give me the strength I need." It was a plea from the heart, and fresh tears washed down her face.

"We will help each other, my husband. You will be strong because you have to. I will be strong because Tag and this child need me."

Windhawk looked for the first time at the baby. He had just assumed since Joanna was nursing the child that it was his own daughter. When he looked into Joanna's eyes, she could see the pain written there.

"Is the child well?"

"Yes, Morning Song's daughter will thrive and

49

grow. She will not know one day of unhappiness if I can help it. She will be as my own daughter."

Windhawk was moved by her words, and he looked upward, feeling his grief like a knife in his heart. "How is your brother?"

"He has not regained consciousness."

Windhawk stood up. "I fear for my mother's sanity. Her grief is such that she is not thinking clearly. I fear what she might do. I have tried to talk to her but, she will not listen." Joanna could read the helpless expression on Windhawk's face.

"I will go to her. You stay with Tag," Joanna said, standing up and wrapping the baby warmly in a blanket.

Windhawk watched her leave the lodge with the baby, wondering how he would have stood the pain had it not been for Joanna. She was the one from whom he drew his strength. Everyone thought he was the strong one, but Windhawk knew that in many cases it was Joanna he relied on for strength.

The inside of Sun Woman's tipi was in shadow, with only the cook-fire to give off light. Joanna saw her mother-in-law lying on her mat, surrounded by her friends. Joanna's heart went out to her as she watched her rock back and forth, chanting the death cry with tears streaming down her face.

"Please leave now—I will take care of my mother," Joanna told the other women. She watched as they filed out one by one, and when the last one had departed, she laid the child down and dropped on her knees beside Windhawk's mother, pulling her into her

50

arms.

"I remember a time when you once helped me, my mother. You held me in your arms and allowed me to cry out my unhappiness. I will now do the same for you."

Sun Woman's body was trembling, and Joanna tightened her arms about her. "Cry, my mother. Cry for the life that was ended too soon. Cry because we will miss Morning Song's laughter. Get all the sadness out of your heart so you can then remember only the joy that she brought into your life."

"Joanna, Joanna, I cannot go on living without her. I have lived too long when I begin outliving my children. Allow me to die!"

"You must not talk like that! Morning Song would not want you to die. Do you not know that if you die you will take some of Morning Song with you? As long as you live, a part of her will live also."

"I will not live! The pain is too great! I will take this knife and plunge it into my heart!" Sun Woman cried, picking up a weapon that lay beside her on the buffalo robe.

Joanna grabbed Sun Woman's arm to keep her from hurting herself. She knew that Windhawk's mother was acting irrationally, and Joanna would have to do something quickly or her mother-in-law might well do something harmful to herself. Applying pressure to Sun Woman's arm, she forced her to drop the knife. The older woman collapsed in a heap, crying hysterically.

Joanna picked up the baby and knelt down beside Sun Woman once more.

"There is someone here who will need your love and

strength, my mother. Would not Morning Song want you to love and care for her daughter? Will she not find a sweeter rest knowing that the woman who loved and raised her will help do the same for her own daughter?"

Sun Woman's head snapped up. "What daughter? What are you saying to me?"

Joanna realized that in her grief over Morning Song's death and her worry over Tag she hadn't told Sun Woman about the baby. "Did you not know that Morning Song had her baby this morning?"

Joanna pulled back the blanket and showed the infant to Sun Woman. "Look, she has Morning Song's hair. It is as black as the midnight sky. Hold her, my mother. Give *her* the love that you once gave to her mother!"

Sun Woman's hand trembled as she touched the baby's soft cheek. Joanna watched as she dried her eyes, and then she handed the baby to her. At first, Sun Woman looked like she might cry again, and then slowly her eyes seemed to brighten.

"I still have a part of Morning Song to love." Her eyes met Joanna's. "You have brought me comfort as no other could have, my daughter. I will live for this child! I will tell her of the goodness of her mother, and she will grow to be just like her."

Joanna stood up and nodded. "Keep the child with you until she is hungry, then bring her to me so I may feed her. I have more then enough milk for both babies. You and I will both love this child, my mother . . . as . . . we both loved Morning Song."

Joanna walked outside knowing Sun Woman would be all right. Her vision became blurred with tears, and her heart was breaking as she stumbled back to her own lodge so she could be with Tag in case he regained consciousness.

Tag awoke feeling a cool hand on his forehead. Everything seemed fuzzy, and he blinked his eyes trying to clear them. There was a tremendous pain in his chest, which seemed to pin him down. He tried to remember where he was and what had happened to him.

"Don't move, Tag, you have been hurt. Lie still."

He heard Joanna's voice and wondered what she was talking about—he didn't remember being . . . !

"Morning Song!" he cried out in agony. "They killed Morning Song!"

"Hush, Tag," Joanna soothed. "Try to go back to sleep—I will sit beside you."

"NO!" he cried, trying to sit up.

Strong hands pushed him back down, and he heard Windhawk's voice. "Drink this," Windhawk told him, raising a cup to his lips. Tag took a sip of the bitter liquid and turned his face away. "Drink all of it, Tag—it will help you sleep," Windhawk urged.

Tag obeyed immediately, wanting to lose himself in sleep. He didn't want to remember that Morning Song was dead. He couldn't bear to think about how she had died in his arms. The foul-tasting liquid soon worked its magic, and Tag felt himself drifting off. In his mind he could hear Morning Song's voice telling him to go back to Philadelphia. He didn't want to go back. He wanted to stay here with her. But he couldn't stay with her . . . she was dead!

"Morning Song," he groaned. He felt a comforting hand clasp his and knew that Joanna was nearby sharing his pain and loss.

For the next few days, Tag slipped in and out of consciousness. Joanna knew Tag didn't want to wake up to face the sad reality of Morning Song's death. Her heart was breaking for him, but there was nothing she could do outside tending his wounds and trying to make him as comfortable as possible. She knew the real test would come as he grew stronger. Then, only time would be the great healer.

With Morning Song's daughter to care for, Sun Woman was better able to accept the tragedy of her daughter's death. Windhawk never again allowed his grief to show. Only Joanna knew about the sleepless nights and his troubled dreams. She realized with a heavy heart that it would be a very long time before this family would recover from losing Morning Song.

It was a week after the tragedy that Joanna felt she had to get away. She had tried to hold her grief inside so she could appear strong for others, but now she wanted time to be alone.

Sun Woman was watching the children, thus giving Joanna the time she needed to find her solitude.

She mounted her horse and rode across the river and into the woods. She allowed her mount to wander at will, paying little heed to where he was going. Finally she halted her horse and dismounted.

It had snowed earlier, but now the clouds had moved away, leaving a bright sunshiny day. Joanna took this time to reflect on all the little things that

Morning Song had done to brighten up her life. Leaning her head against a tree trunk, she allowed the tears she had been holding back to flow. After her tears dried, she just walked about drinking in the stillness that surrounded her. Sitting down on a fallen log, she propped her back against a tree trunk and closed her eyes.

"You all right, Joanna?" Farley, the old trapper, asked.

Opening her eyes, she smiled at him, knowing he had followed her in case she should run into any danger. "I'm going to be all right now, Farley."

He sat down beside her and fixed her with a concerned gaze. "Ifen you want me to go back to the village, I will. Do you want to be alone?"

"No, my dear friend, stay with me for a while."

"I looked in on the boy; his wound ain't bad."

"Tag isn't a boy any longer, Farley. He is a man now, with a man's responsibilities."

"I reckon he'll always be a boy to me."

"I wish there was something we could do to help him get through this."

"There ain't, though. He'll deal with it in his own way. I have watched him growing up, and I'm right proud of him. Nobody's gonna knock that boy 'round without him doing some knocking back."

"I suppose," Joanna said absent-mindedly. Already she was thinking about the ones who were dependent on her back at the village. The babies would soon need feeding, and she wanted to be near Tag when he awoke.

When she stood up, Farley followed her to her horse. Then the two of them rode silently back to the village.

That evening, Tag awoke long enough for Joanna to spoon some soft porridge down him. Then he drifted off to sleep once more.

When the children had been tucked into bed, Joanna lay down beside Windhawk. He drew her into his strong arms, and she rested her head against his shoulder.

"Joanna, it is a strange thing, but I have found that in a time of great trouble, you can always discover what a person is really made of. These last few days I have observed you taking care of everyone, lending your strength to those who needed it. I have seen you so tired and drained you could hardly stand, and yet not once did you complain. I am proud to be your husband. It is time for you to rest and allow me to shoulder some of the burden. Lean on me now, Joanna."

Joanna felt his lips on her forehead, and she allowed herself to relax. Yes, she would lean on Windhawk. From him she always found the courage to go on. He was the strongest, gentlest man she had ever known.

"Sleep, my love. I will hold you all night," he whispered in her ear.

Joanna closed her eyes, knowing that tonight she would sleep without any nightmares to disturb her peace of mind.

As time passed, Windhawk knew Joanna had fallen asleep. When his infant daughter cried to be fed, he got up and placed her at Joanna's breast. Later, he performed the same deed for Tag's daughter, and Joanna didn't stir either time.

The next morning Windhawk took Little Hawk to Farley and the two babies to his mother so Joanna could sleep. He knew she was utterly exhausted, and that if she didn't get some rest she would become ill.

It was late afternoon when Joanna finally awoke. Windhawk had stayed beside her all night and all day. Now he came to her and handed her a dish of food. No words passed between them. There had never been a need for talk between the two of them. What they had to say to one another could be expressed with a smile or a gentle touch.

That evening Windhawk helped Joanna feed the children and put them to bed. He then sat beside her as she spoon-fed Tag some broth.

After everyone had been cared for, he lifted Joanna into his arms and carried her to bed. She curled up next to him, feeling his love reach out to her.

"Have I told you I think you are wonderful, my husband?" she asked softly.

"You have mentioned it once or twice," he replied, resting his face against her red-gold hair.

"Not many men, white or Indian, would have been as considerate as you are, Windhawk."

"It is easy to be kind to someone like you, Joanna. You are always so busy doing things for others, you do not often realize when you are tired yourself."

"Hold me, Windhawk," she said, needing his warmth.

"Every day of our life, my love," he whispered.

Chapter Five

Valley Forge, Pennsylvania, January 1848

"I won't do it, and she cannot make me!" Alexandria Bradford said, stomping her foot and glaring at Tilly, her stepmother's maid.

"I don't think you have any choice, young lady. You are fortunate that your stepmother cares enough about your welfare and wants to see you happy. Rodney is such a dear man, and I'm sure the two of you will deal quite well together."

"What he is . . . is my stepbrother, and I have never liked him. I will not now, nor at any time in the future, marry him!" Alexandria said, pushing a stray mink-colored curl out of her face and plopping down on the window seat. "Rodney reminds me of a fish, with his big lips and bulging eyes. He is horrid, and I will not have him!" she reiterated.

Tilly's mouth gaped open, and she looked like she might have an attack of apoplexy. "You dare to speak ill of dear Rodney when he has always been so kind to you! You are your father's daughter and an ungrateful child."

Alexandria turned her back on the woman and

looked out the second-story window. The trees were bleak and bare, and a thin layer of snow covered the countryside. Alexandria was remembering the day Tilly had come to Meadowlake Farm with Alexandria's stepmother when she had married her father. As time had progressed, the faithful housekeeper, Mrs. Benson, and Colman, the hired man who had served the manor in Alexandria's mother's time, had all been dismissed and replaced with her stepmother, Barbara's, choice of servants.

Alexandria turned back to Tilly and gave her a haughty look. "This is the nineteenth century—there is no way Barbara can force me to marry anyone I don't want to, and I'll not marry Rodney! I have written several letters to my guardian, Mr. Alderman, and when he finds out what Barbara is trying to do, he will put a stop to it. I expect him home from Boston any day now. Having said that, I will say no more. You can go and tattle to Barbara as you always have, and while you are at it, you can report to her that I detest my stepbrother!"

"Be that as it may, miss, you will do as the mistress orders," Tilly said, with a determined look on her face. "Your stepmother has tried to be a mother to you, but you wouldn't allow it. Now that your father's dead, she wants nothing more than to see you happy."

Alexandria stood up, and her amber-colored eyes narrowed. "What she wants is Meadowlake. This is my home! It was left to me by my mother's father and my grandfather. I will not marry my stepbrother just so he and Barbara can get their hands on Meadowlake! I am not worried, because I know Mr.

Alderman will never allow that to happen."

"We'll see, Miss Prim and Proper, we'll see," Tilly stated. "You'll find yourself with a husband before too long. I wouldn't count too much on any help from that trustee of yours. I know for a fact that the letters you wrote to Mr. Alderman never reached him." With a smirk on her face, she sailed out of the room, leaving Alexandria to ponder her words.

When she had gone, Alexandria sank back down on the windowseat and pressed her forehead against the cold windowpane. Tears of hopelessness fell down her face as she reflected on her situation. Alexandria thought of Mr. Alderman, whom her grandfather had appointed as trustee of her estate. He was a kindly old gentleman who tended to the disbursement of the moneys to run Meadowlake. Three months ago he had gone to Boston on an extended business trip, unaware that he was leaving her in the clutches of her unscrupulous stepmother. Alexandria knew if Mr. Alderman was aware of what Barbara was trying to do to her, he would come home immediately. If what Tilly implied were true, then Barbara had intercepted all the letters she had written Mr. Alderman, and she could expect no help from him. Evidently Barbara had gotten her hands on the letters and destroyed them.

Alexandria closed her eyes, feeling the hopelessness of her situation for the first time. She had no one to turn to. Her father had been dead for almost a year, and her mother had died four years before that. Alexandria had not known a happy day since her father's tragic death.

She remembered back three years ago when her father had gone on a business trip to Philadelphia. When he returned, he had brought Barbara and her son, Rodney, home with him and introduced them as Alexandria's stepmother and stepbrother. Alexandria had been fifteen at the time, and she hadn't liked Barbara or Rodney from the start.

She remembered back to happier times before her mother had died. This house had rung with the sound of laughter. There hadn't been any laughter in many months now.

Alexandria's mother had been taken suddenly. The doctor had said it was no more than a mild malady and had put her to bed for a day or two. The mild malady had turned out to be pneumonia, and, within a week, her mother had died.

Alexandria's father had taken her mother's death very hard and had begun to drink heavily. For a time after his marriage to Barbara, he had stopped drinking, but that hadn't lasted more than a few months.

One night last spring, during a terrible rainstorm, her father had been returning from town and his horse had thrown him. A neighbor had found him the next morning and brought him home. Her father had been suffering from a head wound, and he had died without ever regaining consciousness. Alexandria still grieved for the man her father had once been. In the last years of his life he had almost been a stranger to her.

She stood up and, walking over to the vanity table, picked up a hairbrush and began absent-mindedly to brush her rich, mink-colored hair that seem to sparkle

61

with golden highlights. Alexandria had never liked her hair, because she thought it was too curly. The tresses, which were long enough to hang down to her waist, were so curly that they fell only to just below her shoulders. She stared at her amber-colored eyes with distaste. While her eyes might look grand on a feline, they were certainly not becoming in a girl of eighteen, she thought.

Alexandria plucked at the velvet trim on her rust-colored gown, then stood back to survey her image in the mirror over the vanity table. She was small in stature, barely topping five feet. She was small-boned, but her hips were well rounded and her legs were well shaped.

She remembered a time when her father had called her his little kitten and she had felt pretty. Now, beside her voluptuous, overdeveloped stepmother, she felt very insignificant. The face that stared back at her from the mirror had soft, delicate features, and, in spite of her amber eyes, Alexandria thought she might not be too bad looking, although it was hard for her to judge her own looks. The dimples in her cheeks winked at her when she smiled, and her complexion wasn't bad, she told herself.

Alexandria straightened her back and tried to thrust out her small breasts, wishing she had a bosom to show off as did most other young ladies her age. Barbara always told her that she looked more like thirteen than her actual age, and Alexandria thought she might be right. One thing was for certain . . . no young man ever came calling, and she was never allowed to attend any of the functions for the young people in the county. Alexandria knew that Barbara and Rodney kept her virtually a prisoner, and she was beginning to resent it.

Sighing heavily, she placed the brush down on the vanity table and walked toward the door. It was nearing the dinner hour, and Alexandria knew her stepmother wouldn't tolerate her tardiness at meals.

With a stubborn set to her chin, she descended the stairs and walked into the sitting room where she knew Barbara and Rodney would be waiting for her.

"Had you been one minute later, Alexandria, I would have sent Tilly after you," Barbara declared in an angry voice.

Alexandria watched her stepmother walk toward her, noticing for the first time that she was beginning to show her age. Barbara was a very beautiful woman and towered inches above her stepdaughter, putting Alexandria at a distinct disadvantage. Barbara's hair was jet black, with just the tiniest hint of gray at the temples. Alexandria couldn't help but notice the tiny lines that fanned out from Barbara's eyes and mouth.

"Tilly has told me that you have been sulking in your room all day, Alexandria, and I just want you to know I will not tolerate such actions from you, young lady!" Barbara said as her voice raised in volume.

Alexandria merely shrugged her shoulders, and before she could react, Barbara slapped her hard across the cheek. "You have defied me for the last time, Alexandria. From now on, you will know who's in charge around here. You will do as you are told, and I want that clearly understood."

Alexandria held her hand to her cheek where it still

stung from her stepmother's blow. "If by doing as I'm told, you mean marry Rodney, the answer is no, I will not! No power on earth can make me marry him!"

Alexandria's eyes traveled to the gray settee where Rodney sat watching her with a smirk on his face. He was known in the county as somewhat aggressive where the ladies were concerned, but he had often proven to be a coward when he had come up against an enraged father or husband.

He stood up and walked over to Alexandria and flipped a curl from her cheek. "Mayhap you would like me to show you how I persuade reluctant women to do as I wish, Alexandria? I can be very persuasive when the mood strikes me."

Alexandria shivered as she looked into Rodney's gray eyes. She had seen what he was capable of in the past, and she feared that after tonight he would be even more forward and daring in his attempts to get her alone.

Rodney had dark hair like his mother, but while he resembled Barbara in looks, he was far from handsome. His features were too feminine to be handsome. He was very thin, and his shoulders were sloped and rounded. Again, Alexandria shivered as he ran his cold, clammy hand across her cheek, invoking in her a strong distasteful feeling.

"I will have you, Alexandria, with or without your consent. Would it not be better if you were to give in gracefully, and save me the trouble of having to force you?" His voice was low and raspy and seemed to play on Alexandria's nerve ends.

"Why should you want a reluctant bride? There

cannot be much joy in that, even for you."

Rodney smiled, and his eyes followed the graceful line of her neck down to rest on her well-shaped breasts. Looking back into Alexandria's amber eyes, he smiled at her discomfort. "You underestimate your charms. I am not the first man to fall under the spell of those golden eyes. I have seen how men look at you as a treasure to be won. Soon you will be my treasure, Alexandria. I believe after we have been married for a while, you will begin to enjoy being married to me."

When he would have touched her again, she moved back a pace. "Neither of you is fooling me. I know what you're up to! You want Meadowlake, and the only way you can gain control of it is by keeping me under your control. Meadowlake belongs to me, and I will not share any part of it with either of you! I am aware that you have destroyed my letters to Mr. Alderman. When he returns from Boston, he will have you both thrown off Meadowlake."

Barbara's laughter rang out. "I do not think so, Alexandria, because when he returns you will be a married woman, and he will have no right to interfere between you and your husband. Until that time, I control you, Alexandria. Mr. Alderman is merely your trustee of Meadowlake until such time as you marry . . . while I am your guardian. You would do well to remember that."

Suddenly, Alexandria felt very tired. She was weary of Rodney's hiding in darkened corners ready to pounce on her. She was tired of having to lock her door at night for fear he would come into her room and force his unwanted attentions on her. It was not easy to live in a house where her every move was reported back to her stepmother by snooping servants. She had no one to turn to—nowhere to run for safety.

"Take Meadowlake. I give it to you, just allow me to live in peace," she said, sinking down into a chair and leaning her head against the high back.

Barbara leaned against the chair Alexandria was sitting in and fixed her with a cold glare. "You haven't got the power to hand Meadowlake over to us. Your grandfather's will stipulated that in the event of your mother's death, the lands and money were to be handed over to you on your twenty-fifth birthday unless you were married, and, in that event, everything was to be handed to you on your wedding day. It appears your grandfather didn't care much for your father, or perhaps he didn't trust him."

Alexandria closed her eyes. No, she thought, her grandfather hadn't liked her father at all after he had started drinking. He couldn't have known that the will he had drawn up to protect his granddaughter now placed her in jeopardy.

"I will ask you to remember that this is my home. I'm sure there is some way I can prevent you from controlling me. I am prepared to allow you both to stay here, but only if you do not try to force your will on me," Alexandria said with a show of bravado.

Rodney slumped down on the settee, looking very much like a man who would soon have his own way. "Unlike your grandfather, your father left no will; therefore, my mother is your guardian. Until you are either married or you reach the advanced age of twenty-five, she controls your life, Alexandria."

Alexandria had heard this all before; in fact, she was weary of being reminded every day that she was subservient to her stepmother's wishes. "I can do little about my plight, but I still have the say over whom I will marry." She fixed Rodney with a golden gaze. "At the risk of repeating myself, I will neither now, nor in the future, marry you. I would sooner marry the lowest creature on earth than you!"

Rodney's eyes flamed with anger, but before he could speak, his mother jerked Alexandria up by the shoulders, her fingers digging painfully into Alexandria's tender skin.

"When I married your father in Philadelphia, I thought him to be a man of means. Had I known at the time that all he had really belonged to his daughter, I would have looked elsewhere for a more suitable husband. I have no intentions of being cheated out of what belongs to me. I will see my son installed as master of this estate, and there is nothing you can do about it!"

Alexandria tried to get free of Barbara's grip, and when her stepmother released her she fell backwards onto the floor, showing a fair amount of fluffy-white petticoats.

"Get out of my sight, Alexandria! Go to your room and don't allow me to see your face until you can behave as a proper young lady should!"

Alexandria sprang to her feet and faced her adversary.

"You are no lady, nor would you know one if you saw her. I have stood by while you insulted my father at every turn. I watched you crush him without ever voicing any objection. But you will find I am not as easy to crush as my father was. As much as I loved him, I know now that he leaned on my mother, who was the strong one. I am my mother's daughter!"

"Take her to her room!" Barbara screamed. "I will no longer tolerate her disrespect!"

Alexandria watched as her stepmother's face became livid with rage. Rodney stood up and took her hand, pulling her from the room. Alexandria tried to protest, but when she did, Rodney swung her around and lifted her into his arms. She kicked and squirmed as he ascended the stairs, and when he reached her bedroom, he carried her inside and deposited her onto the bed none too gently.

Alexandria quickly scrambled to her knees as he dropped down on the bed beside her. "I think the time has come to teach you some manners, little girl. Mayhap you won't act so haughty after I deflower you." His hand ran down the front of her dress, and Alexandria cringed inside. "No, I don't think you will be so high and mighty once I have made you a woman."

Alexandria tried to scramble off the bed, but he caught her skirt and jerked her backwards. She landed beside Rodney, and he pinned her arms over her head.

"Damn these petticoats," he muttered, trying to loosen her gown, while Alexandria struggled with all her might.

"Don't touch me!" she cried, trying to struggle free.

His grip only tightened on her wrists. "I will do

more than touch you, you little wildcat. You have had me panting after you for the last two years, and you know it, don't you, Alexandria?"

"I detest you!" she cried, feeling as helpless as a newborn baby. "You think you are above the law, but I still have friends in this county. They will see you thrashed if you touch me."

His loud, boisterous laughter startled her. "You have no friends left. Your father alienated all your neighbors when he married my mother. They didn't take too well to his marrying beneath him, did they?" he said, grabbing the front of her gown and ripping it open.

Alexandria gasped and tried to wiggle free so she could cover her nakedness. She felt a shudder wrack her body as he reached out and caressed her exposed breasts, and her face flushed red with shame.

"Damn, you are lovely," he said, looking into her eyes. "I have waited a long time to have you."

"I'll scream!" she threatened.

"Go ahead," he taunted. "Who would come to your aid? The servants are all loyal to me and my mother."

Just then the door was pushed open, and Barbara stood there with an angry frown on her face. "Get out of this room, Rodney. Do you want the servants to spread tales about how you raped a helpless girl? The high and mighty neighbors would love that little tidbit of gossip, wouldn't they?"

Rodney had the good grace to look shamefaced— but only because he had been caught. "I was merely trying to teach her a lesson, Mother."

Barbara looked at her stepdaughter and felt jealousy at her innocent beauty. The years of her own beauty were fast fading, and she envied Alexandria for her unspoiled loveliness. The chit didn't even know that she was beautiful, she thought in disgust.

"I think we will take a little trip to Philadelphia. There we will meet with no opposition to our plan. The two of you will be married very soon now."

Rodney stood up and adjusted his rumpled clothing and smiled down at Alexandria. "How will you like being married to someone beneath your station, as your father was, my dear? I don't think you will fight against the marriage once we reach Philadelphia. Perhaps by the time we return to Meadowlake, you will be as docile as a newborn lamb."

Alexandria was too shocked to reply. She knew there would be nothing she could do to keep Barbara and Rodney from taking her to Philadelphia.

Her stepmother read the hopelessness in her amber eyes and smiled maliciously. "I think, Alexandria, I will have Tilly stay with you while we pack. Tonight I will sleep in your room to make sure you don't take it into your head to leave us suddenly. First thing bright and early tomorrow morning, we will be on our way to Philadelphia."

Alexandria pulled the coverlet over her and laid her head back against the pillow. She could feel herself being drawn more and more tightly into a situation she had no control over. When Barbara and Rodney left, closing the door behind them, Alexandria buried her face in the pillow and cried out her misery. Somehow she had to find a way to escape Barbara and Rodney before they reached Philadelphia, or she wouldn't ever be free. Tears of hopelessness washed down her face, and she wondered to whom she could turn for help. There was no one. The neighbors really had stopped coming around after her father married Barbara, so she couldn't ask them for help. If she was going to get away, she would have to save herself, she thought with stubborn determination!

She dried the tears from her face and sat up. Yes, she was her mother's daughter, and she wouldn't give up until she was free!

Chapter Six

Tag opened his eyes, trying to focus them amid his confusion. It took him a few minutes to realize that he was in Windhawk's lodge. He sat up slowly, searching for his sister. With a sweeping glance, he discovered that he was alone in the lodge. He found to his relief that the pain in his chest wasn't nearly as acute as it had been, and he was hungry. It took several tries and considerable effort, but finally he managed to stand up by holding on to the lodgepole.

He noticed that his chest was wrapped and bandaged, and knew that it was Joanna's handiwork. He had vague, shadowy memories of her feeding him and forcing liquids down his throat.

Tag staggered toward the opening, pushed back the flap, and walked outside. His glance automatically went to his own tipi. No smoke rose from the top opening as it did from all the other tipis, and he realized for the first time that Morning Song wouldn't be there to greet him.

Tag was wearing only a breechcloth, and he began to feel the cold. It was snowing lightly, but a strong wind whirled the flakes about so they weren't sticking to the ground. Turning around, he stumbled back into the lodge. He was feeling weak and shaken so he sat down beside the cook-fire to get warm, hoping his body would soon stop trembling.

That was where Joanna found him when she came in a short time later. When she saw her brother with his face buried in his hands, her first instinct was to rush to him and take him in her arms to give him comfort, but she realized just in time that sympathy was not what he needed at the moment. What he needed was her strength.

"I am glad you are finally up, Tag. I hope you are hungry," she said, trying to sound cheerful.

Blue eyes locked with blue eyes, speaking a language that could not be put into words. Their eyes told each other of their sorrow and spoke of the comfort they could find in each other.

Without another word, Joanna walked to the cook-fire, sliced a piece of meat from the roasting spit, placed it in a dish, and handed it to her brother.

"It's snowing again," Joanna said.

"I know."

"Do you want to talk?"

"Yes, Joanna, I want to talk, but not about . . . Morning Song. Speak to me of the weather. Talk to me about the gossip that is circulating about the village. Say anything, Joanna, but don't mention Morning Song."

Joanna held back her tears, knowing he was dealing with his grief in the only way he could. She wished she could hold him and tell him everything would soon be all right, as she had when he had been a child . . . but he was no longer a child, and there were no magic words that would make the pain of grief go away.

"I think I know what you need, Tag. There is someone who needs you as much as you need her. She will help you get through this," Joanna said, standing up and walking over to the cradle where his daughter lay.

Tag watched as she picked up the baby and carried her over to him. He felt guilty that he hadn't even given the baby a thought. He hadn't even known that his own baby was a girl. When Joanna handed the infant to him, he hesitated for only a moment before he took her in his arms. Staring down into the tiny face, he felt nothing but emptiness.

"I will just leave the two of you alone to get acquainted," Joanna told him.

Tag didn't even notice that his sister had left as he held the baby awkwardly. He felt panic for the moment, since he knew very little about babies. He watched as his daughter opened her eyes and began to cry. Her cry seemed to reach inside him, and he realized that she was a part of Morning Song. Lifting her to his face, he kissed the smooth cheek as fatherly love washed through his heart. His tears wet the baby's cheek as he found an outlet for his grief. Tag knew that he would never cry for Morning Song again after today, even though she would always be a part of him, no matter where he went or what he did. As he rocked his tiny daughter in his arms, her crying stopped, and so did his. Joanna had been right . . . this tiny bit of humanity who was a part of him and Morning Song had helped him face his loss and given him the courage to go on.

When Joanna returned a short time later, she found

Tag curled up on the bearskin rug beside the fire, holding the baby in his arms—both he and the child were fast asleep. Bending down, she pulled a fur cover over them both, hoping Tag had come to terms with his sorrow.

Each day Tag seemed to grow stronger. It wasn't long until he wasn't satisfied staying in the lodge with Joanna and Sun Woman fussing over him. He began to ride out with Windhawk and the other warriors, and Joanna knew he was becoming more like his old self. No one ever spoke to him of Morning Song, because that was the way he wanted it. He spent hours with his daughter, but he refused to give her a name. He told Joanna that, for the time being, he would just call her the little princess. After a while, everyone adopted the name as well, so Tag's daughter became known as the little princess.

One morning when the wind had died down, and the snow clouds had moved away, Tag went for the first time to the tipi he had shared with Morning Song. He spent most of the day inside, and when he came out the whole village gathered around in amazement as he lit a torch and burned the tipi to the ground.

That night Tag, Joanna, and Windhawk sat around the lodge, talking quietly. Joanna could see that her brother was well on his way to recovering from his wound. She hoped he would soon recover from his loss.

"I have decided that I will leave for Philadelphia in two days' time," Tag said, looking at Joanna.

Joanna wanted to beg Tag to reconsider, but the

look Windhawk gave her silenced her just in time.

"I thought that is what you might be planning to do, Tag," Windhawk said hurriedly, not trusting Joanna to keep her objections to herself. "Have you thought this through and know it is what you want to do?"

"Yes, I have to. The two white men who . . . shot Morning Song were sent by Claudia and Uncle Howard to kill me. I heard them talking about it." He looked into Joanna's eyes. "You understand I have to go, don't you, Joanna?"

Joanna's mouth flew opened in horror as the truth of the situation hit her. She hadn't considered for one moment that Tag has been the intended victim of the men who had shot Morning Song. It was hard to believe that her uncle and Claudia would go to such lengths to harm Tag.

"Yes, Tag, I can see that you have to go. I wish I could go with you. I hate the thought that you will . . ."

Windhawk touched Joanna's hand, and she knew he was telling her to let Tag go. "You must do what you must do, Tag," she said in a soft whisper.

"I would ask something of you, Joanna. I can leave with peace of mind if I know you will be caring for the little princess. Before Morning Song died, she asked me to give the baby to you."

"I will love and care for the little princess as if she were my own daughter, Tag. But one day, when this is all settled, you must come back for her. Not so much that she will need you, but that you will need her."

Tag nodded his head, and his eyes traveled to the cradle where his daughter slept. "I'll be back, you can depend on that, but it may be a long while before I return. Tell her about me and her mother. Never allow her to forget that I . . . love her." Tag's eyes were full of sorrow as he looked at his sister. "Joanna, I have to go back—try to understand. Morning Song made me promise before she died that I would go to Philadelphia. Don't you see it's something that I have to do?"

"I always knew this day would come, Tag." Joanna turned away so Tag wouldn't see the tears in her eyes. "I think I will go to visit Farley," she said, rushing from the lodge before she made Tag feel worse by her tears.

Tag half-stood to go after her, but Windhawk stopped him. "Let her go. She will be back soon."

Tag sighed heavily. "Help her understand that I am doing the right thing, Windhawk."

"She knows. Did she not prepare you for this for many years? I also prepared you to return to face the man who has wronged you. You are strong and brave, Tag. You can meet any man in a fight and come out the winner." Windhawk clasped Tag's arm. "You will be missed by the Blackfoot. Send word to your sister, so she will know how you are doing."

Tag nodded in agreement, and they both lapsed into silence. Although Windhawk wasn't old enough to be Tag's father, he had taken on the role in Tag's life for many years, and Tag wanted him to know how much he valued his strong guidance.

"Windhawk, I . . ."

"Do not speak it," Windhawk interrupted. "There has never been the need for words between the two of us. Just remember that your sister and I will always be here for you."

"You do not mind my leaving the little princess with you?"

"As she begins to grow, I will say the things to her that you would say if you were here. I will love my sister's daughter as if she were my own."

"Windhawk, my uncle and Claudia will pay for Morning Song's death. You can depend on that."

Again both men lapsed into silence. There was no more that needed to be said.

Joanna rushed into Farley's tipi and threw herself into his arms. "He's going, Farley! Tag's leaving!"

Farley patted her awkwardly on the back. "You always knowed he would go, Joanna. This can't come as news to you."

"I know, Farley, but this is so sudden. I'm afraid for him. The men who killed Morning Song were sent by my uncle and Claudia to kill Tag!" she cried, tears streaming down her face.

Farley studied her face closely. "Are you telling the right of it?"

"Yes, Tag overheard the two men talking about it."

"I been having me a hankering to see this here Philli-whatever it's called. I 'speck I'll just mosey on down there with Tag to see what's going on."

Joanna threw her arms around Farley, laughing and crying at the same time. "Thank you, Farley, my dear, dear friend. I will feel better knowing you will be with him."

Farley winked at Joanna. "It could be young Tag that will have to look after me. When them big city women get a look at me, they might want to take me home with 'em and domast-a-kate me."

Joanna kissed his rough cheek. "I will miss you. Come home to me soon."

The whole village had gathered to see Tag and Farley off. Tag mounted his horse and looked at the sea of faces that he knew so well. Many of his boyhood friends raised their hands in a silent salute of farewell. Tag had already told his daughter, Joanna, and Windhawk good-bye in private. His eyes now sought his sister's, and he saw the tears swimming in their blue depths. Windhawk placed his arm about Joanna and drew her to him. Tag knew he was leaving behind all that was dear to him. He would be riding into the unknown, where he would meet with hostile forces and people who wanted to see him dead, but there was no turning back. The road had been mapped out for him years before—he now had to follow it to the end.

Suddenly, the crowd moved aside to make a path for Sun Woman, who was trying to reach Tag. He had feared he would have to leave without telling her good-bye, for when he'd gone to her tipi she hadn't been there, and no one he asked had known where she was.

When she reached his side, she was breathing hard, as if she had been running. "I feared you would have left before I could get back, my son."

Tag smiled down at her kindly. As the mother of his wife, she had not spoken to him in the two years he had been married to Morning Song. Now, there was no longer any need for her to remain silent.

"I had searched everywhere for you but could not find you, my mother."

"Night Falcon," she said, calling him by his Indian

79

name. "I heard that you were returning to the white world, so I give you a gift to take along with you," she said, handing a leather pouch up to him. The bag seemed to be very heavy, and she was having trouble lifting it.

"What is this, my mother?" he inquired.

"I went to our sacred mountain and filled the pouch with the yellow rock that the white man craves. I know Morning Song would want you to have it, since you are going back to the white world."

"I could never take . . ."

"Do not speak, my son. Use it to find and destroy my daughter's murderers. Do this for me."

Tag leaned forward and kissed Sun Woman on the cheek. "It will be as you say, my mother. Help Joanna take care of the little princess for me."

"Come back soon, my son. You must not tarry long in the white world. Your daughter does not yet have a proper name—you must hurry home so you can name her."

"It is so, my mother," he said kindly.

Looking beyond Sun Woman, Tag caught Joanna's eyes and sent her a silent message of love. He then turned his horse and rode out of the village with Farley at his side.

Joanna ran into the lodge and threw herself down on the bed, crying. She felt strong arms go about her, and Windhawk lifted her into his arms, cradling her as if she were a small child.

"There has been so much sadness lately, my Joanna. Put it out of your heart. Take my hand, and together we will overcome all the pain."

She wiped her eyes and looked up into her husband's handsome face. His dark eyes caught and held hers, and she leaned forward to touch his lips. Yes, with Windhawk beside her she could overcome anything. He would help her heal.

As Tag left the Blackfoot village behind, he stared straight ahead. Each mile he traveled brought him that much closer to the enemy. His blue eyes were laced with hatred, and the hands that gripped the reins were white about the knuckles from the pressure he was applying to them.

Farley kept pace with Tag, knowing that he would have to keep a close watch on him.

They rode in silence for days, not even talking much to each other when they made camp at night.

Many times Tag wanted to turn his horse and ride back to all that was dear and familiar to him . . . but a force stronger than himself kept pushing him onward. That force was the power of revenge!

Chapter Seven

February 1848

Taggart James leaned against the rail of the barge and stared down at the muddy water of the Missouri River without really seeing it. There was wild, unleashed fury in his heart, and he was driven almost past the point of reasoning by the need to punish Claudia and his Uncle Howard.

His deep violet-blue eyes were cold as he glanced at the shoreline, willing the barge to move faster so he could reach his destination. He sighed inwardly, knowing it would still be weeks before he reached Philadelphia.

Closing his eyes, he could still see Morning Song's lovely face and hear the sound of her laughter. He clenched his fists together tightly, and with sheer will power resisted the urge to slam them against the wooden railing.

Had it only been four months since Morning Song had died in his arms? It seemed like a lifetime ago, and yet the hurt was still so acute. Wild, jumbled thoughts tripped through his mind, and he wanted to strike out against anything to relieve his agony.

Sitting down on a wooden crate, Tag leaned his head against the railing, while his mind drifted back in time . . .

As the cold icy winds blew off the river, Tag remembered himself as a twelve-year-old boy standing at his mother's gravesite, holding on to his sister's hand and feeling lost and helpless. Later, he and Joanna were to learn that their father was also dead. That was when the trouble had all began. He and Joanna had been forced to flee their home in Philadelphia. How long ago that seemed now. So much had happened since then.

His eyes narrowed, and he glanced up at the sky as a cloud drifted across the sun, throwing the land into darkened shadow. He would have his revenge on his Uncle Howard and Claudia. His lip curled into a sneer when he thought of Claudia. After Tag's Aunt Margaret had died, his uncle had married Claudia Maxwell, who was a jealous, bitter woman. Tag never had understood why Claudia hated Joanna so bitterly and would do anything to hurt her. Claudia had tried on several occasions in the past to harm Joanna, but had miraculously failed. Tag thought of the time Claudia had helped Howard Landon capture Joanna, but fortunately Windhawk had rescued her.

Farley, the old trapper, stood in the shadows watching Tag. The young man and his sister, Joanna, were very dear to him. His heart was heavy that Tag had lost his lovely young wife. As Farley gazed upon Tag's face, he saw the agony in his blue eyes. Tag was a tall man with broad shoulders and narrow hips. His body was muscled from the training as a warrior he had received from the Blackfoot. His face was handsome,

83

except for the coldness in his eyes. He was still dressed in buckskin breeches and shirt—around his shoulder-length hair he still wore the leather headband about his forehead. He had a haunted look about him, and though he had the coloring of the white race, Farley knew that he had the training and the outlook of an Indian.

Farley had known Tag and Joanna since they had been traveling with the ill-fated wagon train that had been attacked by the Blackfoot. Although he was very close to them, he had never been told why Tag and his sister had fled their home in Philadelphia, but he had heard enough over the years to know it had something to do with their aunt and uncle.

The old trapper made sure the horses were securely tied to the barge railing before he moved over to sit down beside Tag on the wooden crate.

"It 'pears it might rain 'afore we reach shelter, but I don't think so. I'm most often right 'bout the weather," Farley said, looking overhead at the dark clouds.

Tag nodded his head as if he hadn't really heard the old man.

Farley crossed his legs and let out a spew of tobacco juice, then wiped his mouth on the back of his hand. "I figure we'll be making Independence 'afore dark," he said, trying to draw Tag out of his dark mood.

Tag lifted his eyes and studied the old trapper. No one knew for sure how old Farley was, though his beard and hair were completely white. He was a wiry man who seemed to amble instead of walk. Tag loved the old man as the grandfather he had never had. He knew that his sister must have asked Farley to accompany him to Philadelphia. Suddenly, Tag felt the urge to talk to someone, and he knew Farley was a good listener.

"Have you ever been in Philadelphia, Farley?" Tag asked in the Blackfoot language he had become so accustomed to.

"Nope, never had the urge. I 'spect you might ought to speak in English, Tag. The rest of them passengers is beginning to stare at us a bit," Farley cautioned.

Tag nodded in agreement—the last thing in the world he wanted to do was to call attention to himself. "I remember very little about Philadelphia myself, Farley. I can recall my mother's face very clearly, but my father's face is a blank to me," he said, lapsing into English.

"That's only natural, since they's been dead so long. I 'member Joanna once telling me that the two of you grew up in England."

"Yes, my father had a large shipping business in England, and when I was quite young he relocated us to America. When he and my mother died, Joanna and I were both too young to run the company. My father's sister, Margaret, and her husband came to live with us."

Farley watched Tag's eyes narrow, and he knew Tag was remembering more than he was saying. The old trapper had never been one to pry, but he felt that Tag needed to talk now.

"I always wondered why you and Joanna was traveling on that wagon train. You'll recollect that was the first time I ever seed you and your sister."

Tag smiled at the old man. "Yes, I remember quite

well. I thought you were an awesome figure as you told us about being married to a Blackfoot woman and living among her people. Little did I know at that time that I, too, would live with the Blackfoot and be married to . . ." His voice trailed off, and Farley watched the naked pain in Tag's eyes. Wanting to distract his troubled thoughts, Farley touched his arm.

"Tell me 'bout your aunt and uncle."

The sadness in the depth of Tag's blue eyes turned to cold hatred. "They . . . my aunt and uncle moved into our house and just took over. My Uncle Howard wanted to send me to sea when I was but twelve, and he told Joanna that if she didn't cooperate with him, he would see that I never returned from the sea. You can imagine how Joanna reacted to that."

Farley knew without being told that the uncle had made advances toward Joanna. He could well imagine what the two young people had been forced to deal with before they ran away. "That's when the two of you left, was it?"

"Yes, with the help of our servants, Franny and Simon, we escaped one night through an upstairs bedroom window. Later we joined the wagon train, hoping to reach our father. We didn't know at that time he was dead."

"Ifen I'm hearing you right, you're saying that your aunt and uncle just up and took all that by rights belongs to you and Joanna."

"Yes, and for a long time I didn't care if they had it all. I . . . was happy with Morning Song, and I knew that as my wife she would never be accepted by Philadelphia society. Rather than see her hurt . . . I was willing to live out my life in the Blackfoot village with her." Tag's eyes seemed to blaze with a blue fire. "Had my uncle but known, he could have had it all. I doubt that I would ever have challenged him. He made a fatal mistake when he sent those two men after me. Had they not killed Morning Song . . ." Tag raised his hands in a hopeless gesture.

"Wanna talk 'bout Morning Song?"

"Yes, I think I can now. We were riding that day, acting like two carefree children. When I was with Morning Song, I always felt this overwhelming happiness, and she made me feel good about life. We had everything we could ever want . . . I was almost content. To be honest with you, though, I had begun to feel restless, and Morning Song knew I was thinking about my uncle. She made me promise before she died that I would settle this thing once and for all. I think she knew I would never be completely happy until I confronted my uncle."

"What happened that day, Tag?" Farley asked, knowing Tag had not told anyone, not even Joanna, much about how Morning Song had died.

"As I said, we were riding, and suddenly I heard a shot ring out. I turned to Morning Song to ask if she had heard the shot, and that was when I realized she had been hit. I lifted her into my arms, carrying her behind the cover of some rocks, where she gave birth to . . . my daughter . . . and then died in my arms."

The agony Tag felt plainly showed in his eyes, and Farley placed a comforting arm on his shoulder. "Ifen you don't want to, you don't have to say no more, Tag."

"No, it's all right. I need to tell someone about

what happened. Morning Song . . ." Tag swallowed convulsively before he could continue. "She . . . looked at me with those beautiful soft eyes . . . she knew she was dying. She . . . was bleeding a lot, and I couldn't stop the blood!"

Tag stood up and leaned against the railing, and Farley rose to stand beside him. "She . . . said she loved me and asked me not to grieve for her . . . I held her as she died! Morning Song made me swear I would go back to Philadelphia."

Farley could feel the tears in his eyes, and he wiped them away on the back of his hand. "What happened then, Tag? Was that when you killed that white devil?"

"I could hear two riders coming, so I waited for them to draw even with me. I had no weapon, except my knife. I heard them talking and realized that they were looking for me. When they drew rein, they were no more than three horse lengths away from me, and I waited for my chance."

Tag held up his hand, indicating he couldn't talk about it anymore. "I killed one man, and Windhawk killed the other." He lapsed into silence, as if he were reliving the scene in his mind. "It was Claudia who sent them after me, Farley. She will pay dearly for Morning Song's death!"

Tag had hardly spoken above a whisper, and Farley knew that he was making a solemn promise to his dead wife.

"That vermin, Claudia," Farley spat out. "I never knowed why your uncle got tangled up with the likes of her."

"Neither do I, but apparently he married her after

my aunt died," Tag replied, remembering how much Joanna had suffered at Claudia's hands in the past.

"Why do you 'spose your uncle sent those two men after you, Tag?"

"I don't know, but I intend to find out."

"What's the plan?"

"I don't have one, Farley. You remember Simon, my servant? He has been waiting for many years for me to return to Philadelphia, keeping an eye on my uncle's movements. I suppose the first thing to do will be to contact him. He has been saving my mother's jewels for me in case I need to sell them to fight my uncle and Claudia. Since Sun Woman gave me the gold, I won't have to sell the jewels after all."

Farley smiled when he looked into Tag's face. "Sun Woman's quite a person, but then, so is her son. I never knowed a finer man than Windhawk, be he white or Indian."

"Yes, I agree." Tag shook his head. "I know about the cave where the gold was found . . . Morning Song once told me about it."

"You surely won't have to worry 'bout selling your mother's doodads; Windhawk gave me gold, too. I reckon he didn't know his mother had the same idea," the old man said.

Tag thought how like Windhawk it was, to secretly give Farley the gold, knowing it would help them when they reached Philadelphia. It was because of Windhawk's training that Tag feared no man. The Blackfoot chief had instilled confidence in Tag as a boy, and he knew he would need to call on that strength many times when he reached Philadelphia.

It was as if there were two people inside of Taggart

James—one was an educated white man, the other was a Blackfoot warrior. Joanna had always insisted that he study his lessons, and Tag knew he would be able to function in the white world even though he hadn't been there since he was a boy. There had been times in the past when he had lost patience with his sister when she had grilled him on how to act like a proper gentleman, but now he knew her training would place him in good stead. The other side of him—the Indian side—was that part of him where all semblance of "civilization" was stripped away, enabling him to live in the wild, untamed Blackfoot territory where a man's strength and courage were his only chances of survival. A weak man or a coward could never live for very long in Blackfoot country.

"Are you aiming to just go marching up to your uncle and demand he get out of your house and turn the business over to you?" Farley wanted to know.

"No, I realize I cannot do that. If my uncle wanted me dead, he must feel very confident that he can get his hands on my father's fortune. Chances are he had convinced some ne'er-do-well lawyer to help him in his takeover. I don't want them to discover my presence just yet, so I will have to assume another identity until I feel out the situation. I doubt that either Claudia or my Uncle Howard would recognize me, since neither of them has seen me since I was twelve. Let us hope so, anyway."

"That's kinda what I thought. Don't you fret none. I intend to stay right beside you in case of trouble," the old trapper told him.

Tag smiled. "I know Joanna asked you to come with me. How did she ever convince you to return to the civilization you detest so much?"

"Twern't hard. Your sister has always got what she wanted out of me. 'Sides, I wasn't 'bout to let you go into this without a friend at your back."

Tag stared down at the river, which was churning and turning beneath the barge. The first drops of rain had started to fall, and he pulled his jacket around his shoulders. "You are a good friend, Farley, but you sure as hell can't predict the weather. You said that it wouldn't rain until we reached shelter."

The old man grinned, showing a surprising amount of white teeth. "Ifen I can't tell the weather, at least I sure as hell am good looking."

Tag chuckled. Talking with Farley had put him in a happier frame of mind. "I guess you and Windhawk have been the best friends anyone could ask for." Tag was quiet for a moment before he continued. "I sure will miss Joanna, and I . . . know I will never forget Morning Song."

"What 'bout the child, your daughter? You ain't once mentioned her."

"I . . . Joanna will take good care of her. It was Morning Song's wish that I give . . . our daughter to Joanna."

The old man shook his head. Tag was so eaten up with grief and hatred that he gave little thought to his daughter. Farley could feel trouble coming for Tag, and when it came, he would stand by him all the way. If anyone wanted to harm Tag, they would have to go through him first!

Tag's horse, Navaron, whinnied, and Tag rubbed his silky coat to soothe him. By this time next week he and Farley would be deep in civilized country. Tag hoped he would remember all that Joanna had taught him about the way a gentleman would behave. He hoped Claudia and his Uncle Howard wouldn't be expecting him so soon. If they weren't looking for him, it would give him an advantage over them. He did have one thing in his favor—Claudia and Uncle Howard hadn't seen him since he was a boy. They had no notion how he now looked.

Tag's mind returned to the time Windhawk had bestowed the name Night Falcon on him. It had been just after the Blackfoot village had been attacked by their old enemies the Assiniboin. Tag had been only a boy then but he had helped get the women and children away to safety before the enemy struck. Later, Windhawk had honored him in a ceremony and given him the Indian name.

Tag smiled without humor. "Farley, I will just turn my Indian name around and pretend to be a gentleman from England named Falcon Knight."

Farley nodded his head. "That 'pears like a good idea to me."

As the barge bumped against the shore, Tag disembarked, feeling an urgency to reach Philadelphia as quickly as possible.

When he mounted his horse, he turned around and glanced back the way they had just come. He then squared his shoulders and nudged his mount forward. His destiny awaited him in Philadelphia—there would be no turning back!

Chapter Eight

Alexandria paced the floor of the tiny upstairs bedroom, remembering the carriage ride that had brought her from Valley Forge to Philadelphia. It had been a nightmare. Her stepmother hadn't allowed her out of her sight for a moment. In the two days it had taken to make the journey, she had been forced to endure sitting across from Rodney while he stared smugly at her and made suggestive remarks. He had often brushed against her leg and given her his strange smile that sent chills down her spine. Alexandria had considered trying to run away, but Barbara and Rodney hadn't given her any time to herself, and besides, there was nowhere to run.

Every so often, she would go to the window that overlooked the street. There were a number of other houses that were very similar to Barbara's sister's house, where she was now staying. This wasn't what one would call the more fashionable part of Philadelphia, she thought, watching several young boys playing on the cobblestone streets. Even though the weather was still quite cold, she noticed that their coats were tattered and threadbare, and some of them wore no shoes.

Walking back to the bed, she sat down and wrinkled her nose at the soiled bedcovering. Her mother had always remarked that water was free and soap was cheap, and even the poorest of the populace could afford to be clean. But that wasn't the case in this house. The bare wooden floors looked like they hadn't been washed in months, or even swept, for that matter. The once white walls were soiled and dingy, and the curtains at the windows were tattered and stained.

Alexandria hugged her arms about her, feeling cold and miserable. She had arrived in Philadelphia two days ago and had been forced to remain in this room since yesterday morning.

Twice her stepmother had come into the room to ask if Alexandria was ready to be sensible and marry Rodney. Each time Alexandria had refused. The last time Barbara had told her that her son had found a man of the cloth who was willing to perform the ceremony, and that, by tomorrow, she would be married whether she wished it or not.

Alexandria heard a scratching sound on the door and waited for whoever it was to enter. She was surprised when one of the young boys she had seen playing in the street poked his head around the door and smiled at her.

"Hello, are you really gonna marry my cousin Rodney?" he asked.

"Hello, yourself, and no, I am not going to marry your cousin." Alexandria thought the boy might be somewhere around twelve or thirteen. He was so ragged and dirty that her heart went out to him.

"I'm glad you ain't gonna to marry Rodney. I don't

94

like him much."

Alexandria smiled. "I don't like him much myself. Come and sit beside me, and we can talk," she said, moving to the foot of the bed so he would have room.

He looked shy for a moment, then he walked toward her hesitantly. Alexandria patted the bed, and he plopped down beside her, holding his tattered cap in his hands. "You are much too pretty to be married to Rodney. Why don't you just run away? I've heard them talking below, and they found a man who will join the two of you together without asking no questions."

"I know—Barbara told me. Did you hear them mention when the marriage would take place?"

"They said something about tomorrow night," the young boy said, confirming what Barbara had already told her.

"What's your name?" she asked.

"Name's Johnny. I know yours is Alexandria."

Alexandria nodded. "Johnny, do you think you could help me get away?"

The young boy looked taken aback for a moment. "I can't help you . . . my ma would give me a licking if she knew I even thought such a thing."

"I would pay you, Johnny. Have you ever had a five-dollar gold piece?"

Johnny's eyes brightened. "Nope, but I saw one once. My ma was doing some sewing for a grand lady like you, and the woman paid her two five-dollar gold pieces."

Alexandria reached into the pocket of her gown and withdrew some coins and showed them to the boy. "If you will help me, I will give you this money."

Johnny studied the money in her hand and then looked back to her face. "I'd surely like to help you, and not just for the money. I don't think it's right what they're doing to you, but they're keeping too close an eye on you."

Alexandria took his hand and held it tightly. "You are the only one I can turn to, Johnny. There is no one else I can ask. Please say you will help me."

Johnny stood up and stared down at the toe of his scuffed brown shoes. "It ain't the money that I'm wanting. I'll help you for nothing. What can I do?"

Alexandria reached out, raised his chin, and smiled. "I don't know. Perhaps you have some ideas."

Johnny's face brightened. Alexandria had won the little boy's heart with her smile. He found himself willing to do anything that would save her from his Aunt Barbara and Cousin Rodney. "We could sneak you out of the house tonight, and you could run away . . . no, that wouldn't do no good. Dressed in those fancy trappings you're bound to get into trouble." Johnny was quiet for a moment, and then he smiled. "I betcha you could fit into some of my britches and shirt, then everyone would think you was a boy!"

"I don't think that would be a very practical idea," Alexandria said laughingly. "I doubt that anyone would believe I was a boy."

"Yeh, I reckon you're right. I'd better go now— Ma's sure to give me a licking if she finds me in here with you. I'll try to come back tonight."

Alexandria nodded, watching helplessly as Johnny left. Getting to her feet, she walked over to the window and gazed out at the setting sun. It was a dismal landscape, and Alexandria could feel the hopelessness of her situation. If young Johnny had been telling the truth and Barbara had found an unscrupulous minister to perform the marriage, there would be nothing she could do to save herself.

She turned around, facing the door. When Johnny left he hadn't locked the door! What would stop her from just walking down the stairs and out the front door? But then where would she go, and what would she do? She didn't have much money, and Johnny had been correct when he said she couldn't go about dressed as she was.

Turning back to the window, she stood watching the last dying rays of the sun reflect off the windows of the house across the street. Was it possible in this day and age for a young woman to be forced into marrying someone she detested? Couldn't she just tell the preacher when she saw him that she didn't want to marry Rodney? No, evidently Barbara had been very selective in the minister she had chosen to perform the ceremony, knowing she would meet with resistance from Alexandria.

Walking over to the door, Alexandria opened it quietly, went out into the hallway, and looked about cautiously. Seeing no one in sight, she moved quickly to the stairs. Her foot had barely touched the top step when Johnny's mother appeared at the bottom of the stairs. Her face was grim, and she motioned for Alexandria to return to the bedroom. Knowing it would be of little use to rebel, Alexandria did as she was told.

An hour passed, and Alexandria could hear the sound of laughter coming from below. Again she started the restless pacing. The door opened, and

Alexandria turned to face Rodney, who carried a tray of food.

"You may as well take that back to the kitchen, Rodney. I am not hungry."

He placed the tray on a chair and walked over to her. "Your uppity ways won't get you anywhere with me. I was told by my mother that you have eaten nothing today. It doesn't serve my purpose for you to starve yourself. I want a bride who is strong and able on my wedding night."

"I'll never be your bride, Rodney! Never!"

He advanced toward her and reached out to touch her face. "Oh, you will be my wife, like it or not. I think you will like it, though. I know how to treat a woman."

"I will never allow you to touch me. You are disgusting!"

His gray eyes clouded, and he pulled her against him tightly. "I think I'll just give you a sample of what's in store for you right now, Alexandria."

She twisted and turned, trying to get free, but his grip only tightened. "Squirm all you want to, Alexandria, you will never be free of me. I think you and I will celebrate our wedding tonight instead of tomorrow night."

Alexandria could smell the whiskey on his breath and knew he was more than a little drunk. Her skin seemed to crawl when she looked into his eyes. "Let me go, or you will regret it," she told him, jabbing a knee into his groin. He muttered an oath as Alexandria jerked free of him and ran toward the door. She felt the door knob in her hand and was about to wrench the door open when he grabbed her by the shoulder and pinned her against the wall. "Fight all you want to, Alexandria. In the end it won't get you a damned thing."

"Release me this moment, or I'll scream! I swear I will!"

"Beautiful Alexandria, no one in this house will care what I do to you. Don't you know that by now?"

Alexandria squirmed and struggled and finally managed to get free again. She saw that Rodney was blocking the door and the only way to save herself would be to fight. Picking up the lamp on the nearby table, she raised it over her head.

"Come one step closer, and I'll throw this at you! I swear I will!" she threatened. This time Rodney had pushed her too far, and she would do whatever she must to save herself. Her hands were trembling, and she bit her lower lip to stop its quivering.

Rodney uttered a strangled oath and staggered in her direction. Not pausing to think, Alexandria threw the lamp, and it seemed to explode into a fire. Rodney screamed and grabbed his face as the flames licked at his clothing and spread quickly up to his body.

Alexandria jerked the coverlet from the bed and tossed it about him, trying to smother the blaze. When the bedroom door burst open, she had extinguished the fire, and her stepmother stood as if paralyzed with a look of horror on her face.

"Send for the doctor!" she screeched as others came into the room.

Alexandria stood up, feeling sick as her stepmother removed the charred bedcovering. Rodney's clothing was still smoking, and his face looked like a cooked piece of meat. He was moaning softly, and she backed away, shaking her head in horror, knowing she was responsible for what had happened to him. Even though she despised Rodney, she hadn't wanted to harm him in such a horrible manner. She had only wanted to make him leave her alone.

Alexandria watched as Barbara and her sister lifted Rodney onto the bed. She was horrified that she had been the instrument of so much pain to another human being, but she wasn't sorry that she had save herself.

After Rodney had been made as comfortable as possible, his mother sat beside him, waiting for the doctor, while Alexandria hovered in the corner, not knowing what to do. Suddenly Barbara's eyes fell on Alexandria, and she started screaming. "Take her below and lock her in the basement! I will see that she is punished for what she did to my son!"

Alexandria was too stunned to react. She allowed Barbara's sister to lead her from the room. She was still in a daze when the woman shoved her through a door, and she went stumbling down the wooden steps into the darkened basement. Pain shot through Alexandria's body as she hit the dirt floor hard and her head slammed against the wall. Moaning, she looked up the steps to see the woman outlined in the dim light coming from the kitchen.

"You will pay for this night's work. We will see that you swing from the gallows if my nephew dies," the woman said before slamming the door and shooting a bolt into place.

The basement was dark and damp and smelled of rotting potatoes and mildew. Alexandria sat up as pain seemed to course through her body. Her worst pain seemed to come from her knee. Feeling along her leg, she discovered it was bleeding. She must have knelt in the broken glass from the lamp when she was putting out the fire. Alexandria scooted along until she came to the wall, then leaned back against it, biting her lip to keep from crying out in pain. It was pitch black, and the wall she was leaning against felt damp and moldy.

Alexandria raised her skirt and ripped off a piece of her petticoat. She then wrapped it about the cuts on her knee, hoping to stop the flow of blood. In her mind, she could still see Rodney with his body engulfed in flames. How could anyone survive after being so horribly burned? Would the authorities believe her if she told them the truth? She shook her head. They might have listened to her back in Valley Forge, but she doubted that she could make them believe her here in Philadelphia where no one knew her.

Alexandria was cold and miserable, and she huddled closer to the wall, trying to keep warm. She tried not to think about the scurrying sounds of little feet she could hear in the dark recesses of the basement, knowing it was probably rats. Her body was trembling from cold and fright. There was no one to care what happened to her. There would be no one to know should she just disappear from the face of the earth.

In spite of the cold and dark, Alexandria finally cried herself to sleep. She didn't know how much time had passed when someone shook her by the shoulder, waking her from a fretful sleep.

Alexandria opened her eyes and saw Johnny holding a candle up to her face.

"Are you hurt?" he asked, with concern written on his young face.

"Don't worry about me. How is Rodney?"

Johnny shook his head. "It don't look good for him. The doctor don't think he will live out the week."

"Johnny, I didn't mean to do it. He was . . . I only wanted to . . . "

"You don't have to be explaining to me. I got ears . . . I know what he was trying to do to you while all the rest of them stood outside the door sniggering and laughing. He don't deserve to live."

"You mustn't say that, Johnny! It was horrible what I did to him. I will never forgive myself for what happened to Rodney."

"My ma always says the good Lord helps those that help themselves. I guess you helped yourself in the only way you could."

"What are they going to do with me, Johnny?"

"I heard my aunt talking to my pa. She said they would have you committed to an institution for the insane. That way she could hold on to your farm, and you'd be locked away for good."

Alexandria gasped in horror. "I'm not insane, Johnny! They can't do such a thing to me!"

"That's why I'm here. In the morning, bright and early, some men will be coming to carry you away. If you are going to escape, it will have to be tonight."

"What can I do?"

"I brung you some of my clothes, and my ma's scissors. I 'spect the best thing will be for you to dress like a boy like we said earlier."

"I couldn't . . . that wouldn't be proper."

"I don't think you can worry about what's proper."

Johnny tossed some clothes in her lap, and Alexandria studied his face.

"I have nowhere to go," she said in a small voice.

"Anywhere will be better than the asylum," he told her. "Now get into these clothes while I turn my back. Time is against you."

That was all the prodding Alexandria needed. She quickly stripped off her clothing and donned Johnny's britches and shirt. Then she exchanged her leather slippers for his boots.

"You can turn around now, Johnny. How do I look?"

He set the candle down and walked around her, studying her critically. "You still look like a girl to me." Reaching into his pocket, he withdrew his mother's scissors. "I guess when I've cut your hair you'll look more like a boy."

Alexandria nodded her head in agreement, but she couldn't help cringing when he began snipping off her long tresses. In no time at all, Johnny had snipped off all her curls. Standing back, studying her speculatively, he grinned.

"If I didn't know better, I'd say you was a boy."

"Now what shall I do?" Alexandria asked, looking to Johnny for guidance.

"I'm going to bury your gown along with the hair I cut off near the back of the basement. All I can tell you is to light out. I don't know where you can go. Do you have any friends back in Valley Forge who'll hide you out until this thing passes?"

"N . . . no."

"Look, it's gonna be light before long. You gotta get as far away from here as you can. I done all I can

103

to help you."

Alexandria put her hand on the boy's shoulder. "Will you get into trouble for helping me?"

"I might get a licking from my ma, but that's nothing compared to what you'll get if my Aunt Barbara finds you here when it comes daylight."

Alexandria picked up her discarded gown and reached into the pocket, pulling out the coins she had offered him earlier. "Here Johnny—I want you to have this money for helping me."

He closed his hand over hers. "No, you'll need it much more than I will. It will be my reward knowing that you escaped my aunt and cousin. Now hurry before the house begins to wake up. I'll just bury these things," he said, taking her gown from her.

Alexandria hastily kissed him on the cheek, then hurried up the basement stairs. The kitchen was dark, and she bumped noisily against a table. Fearing she might have awakened the whole household, she dashed into the hallway and out the front door. She ran down the streets, not daring to look back for fear she was being pursued. Darting around corners and across cobblestone streets, Alexandria ran until she was totally exhausted. Leaning against a tree, she waited to catch her breath. She was in a strange city, and she had no one to turn to for help, but at least she was free!

Chapter Nine

Philadelphia, March 1848

The Fox and Hound Inn was bustling with activity. It was long after the dinner hour, and yet the room was filled with customers since a ship had recently docked and its crew was taken advantage of their first night in port. A cold wind howled outside the tavern, and a light snowfall was drifting earthward. Inside the tavern a warm, cheery fire was crackling in the big open hearth. The sound of merriment and laughter was deafening as a small, insignificant figure huddled in one corner of the taproom, trying to appear as inconspicuous as possible.

Alexandria Bradford could feel the hard wooden floor beneath her, and she shifted her weight, removing a splinter that had been prickling her tender skin. She watched as a pretty tavern maid moved from table to table, serving food and ale with a warm smile. Alexandria could smell the mutton pies and leg of lamb, and her stomach growled in hungry protest.

Pulling the wool cap down lower over her head, she leaned back against the wall and studied the people in the room. The seamen weren't hard to detect, with their knee-length trousers and colorful shirts. Their faces seemed to be permanently creased from the hours they spent on the decks of ships, exposed to the sun and salt water.

Alexandria observed the tawny-haired tavern wench laughing while side-stepping one of the sailor's over-amorous overtures. Alexandria had never been exposed to the kind of people who frequented the Fox and Hound, and she felt fear deep inside. She hoped her disguise was good, and that no one would suspect that she was a female!

Alexandria shuddered, remembering all she had been told about sailors' shanghaiing unsuspecting men and boys, forcing them to sail on their ships. She huddled closer to the wall, hoping no one would pay her any attention.

Alexandria was cold, wet, and hungry, but at least she was free. She didn't know what she would do or where she would go, but for the moment she had escaped her stepmother. She remembered the sight of Rodney's charred body and shivered. Surely he would be dead by now, and the authorities were probably searching for her—if they found her, she would more than likely hang for murder.

She had spent her last coin on food the day before, and her plan was to try and hide until the tavern closed, then sneak over to one of the tables to eat what someone had left on his plate. If she wasn't discovered, she might even be able to sleep beside the hearth. The night before she had crept into a carriage house and slept in one of the carriages. She had intended to be gone before she could be discovered the next morning, but she had been so tired she hadn't awakened until someone discovered her and tossed her none too gently into the street.

Alexandria felt herself nodding off, and she fought to stay awake. She warned herself that she must not make the same mistake that she had the night before—if she did, she would surely be thrown out into the cold to freeze.

She tried to think of happy thoughts to keep her awake, but all she could think of was how hungry she was. Looking across the room, she saw an empty table with the remains of someone's uneaten food.

Standing up, she looked about carefully to see if anyone was watching her. The sailors seemed to be distracted by the pretty tavern maid. Now was her chance, she thought. Inching herself along the wall, she kept her eyes on the table nearest her destination where three men were laughing and talking loudly. Taking a cautious step and then another, she finally was in reach of the table. Grabbing a half-eaten leg of lamb, she started to run back to her darkened corner, but before she could move, she was grabbed from behind and swung around to face a huge mountain of a man with a red beard. She squirmed as he lifted her up and dangled her in midair.

"Look what we got us here, men," the sailor said in a loud, boisterous voice that seemed to draw everyone's attention to Alexandria. "If this here lad was a fish, I'd sooner toss him back to sea. He ain't big enough to keep." The red-headed man's laughter was joined by the others', and Alexandria bit her lip in vexation.

"What think you, men—should we take the lad here back to ship and present him to the good captain as a cabin boy?"

"Aye," came the reply. "The last lad we had died of the fever; this here scrawny lad will take his place."

Alexandria began to feel real panic now. She kicked her legs and twisted in the man's iron grip, but this only served to amuse him. "Ho, men, this lad has spirit!" he laughed loudly, dropping Alexandria to the floor, where she landed hard on her backside.

Standing up, Alexandria started to inch slowly away from him, only to back into another wall of human flesh. The giant red-headed man reached down for her and lifted her up into the air again. Alexandria realized she still held the leg of lamb in her hand, so she drew her arm back and hit him hard across the face with it. He howled out in pain and immediately dropped her, and she landed atop one of the tables, with her face buried in a plate of food.

"Damn you," the man bellowed as he grabbed Alexandria again and raised his fist ready to smash it into her face. She closed her eyes, waiting for the blow to fall, when a quiet, clipped, accented voice called out from the doorway.

"Put the boy down . . . *now!*"

Alexandria turned to look at her would-be savior and gasped in surprise. His appearance in no way resembled his cultured English accent. The stranger was a tall, golden-haired man, but she couldn't see his face very clearly, since it was cast in shadows. He stepped into the light when he walked toward the red-headed man, and Alexandria was surprised to see that he was not only extremely handsome, but young as well.

"I said put the boy down!" the newcomer said. He

hadn't even raised his voice, and yet there was something in the way he spoke that chilled the red-headed sailor to the bone.

"You think you be man enough to make me, stranger?" the red-headed man said, knowing he couldn't back down in front of his companions. He shoved Alexandria off the table and sent her sprawling across the floor. "There, I put the boy down. Was it to your liking?"

Alexandria scrambled to her feet and was immediately pulled aside by the tavern wench, who handed her a cloth with which to wipe the food from her face. "Who is he, lad?" the tawny-haired woman asked with a gleam in her eye. "Be he your father or brother, mayhap?"

Alexandria wiped her face hurriedly before looking back to the golden-haired man in confusion. She couldn't help but think how out of place he looked dressed in buckskin. He appeared lean and hard. His handsome face was deeply tanned, and Alexandria thought he might be the perfect male specimen. For just a moment, his eyes settled on hers, and Alexandria saw the coldness in their blue depths.

"No, I have never seen him before in my life," she whispered, wondering why he had come to her rescue.

The tavern wench's eyes rested on the stranger hungrily. "Now, there's a man I could get fond of real quickly. I wonder who he is? It's for sure he ain't from around these parts, and he ain't from the sea."

"Be you ready to die, stranger?" the red-headed giant said, circling around the newcomer.

"I think not," the golden-haired man replied, watching the man carefully. "You can leave now, and

109

I will overlook your treatment of the boy. We'll just say you consumed too much rum, and let it go at that."

The sailor laughed contemptuously, knowing he had at least forty pounds on his challenger. "Let's not say that. Let's say I was gonna take the lad back to the ship with me, and I still am, lessen you think you're man enough to stop me."

"No, you aren't. The only way you will take that boy is if I'm dead." The threat was spoken softly, but it carried all the impact of an ultimatum.

"I think one should know the name of the man who's about to do him in. My name's Bob Travers, and I'm mate aboard the *Lucky Maiden* that just made port from England tonight—you got a name?"

By now, several of the red-haired man's friends had gathered around, and one of them reached for the knife he had tucked into his belt. Before he could withdraw it, however, an old man, also dressed in buckskin, placed the barrel of his rifle at the back of the man's neck. "Ifen I was you, I'd kinda ease off, and that goes for the rest of you, too. This don't concern none of you."

No one wanted to dispute the old man's argument. As far as they were concerned, Bob Travers was now on his own.

Tag's eyes narrowed, and Bob saw more than he wanted to in the blue depths. The coldness he read there sent a chill down his spine. He might be bigger than this man, but he knew he would have to prove his strength. He could see his mates watching with interest to see what the outcome would be. The first law of the sea was that a man had to prove himself in a fight. Bob knew he couldn't back down now, no matter how much he wanted to.

"My name isn't important. I give you one more chance to reconsider, Bob Travers," Tag said, leaning against the wall and crossing his arms over his chest. He stared at Travers with his piercing blue eyes, and the sailor knew he wouldn't have an easy conquest in this man.

In that moment, Bob leaped forward, but Tag smoothly sidestepped him and brought his elbow down against his back, knocking him to the floor. Before the luckless Bob could gain his feet, Tag leaped on top of him and pinned him beneath him. The hapless sailor knew he had been bested. He hadn't even been allowed to deliver one punch to the young man. He struggled, thinking he could throw the man off, but he was astounded at the strength of the golden-haired man.

"I know when I'm beat, stranger. Let me up, and we'll call it your fight."

Tag nodded, and with quick agility he stood up and offered the red-headed sailor his hand. "I think I'll just ask you to leave now," Tag said, nodding toward the door.

Bob's laughter roared out as he took the offered hand and allowed Tag to help him stand. "No hard feelings. When a man betters me, I'll admit it. I always like to know the name of the man who bested me, though."

Tag wasn't in a forgiving mood. He looked at Farley, who had lowered his rifle. "My friends call me Falcon . . . you can call me Mr. Knight."

Again Bob's laughter boomed out, and he slapped Tag on the shoulder. "It's pleased I am to meet you,

Mr. Knight. If ever you be needing a friend, you can always call on Big Bob Travers."

The big man gathered up his coat and motioned for his friends to follow him. Soon the tavern was empty but for the serving maid, Alexandria, and the two strangers.

Alexandria watched as the two men sat down at a table and the serving wench hurried over to them. Alexandria noticed that the pretty maid sidled up to the man who called himself Falcon Knight. She wanted to let him know how grateful she was that he had come to her rescue, but she didn't know if he would welcome her thanks. She waited until the serving maid took the two men's orders and left the tap room before she approached him.

"M . . . Mr. Knight, I want to thank you for saving me tonight. I don't know why you bothered, since I'm nothing to you, but I thank you all the same."

When his blue eyes settled on her, Alexandria drew in her breath. Never had she seen eyes that held so much coldness in their depths. For a moment she read many things in his eyes that she couldn't define: compassion, sadness, understanding, suffering. All those emotions were there in those expressive eyes, only to disappear when his eyes narrowed with a look of indifference.

"What's your name, boy?" the man asked, studying Alexandria with little interest.

"I am called Al . . . Alex."

"Well, Alex, it isn't really my practice to interfere in other people's problems, but I myself was almost sent to sea as a cabin boy when I was about your age. Just consider the matter ended and run along home."

Tag felt pity for the ragged little boy who had been treated so roughly. He was a dirty little beggar, and he couldn't tell much about his looks because his face was so smudged. He watched in irritation as the lad removed his tattered cap and twirled it around nervously.

"You see, sir, I don't have a home to go to. My mother and father are both dead, and I don't have nowhere to go. That was why I came in here. I wanted to get out of the cold and hoped I might pick up a crumb of bread." Alex didn't feel the least bit guilty that she was playing on the man's sympathies by acting the poor waif—after all, everything she had told him was the truth. She couldn't be blamed for omitting some of her story or for pretending to be a boy. Mr. Knight had been kind to her tonight; perhaps, he would give her a bite to eat.

"Climb up at the table, boy. From the looks of you, it would 'pear you could do with a good meal," the other man said. For the first time, Alexandria looked at the old man who was Mr. Knight's companion. His eyes were kind, and she could tell he had been moved by her woeful tale. Alexandria hurriedly sat down beside him before Mr. Knight decided to voice any objections.

"You sure are a scrawny little thing," the old man said. He reached across the table and offered Alex his hand. "My names Farley, Alex. You got a last name?"

She took the old man's hand and shook it. "Just Alex, nothing more. What's your last name?"

"Just Farley, nothing more."

By now, the serving wench had returned with a tray

113

of delicious-smelling food that made Alex's mouth water.

The golden man, which was how Alex thought of the man who had saved her, motioned for her to dig in to the food. He smiled slightly as she grabbed a bowl of stew, picked up a spoon, and started shoveling it hungrily into her mouth. Alex had only finished a portion of the stew when she pushed the bowl aside. She had been hungry, but it had taken very little food to fill her.

The two men ate quietly as Alexandria pushed her plate aside and laid her head down on the table. Suddenly, she began to feel tired, so she closed her eyes and felt herself drifting off to sleep.

"Poor little mite," Farley observed. "Do you reckon he was telling the truth 'bout being motherless?"

Tag lifted a cup of coffee to his lips and looked down at the curly, mink-colored hair. "Who can say? I suppose the least we can do is allow him to sleep in our room tonight, but I want him gone first thing in the morning. I don't need to adopt anyone else's troubles. I have plenty of my own."

The serving maid came over and stood beside Tag. She rubbed her body against his and gave him a promising glance. "My name's Molly. If there be anything you want . . . anything at all . . . you have only to ask for me," she said, giving Tag a smile that was an obvious invitation.

Farley grinned at Tag, and Tag gave him a heated glance before turning back to Molly. "All we will need is a place to stay for a few days."

Molly smiled, thinking that since this incredible man would be staying around, she might get the

114

chance to know him better. "I'll just show you to your rooms up them stairs."

Tag stood up, hoisted the young boy to his shoulder, and followed Molly, who was swinging her hips enticingly.

Farley grinned to himself when he noticed Tag watching Molly closely. He laughed aloud when Tag almost bumped into the railing. "It wouldn't hurt none ifen you was to watch where you was going," he said in amusement.

Tag gave Farley a dark glance, not caring much for the old man's humor.

Once inside the room, Molly lit the lamp, then Tag nodded for her to leave. He dumped his burden on the bed and stood staring down at him. He resented the fact that the young boy had struck a cord of pity in his heart. The last thing he needed was to be saddled with some lad who apparently couldn't stay out of trouble.

There were two beds in the room, and Tag sat down on the bed where he had placed the boy to remove his boots, leaving the other bed for Farley.

Farley dumped his pack on the floor and tested the bed gingerly. He lay down, fully clothed, and propped his hands behind his head. "Now this here is what I call living. I ain't slept in a real bed in . . . hell, I can't even remember when!"

Tag looked about the room in distaste. Although it seemed clean enough, he wasn't too impressed with the meager furnishings. He stripped his shirt and breeches off and stood clad only in his breechcloth. "I meant what I said about the boy, Farley," he warned. "Tomorrow he goes."

Farley grumbled to himself and turned over on his side.

Tag blew out the lamp and moved the boy over so he could lie down beside him, resenting the fact that he had to share his bed with a dirty little street urchin.

"That were a stroke of genius you turning your Indian name 'round and using it. I kinda like the sound of Falcon Knight," Farley said behind a yawn.

"I can't say I'm crazy about it, but I can hardly use my real name, can I?"

"Nope, I reckon not."

"I think we better not talk about it just now. The boy might awaken," Tag said, yawning.

"I 'spect," Farley said, drifting off to sleep.

Alex was dreaming that she was warm and protected. She could feel a hard, muscular body next to hers, and she sought to move closer to that warmth. She was only half awake when the man turned in his sleep, and she curled up around his body, falling to sleep once more.

Farley let out an oath and jumped out of bed. Grabbing the covers, he threw them on the floor and lay down on them. "I can't sleep on anything that moves," he muttered to himself, thinking a soft bed wasn't all he had thought it would be.

A light snow had begun to fall past the window and a chilled wind was blowing outside the small room. Alexandria sighed contentedly in her sleep. For the moment, her troubles were forgotten, and, for the first time in months, she slept an untroubled sleep.

Claudia Landon slipped out of her gown and walked toward her satin-covered bed. She smiled at

116

the man who lay there naked, waiting for her. Melvin Garner was her lawyer, and the only man to whom she could speak her mind.

"I'm sorry to be late, Melvin, but I had to see about poor old Howard."

"You'd better see that he is well and happy, Claudia. If he dies, you will be out of a home, and me along with you."

She laughed and dropped down on the bed beside him. "You are even more unscrupulous than I am. Don't worry. Howard will live a very long time, and Tag and Joanna will soon be dead."

"I wouldn't count on that, Claudia. The three men you sent after him didn't accomplish what you paid them to do. Two of them are dead, and the other one won't even talk about returning to finish the deed."

She lay down and rubbed her body against him. "You will just have to find someone else to send. You are the lawyer—you handle it."

"There is no one else to send. I have come to believe that the boy and his sister will never return. It appears to me that if they were coming back they would already have done so."

"Did the man see Tag?"

"He's not sure. He saw Gibbs shoot a white man before he died, but Jude doesn't know if it was Taggert James, and he couldn't find out if he died from his wounds. Jude said he was hiding in the woods and couldn't get near enough to see clearly."

"I don't know, Melvin. Joanna might not ever come back, but Tag will, if he's alive. You can bet your life he'll come back if he's able."

"I hope he does, Claudia. It would be far easier to

117

deal with him here in Philadelphia than to get at him in the Blackfoot country."

"He's a man now," Claudia speculated.

"Yes, and if he ever finds out that we forged those papers giving Howard and you power of attorney, he will see you and me swing from the gallows."

"It would have been simpler if you had just made me the guardian."

"I couldn't do that. Howard Landon was a shrewd man. He had those papers so well written that there was no way I could write him out without running into trouble. No, your best bet is to keep him alive, because when he dies, you have no legal standing whatsoever."

"All he does is stare at that portrait all day. It gives me the creeps, Melvin."

"I've seen the picture of the girl—Joanna. I wouldn't mind staring at her all day myself."

Claudia raised her hand and struck him hard across the face. "Don't you ever say that again! I loathe Joanna, and I will not have you telling me of her beauty!"

Melvin realized his mistake and pulled Claudia tightly against him. "How could I think of anyone but you when you are naked in my arms?" he breathed.

Claudia closed her eyes, willing herself to feel something for Melvin. No one made her feel alive anymore. She knew that all the James wealth hadn't made her happy. What she wanted most in the world had always evaded her. But if anyone had asked her what she really wanted to make her happy, she couldn't even have told him.

It was as if she were living her life in a shell, waiting

for something to happen. She had to live with the threat day and night that Taggart might return.

She pushed Melvin away and stood up, walking over to the window. Looking out on the front lawn, she watched the snowflakes drift down. Tag was out there somewhere. He might not come tomorrow, or even next year, but deep down she knew he would come . . . oh, yes he would come!

Chapter Ten

Alexandria felt safe for the first time in many days. She curled up against the warm body pressed close to her and sighed contentedly.

Tag awoke and stared into the darkened room. Like Farley, he wasn't accustomed to sleeping on a soft bed. Many troubled thoughts danced through his mind. He and Farley had only arrived in Philadelphia that day, and everything was strange to him. Now that he was here, he was anxious to face his Uncle Howard and Claudia, but he knew he must bide his time until just the right moment. Tomorrow he would have to buy new clothing for himself and Farley. The last thing he wanted to do was to stand out in a crowd.

He shifted his weight when the boy gouged him in the ribs with his elbow. Tag pushed the boy over, but he rolled back against him, so he turned his back. He didn't know what he was going to do with the boy. He had his own problems, and he didn't need anyone else's. Tomorrow he would give the boy some money and send him on his way, he thought.

At last Tag's eyelids became heavy, and despite his discomfort, he drifted off to sleep.

Alexandria awoke during the night and moved

against something warm. For the moment she had forgotten where she was. Reaching out her hand, she felt it brush against someone's face, and she felt the stubble of a beard! She sat up quickly and looked about the darkened room. Hearing someone snoring loudly, her eyes went to a dark form that was lying on the floor in front of a window. When her eyes became accustomed to the dark, Alexandria could see the old man, and then she remembered the events of the evening before.

Thinking it might be a good idea to leave now that both men were asleep, she threw the covers aside. When her foot touched the cold wooden floor, she shivered. She remembered that these two men thought she was a boy, and she lay back down, trying to decide what would be best to do. If she could stay with these men, she would not have to forage for food and a warm place to sleep at night. Perhaps she could convince them to allow her to stay with them for a while.

Alexandria relaxed and pulled the covers over her. Turning her head, she looked at the tall, golden-haired man who lay beside her. Most of his face was in shadows, but she could see his outline and again thought he was the handsomest man she had ever seen. Somehow, she felt safe with him. Had he not rescued her from the sailor tonight? If she could convince him to let her stay with him, she would also be safe from her stepmother's pursuit.

Alexandria continued to study the man's features in the half-light that came from the window. He moved his head slightly, and the moonlight fell on his golden hair. Alexandria was so near him she could feel his

121

warm breath on her face. He moved again, and his face touched hers, causing her to draw in her breath. Suddenly, something akin to pain seemed to touch Alexandria's heart, and she pulled away from him, frightened by strange emotions she had never before felt. She quickly turned her back and inched as close to the wall as she could get. Placing her hand over her heart, she found it was pounding erratically. What was happening to her? Not trusting the emotions she didn't understand, Alexandria squeezed her eyes together tightly, trying to find the elusive sleep she needed so badly, but it wouldn't come. When the first streaks of daylight hit the eastern sky, Alexandria was awake to witness the sunrise that turned the room to a rosy glow.

Slowly, she eased herself off the bed, taking care not to wake the two men. If she was going to convince them to allow her to stay, Alexandria knew she would have to make herself useful to them.

Running a hand through her tousled hair, she tried to straighten it as best she could. Tucking her shirt into her trousers and slipping into the scuffed brown boots, she tiptoed across the room, heading downstairs to the tap room.

Tag awoke and sat up looking about him. He saw Farley sprawled out on the floor and smiled to himself. The old man wasn't taking too well to civilization. Seeing movement out of the corner of his eyes, Tag swung around and saw the young boy he had befriended last night before going through his leather satchel. With his Indian quickness, he leaped across the room and grabbed the boy by the scruff of the neck, dangling him in the air.

"It's fine thanks I get for saving your miserable hide if you are going to rob me in my sleep," he said through clenched teeth. "I would have been better off had I allowed them to ship you out to sea. Perhaps then you would have learned some manners. I have no liking for a thief!"

Alexandria kicked and squirmed. "I'm not a thief! I was going to give your soiled clothing to Molly so she could have them laundered for you."

Tag plopped her down on her feet and looked at her skeptically. "Why do I not believe you? What made me believe you were going to rob me?"

Alexandria met his gaze squarely. "I was not going to rob you," she insisted, "and I don't lie, either. I thought if I was of help to you, you would allow me to stay."

Tag's eyes narrowed, and for the first time he noticed that the boy had the most unusual eyes he had ever seen—they were golden with brown flecks in them, and there was such sincerity in the liquid depths that Tag believed him.

"I'll see that you have a good meal and money in your pocket, but you can't stay with me."

Alexandria felt tears sting her eyes, and she could see the hardness in his gaze. "Please allow me to stay with you, Mr. Knight. I am very strong and will work very hard to please you." She lowered her head. "I haven't anywhere to go."

Farley had been listening to the conversation, and he now stood up, scratching his grizzly white head. "I don't think this little mite will be much trouble to us. Why don'tcha let him stay around a bit."

"What do you call last night if it wasn't trouble,

123

Farley?" Tag said heatedly. He knew Farley. If he allowed it, the old man would take in every stray and homeless waif they came upon.

Farley saw no weakening in Tag, and he shoved the boy toward the door. "Get on below and see to our breakfast."

Alexandria brightened. "I went down earlier and attended to your meal. Shall I go and bring it up now? I also told them to send up a tub of hot water, knowing you would want to bathe," Alexandria said, with hope in her heart, looking from the old man to Mr. Knight.

Tag shrugged his shoulders. "You can stay for the day, but that's all. I will not take the responsibility for you."

Farley winked at the boy and watched the young face brighten. He chuckled to himself when the lad ran to the door. "I'll be so useful to you, you won't be able to get along without me—you'll see!"

When the boy had disappeared out the door, Tag turned his gaze on Farley. "I meant what I said, Farley. I came here because I have my own troubles to work out. The last thing I need is someone else's troubles."

Farley stretched to his full height, trying to ease his muscles, which ached from sleeping on the hard floor. "How much trouble can a small boy be? 'Sides, he might be of help to us. He'll know the lay of the town and some of the locals."

Tag walked over to the window and looked down on the street below. In the distance he could see the Delaware River and the big ships riding at anchor. "There is more to that boy than he's saying. He isn't the street urchin he claims to be. No boy brought up on the streets speaks such educated English, Farley."

Again Farley chuckled. "We won't be holding a edjucation agin him. I can tell he's plenty scairt, and I don't intend to turn him out in the cold. Hell, it's snowing out there! He could freeze to death."

Tag turned back to Farley. "If he stays, he will be your responsibility. Is that clearly understood? I haven't the slightest intention of getting him out of any more scrapes."

Farley reached down and picked up the bedclothes he had slept on the night before and tossed them on the bed. "I heard you. What's your plan?"

"The first thing I must do is try to cut through years of deception. I suppose the first order of business will be to purchase new clothes."

Farley nodded. "I reckon you can't just go up to your uncle and demand he turn your house over to you."

"No, that wouldn't be wise. I will ask around and determine what the situation is first. I know my uncle well enough to realize that when he finds out I'm here, he will send an army of men to deal with me. He is too much the coward to face me alone."

"That's one reason why you ain't gonna use your real name, ain't it?"

"Yes, to do so would be foolishness. I don't want my uncle to know I'm here until I'm ready to reveal myself to him. That's another reason I don't want the boy around. Suppose you let my real name slip out and Alex were to pick up on it?"

"I ain't gonna do that. I wasn't born yesterday," Farley replied in an irritated voice. "Hell, ain't I proved that I can be trusted by now?"

Tag smiled slightly. "Yes, you have proven your worth many times. If you still insist on it, the boy can stay. Just keep him out of my way."

Farley grinned his toothy grin. "Like as not that young scamp will be underfoot, but he's not gonna be too much trouble. He'll be too thankful that you took him in to be any trouble."

Tag gave him a doubtful look just as the door opened and Molly entered the room, carrying a tray of food, with Alex right behind her. With an authoritative manner that surprised Tag, Alex cleared strewn clothing from the small round table and ordered Molly to place the tray there. While Tag and Farley ate, she proceeded to gather up all their soiled clothing and hand them to Molly to be laundered.

Alex noticed the way Molly was looking at Mr. Knight and felt a prickle of jealousy that startled her. Pushing the woman toward the door and casting her a heated glance, she ordered her to see to the laundry and have a tub for bathing brought to the room at once.

"Have you et, boy?" the old trapper inquired, shoveling a spoonful of fluffy yellow eggs into his mouth.

"Yes, sir, I ate before you awoke. Is there anything else you would like me to see to?" she asked, wanting to make herself as useful as possible.

Tag raised his eyebrow. "From the looks of you, you could use a bath. After Farley and I have finished, you will bathe yourself. You may not be accustomed to being clean, but if you are to share a room with me, you will take a bath. Is that clear?"

Alex bit back her heated retort and lowered her head so he couldn't see the anger on her face. She was beginning to be irritated by his high-handed manner. He acted as if he were above all others and as if everyone had been placed on earth to do his bidding.

Farley laughed and stood up. "I'll be moving to another room so I won't offend your sensitive nose, T . . . Falcon. I don't never bathe in the middle of the winter. One could catch their death that way."

"You know I didn't mean you, Farley," Tag answered in an irritated voice as he stood up and threw his napkin on the table.

The old man laughed as he walked to the door. "I'm gonna scout out the lay of the land. Don't look for me back 'til you see me coming."

When Farley had gone, Alex went to the table and started stacking the dirty dishes. Out of the corner of her eye, she saw that Mr. Knight was pacing back and forth. His actions were making her so nervous that she dropped a plate, and it smashed on the floor. She quickly dropped to her knees and began picking up the fragments.

"Damn it!" he swore. "Do you have to be so clumsy?"

Once again Alex bit back an angry retort. Dropping the broken pieces on the table, she gave him her sweetest smile. "I'm sorry, sir, forgive me. It won't happen again—you have my word."

He looked into her golden eyes and saw the mockery mirrored there. "There is more to you than meets the eye, Alex, but I just don't have the time or the inclination to find out."

Alex was glad the timely knock came at the door.

Rushing across the room, she admitted two men. One carried a galvanized tub, and the other carried two pails of water. Instructing them where to put the tub, she waited until they departed before speaking to Mr. Knight.

"I'll just make myself scarce while you bathe, sir," she said, backing toward the door. She caught her breath as she noticed he had already stripped off his shirt.

"No, stay. You can wash my back, and I want to make sure you don't disappear before you have a bath."

"I . . . never . . . I don't."

Tag watched her face turn red and laughed. "A street urchin who is shy! I thought you said you would be willing to serve me in any way I asked." She could read the laughter in his deep blue eyes. It was the first time she had seen the smile reach his eyes, and her heart seemed to be thundering against her ribs. Knowing she must cover up her embarrassment so he wouldn't become suspicious, she nodded nervously.

"I'll wash your back," she said in a small voice.

He tossed his shirt aside, and before she knew what was happening, he had stripped off his buckskin breeches. Alex knew she should look away, but she couldn't keep from staring at him. He was clad only in a breechcloth, and his magnificent body was tanned and golden all over. Her eyes fastened on his broad chest, which was covered with curly golden hair that narrowed to a vee before disappearing beneath his breechcloth. She could feel her breath coming out in short pants as she watched his hand move to the only other article of clothing he wore. She looked at his

128

face quickly and was grateful that he was not watching her. She had never before seen a naked man, and she watched, fascinated, as he tossed the discarded breechcloth aside and stepped into the tub.

"You will find soap in my leather bag. Bring it to me," he ordered.

Alex looked at him in confusion for a moment before doing as he bid. Her hands were shaking so badly she could hardly control them as she reached into the bag and withdrew the soap.

"Well, don't dawdle—bring it here," he said in irritation.

Alex walked across the room and placed the soap into his outstretched hand. When her fingers brushed against his, she felt as if a bolt of lightning had hit her, and her skin seemed to tingle.

"Make yourself useful and wash my back," he told her, handing the soap back to her.

Alexandria quickly dipped the soap into the water and began lathering his back. She could feel the muscles beneath her fingers and began to tremble all over. She was unaware that she was lathering his back in a caressing motion until he spoke.

"I think I'll keep you around just to wash my back. It would seem you have had some experience." He laughed when he saw her face redden again. "I don't think I have ever met a boy as shy as you are. Good lord, haven't you been around a man before?"

"Yes, of course," she said in a clipped tone. Splashing water onto his back, she rinsed the suds away, then hurried across the room. She hated the way her heart was racing and the dry taste in her mouth. She began straightening up the beds, not daring to look in his direction. Alexandria could hear the water splashing, and she knew he had stepped out of the tub. Ducking down to the floor with the pretense of straightening his clothing, Alexandria could feel her face burn hot. Perhaps it hadn't been a good idea to stay here with these two men. After all, what did she know about them? They might be thieves or . . . something worse, for all she knew. She thought of the old man who called himself Farley. His eyes held a light of kindness, and she couldn't imagine his doing anything that was dishonest, but Mr. Knight was another matter. She had often seen the coldness in the depths of his startlingly blue eyes. She knew instinctively that he could be a very dangerous man.

"Alex, bring me something to dry on and hurry. I don't have all day."

She bit her lip to keep from telling him to get it himself. Walking toward him with her head downcast, she held out the drying cloth to him. When she heard his amused laughter, her head snapped up, and she stared into dancing blue eyes.

"Alex, you are the damnedest boy I have ever seen. If I had the time, I could teach you not to be so timid. You will never get anywhere in life if you are afraid of your own shadow."

Alex set her chin stubbornly. "I am not afraid of anything, least of all you."

Tag raised a doubtful eyebrow. "Be that as it may, I want you to take those filthy rags off and scrub yourself until you are clean."

Alex took a step backwards. "I will not! You can't make me!" She realized the moment the words had left her mouth that she had made a fatal mistake. She

130

watched as his eyes blazed, and he reached out, grabbing her by the arm.

"You will find, young man, that if you are to stay with me you will do exactly as I say, or I'll toss you out on the street. Do you undress, or shall I do it for you?"

The drying cloth he had wrapped about his waist had slipped off, and Alex looked quickly away from his nakedness. "If you will leave the room, I will do it myself," she cried in a panic-laced voice. She didn't know what he would do if he were to discover she was a female. She was startled when his amused laughter rang out.

"Do as you will. I have no time to coddle a baby, anyway." He released her and strolled across the room where he quickly dressed. Alex plucked at a thread that hung from her shirt, wishing he would hurry up and leave. He disturbed her peace of mind too greatly, and she wanted to be alone to examine her feelings.

His footsteps were so light she didn't realize he had left until she heard the door slam. Breathing in a sigh of relief, she leaned over and gripped the side of the tub. Never had she had these feelings where a man was concerned. With her stepbrother she had felt only revulsion and dislike. What was happening to her?

Fearing Mr. Knight or the old man might return at any moment, Alexandria quickly removed her cameo necklace and placed it on the table. She then stripped her clothing off and climbed into the tub. The water was so soothing she wished she could just lean back and take a long, leisurely bath, but she knew she didn't have that luxury. Mr. Knight might return at any moment. She quickly lathered her hair, knowing she must hurry.

Alexandria had many strange new emotions and feelings to reflect on. It didn't matter to her that she was deceiving the two men. She would do what she must to keep her stepmother from finding her. For now, she knew her best protection would be to stay with Falcon Knight. He had come to her rescue before; she hoped he would do it again if the need should arise. There was something about him that made her trust him.

After she climbed out of the tub, Alexandria quickly dried herself. She hated to put her dirty clothing back on, but she didn't dare wash it, fearing it wouldn't be dry before Mr. Knight and Farley returned.

Alexandria buttoned up the shirt and stuffed the tail down into the trousers. She didn't know what would happen from one moment to the next, but for now she had a roof over her head and food to eat. She could do no more than take one day at a time. She realized she would have to watch her temper. It wouldn't do at all to antagonize Mr. Knight. She knew he wouldn't hesitate to make good his threat and toss her out into the street if she displeased him.

Chapter Eleven

Tag made his way to the livery stable in back of the Fox and Hound Inn to hire a horse, since he wanted to give Navaron a rest after the long journey. He couldn't help but notice how much Philadelphia had grown since he had lived there as a boy. The town had changed so much, he had to ask directions to reach his destination.

As he rode up the hill high above the city into the better part of town, the scenery became more familiar to him. The magnificent old houses with their iron gates stirred memories he thought had died long ago. He had to curb his urge to ride to his own home and confront his Uncle Howard. Tag knew he would have to be patient if he were to win against his uncle and Claudia.

Riding through a wide iron gate, he stopped before a two-story stone house that proclaimed its owner's wealth. He dismounted and tied his horse to the hitching post. Climbing the steps, he reflected on his mission here today. This was the Thatcher mansion. Harland Thatcher, at one time, had been in love with Tag's sister, Joanna. But it wasn't Harland he had come to see today—it was his father's old retainer,

Simon, whom he sought. Simon had helped him and Joanna escape from their uncle and aunt when Tag was a twelve-year-old. Simon had taken the job as servant to the Thatchers so he could keep an eye on Tag's uncle. He had been given Tag's mother's jewels for safekeeping, and Tag had now come to collect them and find out if Simon had learned anything that could help him in dealing with his uncle.

Rapping on the door, Tag waited impatiently for an answer. In no time at all the door was opened, and a middle-aged housekeeper in stiff white apron and mobcap stood staring at him, open-mouthed.

"Yes?" she said in a stiff manner while looking him over from head-to-toe with obvious disapproval. For the first time, Tag realized he had made a grave mistake. He had forgotten he was dressed in his buckskin shirt and trousers, and he should have gone to the back door since he was here to see Simon. He silently cursed his foolishness. He had been too long away from the niceties of life and had forgotten one very important thing—one never came to the front door when wishing to see one of the servants. Tag realized it was too late to cover tracks this time. He would just have to be more cautious in the future.

"I am making inquiries about Simon Green, ma'am. I was told he was employed here."

The woman's eye's widened in surprise. "I . . . yes, he was. If you will come to the back door, I'll let you in. Just go around the side of the house there."

Tag was puzzled by her strange behavior, but he did as she asked. He could feel something was wrong, but he didn't yet know what it was.

When he reached the back of the house, the door

swung open, and the same woman was there to greet him.

"Come into the kitchen where we can talk. I have sent the cook away so we won't be disturbed."

Still puzzled, he entered directly into the kitchen. The woman motioned for him to be seated at the wooden table and poured him a cup of tea before sitting down across from him.

"Is your name Taggart James?" she inquired, lowering her voice.

"Why should you think that?" Tag asked suspiciously, looking into the older woman's periwinkle-blue eyes and seeing tears swimming there.

"I think I should tell you Simon is dead. He was buried no more than a fortnight ago. His last dying thoughts were of Taggart James and his sister, Joanna. I know you are he and I also know you have to be cautious."

"How would you know?" Tag asked, feeling a pain of sadness in his heart for the man who had served his father for so many years. "Simon would never have discussed me and my sister with you or anyone else."

The woman reached out and touched Tag's hand. "You are right . . . my Simon would never have discussed your troubles with just anyone . . . but you see, I was his wife. We were married but three short years ago, and my husband knew he could trust me."

Tag looked into bright, earnest eyes and knew the woman spoke the truth. "I am grieved about Simon, Mrs. Green. He was almost like family to me and my sister. I hope he didn't die in pain."

Mrs. Green dried her eyes on her snowy white apron. "No, the end came quickly. One day, he was well; the next, he was gone."

"Please accept my condolences, Mrs. Green."

She dabbed at her eyes once more and nodded. "Simon charged me to give you a packet you left in his keeping, along with some information he had learned. We shouldn't be talking here. I'm off duty at six. Can we meet and discuss it then?"

"Yes, where shall I meet you?"

"My sister lives on Hargrove Road. It's the last house before you come to the river. Can you be there at seven?"

"Yes, I'll be there," he said, standing up.

Mrs. Green stood also and walked him to the door. "I would caution you to have a care. You are not safe. Simon's one wish was that you and your sister get back what was stolen from you."

Tag towered over the woman and smiled down at her kindly.

"I have lost a dear friend in Simon, but it seems I have found an ally in you, Mrs. Green."

"I will do whatever I can to help you, Mr. James. Take care and don't do anything foolish again."

He laughed. "Like going to the front door?"

She smiled. "There was no harm done since I was the one who answered your knock."

As Tag rode back to town, he felt a great loss at Simon's passing. Although he hadn't seen him in many years, they had often corresponded through the trading post at Fort Union, and Tag had felt close to him.

Looking down at his buckskins, Tag realized that he would have buy new clothing. His manner of dress set him apart from rest of the population, and he knew he must become just one of the many on the streets of Philadelphia.

Alexandria had straightened the room and carried the dirty dishes down to the kitchen. When she was on her way back upstairs, Molly called out to her.

"Hold, lad. I want to talk to you."

Alexandria turned to face the pretty serving girl. She didn't much like Molly and didn't really want to talk to her.

"You surely fell into a good thing, didn't you, boy? It appears that Mr. Knight took you under his wing."

"I am working for him," Alexandria replied through stiff lips.

"I'd like to work for that handsome man," Molly said, tossing her tawny hair. "Leastwise, I'd like to work beneath him while he's on top." The serving maid's lewd laughter rang out and Alexandria felt her face redden. Turning her back, she ran up the stairs to escape any further conversation with the woman.

When she was inside the room, she leaned against the door, while wild thoughts danced through her mind. What would it feel like to have Mr. Knight make love to her? She tried to clear her mind of her daring thoughts. Never before had she wanted a man to touch her. Now all she seemed to think of was the way he smiled when he was amused, or how his blue eyes could turn quickly to swirling blue storm centers when he was angry.

Scolding herself, Alexandria closed her eyes. Mr. Knight would never look at her as a woman. He thought of her only as a boy whom he no more than tolerated. Walking to the cracked mirror that hung on the wall over the wash basin, she looked at herself critically. Her hair was too short, for one thing; it curled in ringlets all over her head. She looked at her golden-colored eyes, which were fringed by long, silky lashes, wishing they were a different color. Her stepmother had often told her that her eyes were too catlike and that no one could look at her without shivering. Sighing heavily, she looked at the outline of her body. She was much too skinny. Most girls her age were nicely rounded. She wasn't very tall and reached only to Mr. Knight's shoulder. Alexandria couldn't tell if the face that stared back at her was pretty. The only man she had ever been around had been her stepbrother, and he hadn't been a very good judge, since he liked anything in petticoats. For the first time in her life, she wished with all her heart that she *was* pretty.

Alexandria hadn't heard the door open softly and didn't know that Mr. Knight had entered until she saw his reflection in the mirror behind her.

"What do you see reflected there, Alex?" he said in an amused voice.

Her golden eyes met his blue ones. "I don't know. What do you see, Mr. Knight?"

He smiled slightly. "I see a boy who is much too pretty to be a boy."

"What . . . do you mean?" she asked, spinning around to face him, fearing he had learned her secret.

"I mean," he said laughing, "that when you grow up, you will always have a string of attractive women trailing after you." He paused, "That is, if you can learn some niceties and take a bath more often."

Alexandria's chin jutted out angrily. "You don't

know anything about me! You shouldn't go around making snap judgments about someone you have only just met."

He gave her a lopsided smile. "I think I know you well enough. Some day you want to tell me your story."

"I have nothing to tell."

He grabbed her by the arm and led her to the bed, where there were numerous parcels laying in a heap. "You will find some new clothing for you among those boxes. See that you put them on and make yourself more presentable."

She threw her head back. "I will not accept anything from you. I will not wear anything you bought."

He tilted her chin up, and she saw his blue eyes flash. "Must I remind you again that I will toss you out if you don't do as you are told?"

"I . . . will put them on, but later," she said, quickly reconsidering. The last thing she wanted was to be sent away to fend for herself.

"How old are you, Alex?"

She considered telling him the truth. "I'm thirteen," she answered, knowing he would never believe she was eighteen.

"You will get over being so shy when you have been with your first girl."

"I won't ever . . ." She bit her lip and suffered his laughter.

"Oh, yes, you will, Alex. If I were to turn you loose with Molly downstairs, she would make a man of you soon enough."

"It's sinful . . . what you are suggesting. No nice gir . . . boy would do what you suggest out of

139

wedlock. That's disgusting!"

Amusement danced in his blue eyes. "I can see you have been properly brought up after all, Alex. I think the time may come, however, when you will change your way of thinking."

"Never!"

Tag reached for one of the parcels and withdrew a blue suit coat and threw it around his shoulders. "What do you think, Alex? Will I look the proper gentleman dressed in this?"

She looked at the light blue fabric and knew that it was from one of the better shops in Philadelphia. "Yes, I suppose, but why would you want . . ."

He held up his hand, cutting her off. "Yours is not to question, but to do as your are told. I bought a pair scissors—do you think you can cut my hair in a reasonably fashionable style?"

Alex nodded. "But I don't see . . ."

"Here, I'll sit in this chair, and you can do your worst right now."

Alex reached for the scissors and felt a lump in her throat. What a pity it was to cut his beautiful hair, she thought. She somehow felt sad that, with his hair cut and dressed in the suit, he would be just like other men. No, he would never be like any other. He would always stand out as different and unusual. She detected something about him that set him apart. Perhaps it was that he was so handsome, but she didn't think so. It was more that he was so . . . male. At times, she got the feeling that he wasn't of this world.

Taking a golden strand, she snipped it off. Hoping he wouldn't notice, she pushed the golden strand into her pocket, not knowing herself why she wanted to keep it. In no time at all, the haircut was completed, and she looked at him with satisfaction, thinking she hadn't done too bad a job.

"Has Farley been back?" he asked, brushing the loose hair from his shoulder.

"No, I've been here all day, and I haven't seen him."

"I have to dress and go out for a while. Should Farley return, tell him to wait until I get back—is that clear?"

"Yes, but can I not go with you?"

He stripped his shirt off and tossed it on the chair. "No, I have business to attend to. You just go downstairs and see that they give you some food. I think it would be a good idea for you to avoid the tap room. You don't want a recurrence of last night."

She nodded, picking up his discarded shirt and folding it neatly.

"Tell Farley he will be sleeping in the next room. You will be sharing it with him."

Alex opened her mouth to protest, but his look silenced her. "I want you to tell Molly that she is to come to my room tonight after she gets off work. Do you understand?"

Alexandria spoke before she had time to think. "I understand, all right. How can you . . . with a woman like her . . . ?"

Tag pulled on a shirt and chuckled. "For the obvious reasons. You will find you don't just walk up to a nice girl and ask her to spend the night with you."

Alexandria turned away, feeling crushed. For some reason, she couldn't stand the thought of his holding Molly in his arms. "I don't see why you need a woman at all," she said through tight lips.

"When you are older, you will know that a man has certain urges that must be satisfied."

Alexandria turned back to face him, only to discover that he had replaced his buckskin trousers with soft blue tight-legged pants. "You don't love Molly." She couldn't help but state her opinion.

Tag sighed indulgently. "Love has nothing to do with it, Alex. I don't have time to go into man-woman relationships with you now. Just see that Molly comes to my room tonight."

She watched as his eyes took on a look of sadness. When he spoke, it was more as if he were speaking to himself. "I have only loved once. I doubt I shall ever love again."

Alexandria wanted to ask him about the woman he had loved, but she dared not. She watched as he sat on the edge of the bed and pulled on a pair of black leather boots. When he stood up, she studied him closely. Gone was the handsome golden man, and in his place was a well-dressed gentleman.

"What do you think, Alex? Do I come up to scratch?"

"You look very nice," she said, still too angry to hand out a compliment. She jumped when he tweaked her nose and walked toward the door.

"Don't forget to tell Molly," he reminded her before sweeping out of the room.

She wanted to shout at him that if he wanted Molly he could tell her himself, but the door slammed behind him. Sitting down on the bed, Alexandria propped her head on her folded hands. It wasn't her place to question Mr. Knight's morals. If she knew what was good for her, she had better do as he asked or be tossed out into the street as he had threatened on several occasions.

It wasn't until much later in the evening that Alexandria went to find Molly. She was halfway downstairs when the sound of the servant girl's laughter reached her. Glancing down into the tap room, she saw the woman perched on a heavyset man's lap while he fondled and caressed her openly. Setting her jaw stubbornly, Alexandria climbed back up the stairs. If Mr. Knight wanted a woman like Molly, then he would just have to do the asking himself. She had no intention of approaching that woman. Let him throw her out! She would just have to find a job of some kind. She could take care of herself; she didn't need him!

Farley came in a short time later, and Alexandria told him Mr. Knight wanted them to share the room next door. The old man went to bed early, so Alexandria tiptoed into the room and saw him sleeping on the floor as he had the night before. She made her way to the bed, and curled up on it, lost in total misery. She didn't know where she was going from here. Alexandria was afraid that the authorities would be searching for her, and she knew she would have to be very careful not to get caught. With that thought in mind, she drifted into a troubled sleep.

Tag sat at the kitchen table and unwrapped the parcel that contained his mother's jewels. Mrs. Green exclaimed over the valuable pieces that had been left in her care.

"I never knew what the packet contained, but

143

Simon told me to protect it and never tell another living soul about you and your sister."

He reached out his hand and squeezed hers. "I cannot thank you enough. If only there was some way to repay you for your kindness."

"I need nothing but your thanks. I have come to feel that I know you and your sister, Joanna, from hearing about you from Simon. Is your sister well?"

"Yes, Joanna is happier than anyone I know. She has a good life."

"Simon was always worried about her. He seemed to think she had lost some of her reasoning."

Tag laughed, remembering how upset Simon had been when Joanna chose to stay with Windhawk. "I can assure you my sister has all of her faculties." Then Tag became serious. "Did Simon leave me any message?"

"He was afraid to write anything down, so he told me what to relay to you. Your uncle is an invalid and is bedridden. I am told his speech is garbled, and one can hardly understand him."

"If that is so, then who sent the two men who tried to kill me?"

"Humph, likely as not, it would be his wife. I hear tell Claudia Landon is a regular terror. Simon told me to warn you that she is the one to look out for, because she is vicious and cruel. Hers is the hand that runs your shipping company. She had employed a lawyer who is at her beck and call. Simon seemed to think that he must have drawn up papers falsifying your signature. Otherwise, she would never have been allowed to have free reign over the James Import-Export Shipping."

"What's the name of her lawyer?"

"I've written it down on this piece of paper for you, as well as the location of his office. Simon thought it would be best for you to proceed slowly and allow no one to know your true identity for now."

"What's to stop me from going to my father's old lawyer, Mr. Barker, for help?"

"You can't. He's dead. Simon said he died mysteriously in a fire that destroyed all his important papers. Simon told me your father's will and all the documents relating to your inheritance were also destroyed. Simon went to the city registrar one day to find out if the will had been admitted for probate and found there was no such document. You can see this Claudia Landon covers herself very well."

"Yes, apparently she does. This might be more difficult than I first anticipated."

"What are your plans?"

"I think the best way to proceed will be to assume a false identity. I have been thinking about setting up a household and establishing myself as having just come over from England."

"Have you money to do this?"

"Yes, money will not be a problem."

"Allow me to help you. I think Simon would want that. You will need a housekeeper—I can fill that role. I believe you should have people around you that you can trust."

He took her hand and squeezed it. "I would be very grateful if you would fill that role for me, Mrs. Green. Tomorrow I shall search for a house to rent. It will have to be something big and showy."

Mrs. Green's face brightened. "I know just such a

house. The Carsons own it, and they have gone to Paris to live. You could make inquiries about their mansion."

Tag nodded. "Tell me everything Simon found out about Claudia Landon, Mrs. Green."

"I know what the gossips say, and it doesn't bear repeating. She wears expensive gowns and jewels, attracting men like bees to a honeypot. Simon would get so angry, knowing that it was your money she was using to deck herself out in finery."

Tag stood up. "I want to thank you for all your help. I will send word to you as soon as I find out about the Carson home. Are you sure you want to leave your present employment to work for me?"

She walked him to the door and took his hand. "I will feel like I am fulfilling a wish of Simon's by helping you. He lived for the day you would return, so he could help you. If you will allow it, I will take his place."

On an impulse, Tag leaned forward and kissed her wrinkled cheek. "I will indeed consider it a pleasure to have you, Mrs. Green."

Her eyes were brimming with tears. "I shall serve you well, just as my Simon would have, had he lived, Mr. James."

"I am going by the name of Falcon Knight for now, for the obvious reasons. I'll be getting in touch," Tag said, reaching for the doorknob.

"Oh, one other thing. Some of your father's dock-workers told Simon that there was a stranger hanging about the shipyard asking questions about you and your sister. Simon didn't seem to think he had any connection in any way to your uncle and Claudia."

"Did he have any notion who the man was?"

"No, but Simon tried unsuccessfully to find the man. He was puzzled by the incident right up to his death."

As Tag rode back down the hill, he had many things on which to reflect. The revenge and hatred he carried in his heart cried out to be satisfied, but he was smart enough to know he must proceed cautiously. There was more at stake here than revenge. He would have to outsmart Claudia and bring her tumbling down. Windhawk had taught him patience, but right now his patience was strained to the limit.

Alexandria stirred in her sleep, and her hand automatically went up to touch her mother's cameo necklace which she had worn since her mother's death. It had always given her comfort and made her feel closer to her mother. Alexandria came awake with a start! The necklace wasn't there! She felt around in the bed, hoping it had come off in her sleep. When she didn't find it there, she dropped to her knees and searched the floor, hoping she wouldn't wake Farley. She became desperate when she couldn't find the necklace. Alexandria tried to remember the last time she had seen it. Standing up and sinking down on the bed, she remembered removing it that morning just before she had taken a bath.

Suddenly, Alexandria knew she had to go to Falcon Knight's room and search for her necklace. She couldn't take a chance on his finding it in the morning. It might make him suspicious. She didn't know what time it was or even if Mr. Knight had returned.

Not wanting to awaken Farley, she dared not dress.

The old man had given her a long shirt to sleep in, and it covered most of her body, falling to well below her knees. She knew the hallway would be in darkness, and if she were in luck no one would see her.

All she knew was that she had to get her mother's necklace back!

Chapter Twelve

When Tag reached his room, he didn't bother to light the lamp. Stripping off his clothing, he lay down on the bed, lost in thought. Lately, he hadn't allowed himself to think about Morning Song and his daughter. Tonight, for some reason, the loneliness seemed to lie heavy on his heart. What was he doing in Philadelphia when all he really wanted to do was to return to the Blackfoot lands?

He could feel the restlessness stir from deep within his body. It had been a long time since he had been with a woman, and he felt an ache deep inside that needed fulfilling. He wondered if Alex had given Molly his message. Sitting up, he reached for the bottle of rum Farley had left on the night table. He hadn't had much experience with strong spirits, since Windhawk didn't like his braves to drink the white man's liquor. Removing the cork, he took a deep drink and almost choked when the fiery liquid burned a path down his throat. Coughing, he tried to catch his breath. When the burning stopped, he took another deep drink, hoping it would help him through the lonely night. Suddenly he remembered Morning Song's sweetness, and he knew he didn't want to be with Molly.

After a few more deep swallows of the rum, Tag felt his head begin to swim. Lying down, he felt his whole body relax. He was tired and felt himself nodding off.

Alexandria clung to the darkened shadows in the hallway, thinking she should have dressed before she left her room. What would she do if someone were to come along and find her dressed only in the shirt? She considered returning to the room she shared with Farley, but decided it was important that she retrieve her cameo necklace.

She listened outside Falcon Knight's door, not knowing whether to go in or not. She couldn't tell if he had come in yet, but she hoped he hadn't. Alexandria tried the door and opened it easily. She thought the hour might be somewhere around midnight, and she hoped that if he was in the room he would be asleep. As she strained her eyes in the darkness, Alexandria could see Mr. Knight's outline on the bed.

She remembered placing the necklace on the bed-side table, so she moved across the room quietly, hoping he wouldn't awaken. The room was too dark to see the night table, and she reached out her hand, not wanting to bump into it.

Before she knew what was happening, Alexandria felt his hand tighten on hers, and she was pulled forward to land on top of him.

She tried to struggle as his lips fastened on hers, but he gripped her about the waist, pulling her tighter against his body.

"You're not Molly," he growled against her lips.

"Who are you?"

Alexandria tasted the liquor on his lips and feared he must be drunk. She dared not speak because she was afraid he would recognize her voice.

"I like a woman who doesn't talk much," he said, nibbling on her neck and sending shivers of delight coursing throughout her body. She knew she should say something, but her throat seemed to close off, and she couldn't make a sound. When his hand went up to tangle in her hair, he pulled her head forward, and she felt his lips brush against hers. Alexandria's body felt cold and hot at the same time. Her senses were being awakened for the first time by a man's touch. Against her will, her lips parted as he probed her mouth with his tongue. She thought if he didn't stop, she would swoon. Never had she imagined a man's kiss could render her so helpless.

Alexandria felt him roll her over and push the shirt she was wearing up to her waist.

Now she felt panic! When she tried to push him away, he only laughed. "Don't play games with me. Don't you think I know why you came to my room? Molly couldn't come herself, so she sent you."

Alexandria shook her head, but he paid not the slightest heed. She was about to speak when she felt his hand move up her stomach to cup her breast.

"Your skin is so soft," he breathed in her ear. "I have an ache deep inside that you can ease, my silent one."

Alexandria was now incapable of speech. Where before she would have fought him, she now wanted nothing more than to soothe the ache he talked about.

"I need someone," he whispered hotly against her

ear. "Help me find a few hours of forgetfulness," he said in an agonized voice. "I have loved but one woman in my life, and I will never love again. Help me get over the pain of losing her."

Alexandria reached up and caught his face in her hands and guided his mouth down to hers, feeling his sadness in the depths of her heart. She would give him anything he asked. She now admitted to herself that she had been drawn to this man since the first moment she had seen him. In her innocence, she gave no thought to what was to follow. All she knew was that he needed her.

As his lips covered hers, she heard a groan escape his throat, and it touched off a mountain of feelings that rushed to the surface. She *loved* this man who had told her that he had once loved another and would never love again.

She was soft in his arms as he lifted her up and pulled the shirt over her head. When he pulled her back against him, naked flesh collided with naked flesh. A whimper escaped her lips when she felt his mouth move down her throat to tease the nipple of one breast, then move on to taste the other.

Tag was surprised to feel the overwhelming desire that ran through his body. Momentarily, he tried to deny that this strangely silent woman had reached deep inside him and touched his emotions. It was too dark to see her face, so he traced its outline with his lips. "So sweet, so lovely," he breathed in her ear. "Have you come to torture me?"

Alexandria shook her head, and it invoked soft laughter from him. "Oh, I think you have. In your profession, you have been trained to please a man,

152

have you not?" he whispered softly.

Alexandria felt a thrill go through her body at the knowledge that she was pleasing him. Not realizing what was to come next, she hoped he wouldn't be disappointed when he discovered she was untested in lovemaking.

As he shifted his weight on top of her, she felt her body sink into the soft feather mattress. When his swollen manhood touched the inside of her leg, she began squirming with a burning need that cried out to be fulfilled.

"You stir my blood, my silent one. Feel how you excite me," he said, taking her hand and placing it on his swollen member. Alexandria heard him gasp as her hand gently grasped the throbbing flesh. Pulling her further beneath him, he thrust forward and entered her virgin body. Alexandria bit her lip to keep from crying out in pain.

"What the hell!" he said, pulling back. "Who are you? You have never been with a man before. You can't be a friend of Molly's."

When she realized he was about to withdraw from her, Alexandria moved forward and pulled him toward her. Raising her head slightly, she found his lips and smothered the moan that issued from his mouth. After that, everything became a new plane of pleasure for Alexandria. She had entered a world of touching and feeling she hadn't even known existed. The love she felt for this man she hardly knew seemed to be the driving force in her life. She would live to bring him pleasure. After having no one to care for in so long, she now had a purpose in life.

Alexandria kept her silence as he took her into a

153

world of pleasure and sensuous feelings. His hands caressed her body while his lips bruised her mouth with savage kisses. His smooth, fluid motions reached deep inside her body and aroused her beyond her wildest dreams. Alexandria could now feel the tension mounting, and she knew they were on the brink of something new and even more exciting. As his lips covered hers, she thrust her hips against his and felt his body shudder. Whatever the unknown promise of fulfillment was, it had not been obtained. He kissed her deeply and clasped her tightly against him, and she felt him relax.

"Sweet, little innocent one, I have never felt this way before. You gave me pleasure as no other ever has. . . ." Tag stopped himself just in time. He had been ready to admit that he had never felt such joy and fulfillment. This strangely silent woman had aroused his body as Morning Song never had, and he felt in some way he had betrayed his dead wife. In spite of himself, he clasped the mysterious woman to him, brushing a stray curl from her face. He was trying not to think about what had just happened to him, but she excited him almost beyond belief.

Alexandria curled up in Falcon Knight's arms, feeling a soft, warm feeling descending upon her. She was still puzzling over what had happened between the two of them, when her eyes drifted shut, and she fell into a peaceful sleep.

Alexandria awoke and blinked her eyes. The room was shrouded in darkness, and she tried to remember where she was. She tested her lips with her fingers and found them to be swollen and sensitive to the touch—in fact, her whole body felt somehow different.

Suddenly she remembered what had taken place with Falcon Knight, and she sat up quickly. She must have fallen asleep because she was still in his room. Reaching out her hand, she discovered Falcon no longer lay beside her. Her gaze swept the room and she saw his dark, shadowy outline sitting in a chair near the window. Somehow, even from across the room, she could feel his troubled thoughts and wanted to reach out and bring him comfort.

Getting out of the bed, she walked hesitatingly toward him, not knowing how to approach him.

"I was wondering when you would wake up," he said in a deep voice. Falcon reached out and took her hand and drew her down in front of him. "I think we should talk, don't you?"

Alexandria nodded, knowing he couldn't see her features, but he would be able to see the movement of her head.

"I don't know who you are or what you are doing in my room. Had I known you were untouched, I would never have taken advantage of you. Understand me—I don't feel guilty for what happened between us, since you are the one who came to me. Is that understood?"

Again Alexandria nodded. She knew that in spite of his statement, he was feeling guilty, and she wished she could put his mind at rest. For some reason he was troubled because he had been the first man to be with her. Alexandria wanted to reassure him that she didn't blame him at all. Reaching out her hand, she placed it against his cheek.

When Tag felt her hand on him, he jerked away

from her as if she had burned him with her touch. He grabbed her hand, gripping it tightly.

"Tonight you were introduced for the first time to a man's body. Is your appetite such that you want to learn more about the lust that exists between a man and a woman?" His tone was harsh and accusing.

Alexandria shook her head, trying to pull her hand out of his grasp. Falcon had completely misunderstood her. She had only wanted to bring him some measure of comfort, because she knew he must be suffering from something that happened to him in the past.

Tag grabbed her by the waist and pulled her against his hard body. "If it's lust you want, little no name, I can give it to you."

His lips came down on hers, and he ground her mouth against his. Alexandria struggled with all her might, but still he held her fast. Suddenly Alexandria's struggling ceased as his hand moved up her silken thigh and he heard the sigh coming from deep inside her throat.

Tag hadn't meant to make love to her a second time, but the feel of her soft breasts pressing against his chest sent the blood pounding in his temples. He tried to think of Morning Song's face, but all he could think of was this woman who had no face and no name. So far he hadn't even heard the sound of her voice, and still his blood seemed to rise to the boiling point at her touch.

He stood up, still kissing her, lifted her into his arms, and carried her to the bed. He placed her down, following her onto the soft mattress.

She twined her silken arms about his neck and he

felt like a man who had come upon an oasis after thirsting for water on an endless desert. She was reaching inside him and tapping emotions that he hadn't even known existed. Even though she had never been with a man before him, she stirred his body to the boiling point.

Alexandria suppressed a deep moan as he thrust forward inside her. He guided her hips so they were moving in unison with his, stirring her to the depths of her being. As had happened the time before, she felt a deep yearning building up deep inside her, and she arched her hips up, seeking release from the unknown pressure.

She felt the tension mounting as Falcon drove deeply into her. She heard him groan and felt their bodies shudder simultaneously. Alexandria seemed to go limp beneath him, in awe of what had just happened to her.

He was sprinkling kisses over her face and murmuring softly. "Sweet, oh so sweet."

Alexandria felt his fingers lace through her hair, and he drew her face up to his. When he lowered his head to taste her honeyed lips, she felt her heart swell inside her breast.

Tag kissed and caressed her, wondering what there was about this woman that had touched him so deeply. When he had made love to her, he had only sought a release. He had neither wanted nor expected to experience such a deep fulfillment. Suddenly he thought of Morning Song and jerked his head up. Somehow he felt the need to hurt this woman who had caused him to forget Morning Song twice tonight. He thought that in causing her shame, he would relieve some of the guilt he felt for desiring her.

"Did I satisfy your lust?" he asked in a harsh tone. "If you feel the urge again you can always come to me. We have hardly tapped the surface tonight. There are many things I could introduce you to," he said insultingly.

Alexandria watched him move away from her and felt the sting of his words. She wanted to crawl off somewhere and hide—she wanted to voice her anger by telling him that he, to, had felt the lust he seemed to condemn in her. Standing up on shaky legs, she did neither.

Tag fumbled in the dark to find his britches. Pulling out a roll of bills, he thrust them into her hand. "I don't know the going rate, but this should cover it," he said coldly.

Alexandria suddenly felt soiled and dirty. As the tears blinded her, she threw the money on the bed, scooped up the shirt she had been wearing, and pulled it about her while dashing to the door. She feared he would follow her, so she quickly ducked into the room she shared with the old man.

As she sat on the edge of the bed, the tears fell down her face. What kind of woman was she? She was no better than Molly. Lying down, she curled up into a knot and cried brokenheartedly. She knew she loved Falcon Knight, and he thought of her only as a harlot. She was so unhappy she couldn't even lose herself in sleep. She heard Farley when he turned over and mumbled something in his sleep.

When the first streaks of morning announced the coming of a new day, she was still awake.

* * *

The next few weeks were busy for Tag. He consulted a lawyer, using the name of Falcon Knight and saying he was from England. Through the lawyer, he had managed to rent the Carson mansion.

Mrs. Green turned out to be a godsend. She handled the hiring of servants and made the house ready for occupancy. Tag and Farley spent several days buying horses and new clothes, while Alexandria trudged along beside them, uncharacteristically silent.

The day finally arrived when everything was ready for them to move into the house. Alexandria walked into the marble-floored entryway and gazed at the high ceilings. She had never seen such a beautiful house and excitedly went from room to room exclaiming, over and over again, how lovely everything looked.

Since the night she had spent with Mr. Knight, she felt shy in his presence. Often her eyes would follow him, and she would remember how it had felt when he had caressed her body and whispered passionate words in her ear. She felt an uneasy craving whenever he was near, and she tried to hide those feelings, from herself as well as from others. Sometimes at night Alexandria would awaken and find she had been dreaming about him, and her pillow would be wet with tears.

Alexandria knew by now that there was something mysterious about Mr. Knight. She had heard him telling people he had just arrived from England, and she knew that was not the case. She had decided that it didn't matter to her what his background and purposes were—whether he was a thief or a scoundrel,

159

she would never betray him.

She was standing on the landing looking up at the painting of a sunset, when Farley came up behind her. The old man had become very dear to her, and she could tell he was also fond of her.

"I never did take to cheap imitations. That there sunset ain't nothing like the ones you can see in Blackfoot territory."

Alexandria turned to the old man and studied his face closely. "Is that where you and Mr. Knight came from? Is that why you were both dressed so strangely when I first met you?"

The old man's eyes became guarded, and a secretive light gleamed in the sparkling depths. "I never said I'd been to Blackfoot country."

"You implied it."

"Listen here, boy, ifen you care 'bout . . . Falcon, you won't ask no more questions. I'm a-telling you now ifen word gets back to certain people 'bout him, he's as good as dead. I seed that you are fond of him, and don't forget that he took you in. Keep your mouth shut, and don't go asking no more questions."

"Farley, I would never do anything to endanger Mr. Knight. Don't you know me well enough by now to see that?"

He studied her face closely. "I seed a lot more than you think I do. I could ask you some questions that might surprise you, Alex."

"I don't know what you mean," she said, lowering her eyes for fear he really could see too much about her.

He chuckled lightly. "I think you know, but my young friend has been too busy with his own problems to notice what's right before his eyes." Farley walked away, smiling to himself and leaving Alexandria to wonder if he had discovered she wasn't a boy at all. Somehow she sensed that even if he did know her secret, he wouldn't tell anyone.

Chapter Thirteen

Spring was in the air, and the flowers in the garden were in full bloom, and the scent of honeysuckle filled the air. As Alexandria walked out the back door, she noticed that the dogwood trees were in bloom. Their dainty pink and white blossoms were waving slightly in the soft breeze.

She was a farmer's daughter and had a feeling for the land. Without realizing she was doing it, she bent down and began pulling weeds out of the rose garden.

"Can it be that our Alex is a gardener at heart?"

Alexandria stood up and clasped her hands behind her as if she had been caught doing something wrong. "I don't like to see weeds choking the flowers out," was her only reply.

She noticed that Falcon was dressed in a blue cutaway coat that enhanced the color of his eyes, and his smile made her heart flutter.

"Have you been keeping yourself busy, Alex?"

"Mr. Knight, I've been wanting to talk to you about something. I feel so useless doing nothing."

He eyed her closely. "You don't have to address me as Mr. Knight—you can call me Falcon. Now tell me, what are you qualified to do, Alex?"

"I . . . could tend the garden for you, Mr. . . . Falcon."

"Is that what you want to do?"

"Yes, if you wouldn't mind."

Tag rested his hand on the boy's curly head. He had grown quite fond of the little scamp and realized for the first time that Alex didn't know any boys his own age.

"I don't think tending the garden is what I have in mind for you. How would you like to become a gentleman?"

"I don't know what you mean."

"I have decided to go to a lawyer and have myself declared your guardian. You will be sent to the best boy's school. If you like, I will even send you to England. Would you like being my ward, Alex?"

Alexandria shifted her feet uncomfortably. "I don't know . . . I hadn't thought about it."

"Why don't you give it some thought. All you need to do is give me your mother and father's name, and I'll have the papers drawn up."

Alexandria could feel the wall of lies that stood between them. He was being so kind to her, and all she had done was take advantage of his kindness and repay him with deceit. "May I think about it for a while?"

"Of course. Did I not say so?"

Not knowing what else to say, she bent down to pull another weed.

"Alex, I have been meaning to ask *you* something. Do you know anything about a girl who came to my room one night back at the tavern?" Tag said, dangling her mother's cameo necklace before her.

163

The question had come so unexpectedly that she was taken unawares. Alexandria wanted to reach for the necklace, but she didn't dare. Many times in the past few weeks she had wanted to ask him about the necklace, but she hadn't wanted him to become suspicious.

"Yes, I do know her, and if you will give me the cameo, I will see she gets it back," she said, hoping he would do as she asked.

"I have been trying to find her. I asked at the inn, but no one seems to know anything about her. You were my last hope."

"I . . . told you I know her. Give me the necklace, please. I'll see that she gets it. Don't you trust me?"

Tag took her by the shoulders and raised her up to face him. "No, I think I'll just keep it until I see her again. Tell me all you know about her. What's her name? Where does she come from?"

"I cannot tell you," she said pulling away from him. "Why do you want to know?"

His eyes rested on her face for a moment. "I don't even know myself. I can't seem to get her out of my mind."

"What do you want me to do?" Alexandria asked, with hope in her heart.

"Tell me where I can find her. I must see her again!"

"No, I can't do that."

"Why?" he asked in an irritated voice. "Why all the secrecy?"

"She doesn't want to make her identity known. I can tell you nothing more about her."

Tag was quiet for a moment as he glanced back

toward the house. Then he looked at Alexandria. "I would like you to go to her and ask her to come to me. Tell her to meet me here in the garden tonight."

"I don't know," Alexandria said, and her heart seemed to be pounding against her ribs. "She doesn't want you to see her face."

"Why not, damn it? She wasn't scarred or disfigured—I could tell by tracing the outline of her face that she was very beautiful."

Alexandria felt her heart skip a beat. "I will send her to you, but she won't come to the garden because there is too much light here. She will come only after the household has gone to bed. You must have no light in your room, and the curtain must be drawn so no light is showing through."

Tag's eyes narrowed. "Damn it! I don't like all this secrecy."

"If you want to see her again, you must abide by her wishes. Otherwise, I know she will not come."

Tag was quiet for a moment. He couldn't understand the reason for all the mystery, but he definitely did want to meet the woman again. Since the night she had come to him, he had been unable to get her out of his mind. Perhaps it was the mystery that stirred his blood to the boiling point . . . perhaps if he had been able to see her face he would have forgotten about her by now.

"Tell her it will be as she wishes. Are you sure she will come? I said some very harsh things to her before, which I didn't mean."

"She will come," Alexandria said, turning her back to him lest he read the excitement that sparkled in her golden eyes!

* * *

Alexandria climbed out of the bath and quickly dried herself. As she stepped in front of the mirror, she noticed that her amber-colored eyes were fever-bright. Her hand was shaking when she reached for the brush and ran it through her mink-colored hair.

Was it wrong and sinful to go to Falcon, knowing what he had in mind for her? How could anything that felt so right be sinful? Falcon had said that he needed her. Had he not been kind to her and taken her in off the streets?

She would have been sent off to sea had he not come to her rescue. Didn't she owe him something for all he had done for her? She turned away from the mirror, no longer able to look at herself. She wasn't being noble in going to him—she was going because she couldn't stay away. Ever since the night he had held her in his arms and whispered passionate words in her ear, she had been his and his alone. Lately, she had begun to feel guilty for deceiving him, but she had gone too far to pull back now. Today when he had so generously offered to make her his ward, the impact of her guilt had hit her full force. Alexandria realized the deception couldn't go on forever, but would it be so wrong to take what happiness she could for the moment? When the time came to leave, she would just disappear from Falcon's life forever.

Looking at the trousers and shirt that hung over the back of the chair, Alexandria frowned in distaste. She couldn't go to him dressed as a boy. He would know right away about her deception if she did that. Seeing the soft blue velvet spread that covered her bed, she picked it up and draped it about her shoulders.

Laughing delightedly, she unfastened a golden-colored tassle from the canopy above and tied it about her waist.

Moving before the mirror once more, she drew in her breath. The blue of the velvet caused her skin to appear white and creamy. Alexandria was startled to see how her amber eyes sparkled with fire. She was in love, and it made her appear beautiful.

Suddenly, Alexandria wished she could end this farce and tell Falcon the truth about herself. Shaking her head, she knew that would not be possible. She couldn't bear to have him angry with her. Had he not said to her just today that he didn't like secrecy? Didn't he have enough troubles without being burdened with her problems?

Alexandria walked to her bedroom door and looked out. Falcon had kept his word—the hall was in darkness, and there seemed to be no light coming from downstairs. She stepped into the hallway, heading for Falcon's bedroom, using the wall as her guide in the darkness. When she reached his bedroom, she felt panic. What was she doing? What if she were discovered? Knowing she wanted to be with Falcon more than anything, she found the courage to turn the doorknob.

The inside of the room, like the hallway, was shrouded in complete darkness. Closing the door, she stood, undecided, not daring to speak lest Falcon recognize her voice.

Out of the darkness, a hand reached out and touched her cheek, tracing the outline. "I half-feared you wouldn't come tonight," Tag said in a deep, meaningful voice.

Alexandria melted against him when his arms encircled her. She felt a shudder wrack his body and realized he was as excited as she.

"Can you not talk, or do you not want to?" he asked, laying his face against hers.

She only shook her head.

"No matter," he said, leading her toward the bed. "Speech is not necessary between you and me."

He eased her onto the bed and lay down beside her. "I find myself wanting to know all about you," he told her, while pulling her head to rest against his shoulder. "Will you answer some questions for me by nodding your head?"

She nodded her agreement.

"You had never been with a man before me . . . this I know. Have you . . . been with a man since me?"

She shook her head no and heard his sharp intake of breath.

"How did you find out about me? Did Alex tell you?"

She nodded yes.

"You are a friend of Alex's?"

Again, she nodded the affirmative.

"There are so many things I want to know about you. What color is your hair, and your eyes? Do you have any family? Where do you come from, and where do you go when you leave me?"

She took his hand and raised it to her face, sprinkling kisses over it.

"Oh, sweet, silent one, you do have a way of getting into a man's blood. Suppose I told you that because of that one night with you, I am able to find a glimmer of happiness?"

Tag felt hot tears fall on his hand, and he crushed her in his arms while he kissed the tears away. "Do not be sad for me, little one. Just give me a few hours of forgetfulness. One can ask for no more than that."

She wished she could ask him if he had been with another woman since her, but she dared not. She would do as he asked and give him a few hours of forgetfulness.

Alexandria felt his hand brush against her cheek. "Because I cannot see you, I will have to be content with the sense of touch. He outlined her face with his hands. "You have a beautifully shaped face—your hair is curly and you wear it shorter than most women." She could hear the smile in his voice. "A pert little nose," he said, kissing the tip of her nose. "Your mouth is full and made for a man's kiss." He proceeded to demonstrate by brushing her mouth with his. When his hand drifted down to her shoulder, pushing the velvet drapings aside, Alexandria was mesmerized by the sound of his voice.

"You are small-boned and delicate. I can imagine your skin is a soft creamy white." For a moment, the vision of dark bronzed skin flashed though Tag's mind, and suddenly he felt no guilt where Morning Song was concerned. He knew she would want him to find . . . what? . . . surely not love? He couldn't love someone he had only been with for one night and whose face he had never seen. No, this woman was nothing more to him than an outlet. Why then had he thought of her so often? Why couldn't he get her out of his mind? Pushing his troubled thoughts aside, his hand slipped down her back.

"You have a mole just at the base of your spine. Did you know that?"

He felt her nod her head. Sitting up, he untied her belt and, with a quick jerk, removed the soft velvet in which she was draped. "What kind of a gown is this . . . some kind of new mode in women's clothing?" he asked, dropping it to the floor.

There was no reply.

"You have small hands," he continued, raising her hand to his lips and kissing her fingers one by one. Alexandria thought she would go out of her mind as he explored every inch of her body in such a sensuous way. She could hardly wait for him to move from one part of her body to another.

"Your stomach is smooth and flat," he whispered in a husky voice, sliding his hand downward. "Your legs are perfectly shaped, and your feet are tiny." His fingers followed his assessment, sending shivers of delight across every nerve end of Alexandria's over-heated skin. "I would say you have the perfect body, my silent one," he said, coming back to lie beside her and drawing her naked body against him. "If only I could hear the sound of your voice. I'm sure it would be as lovely as the rest of you. Can you truly not speak? I know that you have communicated with Alex."

Alexandria shook her head no.

"No matter," he sighed. "As I said, words are not necessary between you and me." His head dipped down to brush against her lips, and he heard her gasp. "I want so many things from you . . . I don't even know what they are. Perhaps you are a witch who searches for a man's soul during the night and disappears in a puff of smoke in the dawn hours."

Alexandria smiled and shook her head, lacing her hands through his hair. How different this man was from the brooding, often angry man she had come to know in her other identity as Alex. How could a man have two sides that were entirely different?

She slid her body against his in a bold display of enticement, and he laughingly crushed her to him.

"Yes, I believe you are a witch."

His lips came down on hers with a bruising force, and she slid her hands about his shoulders. Moving forward, Alexandria felt as if her body were being absorbed into his. A deep longing filtered through her body like a slow, burning flame. She could now feel the urgency in him as his lips moved across her face hotly, touching her closed eyelids, brushing against his ear, and then dipping down to nuzzle her neck. She could hear his labored breathing and knew he wanted her. When he thrust forward within her body, she clamped her lips tightly together to keep from crying out. Wave after wave of pleasurable feeling ran through her body like a soft whisper that echoed and reechoed in her heart. Her fingernails dug into his back, and he groaned.

"I thought perhaps it might have been the rum I consumed the other evening that made me think you were special, but I now know that was not the case," he whispered in a deep voice. "It wasn't the rum . . . it was you."

Alexandria felt tears in her eyes at his beautiful words. He would never love her, but she could tell he did have a special feeling for her. She knew she would have to be content with that.

"Sweet, sweet," he murmured against her ear. Alexandria could feel her body building up to a climax, as she had the other time. Groaning, she moved forward, and her body seemed to explode in a feeling unlike anything she had ever imagined, leaving her breathless. As the feeling seemed to lift her higher and higher, she felt Falcon shudder, and they both went limp.

As he rolled over and clasped her to him, it seemed they were both floating on a soft, downy cloud high above the earth.

"I don't know what you are doing to me, little one. You seem to have magic in your fingertips. I would be loathe to give you up. Can you stay with me tonight?" he asked, stroking her breasts until they swelled in his hands.

She shook her head no and sat up, wishing with all her heart that she could stay with him.

"Will you come again?" he whispered, running his fingers up and down her arm.

Alexandria nodded, knowing she would come each time he asked it of her.

"How will I know where to get in touch with you?" he wanted to know. Suddenly, he feared that she would just disappear with the morning mist and he would never see her again. "Shall I tell Alex when I want you to come again?"

She took his hands and placed them on either side of her face while she shook her head yes. She stood up and reached down to the floor, picking up the velvet spread and draping it about her shoulders.

"Tomorrow . . . will you come tomorrow night?"

She said nothing as she made her way to the door.

Tag heard the door open and close softly and he felt a deep sense of loss and loneliness. He was intrigued by his silent lover—no, more than that, he was bewitched. He had the urge to get up and follow her, but he decided against it. He had given his word, and he would keep it. Tag knew he would be looking forward to tomorrow night with urgent impatience.

He was caught between wanting to know more about his mystery lady and wanting her identity to remain a secret. He felt he wasn't really being disloyal to Morning Song if the woman who he made love to had no name and no face. For the first time, he began to examine his feelings for Morning Song. He had loved her above all others . . . and yet . . . he had never felt the overwhelming, unleashed passion with her that he felt with his mysterious love. Love? No! Not love. Lust . . . and yet not lust. He was too confused to examine his feelings too deeply. He had a mission to complete, and he wouldn't allow anyone or anything to get in his way—still, he was looking forward to tomorrow night.

Tag picked up the necklace from the night table and held it against his face. He purposely hadn't returned the cameo to her tonight, wanting to hold on to something that belonged to her.

When Alexandria reached her bedroom, she allowed the velvet covering to slip to the floor. Without lighting the lamp, she walked over to the bath water and stepped into it. By now the water was cold, and it helped to cool her heated skin. Leaning her head back, she closed her eyes. If only she didn't love Falcon. If only they had met under different circumstances. What would he do if he knew she had killed a man? Placing her hands over her face, she let a sob escape her lips. There was no turning back now.

Alexandria knew she was hopelessly in love with Falcon. She would go to him tomorrow night, and every night he wanted her. She thought of the possibility that she might become with child. After all, she had been brought up on a farm and wasn't completely innocent of how babies were conceived. It didn't matter—nothing mattered except that Falcon needed her. She would give to him, and keep on giving, as long as he wanted her.

Alexandria realized that since she had come to know Falcon, she very rarely thought about her own troubles. The life she had led at Meadowlake now seemed long ago and far away to her. She hardly gave Barbara and Rodney a thought. Being with Falcon had given her a sense of comfort and well-being. It was as if she had no past and no future . . . only the here and now.

Stepping out of the tub, she dried herself off and lay down on the bed. Tomorrow she would be Alex again and would have to play a part. She knew that as time passed it would become more difficult for her to conceal her identity.

Chapter Fourteen

It was a beautiful spring morning, and Alexandria was weeding the garden. Her heart felt free and happy as she hummed while she worked. Hearing someone coming down the brick path, she looked up to see Mrs. Green approaching. The older woman smiled brightly at her and shook her head.

"I always know where to find you when the master wants you. All I have to do is search the garden, Alex."

Alexandria stood up and dusted her hands. "Was Falcon looking for me?"

"Yes, but don't you think it would be more respectful if you would call him Mr. Knight, Alex?" Mrs. Green scolded lightly, thinking she was speaking to a young boy.

"Falcon gave me permission to call him by his first name, Mrs. Green."

The housekeeper smiled fondly at the boy. "I suppose it will be all right, then, but you had better run and get dressed. Mr. Knight says to put on one of your best suits."

"Did he say where I was going?"

"The young master doesn't confide in me, but

unless I miss my guess, you had better do as he says."

Alexandria felt excitement that Falcon was going to take her somewhere. For the past week she had hardly seen him at all, since he had been away from the house most of the day. Of course, she had gone to his bedroom twice at night in that length of time, and he had made love to her.

Racing up the path, she entered the house by the back door. Taking the stairs two at a time, she reached her room and stripped off her clothing. She was humming to herself as she put on her best suit. Alexandria wrinkled her nose in distaste when she saw her reflection in the mirror above the washstand. She hated to wear the horrible clothing of a young boy. Her wardrobe was filled with the latest fashions—all were suitable for a twelve-year-old boy.

She was straightening her necktie when a rap came at the door. When she called for whomever it was to enter, Farley poked his head around the door.

"You ready to go, Alex?"

Alexandria stared at the old man in surprise. He was wearing the gray pants and jacket of a coachman and had a matching cap which was pulled low over his forehead.

"What are you dressed up for, a masquerade ball?" she laughed, thinking how strange he looked.

"Yours ain't to question. You'd do well to just follow orders." The harsh words were softened by the twinkle in his eyes. "Today you are to do exactly what you're told, is that clear?"

Alexandria nodded and followed the old man downstairs. When they reached the front of the house, Falcon was standing beside the coach impatiently.

Without a word, he swung Alexandria into the coach and climbed in himself. Alexandria could hear Farley talking to the horses as the coach started off with a jerk.

Tag stuck his head out the window and called up to Farley, "Stop here, Farley."

Alexandria sat on the plush black leather seat across from Falcon, and he gave her a crooked smile. "You look bored, Alex. Perhaps the life of the streets has more appeal than living the life of the idle rich."

"I can take it either way—it's all the same to me."

"Pest," Tag said good-naturedly.

"Why are we stopping here, and why is Farley dressed like a coachman?" she inquired, looking out the window and seeing they were on a fashionable street much like the one on which they lived. Her eyes fastened on the big house that sat several acres back in a grove of dogwood trees.

"Who lives there?" Alexandria wanted to know.

Tag didn't answer her, but merely pushed the door open and gazed up at the big house. Alexandria climbed out and stood beside him, noticing the muscle that was twitching in his jaw.

"Do you know who lives here, Falcon?" she asked again.

His eyes narrowed, and he acted as if he hadn't really heard her. "Oh, yes, I know who lives here. It's been many years since I've been on the inside of this house. It seems that it has changed very little."

"Are we going calling at the house?"

He looked down at her. "Yes, in a way. You are going to go up to the house and introduce yourself as the ward of Falcon Knight. Say our coach has broken down, and we need assistance."

"I don't understand—the coach hasn't broken down." She was further puzzled when Farley began loosening the coach wheel.

The old man grinned at Alex. "It 'pears that it's broken now. You best skedaddle on up to that house and do as you're told."

Alexandria looked from Falcon to Farley as if they had both lost their minds. "I don't understand."

"Damn it, Alex, do you always have to question my every decision? Can't you just once do as I tell you?" Tag said in an irritated voice.

She shrugged her shoulders and pushed the iron gates aside, walking up the coach road. "Alex!" Tag called after her. "Don't mention Farley by name," he said, causing her further puzzlement.

Twice she stopped and looked back to where Falcon and Farley stood watching her. She couldn't see what they were up to, but she would do as she was told all the same. Apparently they didn't trust her enough to let her in on their plans.

When she reached the big ornate door, she lifted the heavy knocker and rapped several times. The door was opened almost immediately by a stiff, sour-faced butler who looked down at Alexandria through bushy eyebrows.

"What can I do to help you, young man?" he asked, noticing that the young boy was fashionably garbed.

"My name is Alex, sir. I am the ward of Mr. Falcon Knight. Our coach broke down in front of your gate, and my guardian wishes to know if we could enlist your help."

"Who is it, Graves?" a feminine voice called out from inside.

The butler turned to address his mistress. "A young lad, ma'am. He says he is traveling with his guardian, and their coach broke down at your front gate."

The door was pushed aside, and Alexandria knew she stood face-to-face with the lady of the house. Her blond hair was coiffured in the latest style and hung down her shoulders in ringlets. Her pink gown could have come from nowhere but Paris, and the black pearls she wore about her neck were certainly not imitation. Her face was pretty enough, but there was a coldness about her eyes that seemed to chill Alexandria to the bone. She judged her to be about ten years her senior.

"What is the name of your guardian, young man?" the woman asked, with little interest.

Alexandria met the woman's eyes without flinching. "His name is Falcon Knight, lately of London, England, ma'am. We are staying at the Carson mansion while we are in this country."

Alexandria watched as the woman's face changed from bored indifference to interest. "I had heard that someone had moved into the Carson place. I had intended to call on you to extend a welcome. Where is your guardian now?" Claudia had been told that a very handsome young gentleman had moved into the neighborhood. Claudia always liked to be the first with an invitation if she thought the person worthy of the parties she gave.

"He stayed with the coach, ma'am," Alexandria said, amazed at the change that had come over the woman.

"That simply will not do. Graves, tell Millard to take the buggy and bring Mr. Knight up to the house. Tell him to do whatever he must to see that the coach is mended."

The butler nodded stiffly and walked away while the lady of the house stared at Alexandria. "Come into the sitting room and tell me all about this guardian of yours," the woman said, taking Alexandria's hand and pulling her forward.

Alexandria stared about her in awe. The Carson house was nice, but this house was built on a much grander scale. As she followed the woman into the sitting room, her feet sank into deep-pile Persian carpet. The settees and matching chairs were covered in maroon velvet.

"Be seated, Alex. My name is Claudia Landon, and I want to ask you all about your guardian before he arrives."

"I am pleased to meet you, ma'am," Alexandria said, bowing formally from the waist.

"My, my, what pretty manners. I assume you went to the best schools in London?"

"Did you decorate this room, Mrs. Landon?" Alexandria asked, changing the subject quickly.

Claudia looked about her assessingly. "No, this is one of the few rooms in the house that I didn't decorate. It was decorated by a former owner. It's not to my taste, but my husband refuses to let me touch this room."

"Will we be meeting your husband, ma'am?" Alexandria asked, trying to make conversation until Falcon arrived.

"No, the poor dear, he is bedridden and rarely

comes downstairs."

"I'm sorry," was all Alexandria could think of to say. She felt very awkward and was still wondering why Falcon had wanted her to help get him into this house under false pretenses.

"Yet, it's a pity," Claudia said, looking at Alexandria with interest. "How did you become the ward of Mr. Knight? Is he a friend of your family?"

"Ma'am, would you mind if I had a drink of water? I am parched from the heat," Alexandria said, still side-stepping Claudia's questions.

Claudia's eyes gleamed angrily for just a moment, then she walked over and tugged on the bellpull, which brought an immediate response. She sent the servant off for refreshments, then sat down and motioned for Alexandria to join her.

Alexandria sat on the edge of the seat, feeling very uncomfortable, knowing she must avoid answering any questions, since she didn't know what Falcon would want to tell this woman.

"Tell me, what does Mr. Knight look like? Is he old or young?"

"I suppose I never paid too much attention, Mrs. Landon. I guess the ladies might think him handsome."

"Indeed," Claudia said with interest.

"Tell me, what business is he in?"

At that moment, the front door opened, and Alexandria breathed a sigh of relief. The butler showed Falcon into the room, and Claudia stood up with a bright smile on her face.

Tag stared long and hard at the woman who had cost him so much. He waited to see if she would

181

recognize him, but apparently she didn't. Of course, the last time she had seen him, he had been only twelve. He noticed that she had barely changed at all, except that she was now dressed more expensively. He felt unleashed anger in his heart knowing it was his money that had bought her finery.

Claudia stared in open admiration at the handsome Mr. Knight. Her heart was pounding loudly as she looked into his deep blue eyes. He stared at her so hard she began to feel uncomfortable.

Tag saw no recognition in Claudia's eyes, and he knew his identity was safe from her. Deciding that he must play a part, he smiled slightly at her. "I'm told your name is Mrs. Landon. I am indebted to you for your kindness, madam," he bowed politely. "I am Falcon Knight, at your service."

Claudia's face brightened as she advanced across the room to him. Holding out her hand, she stared boldly into his eyes when he raised her hand to his lips.

"I am delighted to make your acquaintance, Mr. Knight. Your ward was telling me that you just recently arrived from England."

"You look very familiar to me, Mrs. Landon. Could we perhaps have met in London?"

She laughed aloud, showing her perfect teeth. "I have never made your acquaintance, Mr. Knight. If I had, I would not have forgotten you." Her eyes were assessing him, and there could be no mistaking the invitation she sent him. "I trust my men are seeing to your coach?" she asked, linking her arm through his.

"Yes, thank you, madam. They have been most helpful."

Alexandria watched the shameful manners Mrs. Landon was displaying. She reminded Alexandria of a tigress gazing at her prey with hungry eyes. Looking at Falcon, she felt angry that he seemed to be taken in by the woman. He seemed to be enjoying her fawning over him, Alexandria thought in disgust.

"Come and sit with me, Mr. Knight. I want to hear all about London and what you think of America," Claudia said, pulling him toward the settee.

"Please call me Falcon," he said, sitting down and crossing his long legs. He leaned back and studied her lazily through lowered eyelashes. "All my friends do."

Claudia's eyes ran over Falcon, taking in the wide breadth of his shoulders and the expensive cut of his coat. When she looked into his handsome face, she felt her heart flutter like a young schoolgirl's. It had been a long time since she had felt so alive and interested in a man.

"I will call you Falcon only if you will call me Claudia," she said, touching his arm and feeling the restrained strength of his muscles beneath his well-cut coat. Never had she seen a man who possessed such raw strength. Her heart skipped a beat just thinking how it would feel to have him make love to her. She knew in that moment that she must have this man.

"Is there a Mr. Landon, Claudia?" he asked, looking at her with piercing blue eyes.

"Yes, poor Howard. I was just telling young Alex that my husband is bedfast and has been for several years." She looked deeply into his eyes and felt a quiver of delight. Claudia was hardly able to concentrate on the niceties that were expected of her as hostess. "You can't imagine what it's like being a young woman alone."

"I can imagine it would be difficult, Claudia. Perhaps we can do something to relieve the situation," he said, looking at her lips.

Claudia placed her hand over her heart to still its rapid beating. For the moment she was speechless.

Alexandria stood up with her amber eyes blazing. "If the two of you will excuse me, I will go back and wait with the coach." She didn't try to disguise the anger in her voice and knew she was feeling jealous. She had never seen such a shameful display before, and she couldn't believe Falcon was taken in by it. She felt betrayed, even though she knew she didn't have any right to. Falcon didn't have to answer to her for his actions. Walking across the room, she wanted nothing better than to get away from both Falcon and Mrs. Landon for the moment.

"Alex, haven't you forgotten something?" Falcon called out.

Alexandria turned on her heels and glared at him. "No, I don't think so."

"How about telling Claudia how pleased you are to have met her," he said, eyeing her lazily while a smile played on his lips as if he knew what she was thinking and was amused by it.

Alexandria would have liked to have said it was no pleasure to have met Mrs. Landon, but the look in Falcon's eyes told her she had better reconsider. "Madam, you have been most kind," she said with a quick bow. Then turning away, she walked out of the room.

"You will have to forgive my young ward, Claudia," Tag said, smiling in amusement. "He is a very spirited lad and can sometimes be a great trial."

"It has been my experience that strict discipline will soon pull naughty children into line. Haven't you found that to be the case?"

"No, not at all. I wouldn't want to crush the boy's spirit. Do you and Mr. Landon have children?"

"Goodness, what would I want with children? It's hard enough to look after my husband, Howard. He is about as helpless as a baby."

"I see . . . you sound like a devoted wife."

Claudia thought she heard sarcasm in his voice, but when she looked at him, she could see nothing more than a sparkle in his blue eyes.

"Let's not talk about unimportant matters. I want to hear all about you. Why did you come to the United States?"

"I'm interested in acquiring some property," he answered, looking into the face of the woman to whom all his anger and hatred was directed.

"What kind of property?" Claudia wanted to know, giving him her prettiest smile.

"I was thinking about the shipping industry," he said, looking at her through narrowed eyelashes.

"La, I hope not. I myself am in shipping. I wouldn't welcome the competition."

"I am aware of who you are. Perhaps you would consider selling me your shipping company, Claudia?"

Claudia was thoughtful for a moment. "No, I couldn't do that, although at times it's a real trial for a woman alone to run such a large enterprise."

"I can well imagine. I wonder if you could help me, Claudia," he said, changing the subject. "I am looking for a good lawyer. I need someone who is reliable and trustworthy. Could you recommend such a man to me?"

"Indeed, I can. My lawyer fits that description very well. I will give you his name and address before you leave."

Tag stood up. "I have taken up too much of your time already." Taking her hand, he raised it to his lips. "I thank you for your hospitality, and I will look forward to seeing you again in the near future."

"I am giving a dinner party tomorrow night. I would be delighted if you would attend."

"It would be my pleasure, Claudia," he said, looking deeply into her eyes.

She smiled and touched his hand. "The other women will be pea-green with envy when I show you off."

Alexandria watched Farley pull his cap over his head and sit down in the shade, bracing his back against the coach. She turned her gaze to the big house, watching for Falcon to return and wondering what was keeping him so long. She didn't want to think of him and Mrs. Landon being together.

"I don't like that woman!" she said, kicking out at the wagon wheel.

Farley pushed his cap back and looked at Alexandria. "Be you talking 'bout Claudia?"

She spun around and faced the old man. "Do you know Mrs. Landon?"

"I knowed her."

"How can that be? Falcon only met her today. I don't understand any of this."

186

"Look, he be coming back now," Farley said, standing up and climbing onto the coach. "You better be getting inside . . . he'll want to be leaving right away."

As Tag approached the coach, he saw a man watching him from just beyond the gates. He wouldn't have thought much of the incident if the man hadn't ducked out of sight when Tag drew near. All he had been able to tell from that distance was that the man had been dressed as a sailor. He remembered Mrs. Green's telling him about a sailor who had been hanging around and asking questions about him and Joanna.

Climbing into the coach, he looked out the window, but the man was nowhere in sight, and Tag dismissed him from his mind as unimportant. When the coach pulled away, he saw the sailor step into the road, staring after the coach.

"I hope you know you made a proper fool out of yourself over Mrs. Landon!" Alexandria said hotly.

He smiled. "Did I, Alex? I thought I was rather clever in my dealings with her."

She didn't understand when he leaned his head back and laughed deeply. "This is going to be easier than I thought. I believe the lady in question is more than a little attracted to me. I don't think I ever considered that possibility before."

"Why should that surprise you? Since I've known you, all the ladies seem to make fools of themselves over you," Alexandria said, turning her face away, fearing her jealousy would show in her eyes.

"Alex, Alex," he said in amusement. "You have a lot to learn about the opposite sex."

"I have a lot to learn about men like you. I don't know how you can be interested in a woman whose husband is a cripple. Have you no shame?"

His eyes narrowed as he seemed to look right through her. "I have no shame and no scruples where this lady is concerned . . . none at all. I will do what I must to get close to her and her husband."

Alexandria closed her eyes and leaned her head back against the seat. Had he been so attracted to the woman that he would do anything to be with her? Alexandria had thought she knew him, but apparently she was wrong. She didn't know what kind of game he and Farley were playing, but whatever it was, she didn't want to be any part of it.

"I am going to need your help, Alex. I wonder if you trust me enough to do anything I ask of you without question?"

She opened her eyes and looked at him. "I don't know. Are you wanting me to do anything outside the law?"

He laughed. "It might appear that I am doing something underhanded, but if I do, it will all come right in the end. Do you believe me?"

She turned her head away. "Yes, I believe you."

"You will do what I ask even though it might be against what you feel is right?"

"Y . . . yes," she whispered, knowing she would do anything he asked of her.

"Good. We are a small force . . . you, Farley, and myself . . . but together we may just win out."

"I suppose if I ask you to tell me what this is all about, you will refuse?"

"Yes; for now, the less you know, the better."

"I think our friendship is all one-sided, if you ask me to trust you, and *you* won't trust *me*."

Tag moved forward and rested his hand on Alexandria's shoulder. "In the short time I have known you, I have come to trust you entirely. I will tell you this, Alex. No matter how it looks, I am doing nothing wrong . . . but it will be dangerous. Guard your tongue and say only what I tell you. Will you do that for me?"

"Yes, Falcon."

He leaned back and smiled. "You are a most unusual and intelligent boy. When this is all over, I'll see that you want for nothing."

Alexandria lapsed into silence and stared out the coach window thoughtfully, listening to the horses' hooves clopping on the cobblestone streets. There were many things she didn't understand, but one thing she was sure of . . . Falcon was in some kind of trouble and she would do anything she could to help him. Anything!

Chapter Fifteen

Falcon had left the house early in the evening. Alexandria was angry and jealous that he had accepted Claudia Landon's party invitation. She had asked him to take her with him, but he had only laughed and told her he wasn't attending a party for children.

After he had gone, she paced the floor. She didn't know what was going on between Falcon and Mrs. Landon, but for some odd reason she thought Falcon might be in some kind of danger. Alexandria knew she couldn't just wait around not knowing what was taking place. She waited until Farley had gone up to bed and all the lights were out to sneak out of the house. She then made her way into the Landon garden.

Alexandria had hidden behind a hedge that gave her a good view of the people dancing inside the house. It was a cold night, and she hoped no one would come into the garden.

She could hear the laughter from inside—Everyone seemed to be having a wonderful time. She wished with all her heart that she could cast her awful boyish clothing aside, don a lovely gown, and join in the merriment. She had never seen women wearing such beautiful gowns before. Her eyes searched the crowd of faces, looking for Falcon, but she couldn't locate him anywhere. Hearing loud voices coming from the doorway, she ducked down so whoever it was wouldn't discover her presence. When the man and woman drew even with the hedge Alexandria was hiding behind, she recognized Mrs. Landon's voice.

"You had better have a good reason for bringing me into the garden, Melvin. My guests will be wondering what happened to me."

"Your guests, as you call them, will think you are off in the bushes with some gentleman. They are accustomed to your disappearing during your parties."

"I don't have to stay here and be insulted by you! You weren't invited to my party tonight, and you can just leave now."

Alexandria heard the man's snide laughter. "Perhaps I have come to save you from yourself. I have been doing some checking on your friend, Falcon Knight, and no one knows anything about him."

"Why should that surprise you? I told you he has only recently come over from England."

"Yes, but isn't it a bit strange that no one seems to have had any contact with him?"

"As usual, Melvin, you are being overcautious. He is exactly what he seems—a wealthy Englishman looking for a way to invest his money in America."

Alexandria heard the man's amused laughter. "Shall we help him find a way to spend his money?"

"No! You aren't to do anything that will make him suspicious. In the past, I have provided you with wealthy men who were fools and could easily be parted from their money. Falcon is different; he is no fool."

Alexandria could hear the sound of struggling, and the woman cried out in pain.

"Why do I think you care more for this man than the others, Claudia? I had better not find out that you are playing me along," Melvin said.

"I don't owe you anything, Melvin. You don't own me!"

Alexandria heard the man's deep, ominous laughter. "I know so much about you. If I should talk to the right people, it would blow you right out of this comfortable nest you are living in, Claudia. Don't think for a minute I wouldn't do it if I thought you were going to betray me."

"You have no right to threaten me, Melvin. If I go down, I'll take you right along with me."

"It would seem, Claudia, that you and I are dependent on each other. Go ahead and play your little game with this Falcon Knight, or whatever his name is. Just watch your step until I can find out more about him."

"I told you to leave him alone. He is exactly what he seems and nothing more."

"You, more than anyone, know why you must be suspicious of every man who is new in town. Must I remind you that Taggart James and his sister aren't dead?"

"Don't be a fool, Melvin. I would know Tag and Joanna the minute I set eyes on them. Falcon Knight is not Tag!"

"I wonder what you would do if the brother and

sister were to show up on your doorstep, Claudia? Would you have the nerve to kill them? You are good at hiring others to do your dirty work for you . . . what would you do if you were confronted with them in the flesh?"

"I would have no trouble ending their lives. I would take the greatest pleasure in seeing Joanna dead."

"I could never understand why you are so obsessed with this Joanna. You really hate her, don't you?"

"Yes!"

"Strange that you should hate the ones who have provided you with such luxuries. Were it not for them, you would still be a trollop, searching for someone to make an honest woman of you. Don't forget I knew you before you became Mrs. Howard Landon."

Alexandria heard a loud slap, and she knew that Mrs. Landon had struck the man. She heard his muttered oath and crouched lower behind the hedge, fearful of being discovered.

"Lawyers like you are easy to find. I could easily replace you."

"You slut! If it hadn't been for me, you would have nothing. Was I not the one who forged the papers that put you in charge of all the wealth you now enjoy? If you ever cross me, I'll see you dead!"

"Where would you be, Melvin, if it weren't for me? You have been paid well for what you did for me. Don't ever forget you have benefited as much as I have from the James money. Now I'm going back in to my guests. I suggest you leave immediately. I'll get in touch with you should something come up."

"You can't wait to get Falcon Knight into your bed, can you? I can remember a time not so long ago when you were after another gentleman, trying to entice him into your bed. I wonder whatever happened to him?"

By now they had moved away from the hedge, and Alexandria could no longer hear their conversation. She found she was trembling all over. What she had overheard had not been meant for other ears, and she knew she would be in grave danger if Mrs. Landon and her friend ever found out she had been listening to their conversation.

Alexandria knew she should tell Falcon what she had heard, but how could she? Wouldn't he be angry with her if he knew she had sneaked into the Landons' garden?

Standing up cautiously, she watched as Mrs. Landon and her gentleman friend disappeared into the house. She decided it would not be wise to tarry any longer. Melting into the shadows, she made her way back the way she had come earlier. Somehow, she would have to gather the courage to tell Falcon what she had overheard in the garden tonight. She realized she was jealous of Claudia, and perhaps if Falcon knew what the woman was really like, he wouldn't see her again. Would he believe her? Alexandria shook her head. He might not believe her as the boy Alex . . . but he just might listen to her if she spoke to him as his silent lover.

Claudia saw Mr. Knight surrounded by a group of women, and she elbowed her way toward him. Linking her arm with his, she smiled at him possessively.

"Are you having a nice time, Falcon?" she crooned, giving him a provocative smile.

"Indeed, I am, but the hour grows late and I have an appointment. Will you forgive me if I leave now?"

"Would your appointment be with a lady?" she asked, giving him a hurt look.

Tag could hardly stand for her to touch him, and he felt distaste as she licked her lips and smiled slightly. "Now that would be telling, wouldn't it?" he replied, wanting to leave as soon as possible. He had found that the kind of parties that Claudia gave weren't at all to his taste. There had been dancing in the ballroom, and he had been forced to beg off since dancing was the one thing that Joanna had neglected to teach him. He knew there had been much speculation as to why he didn't partner anyone in the dance. That was one thing he had overlooked, and he knew he must rectify it at once. He couldn't afford to make another mistake like that one.

"She is very fortunate, whoever she is," Claudia said. "I had hoped that you and I . . ."

He smiled at her and bowed politely, cutting her off. "Until next time," he said, moving toward the door.

Tag had no way of knowing he had only heightened Claudia's interest by being so elusive. She stared at his retreating back, knowing she had never been so drawn to a man before. She wasn't one to give up easily, and she was determined that she would have him before too long.

When Tag reached the house, he went directly to Alex's room and rapped on the door. The evening had left a bad taste in his mouth, and he found himself wanting to be with his silent lover. He would send Alex to bring her to him. She was so sweet and loving—perhaps she would help ease his troubled thoughts. When there was no answer to his knock, Tag thought the boy was asleep and decided against waking him.

When he entered his own bedroom a short time later, he didn't light the lamp but sat down in a chair and leaned his head back, staring into the darkness. He wished there was some shortcut he could use to see that justice was done, but he couldn't see any way to get the information he needed from Claudia other than to try and get close to her.

Hearing a movement near his bed, Tag tried to see in the darkness. He could only see a shadowy form moving toward him, and he knew his silent lover had come to him. As she knelt down in front of him and began removing his shoes, he reached out and touched her soft cheek.

"How did you sense that I needed you tonight?"

She laid her cheek against his hand, wishing she could tell him that she needed him also. Hearing his deep intake of breath, she set his shoes aside and stood up.

Taking her hand, Tag pulled her into his lap. "Why is it that lately when I am troubled I need you? I feel like I could tell you anything and you would understand."

She placed his hands on either side of her head and shook her head yes. His soft laughter made her heart gladden. She was glad she could bring him joy and a release from whatever was troubling him.

"I find myself wanting to know all about you. If only I knew your name. I have never been so intrigued by a woman before. Perhaps you are becoming an obsession with me. If I could see your face, what would I see?"

Alexandria smiled at his words and laid her head against his shoulder. She wished she dared tell him that in a world of ugliness he had brought her a ray of hope. Would he turn away from her if she declared her love for him?

Kissing her on the cheek, he stood up and set her on her feet. "I have a dilemma that you can help me with, my silent lover. Can you teach me how to dance?"

She was shocked for the moment, wondering why he should ask her such a thing. Surely a man of his obviously wealthy upbringing would have learned how to dance by now.

"I can sense your disbelief, but I can assure you that I am serious. I never learned to dance. Will you teach me?"

Before she could react, he took her hand. "I will hum a lively reel, and you will lead me through the steps." So saying, he began humming in a deep baritone voice, and she guided him through the first steps. Her heart felt crushed and trampled on, knowing that he wanted to learn to dance so he could dance with Mrs. Landon. Was he attracted to that kind of woman? Was he only using her? She had no claim on him, she reminded herself. If he wanted to learn to dance, she would teach him, but she decided she would never come to him again after tonight.

She had written him a note warning him about the conversation she had overheard in the garden, which she would leave where he could find it in the morning. If he chose to ignore the danger signals, then she could do no more to help him.

When they made a wide swirling turn, they bumped into a chair, and he stopped long enough to push the furniture against the wall, giving them more room to dance. For each dance, he hummed the tune, and she guided him in the steps.

It soon became apparent to Alexandria that Falcon was learning the dance steps quickly. They were dancing well together, gliding about the room as if their bodies were one. Finally, he drew her into his arms and rested his lips against her temple.

"You stir my blood, little one. I have no desire to dance with anyone but you."

Alexandria's body became soft against his as he raised her head and covered her lips with his mouth. Love so strong she wanted to shout it to the world encircled her heart as he picked her up in his arms and placed her on the bed.

"I have a desire to do more than dance with you. I was forced to face a very unpleasant evening. Help me wipe it from my mind, little one," he said, pushing the velvet covering from her shoulders.

Alexandria buried her face against his chest, feeling the soft golden hair tickle her cheek. Her heart was filled with so much love for this man that she could sense his unrest and wanted to bring joy into his life. Somehow she would put her shyness aside and give all of herself to him tonight. Alexandria turned over on her side and ran her hand down his chest and over his hips in a slow, circular motion.

"You have a magic about you, little silent one," Tag groaned. He felt his body tremble as she moved her satiny breasts across his chest and brushed her lips against his ear. He felt as if his body was on fire as she kissed his closed eyelids and then allowed her mouth to move down to his lips. Another groan escaped him when she nipped at his lips with her teeth. Alexandria was determined to erase all thoughts of the other woman from Falcon's mind.

He was fascinated by her actions tonight. Before, he had always been the one to guide her in the act of lovemaking. She seemed to know just what to do to excite him now, with a touch or a caress. She almost destroyed his mind as a soft purr escaped her lips and her tongue traced the outline of his mouth.

Alexandria ran her hand over Falcon's chest and gently pushed him back against the pillow. In a daring attempt to please him, she slid her body on top of his and nipped at his ear.

"Love me, little silent one," he groaned as he felt her breasts pressed against his chest. He felt her satiny legs move to either side of his hips when she straddled him, and he gasped with pleasure as she guided his pulsating manhood into the soft, warm recesses of her body.

Wave after wave of pleasure passed over Tag's body as she began her slow up-and-back motions. Never before had he felt such a deep pleasure. It was as if he were floating in an endless sky, and his body was more alive than it had ever been before. Her soft lips that were always silent sought his eagerly, and he clutched her tightly to him. Tag realized in that moment that before he had met this silent, mysterious woman, he hadn't truly been alive. Turning her over, he crushed her into the soft mattress and plunged deeply inside her, feeling as if the two of them were the only people in the whole world.

Tag realized that, after tonight, he would never be satisfied until he found out who she was. He wanted her in his life, not as a shadowy, silent dreamlike figure that came to him in darkness, but as someone whom he could reach out and touch whenever he wanted. He found, to his surprise, that he needed her at all times!

Alexandria felt the soft groan rising in her throat and clamped her lips tightly together to keep from voicing her pleasure. She admitted to herself that she lived for these nights when Falcon made love to her. It was becoming more difficult all the time to keep her silence. It was becoming almost impossible to play the part of Alex in the daytime. Many times she would become aware that her eyes were following him hungrily, and the love she felt for him cried out to be voiced.

As Falcon took her body soaring into the sky, she sprinkled kisses across his throat. She hadn't known one could feel such deep love and longing for a man. When his lips settled on one breast to tease and caress the nipple while his fingers brought the other to a hard rosebud peak, Alexandria thought she would cry out from the beautiful feelings that spread throughout her body.

"I need you, I need you," he breathed hotly in her ear.

Alexandria felt Falcon drive deeper into her, and his body began to tremble in total fulfillment, stirring an answering fire and fulfillment within her.

He kissed her and held her so tightly she thought her ribs would break. When he rolled over, he carried her with him and caressed her lightly while kissing her eyelids, her lips, and her throat.

Alexandria curled up in Falcon's arms, feeling strangely contented and at peace.

"You have never spoken one word to me, little one, and yet I can sense your goodness. After what I have been through tonight, you are like a breath of fresh air to me. I want to breathe in your goodness to sustain me in the days ahead."

She raised her face to him, not understanding his meaning. Tag sensed her unspoken question and buried his face in her soft ringlets. "I cannot tell you what I mean, little one. One day you will know what I am doing, and why I must keep my own counsel. I do not ask you why you only come to me under cover of night—therefore, you must not question me about my private life."

Alexandria closed her eyes, knowing they both had secrets they couldn't share with each other. She lay silent for a long time, until she could hear his steady breathing and knew he was asleep. Easing herself off the bed, she placed the letter she had written to him on the pillow and slipped silently out of the room.

Tag awoke the next morning when the early morning sunlight came streaming into his room. Reaching out his hand, he came fully awake when he discovered he was alone. Raising up on his elbow, he wondered if he had imagined the night before when he had danced with his silent lover and she had taken him to the heights of ecstasy.

His eyes narrowed in puzzlement when he saw what

appeared to be a letter lying against the pillow where she had slept. Picking it up, he started to read:

Dear Falcon,

I wanted to warn you about Mrs. Landon and her lawyer, Melvin. I overheard them discussing you and want to alert you that they are checking on your identity. Please beware, for I know they are not your friends. I heard them talking about forging papers and trying to kill someone named Taggart James and his sister, Joanna. This led me to believe they are dangerous and unscrupulous. You must beware. I will not come to you again, but I shall never forget you. Take care of yourself.

Xandria

Tag reread the letter, trying to make sense of it. So her name was Xandria. How could she know about Claudia? Why had she chosen to reveal her name to him, if indeed it was her real name? What did she mean she wouldn't come to him again? He would tear the whole damned town apart searching for her if he had to. Alex would know how to get in touch with her. He had to talk to her and find out how she knew about Claudia. Could Xandria know his true identity? No, that was impossible.

Pulling on his trousers, he walked to Alex's room and rapped on the door. When there was no answer, he pushed the door open to find the room empty. He knew where he would find the boy and rushed down the stairs, heading for the garden. He wanted some answers, and he suspected that Alex could furnish them for him.

Alexandria was gathering a bouquet of red and white tulips when she heard footsteps on the garden path. She turned to see Falcon approaching. His features were stormy, and she could tell he was irritated about something by the stubborn set of his jaw.

For a moment she feared he had discovered who she was and was angry with her for deceiving him.

"Alex, I want to talk to you," Tag's voice boomed out. "I have had just about enough of your little game!"

"I . . . don't know what you are talking about."

"Don't you? Who in the hell is Xandria, and why does she finally tell me her real name?"

"Did she?" she asked, relieved to find he hadn't discovered her identity after all.

"You know damn well who she is, and I think it's time you told me."

"I cannot do that. To do so would place her in danger."

"Would you rather I ask around and find out for myself? I now have a name to go on."

"No! Please don't do that. You can't know what the consequences would be if you were to do such a thing. Xandria must have trusted you, or she would never have told you her name. Will you betray that trust?"

"You could tell me about her, and it wouldn't be betraying a trust."

"No, Falcon, do not ask it of me. I can only tell you

that she is running away from something that is very bad. If you were to start asking questions about her, she would be in very grave danger."

Tag gripped Alex tightly by the shoulders. "If she is in danger as you suggest, why doesn't she trust me? I would protect her."

"I cannot answer for her. You must just forget you ever knew her."

"No! I cannot do that. You must go to her and tell her I want to see her tonight."

"She has gone away. I doubt that she will ever return," Alexandria said, knowing it was best if she never came to him again as Xandria. He was beginning to be too suspicious.

"Can you tell me how it is that she should know about Mrs. Landon?"

"I can only tell you that she is afraid that you will come to harm from Mrs. Landon and her lawyer friend."

"Tell me all you know. I cannot tell you how important it is to me."

"I will tell you what I can, which isn't very much. What would you like to know?"

"Is her real name Xandria?"

"Yes, in part."

"What the hell is that supposed to mean?"

"I mean I can't tell you her entire name," she answered hurriedly.

"Did Xandria ever mention someone named Taggart James to you?"

Alexandria hesitated for a moment. Could she tell him what she had overheard without casting suspicion on herself? "She did tell me that she overheard Mrs.

Landon discussing this James person and his sister, Joanna. She told me they said something about forging some papers, and that if they, the James's, showed up, they would have to be . . . killed."

"Anything else?" Tag wanted to know.

"Yes, the lawyer questioned if you could be this Taggart James, and Mrs. Landon said you weren't. She assured him she would know the Jameses if they should show up. Does any of this make sense to you?"

Tag nodded his head, and a faraway look came into his eyes. "Yes, more than you can guess. If Xandria should return, will you tell her I want to see her?"

"Yes, but I don't think she will."

Tag felt his heart contract. He felt such a deep sense of loss that it was almost like a physical pain. He looked at Alex and found the boy watching him. Pushing his troubled thoughts aside for the moment, he smiled at him. "Alex, are you above a little thievery if it's for a good cause?" Tag asked, smiling slightly.

"What cause?"

"Again I must ask you to trust me. I have a notion to break into that lawyer's office tonight and see if I can find anything of interest."

"That would be unlawful, wouldn't it?"

"Perhaps, but I think the end will justify the means. What do you say . . . will you go along with me and Farley?"

Alexandria stared at him for a moment. She knew that if he were going to be in danger, she wanted to be at his side. "I will go with you."

He laughed and ruffled her curls. "I found a true and loyal friend when I rescued you from that sailor, did I not, Alex?"

"I am your friend, Falcon. I would do anything you asked," she replied, her golden eyes shining earnestly.

"Anything but tell me where to find Xandria," he corrected.

"Yes, anything but that. Would you trust me if I were to betray a friend?" she questioned.

"You could never betray Xandria to me, Alex. I would never do anything to harm her. I have come to care a great deal about her."

There were many questions she would like to have asked him, but she didn't dare. "When will we go to the lawyer's office."

"Like I said earlier, we will go tonight. We will wait until everyone has gone to sleep, then you, Farley, and myself will sneak away. I have been watching his office, and there is a small window in the back that should be large enough for you to climb through. You will then open the back door and let me in. How does that sound to you? Does it test your sense of adventure?"

"It sounds crazy and dangerous to me," Alexandria admitted.

"It won't be as dangerous as you think. We will have Farley on the outside to alert us in case of danger."

"It still sounds crazy to me. What could that man have that would be of interest to you?"

"He holds my life in the palm of his hand. If I want the advantage, I must find some papers."

Alexandria didn't understand at all, but as she had told him, she would do anything he asked of her. She knew deep in her heart that he was an honorable man and that anything he did would be for a good reason.

"I'll be ready when you are," she said, walking toward the house and leaving Tag with a puzzled expression on his face. Sometimes Alex seemed older than his young years. Tag knew he would trust the boy as he did Farley. There were only the three of them in a hostile environment. He knew that if Claudia found out his true identity, he might never get his inheritance back, and he would have trouble even staying alive.

If luck was with him tonight, he would find the papers that were so vital to him. He smiled, thinking if he were fortunate enough to find the documents, what Claudia's reaction would be when she discovered them missing!

Chapter Sixteen

Farley led the horses around to the back of the law offices of Melvin Garner and watched as Tag and young Alex cautiously approached the back door. He placed his hand on Tag's horse to gentle him and looked skyward. The bright moonlight shed its light on the town, casting the back of the buildings in half-light. He had tried to talk Tag out of coming tonight, because of the full moon, but the young man had been set on breaking into that Mr. Garner's office.

Tag looked up and down the deserted alleyway. It seemed unnaturally quiet, and he wondered if he had been foolhardy to try such a daring plan. Glancing down at Alex, he could see the boy was eagerly waiting for him to tell him what to do. He hesitated, not wanting to place the boy in any danger—after all, this was his fight, not Alex's.

Alexandria could tell Falcon was having second thoughts, and she touched his hand. "If you will break the window, I believe I am small enough to fit through. All you have to do is give me a boost up."

She saw the doubt on his face. "I don't know, Alex, I have been wondering if we aren't on a fool's mission. I have no right to ask you to help in this. I must remind you it could be very dangerous."

Alexandria realized that if she didn't do something quickly, Falcon would probably change his mind. She surmised that the papers he wanted must be important to him or he wouldn't have wanted them in the first place.

Seeing a piece of discarded pipe lying on the ground, she picked it up and quickly wrapped her coat around it so there would be less noise when she broke the window. Tag was looking back toward the horses when she moved forward and delivered a heavy blow to the window. The sound of shattering glass seemed to split through the silence.

"What the hell . . ." Tag said, swiveling around.

Alex gave him an impish smile as she agilely climbed up to the window ledge.

"I've changed my mind, Alex, come down right now. You could cut yourself on the broken glass!"

"Shh," she said, smiling down at him. "There will be no danger if you don't alert everyone with your loud voice."

"Alex, come down . . . now!" he commanded.

She only laughed and climbed through the window, taking care not to cut herself. Her feet had no sooner touched the floor when she heard a key grating in the front door. Seeing that she was in some kind of storage room, she quickly ducked down behind a wooden crate.

She prayed silently that Falcon would know someone had entered the building and not call out to her!

Tag saw the light streaming through the window and cursed to himself that Alex would be so foolish as to light a lamp. He was about to call out to him when he heard voices coming from the inside and realized that Melvin Garner must have arrived at his office with a client. He flattened himself against the building, knowing he was too large to fit through the window. There was no way he could help Alex. He hoped the boy wouldn't lose his head and do anything foolish. Surely he would know to hide and stay out of sight. He motioned for Farley to keep the horses quiet. Tag removed the gun from his belt and waited, knowing that if Alex were discovered he must be ready to break down the door to rescue him.

Alexandria peered over the crate and hoped against hope that the two men she could hear talking in the office wouldn't decide to come into the storage room. If they did, they would be sure to see the broken glass from the window that littered the floor and know something was wrong.

Minutes passed with the slowness of hours as she waited apprehensively for the two men to leave. She was certain that Falcon and Farley were aware of the two men by now. Alexandria was comforted by the fact that they wouldn't abandon her should the worst happen.

Sitting down, she leaned her head against the wall and listened to the droning voices in the next room. Up to now, she hadn't paid too much attention to what the men were discussing. Then she recognized one of the voices. He was the same man she had heard talking to Mrs. Landon the night of the party.

"Damn it, I don't care how important the news is you have to deliver to me! I will not pay you one cent more than what we agreed on in the first place!"

"I have news that will concern you and Mrs.

210

Landon, all right. You will want to hear what I have to say, but you will pay my asking price," the other man said.

"Like hell I will! You were paid to kill Taggart James and his sister. Since you apparently haven't done so, I won't pay you anything."

"I think you will, because I can tell you where Taggart James is at this very moment."

There was a long silence, and Alexandria shifted her weight, listening intently.

"All right, if the information is worth hearing, I will double the price. Where is Taggart James?"

Loud laughter drifted back to Alexandria. "Well, sir, it would seem that he's here in Philadelphia. I talked to a trader at Fort Union, and he said that Mr. James and some old trapper known only as Farley passed that way no more than a few months ago, and they was heading here to Philadelphia."

Alexandria opened her mouth in shocked surprise. In that moment, she realized that the man she knew as Falcon Knight was in truth Taggart James! He had to be—there couldn't possibly be another old man named Farley. Nothing made any sense to her. She couldn't understand anything about what was going on, but one thing was clear: Falcon . . . Taggart James . . . was in trouble. She strained her ears so she could hear what else they had to say.

"Where can I find Taggart James?" the lawyer, Mr. Garner, asked.

"Now, that I don't know. All I know is what I told you."

"What about Joanna James?"

"Well, that's the fly in the ointment. That woman is

211

heavily guarded, and she never rides out alone. It would take an army to get to her. I wasn't about to risk my life trying. You didn't tell me she was the wife of Windhawk. Nobody in their right mind would try to harm Windhawk's wife!"

Alexandria heard the clinking of coins and knew the man was being paid for his information. Shortly thereafter the light went out, and she heard the grating of the key in the lock. She waited for several moments before she stood up and walked silently to the outer room. The moonlight was streaming through the front windows, and she scanned the room, looking for the place where Mr. Garner would keep his important papers. She now knew what Falcon wanted, and she was determined to find it for him.

Knowing the danger to herself should the two men return, Alexandria took her courage in hand and lit the lamp. She knew full well that Falcon would be waiting for her to let him in the back door, but she decided it would be far better if she were to find what he wanted on her own. That way, if the men did return, only she would be in danger.

Seeing a box of loose files stacked against the wall, she disregarded them, knowing Mr. Garner wouldn't keep Taggart James's files there—no, they would be locked up somewhere. Placing the lamp on the floor, she tested the desk drawers until she found one of them locked. Grabbing up a letter opener she found on the desk, she fumbled and pried until the lock broke! She thumbed quickly through the documents until she found several with the name Taggart James written across them.

Alexandria quickly blew out the lamp and stuffed

the documents down the front of her trousers. She then raced toward the storage room. Pushing a box over to the window, she scrambled on top of it and hoisted herself up to the window. Her heart was drumming as she climbed out the window and dropped to the ground.

Immediately, Falcon swung her around to face him. "You little fool, if you ever do anything like this again I will throttle you!" he said, trying to cover up how worried he'd been about Alex's safety.

In the bright moonlight she could see the anger etched on his face. "By your rash action tonight you have cost me the chance to get my hands on some very important documents. Once they discover the place has been broken into, we won't have a chance to go in again."

"Shouldn't we be away in case they come back?" she asked, knowing she had what he wanted.

His face held a grim expression as he turned and stalked away, heading for the horses. As they rode back toward the house, Alexandria tried to figure out what was happening. Why would Mr. Garner hire men to kill Taggart James who was really . . . Falcon Knight? Joanna must be Tag's sister, but who was Windhawk? She was beginning to realize that her life and Falcon's were a tangled web of deceit. If it wasn't so serious, Alexandria would think it was amusing that neither of them was who he claimed to be!

Alexandria glanced sideways at Falcon, and though his face was half in shadows, she could tell he was still angry with her. Her hand went down to the documents she had tucked into her trousers. He would forget all about his anger once she showed him the papers.

When they reached home, Farley led the horses to the stable while Falcon took Alexandria by the arm and led her toward the house, forcing her to run to keep up with his powerful strides. When they were inside the house, he led her into the study and pushed her down into a chair without looking at her.

Alexandria watched as he paced back and forth, and she smiled to herself. "You're angry with me, huh?"

He stopped before her, and she saw the anger drain out of his face. "Damn it, Alex! You could have been . . . didn't you realize the danger you were placing yourself in? Mr. Garner is a dangerous man! He wouldn't have hesitated to kill you if he had found you in his office tonight. I hope you have learned your lesson."

"You were worried about me?" she inquired, feeling warm all over.

"Hell, yes, I was worried! You always seem to be getting yourself in trouble. Tonight I thought I was going to have to go in shooting to get you out. One day you are going to get yourself into trouble and I won't be there to save you. What will you do then?"

"It was your idea that I climb through the window, Falcon . . . not mine," she reminded him.

Alexandria watched as he doubled up his fists and raised his head to look at the ceiling. "I don't know where to turn. I guess I thought it would be so easy, but . . . oh well, I'll just have to try another tactic."

"Were the documents you wanted so important?"

His blue eyes rested on her face. "You can't imagine," he whispered. "I doubt that they would have

214

been kept in Mr. Garner's office anyway. Most probably, Claudia has them with her."

Alexandria reached into the front of her trousers and withdrew the papers, holding them out to him. "Could this be what you wanted?"

He looked at her with with a puzzled expression. Alexandria watched as he read the name scribbled on the front, and his eyes widened in shocked surprise. He flipped through the documents, and she watched a smile spread over his face. When she caught his eye, she noticed the tension appear to drain from his face, and relief seemed to be reflected in the blue depths of his eyes.

"Alex, how did you know this was what I wanted? How did you get them?" He sat down in a chair and stared at the papers in amazement.

Alexandria moved over to him and dropped down on her knees before him. "I wasn't sure until tonight when I overheard Mr. Garner talking to a man in the outer office. I know you are Taggart James."

He watched her closely. "What makes you draw that conclusion, Alex?"

"Mr. Garner was talking to a man about you. Apparently, he and Claudia Landon had sent the man to kill you and someone called Joanna. The man told him that he couldn't get close enough to Joanna to kill her and that she was married to someone named Windhawk whom the man seemed to fear."

"I see nothing in that that would make you believe I am this Taggart James, Alex," he said, still watching her face closely.

"The man told Mr. Garner that he learned at Fort Union that you had come to Philadelphia with an old

215

trapper by the name of Farley . . . you see, the rest was easy. I then realized that the documents you were after would be about Taggart James. I found them in a locked drawer of the desk."

Tag ruffled her mink-colored hair and laughed deeply. "You are a scamp and have caused me nothing but trouble—still, I thank my lucky stars for the night you came into my life, Alex."

She basked in his praise, wishing she dared throw herself into his arms and tell him she wasn't really the boy he thought her to be. She wanted to tell him that she was the girl who had lain in his arms, giving him all she had to give.

"I must caution you, Alex, not to tell anyone what you have learned tonight. I'm sure you gathered from the conversation you overheard that Mr. Garner and Claudia wouldn't hesitate to hire other men to come after me. We must be very careful."

"I don't understand any of this, Falcon. Why do they want you dead? What kind of threat do you represent to them?"

Tag hesitated for a moment, wondering how much he should tell Alex. The boy had proven his worth to him many times over and he trusted him completely, but wouldn't it be best to keep him in ignorance? What if Claudia and Mr. Garner tried to get to him through the boy?

"All I can tell you, Alex, is that Claudia is married to my Uncle Howard, who has stolen all that my father left to me and my sister, Joanna. I have come to Philadelphia to take our inheritance back."

"Who is the woman you said you loved . . . where does she fit in all this?" Alexandria asked.

Tag's eyes narrowed, and he searched Alex's face carefully. "How could you know about the woman I loved? I told no one but Xandria. . . ."

"She . . . Xandria told me," she said hurriedly, realizing the mistake she had made and trying to cover it up.

"I wasn't aware that Xandria discussed our private conversations with anyone else. I wasn't even sure she could talk."

"I . . . she doesn't usually discuss private matters with anyone, but . . ."

Tag took Alex's chin between his hands and turned her face up to him, studying her closely. "What else did Xandria tell you, Alex?"

"N . . . nothing, she told me nothing else."

"Who is Xandria, and what is she to you?" he asked, still staring into her eyes.

"I . . . she is my . . . sister." The lie came hard to Alexandria's tongue, and she wished she could look away from Falcon's deep, piercing gaze.

"I see," he said, taken aback by Alex's revelation. "That could explain many things I haven't understood. What are you and your sister running from, Alex?"

She lowered her head. "I cannot speak of it."

"Don't you know I will help you in any way I can? What can be so horrible that you can't speak of it to me?"

"I . . . Xandria killed a man," she said, tears streaming down her face. "If she is discovered, she will be hanged for murder!" she cried between sobs.

Tag raised her head once more and wiped the tears away with a handkerchief. "Tell me everything, Alex.

I know that if Xandria killed anyone it had to be for a good reason."

"I cannot tell you. Don't ask it of me!"

"Damn it, Alex, don't you know I'll stand behind you and your sister in whatever comes your way. Tell me," he encouraged, brushing a mass of curls off her forehead and smiling down at her.

"I . . . Xandria and I have lived with my step-mother and stepbrother since my father died. My mother's father had left Meadowlake Farm to me . . . and Xandria. My stepmother knew the only way she could get her hands on the farm was to force . . . Xandria to marry my stepbrother, Rodney. She brought me . . . us to Philadelphia, where she held us prisoner in her sister's house. She found a preacher who was willing to marry Xandria to Rodney against her will." A sob tore from her throat as she remembered that awful night when Rodney had come to her bedroom, trying to force his attentions on her. "My stepbrother tried to force Xandria to . . . he was going to . . ."

"I think I know what you're trying to say . . . go on, Alex," Tag urged.

"Xandria tried to get away from Rodney and picked up a lamp, and threw it at him." Alexandria placed her trembling hands over her eyes, trying to block out the memory of that awful sight when her stepbrother had been engulfed in flames. "It was awful—Rodney was on fire! She didn't mean to harm him, honestly she didn't." She took a big gulp of air and dried her eyes on the handkerchief Tag handed her.

"My stepmother locked me . . . and Xandria in the basement. She was going to have me . . . and her

218

declared insane and have us locked away forever."

Tag pulled the boy to him, trying to bring him comfort. "What happened then, Alex?"

"I . . . we escaped, and you know the rest."

Tag raised her face up and studied her closely. "Yes, I believe I do. Have you seen your stepmother or stepbrother since that night?"

"N . . . no."

"Then you don't know if your stepbrother is really dead?"

"I don't think anyone could be so severely burned and live. He must be dead! It was so awful! I didn't mean to do it, but I had to get away from him!"

Tag's eyes widened in shock. Alex was so upset he hadn't even realized what he had just said. Tag lifted the boy's face up to him and studied it with a different aspect. Yes, the features were delicate . . . too pretty to be a boy's; beautiful really . . . even with her hair chopped off. He wondered how he could have been such a fool. He had been so caught up in his own problems that he hadn't noticed what was before his very eyes. Alex was Xandria! Most probably her name was Alexandria!

Suddenly, he was horrified that he might have taken a young girl to his bed and stolen her innocence! He couldn't allow Alex to know he realized who she was—not yet. "I'm going to ask you a question, Alex, and I want you to answer it honestly. How old are you?" He dreaded to hear the answer, fearing she would prove to be a child.

Alexandria raised her face to him. "I haven't been truthful with you. I'm eighteen."

Tag took a deep breath and let it out slowly as relief

washed over him. "I think you have had a hard day, Alex. Why don't you run upstairs and climb into bed. We will talk more later about how to help you . . . and your sister."

She stood up reluctantly. "You aren't mad at me, are you?"

In that moment, Tag wanted to take her in his arms and hold her so he could assure her that everything would be all right. "No, Alex, I'm not angry with you. Go to bed now."

He listened to the soft pad of her footsteps as she left the room. This evening had been a revelation to him. His feelings for the boy Alex had become entangled with his feelings for Xandria. What were his true feelings for her?

Trying to dismiss her from his mind, he picked up the documents with his name scribbled across the front and tried to read them, but his eyes became blurred with tears. Leaning his head back, he closed his eyes. He thought of Morning Song and the life he had once shared with her. They had been like two carefree children playing at life. There had been no major problems confronting them. He thought of Alex, and how she had touched his life. His feelings for her were altogether different from what he had felt for Morning Song. Morning Song had been sweet and gentle, while Alex was wild and unpredictable. He remembered making love to her and admitted that she had made him feel things that he had never felt with Morning Song. Was it love he felt for Alex? If it was, then what had he felt for Morning Song?

He heard shuffling footsteps enter the room and knew Farley had just come in. Opening his eyes, he watched the old man take a chair, propping his feet up on a footrest.

"All hell's broken loose, Farley. No one is who they are supposed to be."

"What's that supposed to mean?" the old trapper asked, eyeing him warily.

"I mean no one with the exception of yourself is who they say they are."

Farley grinned broadly. "I 'spect you found out 'bout young Alex. I wondered how long it would take you to know that he was a she," he chuckled, showing a fair amount of white teeth.

Tag sat up and studied Farley's face. "You mean she told you and didn't tell me?"

Again Farley chuckled. "She didn't have to tell me. I knowed it almost from the first. I can't see how you missed it, though. You must be slipping when a beautiful young gal can convince you she's a boy."

"Why didn't you tell me?" Tag asked sourly, thinking he really was a fool.

Farley scratched his head. "Well, I didn't see as how she was doing any harm, and I figured she was in some kind of trouble. 'Sides, with her running off to your room most ever night, I figured you knowed she was a woman, leastwise, I hoped you did."

Tag's eyed gleamed brightly, and the look he gave Farley warned the old man that he had better watch what he said. "I don't want you to think badly of Alex, Farley. When she first came to me, she had never been with a man before," Tag said, feeling he needed to defend Alexandria.

"I knowed she were innocent—anyone could tell that just by looking at her."

Tag shook his head in bewilderment. "I have just been sitting here reflecting on my life . . . past and present. I know I should do the right thing and marry Alex."

"Is that what you wanna do?"

"Hell, how do I know? Morning Song hasn't been dead that long, and I feel as if I am betraying her in some way."

"Now, how could you feel like that 'less you feel guilty for loving Alex? If your heart weren't in it you wouldn't give it another thought."

Tag stood up and walked over to the window, throwing the curtains aside. "Would you think me disloyal to Morning Song if I told you what I felt for her wasn't as deep or as meaningful as what I feel for Alex, Farley?"

"Come on back over here and sit, Tag. I'm 'bout to talk to you like I would ifen I was your real grandpa."

Tag walked back to the chair he had been sitting in and waited for Farley to speak.

"I watched you and Morning Song together, and I always thought the two of you acted like young children. I always felt this thing tugging at you, and while you will think it was you wanting to face your uncle, I always knowed that a big part of it was that you weren't completely happy." Farley sat forward and lowered his voice. "You see, Tag, you had outgrown Morning Song. I always knowed you loved her like a good friend more than anything else. Joanna thought the same thing, too, but she never said as much to you."

"I don't know, Farley. I have been asking myself if Morning Song were still alive, could I give Alex up and return to her?"

"What did you answer yourself?"

"I would never be able to forget Morning Song. . . ."

"But?"

"I'm damned if I know," Tag answered, shaking his head. "I have never before been this unsure of anything in my life. I feel like all hell's about to break loose."

"Well, the way I seed it is you don't have to make that choice. Sad as it is, Morning Song is dead. You shouldn't forget that you have a little daughter, though."

"No, I never forget that."

"I 'spect you should just sit tight and let nature take its course."

"Farley, Alex doesn't realize that I know who she is."

"Well, you got all the free advice from me you're gonna get for one evening. I think I'll turn in."

"Wait," Tag said, holding the documents out to the old man. "Alex was able to get these for me tonight."

"You know I can't read. Was they the papers you was wanting?"

"Yes, and I never thought anyone could do such a good job in forging documents. If I came forward now and declared who I am, no one would believe me because these are so convincing. I myself could almost believe they are legitimate."

"What do they say?" Farley asked with interest.

"In part, they say that I, Taggart James, give my Uncle Howard and his wife, Claudia, full power to administer my estate in my absence."

223

"The hell you say! That woman and her Mr. Garner done went and committed something unlawful. Ifen you asked me, I'd say you had a good case against them now. I don't know much 'bout the law, but I know enough to see what they did would send them to prison for a long time to come."

"Yes, but I cannot go to the authorities just yet. I need more proof, and the only way I can get that is to spend more time with Claudia."

"I'd sooner stand next to a blackwidder spider than that woman."

"My sentiments exactly," Tag said, standing up and placing the forged documents in his desk drawer.

"By the way, I seed that sailor again tonight."

"Where?"

"He was standing under that big elm tree out front, just gazing up at the house. When I started toward him, he just kinda faded away."

"I wonder if he's been hired by Claudia to keep an eye on me?"

"I don't know, but it surely do seem strange how he keeps turning up everywhere we go, don't it?"

"Let me know if you see him again. By the way, Farley, you are going to have to stay out of sight for a while."

"How so?"

Tag told the old trapper what Alex had overheard that evening in Mr. Garner's office. "As you can see, they know about you, and if Claudia were to see you, she would recognize you right away."

Farley stood up and ambled toward the door. "You can trust me to lay low for a spell," he said over his shoulder.

When Farley had gone, Tag walked back to the window and stared out into the night. It was long past midnight, and the full moon lit the countryside with its brightness. He looked down at the elm tree where Farley had said he had seen the sailor earlier. He watched as a shadow detached itself and moved away from the house. He wondered who the man could be, and why he was keeping such a close watch on him.

Turning away, he blew out the lamp and walked toward the stairs. He was bone weary, but he had so much on his mind, he doubted he would sleep tonight. It was still hard for him to think of Alex as Xandria. What a fool he had been not to see through her disguise right from the start.

When he lay down on his bed he tried not to think about Xandria. He was almost afraid to examine his feelings for her too closely. One thing he was determined to do was help her, if it were at all possible.

Chapter Seventeen

Alexandria lay on her bed, wide-eyed and sleepless. She watched the shadows caused by the wind blowing the branches of big oak tree outside her window dance fleetingly across the wall.

Falcon Knight was really Taggart James, she kept thinking over and over to herself. Tonight, part of the mystery about his past had been unraveled, but there was still many questions to which she would have liked to know the answers. Who was the woman Falcon was supposed to love? No matter how she tried to transfer her thoughts, they always seemed to slip back to the woman Falcon loved. No, not Falcon . . . Taggart James.

Alexandria closed her eyes, and she could almost feel his strong, sensitive hands move over her body. She ached for him to hold her. It mattered that he loved another woman, but she wouldn't let that stop her from going to him. What would happen if she were to go to him right now? Of course, he now knew about her killing her stepbrother, and he might no longer want to be with her.

She sat up and swung her legs off the side of the bed. Perhaps she would go to him once more—just one last time. She had already decided that she would have to leave now that Taggart knew about her past. She knew it would be hard to face him now that he was aware of her guilt. Of course, he wouldn't blame Alex for what had been done to Rodney—she could stay on as Alex! No, that wouldn't do at all. Tomorrow she would have to leave—but tonight . . . tonight she would go to him for the last time as Xandria.

She took off her clothing and removed the velvet cover from the bed, draping it about her shoulders.

Her excitement mounted as she walked down the hall toward Taggart's bedroom. She had to slow her footsteps to keep from running to him.

By the time she reached his door, her knees felt weak, and she didn't know if she had the nerve to enter his bedroom. The irony of her situation hit her full force. Since the very beginning, she had always been the one to go to him. What if he didn't really want her and was too kind to hurt her feelings? In that moment, she knew she couldn't walk through that door. She could only guess at what he thought about her conduct.

Alexandria remembered being shocked at the way Molly, the tavern maid, had thrown herself at Tag. How sanctimonious she had acted then. Now, she realized, she was no better than Molly. Perhaps she was even worse than the tavern maid. At least Molly didn't try to cover up what she was—while Alexandria always crept about in the dark of night when she went to Falcon's room.

She took a step backwards with the intention of returning to her bedroom when the door was flung open and Tag stood staring down at her.

"I had hoped you would come tonight, Xandria. Won't you come in?" he asked, moving back to allow her entrance.

She shook her head and took another timid step backwards. His hand closed around her arm, and he pulled her forward, shutting the door behind them.

"I didn't think you would come to me anymore," he said, giving her a searching glance.

His bedroom was flooded with moonlight, and Alexandria felt shy knowing he could see her so clearly. The other times she had come to him, his room had been in total darkness.

"What am I to do with you, Xandria? You have become a real dilemma for me."

"I . . . am sorry," she said softly. "I do not mean to be a bother to you."

"Ah, so you speak at last," he said, smiling slightly. "In that case I will ask you to answer something that has been puzzling me for a time."

"I will if I can."

"Remember the note you wrote me, warning me of Claudia's treachery?"

"I remember."

"How did you find out about her and Mr. Garner?"

Alexandria ducked her head. "I was hiding in her garden and I overheard Claudia Landon and Mr. Garner talking."

"I see. Was that the night of the party?" Tag asked, remembering how Alex had asked him to take him to the party with him that night.

"Yes," Alexandria whispered. She glanced at his handsome face, which was clearly defined in the

228

moon's brightness. She felt very vulnerable knowing he could see her equally well. "Yes, it was the night of the party," she said softly, wishing she hadn't come to his room at all. "I had to see you one last time, Falcon, before I go away," she blurted out.

He arched an eyebrow. "Oh, so you have decided to go away, have you?" he asked, smiling to himself. Now that he knew she was Alex he didn't feel unduly distressed at her announcement. "I'm glad you have come to me tonight. I have been thinking about you and would like to talk to you seriously."

Alexandria was more than a little hurt that he didn't seem concerned that she wasn't coming back again. Her eyes were clear as she looked at him, masking her hurt. "All right," she said, wondering what he wanted. She suspected he wanted to talk to her about her stepbrother and felt shame that he knew about the horrible deed she had done. "Do you want to ask me about Rodney?"

"Yes, in part. Come sit in the chair by the window so you will be more comfortable." He clasped her arm and led her across the room and sat her down while he stood over her, realizing how beautiful she really was. If her story were true, and he had no reason to doubt it, she had no one to turn to but him. He pulled up a stool and sat down beside her. Since the stool was low, it put him on her eye level.

"Tell me about your stepmother and stepbrother, Xandria," he said in an insistent voice. Tag would still let her play her little game where she pretended to be Xandria. He feared if he were to tell her he knew who she was, she might really run away.

She turned her face away and stared out at the

moonlight. "I don't want to talk about them. It's too horrible to remember."

He took her chin and turned her back to face him. When his eyes softened, Alexandria wished she could reach out and rest her head against his shoulder, knowing she would find comfort there. As if he read her thoughts, he pulled her forward and held her tightly against him.

"Don't you know I would do anything to protect you, Xandria? Why can't you trust me? Alex does."

"Oh, I do trust you, Falcon. I just don't want to burden you with my problems when you have your own troubles."

"It seems you have become my problem, Xandria," he said, brushing her cheek with his lips. She could feel the strength of his arms about her and knew as long as he held her this way, no one could harm her.

"I never meant to be your problem. I don't know what to do anymore. I cannot hide the rest of my life."

"If you will trust me, perhaps you won't have to hide at all, Xandria," he whispered against her ear. "Tell me where your stepmother is staying."

"At the time of the accident, she was staying with her sister, Annabelle Norris, on Front Street. She may since have gone back to the farm in Valley Forge." She pulled back and stared at him. "You wouldn't go to her and tell her where I am, would you?"

"You know better than that, Xandria. I merely want to understand what you are facing. I don't know if you are aware of it, but you yourself just referred to what happened to your stepbrother as an accident. I'm sure if the authorities knew how your stepmother was trying to force you into a marriage against your

230

will, they would be on your side."

"You aren't going to go to the authorities about me, are you?"

Tag noticed the fear that caused her amber eyes to widen, and he wanted to assure her that he would take care of her. He hated the thought that she had been made to suffer at the hands of such unscrupulous manipulators as her stepmother and stepbrother. She had such an endearing quality about her, he couldn't imagine anyone's wanting to hurt her.

"Xandria, I would do nothing to cause you distress. You should know by now that I wouldn't do anything that would harm you."

"Yes, I do know that. I was just wondering . . . do you . . . are you disgusted by me?"

He laughed and tugged playfully at a loose curl that fell over her forehead. "On the contrary, I am enchanted by you. I would have thought you knew that by now."

"I don't know anything for certain anymore. If you had told me a few short months ago that I would come to a man's room at night and allow him to . . ." She lowered her eyes. "I . . . would never have believed such a thing about myself. I am not only a murderess, but a . . . I don't . . . know the word for what I have become."

He smiled and forced her to look into his eyes. "You have become my lover. Is that so hard for you to admit? You came to me at a time when I needed someone. You gave unselfishly of yourself, while asking for nothing in return."

She blinked the tears from her eyes. "That's not quite true. You allowed . . . Alex to stay with you."

"That was easy, Xandria. Alex has become indispensable to me."

"I must go now," she said starting to rise, but he put a restraining hand on her arm.

"I am not finished talking to you yet, Xandria. I have something very important to ask you."

"What is it?"

"I want to ask you if you will do me the great honor of becoming my wife."

Alexandria was taken completely by surprise. She hadn't expected him to offer her marriage. Her amber eyes sparkled with joy as he pulled her toward him. To be his wife was all she could ask for in life. Oh, how she loved him! She felt his lips brush her brow, and she closed her eyes.

Suddenly grim reality settled over her. Falcon hadn't said anything about loving her. He had offered to marry her because he was an honorable man and he wanted to do the right thing by her. No, she couldn't possibly marry him on those terms.

"No, I don't want to be your wife," she said, knowing she had told the biggest falsehood she had thus far spoken to him. "I don't want to be anyone's wife. You don't love me, and I don't love . . . you."

"Are you quite sure, Xandria?"

"Yes, very sure," she said, standing up and moving hurriedly across the room. When she reached the door she opened it and fled into the hallway, fearing if she hesitated she would weaken. She hoped fervently he wouldn't try to stop her. He had just offered her the one thing she wanted most in life, and for his sake, her answer had to be no.

She slipped into her room before the tears reached

her eyes. Leaning against the door, she unfastened the bedcovering and allowed it to slide to the floor. As she climbed into bed, she buried her face in the pillow so her sobs couldn't be heard outside the room.

Hearing a light tap on the door, she sat up quickly. What if it was Falcon? Perhaps he had come to ask her more questions. She quickly reached down to the foot of the bed and gathered up her nightshirt, pulling it over her head. Wiping her tears away, she called out for whomever it was to enter.

"Alex, I have come to talk to you," Tag said moving to the bed and sitting down on the foot, propping his long legs up beside Alexandria.

"It's late, Falcon."

"Yes, but I have a dilemma that you may be able to help me with. Will you help me, Alex?"

"You know I will . . . if I can."

"First of all, I need to tell you some things about myself, Alex. Since I was twelve years old I lived with the Blackfoot Indians. My sister, Joanna, is married to the Blackfoot chief, Windhawk."

"Weren't you frightened?" she asked, amazed at his revelation. She had expected anything but this.

"No, you see the Blackfoot were very kind to me and my sister. They made us feel as if we belonged to them. That's why I married an Indian princess, Morning Song."

"You . . . married an Indian?"

"Yes, and I was very happy until last fall when Morning Song was killed by a bullet that had been intended for me. You see, Claudia is married to my uncle, and they sent some men to kill me and my sister."

233

"Oh, Falcon, I'm so very sorry," she said in horror. "Did you love Morning Song very much?" she asked, knowing she would be the woman he had told her he loved.

"Yes, very much. Before she died, Morning Song delivered our child, which turned out to be a daughter."

"Oh," was all Alexandria could manage to say, with tears in her eyes, thinking how much he must have suffered.

"I tell you this because I want to be honest with you. I want to keep nothing important from you." His eyes sought hers, and she wondered at his reason for telling her about his wife and daughter.

"Where is your daughter now?"

"She is with my sister, Joanna. Before Morning Song died, she made me promise that I would give the baby to Joanna to raise."

"How awful for you. I am so very, very sorry."

"Don't be sorry for me, Alex. I have learned to live with my grief by replacing it with hatred. Perhaps you can better understand now, why I felt I had to return to Philadelphia. You see, the house that my uncle and Claudia live in belongs to me and Joanna. I won't go into any more details, but I think you can see why I have been forced to be so secretive."

"Oh, yes, I do. I will help you in any way I can to see that justice is done, Falcon. You can count on me."

He laughed slightly. "I have come to count on you a great deal, haven't I? Without your help tonight, I might never have gotten my hands on those documents. You can see now why they were so important."

234

"I can't understand how people can be so evil, like Claudia and my stepmother and stepbrother."

"No, Alex, I don't think you can understand. That's one of the things I like about you. By the way, my name really is Falcon. Actually, it's my Indian name . . . Night Falcon!"

"I'm glad you told me about your past, Falcon. I promise no one will hear of it from me."

"I know that." He moved to the center of the bed and took her hand. "Now, I want you to do something for me. I have asked your sister to marry me. I hope you will convince her of my sincerity."

"She won't marry you. I know this."

"Perhaps if you were to tell her that I need her—do you think that would change her mind?"

"No, I don't think so," she answered in a whisper. He had talked about need but hadn't said anything about love, except when he told her about Morning Song.

Tag dropped her hand and stood up, crossing the room. When he reached the door, he turned back to her. "Think about what I said, Alex." With those as his parting words, he opened the door and slipped quietly out into the hallway.

Alexandria stared at the closed door for a long moment. Too many thoughts were whirling around in her mind for her to make any sense of their conversation. She knew now why he wanted to marry her . . . because she had been untouched when she first went to him. He was the kind of man who held honor above all else, and she wasn't about to take advantage of his kindness.

She got out of bed and walked over to the window.

Pushing the curtains aside, she gazed out on the grounds below. She wished there was someone she could turn to for advice, but there wasn't. She sat down in a chair and leaned her head against the padded back. She reminded herself that she was her mother's daughter, and that gave her the courage to do what she knew she must. Alexandria knew that before too long she would have to leave. Tonight had been proof that she had taken unfair advantage of Falcon's generosity.

She moved to the bed and lay down. Yes, her mind was mind up. She would leave tomorrow. When she left it would very difficult, but she must not weaken.

She clasped her hands tightly together, praying for the courage she would need tomorrow.

Chapter Eighteen

Taggart stepped out of the carriage and pulled the collar of his gray coat about his neck to protect himself from the downpouring rain.

"Wait for me, I won't be long," he told his coachman as he walked up the steps to the drab gray stone building. He waited for the answer to his knock and looked about the neighborhood with distaste. In spite of the rain, pathetically ragged children were wading in the stream of water that ran down the cobblestone street.

Tag saw a woman peep through the tattered and soiled curtain at the window, and almost immediately the door was thrown open. The woman, who stared at him open-mouthed, wore a soiled and dingy apron. Her brown hair, which had been drawn back into a bun, had slipped from its pins and streamed down her face.

"If you're selling something, I ain't buying," she said, eyeing the fancily dressed gentleman suspiciously.

"To the contrary, madam. I wish to buy something."

"Huh?" she asked, still suspicious. "What would

the likes of me have that a fine gentleman like yourself would want to buy?"

"First, allow me to introduce myself to you. I am Falcon Knight, and I am interested in purchasing a farm in Valley Forge by the name of Meadowlake."

The woman's face eased into a grin. "Are you now?" she asked, pushing a wisp of hair back off her forehead. "Well, Meadowlake ain't mine to sell. It belongs to my sister."

"Would you mind if I stepped in out of the rain so I could ask you some questions?"

She looked behind him and saw the fine coach and six he had arrived in and nodded. "I reckon as how it'll be all right," she said, moving aside so he could enter.

Tag stepped into the dimly lit hallway and ran his hand through his damp hair. "May I ask your name, madam?"

"Name's Mrs. Annabelle Norris, but you'll be wanting to talk to my sister, Barbara Bradford. She ain't here just now. She took her son in to see the doctor."

Annabelle had never before talked to such a fine gentleman. She and her sister Barbara had been raised in Marysville, on a street very much like this one. While Barbara had been married to Mr. Bradford, she had never introduced him to her poor relations. Barbara had taught herself how to speak properly and knew all the niceties in life, while Annabelle had married a poor seaman and had never tried to better herself.

Tag watched the woman's face carefully. "I'm sorry to hear that, Mrs. Norris. Is her son ill?"

238

"He were for a time. Got burnt real bad a while back, but he's about as fit as rain now."

"That is fortunate. A burn can be serious if it gets infected. How did he come to be burned?"

The woman's laughter crackled out. "He had woman trouble. I told my sister she shouldn't fool around with that fancy piece that was her stepdaughter. The girl had been spoiled all her life by a doting father. My sister tried to be a mother to her, but Alexandria would have none of it. The girl was rebellious and strong-willed. My poor nephew, Rodney, offered to marry her, but that little tart threw a lamp at him, and it nearly caused his death. As it is, much of his body was burned real bad. He has one bad scar on his face, and his hair was all singed off, but it's very near grown back now."

"When do you expect Mrs. Bradford to return?"

"It ain't easy to say. But I can tell you this right now—my sister can't sell you Meadowlake."

"Why is that?" Tag asked, delighted that he was finding Mrs. Norris to be a wealth of information.

" 'Cause it don't belong to them. It belongs to Alexandria—that stepdaughter of my sister's. Seems her grandfather left it to her all legal and proper."

"Then perhaps she is the one I need to talk to. Where can I find her?"

"Well, as to that, I just wouldn't know. She done went and took off. My sister has the law searching for her, but they ain't turned nothing up yet. I can tell you this much, though, if they do find her, she won't be in any condition to sell you nothing. My sister is going to have her committed to an asylum."

"I see. Perhaps I had better forget about buying

239

Meadowlake, then. I have no intentions of getting myself mixed up in family problems."

"Yes, it's just as well, Mr. Knight. My nephew fancies himself a farmer and wouldn't want to be parting with Meadowlake anyhow."

"But, according to you, Meadowlake doesn't belong to him," Tag reminded her.

The woman's laughter crackled out. "That don't make no never mind. When they find that ungrateful Alexandria, they'll most likely have her committed, and my sister, as her guardian, will have full control of Meadowlake."

"I see," Tag said, realizing what Alexandria had run away from. He had gained all the information he needed. Alexandria's stepbrother hadn't died, and Tag saw that with very little trouble she could be cleared of any charges they may have brought against her. "I thank you for your time, Mrs. Norris. I find that I'm not interested in buying Meadowlake, after all. You understand?"

"Yes, of course. It was good to talk to a fine gentleman like yourself. We don't get many like you down here on Front Street."

"I can assure you the pleasure was all mine, Mrs. Norris. I found you to be very informative," he said, bowing slightly and taking his leave.

When Tag was outside, he noticed it had stopped raining, and he breathed in a breath of fresh air. His heart felt light, knowing Alexandria's problems could easily be solved by a good lawyer.

As he started to get into the coach, he noticed a sailor standing across the street. There would have been nothing unusual in this, except that when the man saw Tag watching him, he faded into the shadows. Tag knew that would be the man who had been watching him so closely. He was of half a mind to cross the street and confront the man. He reconsidered when he saw the sailor disappear around the corner. Tag knew it would be futile to try to catch up with him, since the man had such a head start on him.

It was beginning to bother him more than a little that his every move was being watched. The only one he could think of who might be responsible was Claudia. If it was she who had hired the man to follow him, he would have to take care not to do anything that she might find suspicious.

Alexandria found Farley at the kitchen table sampling a hot apple pie Mrs. Green had just taken from the oven. After she wished Farley and Mrs. Green a good morning, she sat down across from the old man and watched him bite into a plump slice of the apple pie. Refusing a slice of pie herself, she watched as Mrs. Green left the kitchen to attend to the cleaning of the upstairs bedrooms.

"Where is Falcon this morning, Farley?"

"I don't rightly know. He ordered the coach brought 'round front bright and early, saying he was going to visit somebody who lives on Front Street."

Alexandria felt fear encircle her heart, knowing without a doubt that Falcon had gone to see her stepmother, Barbara. Horrible thoughts went through her mind as she felt the heartbreak of being deceived. She had trusted Falcon in telling him about her trouble. How could he go behind her back to talk to

Barbara?

"Are you quite sure Falcon said he was going to Front Street, Farley . . . could there be no mistake?" she asked, knowing the bitter taste of betrayal.

"Yep, leastwise that's what I was told. Ifen you need to see him, I 'spect he'll be home afore lunch," the old man said, watching the color go out of Alex's face. He was further puzzled when Alexandria got up from the table and ran out of the room.

Mrs. Green came back into the kitchen, staring back over her shoulder. "What's wrong with that young lad? He pushed past me in the hall like the very devil was chasing after him. Has something upset him?"

"I don't know, ma'am, but I can attest to this being the best apple pie I ever sunk my teeth into."

Mrs. Green's face brightened. "I like cooking for them that appreciates it, Mr. Farley."

Alexandria threw only a few of her meager belongings into the middle of the bed and wrapped them in a bedsheet. Realizing she wouldn't get very far without money, she slipped out of her bedroom and went to Falcon's room. She was relieved to find some money lying on the top of his dressing table. Picking up a quill and paper, she scribbled him a quick note, then dashed back to her room to pick up her belongings.

Slipping silently down the stairs, she left through the back door, keeping the hedge between herself and the house, hoping no one would see her leave. Bitter tears of anguish washed down her face as she reached the roadway and headed toward town.

At the moment, Alexandria didn't know what she would do or where she would go, but she now knew

242

she wasn't even safe disguised as a boy. After walking for a while, she began to think more clearly. She wanted to believe that Falcon had not betrayed her. If anything, he had probably gone to see Barbara to try and help Xandra. Falcon couldn't have known the kind of person Barbara was. Alexandria suspected that before the day was out, her stepmother would come to the house to take her away and no one could save her. Alexandria had never known that one could hurt so badly from a broken heart.

When she reached the bottom of the hill, she crossed the road and shifted her heavy bundle to her opposite shoulder. She would never trust a man again as long as she lived, she thought bitterly. Alexandria wiped the tears from her eyes, feeling an overwhelming sense of loss. She loved Falcon so much, and she knew she would miss seeing him every day.

Alexandria wondered where she would go. The future looked dark and bleak to her now. She had no friends and nowhere to turn. She considered, for a moment, returning to Meadowlake, then realized that would be too dangerous. She would have to rely on her own wits to survive, and she was determined to do just that!

When Tag returned home, he ran up the stairs, taking them two at a time, calling Alex's name. He was anxious to tell her that her stepbrother wasn't dead at all. He wanted her to know that he would soon engage a lawyer who would help her in her fight against her stepmother and stepbrother.

In his haste to see her, Tag opened Alexandria's bedroom door without knocking—he found the room empty. Seeing the floor littered with clothes and the bed in disarray, he was puzzled. Alex was usually so neat.

After questioning Mrs. Green about Alex's whereabouts, he was no closer to finding her. It wasn't until he talked to Farley that he discovered how strangely Alex had acted after Farley had told her where Tag had gone that morning. A thorough search was made of the grounds but still there was no sign of her.

By midafternoon, Tag went to his room and found the note Alexandria had propped against his pillow. Opening it, he read it quickly:

Dear Falcon,

By the time you read this I will be gone. On learning from Farley that you were visiting my stepmother, I felt I had to get away. I took some money I found lying on your dressing table, but I didn't steal it. As soon as I am able, I will pay you back in full. So you won't think me ungrateful, I thank you for taking care of me in the past. I do not thank you for betraying me to Barbara. I hope you will be successful in your endeavor to restore what rightfully belongs to you.

Alex

Tag swore angrily and wadded the paper up, throwing it to the floor. "We'll just see, Alex!" he said aloud, walking to the door and calling for Farley.

All that day, Tag and Farley searched the places they thought Alexandria might have gone. They even returned to the Fox and Hound Inn and questioned Molly, but she swore she hadn't set eyes on the boy

244

since they had moved away.

When darkness fell, it began to rain again. Tag was almost frantic in his search. He could imagine all sorts of horrible things happening to Alexandria. It was after midnight when Farley finally convinced him to return home and renew the search in the morning.

Tag sat by his bedroom window, listening to the rain patter against the windowpane. He prayed that Alexandria was somewhere where she would be safe and dry. He cursed himself for not telling her what he had been trying to accomplish by going to see her step-mother.

Tag placed his hand wearily over his eyes. He hadn't realized until today how much Alexandria meant to him. If anything should happen to her, he would never forgive himself. He would miss the sound of her laughter as Alex, and he would miss the nights she had come to him as Xandria.

"Damn you, Alex!" he called out. "I would thrash you if I could get my hands on you!"

When the sun came up, Tag and Farley renewed their search, but with the same results as the day before. No one they asked had seen a young boy leaving the house or grounds. It was as if Alexandria had disappeared without a trace!

By now Tag was frantic. He didn't know where to go to find her. All he could hope for now was that she would come to her senses and return to him on her own.

Blackfoot Territory

A warm breeze stirred the leaves on the tall cotton-

245

wood trees that grew beside the Milk River. Windhawk guided his horse through the waters of the river, riding at a fast pace. When he reached his lodge, he dismounted, threw the flap aside and entered. Inside he hung his weapons from the lodgepole. Seeing Joanna sitting on the bearskin rug, he crossed the room to stand over her. His dark eyes settled on her flaming hair, and he was awed by the tenderness that surrounded his heart at the sight of her nursing Tag and Morning Song's baby. Bending down beside her, he took the baby's hand in his.

"Morning Song's daughter seems to thrive on your milk, Joanna. It is a good thing that you have enough milk to feed both her and our daughter."

Joanna laid her hand on her husband's hand. "She is so tiny, I just want to hold and protect her from anything that would hurt her. I do not think it would be possible to love her more if she were my own daughter. Look how much the little princess resembles our own daughter. If they were the same size, many could not tell them apart."

Windhawk's dark eyes sought Joanna's, and she saw the troubled expression in their dark depth. "It is not good that you feel too deeply for this child, Joanna. The day will come when your brother will want her to be with him. When that day comes, it will tear at your heart."

"I know what you say is true, Windhawk, but I will face that when it comes. For now, she needs all the love I can give her."

Windhawk bent his head and kissed the child on her soft cheek. "It is as you say. I, too, feel as if she is a child of my body. In her, I feel as if I can hold on to a little part of Morning Song."

The baby cooed contentedly, drawn into the circle of love that encased her small, secure world. The love Windhawk and Joanna had for their own two children was such that it included her.

Later, Joanna walked down by the river and stared toward the horizon. Each day, she watched for her brother's return. The hardest thing she had to endure was the waiting, the not knowing if Tag was safe. She knew her Uncle Howard could be a very dangerous man, and Tag had no one but Farley to help him. Many times in the past months, Joanna wished that she had gone back to Philadelphia with Tag.

She watched until the sun went down, and then turned her footsteps back to the lodge, knowing that the next day she would again return to the river to watch for Tag.

Chapter Nineteen

Alexandria sat in the outer office of the employment agency, running her hand nervously down the seam of her gray gown. She pushed her hair off her neck, hoping to find some relief from the heat. Since she was alone in the room, she lifted her skirt just enough to show the white ruffles on her petticoat and wrinkled her nose in distaste at the heavy brown shoes on her feet. The cobbler who had sold her the shoes had called them a sensible style, and she could think of no better word to describe them. The long-sleeved gray gown she wore was not what one would call stylish, but then she was applying for a position as a maid and hoped she would look the part. Her one other gown was packed in a scarf and rested on the seat next to her. She was weary of pretending to be someone she wasn't and had decided to use her own name. She didn't think it very likely that Barbara would find her if she were employed as a maid. Barbara would have no reason to come to the better side of Philadelphia.

Alexandria still felt pangs of guilt for taking Falcon's money, but she needed enough to live on until she could find employment and support herself. She vowed to herself that as soon as possible she would pay him back every cent.

At that moment, a stern-faced woman wearing wire-rimmed glasses opened the inner door and motioned for Alexandria to enter the room. Gathering up her belongings and swallowing the lump of fear in her throat, she complied. The woman made what was supposed to be a smile, but to Alexandria it appeared more of a grimace.

"I am Mrs. Albita Chandler," the woman said, motioning for Alexandria to be seated in the cane bottom chair across from her desk. Mrs. Chandler picked up the paper before her and scanned it before fixing Alexandria with a cold stare. "Your name is Alexandria Bradford. It says here that you are eighteen and have had no previous experience and have no references. I'm afraid our clients always insist on a reference and usually someone who is older and with more experience."

Alexandria saw her hopes being dashed and took her courage in hand to try and win the stern-faced Mrs. Chandler over. "I may be young, but I was brought up on a farm and am a hard worker. If you will take a chance on me, I promise I won't let you down."

Mrs. Chandler looked at Alexandria over the rim of her glasses. "It says here that you have no family."

"That's right, ma'am. My father and mother are both dead. I have no one." Alexandria saw no pity in the woman's glance and knew she must try another tactic. "My mother died when I was quite young, and I looked after my father and managed the farm and the house for several years. While I have no one to recommend me, I was never afraid of hard work, and

I'm very strong. I have seldom known a sick day in my life."

"I see. You will have to understand this agency's clients are of the most prominent families in Philadelphia. I would be very remiss in my duties should I send them a young girl with no recommendation."

"I'm willing to do any kind of housework, Mrs. Chandler. I can cook, scrub floors, make beds, and tend garden. If you will just give me a chance, I promise I will prove it to you," Alexandria said earnestly.

"Well . . . perhaps I do have something," the older woman said, reaching into her desk drawer and pulling out a sheet of paper. "Mind you, I'm reluctant to send you on this interview. The family in question has gone through three of our ladies in the last six weeks. I'm not one to gossip, but Mrs. Landon is very difficult to work for, and I am about at my wits end trying to find someone suitable for her. You see, her husband is an invalid, and he requires constant attention."

Alexandria dropped her eyes. Could Mrs. Chandler be referring to Claudia Landon? It would be disastrous if she were to be recognized by Claudia. But . . . if she were to be accepted into the Landon household, perhaps she would be in a position to help Falcon!

"What would the position entail, ma'am?"

"As I said, Mr. Landon is an invalid. He has a man who sees to all his personal needs. Should you get the position, you would be required to keep his room clean, serve his meals, and read to him. I see on the form you filled out that you are able to read."

"Oh, yes, ma'am. I can read very well," Alexandria

told her, thinking the woman was dense if she didn't realize she would have to know how to read if she was able to fill out the forms. "My grandmother had been a governess before she married my grandfather. She taught me when I was very small," Alexandria said with enthusiasm.

Mrs. Chandler arched her eyebrow with approval. "In that case, perhaps you might do. For some reason, Mrs. Landon always insists that we send a woman to look after her husband. I must warn you that Mr. Landon isn't an easy man to get along with. I understand he is very demanding, and you will work long, hard hours. Will this be satisfactory to you?"

Alexandria leaned forward. "As I told you, I am willing to work very hard. Please give me this chance, and I give you my word I will do a good job."

"Well . . . all right, but mark my word, you will not have an easy time of it. The pay isn't at all good, but you will have room and board."

As Mrs. Chandler scribbled an introduction for her to carry to Claudia Landon on a piece of paper, Alexandria stood up, thinking she might be in a position to help Falcon. She was determined that she would make herself indispensable to Mr. Landon, and, in so doing, perhaps she could keep her eyes and ears open for anything that might help Falcon!

Farley ducked behind the stable and unsheathed his knife. He then watched quietly as the hedges next to the carriage house parted and a man poked his head out. Farley recognized him immediately as the sailor who had been following Tag for several weeks. Farley had spotted the man a short time before from his bedroom window and had quickly made his way down the back stairs and out to the stable hoping he could take the man by surprise.

The sailor didn't know he was being watched, and he slipped to the side of the hedges now and stared up at the house. With the quietness Farley had learned from the Blackfoot, he eased himself along the stable wall toward the carriage house. When Farley was near enough, he made a flying dive at the man and knocked him to the ground. For a long moment, the two men struggled, until at last Farley gained the upper position and pinned the man beneath him.

"You better speak your piece now, stranger, 'cause dead men don't talk too good," Farley said, placing the point of his knife at the man's throat. "I been watching you hanging 'round, and I don't figure you're up to no good."

"You are mistaken. I don't mean you or the boy any harm. Let me up, and I'll be on my way."

Farley studied the man's face carefully. It didn't take a practiced eye to tell the man was no more a sailor than Farley himself was. The man's hat had come off in the struggle, and Farley noticed his hair was red, but for the white streaks that ran through it at the temples.

"Now, I ain't zackly anxious to let you go 'til you do some talking. What are you doing hanging 'bout here, and what boy are you talking 'bout?"

The stranger looked into Farley's eyes, seemingly unafraid of his threats. "I was referring to the one who calls himself Falcon Knight."

"Falcon Knight ain't no boy. And what do you mean when you say he calls himself Falcon Knight?

252

Do you doubt that that's his true name?"

"I don't know. I wish to hell I did know if he is who he claims to be. It could be I am letting my imagination run away with me and hoping he is who I think he is."

Farley looked at the man suspiciously and jabbed the knife closer to his jugular vein. "Who do you hope he be?"

"I'm not at liberty to say. Would you allow me to get up? You have my word I won't try to escape. I'm not finding this position too comfortable."

"Why should I? You ain't what you'd have me believe. You surely ain't been at sea. I ain't got no edjucation, but I knowd a edjucated man when I heard one. Tell me who you are, and what you want, or I'll run this knife clean up your gullet."

Still the man showed no fear. "Let's just say if Falcon Knight is who I suspect he is, I am someone who is interested in his welfare, and let it go at that."

"No, let's not let it go at that. Who in the hell do you think he is?"

"I'll answer your question with a question? Did Falcon Knight ever go by the name of Taggart James—does he have a sister named Joanna?"

Farley's eyes narrowed. "You ain't in any condition to ask questions, but you sure as hell better answer mine. You ain't got long to live." To prove he meant what he said, Farley pricked the man's skin with his knife. "What do you mean by coming 'round here making such charges? I ain't never made the acquaintance of no Taggart James."

"I have been watching you and the boy for some time, and I have come to know you are a friend of his.

253

If you don't believe anything else I say, believe that I, too, am his friend."

"I don't rightly see as how I believe you. Ifen you was his friend, you'd not sneak 'round like a thief in the night. If you are a friend of hissen, why do you skulk 'round? I 'spect you and me will just go on up to the house and ask him ifen he knows you."

"No, don't do that. I doubt that he would remember me."

"Ifen you be thinking he was that Tag you was speaking 'bout, he won't know you from Adam. 'Cause his name's Falcon Knight."

Farley was surprised to see the man's face ease into a smile. "I don't recall calling him Tag . . . although I often called him that in the past. I asked you if his name is Taggart James. I think you just told me what I wanted to know."

Farley grabbed a handful of red hair and pressed the man's head backwards. "Can you think of any reason why I shouldn't slice your throat right now?"

The man grabbed Farley's wrist, and with a strength that surprised the old trapper, wrestled the knife from his hand. Before Farley could recover, the man pushed him aside and stood up. Farley would have scrambled to his feet, but the man placed a foot on his chest and applied pressure.

"Were I not the boy's friend, I would end your life now, old man. Look after the boy . . . he has enemies." So saying, the stranger threw the knife, and it landed with its point between Farley's legs.

Farley watched as the sailor disappeared, knowing no more about the man who had been sneaking about for weeks than he had before. The old man shook his head. If the stranger wasn't Tag's friend, one thing was certain; thanks to the slip of Farley's tongue, the man—be he friend or foe—now knew Taggart James's true identity.

Alexandria sat in the morning room, facing Claudia Landon. She had prayed the woman wouldn't recognize her dressed as a girl. So far, Claudia hadn't seemed suspicious, although she did look at her in a peculiar way every so often. It took only a short time for Alexandria to realize that Claudia couldn't read. She had taken Mrs. Chandler's letter as a recommendation.

"I hope you will prove more satisfactory than the last three women the agency sent. They were afraid of their own shadows and became nothing but an annoyance to my husband. I think you should know from the onset that my husband is not an easy man to get along with."

"I will do my best, Mrs. Landon. You will find that I am not easily intimidated."

"I would have thought you a bit young, but who knows—the others were well past their prime, and they didn't last very long."

"I would ask that you give me a fair chance. Pray do not hold my youth against me. I will work very hard."

Claudia raised her chin and studied the girl more closely. Her short-clipped hair curled about her forehead, and her face was much too pretty. As a rule, Claudia didn't like to employ servants who were attractive, but she was becoming desperate for someone who would please Howard. "I'll give you a week's trial period, but if by that time I am not pleased with you—you will leave. Is that understood?"

"Yes, that seems more than fair to me," Alexandria agreed hurriedly. She was relieved that Claudia considered her at all.

Claudia's gaze went back to the young girl. There was something about her that reminded her of Joanna, her hated enemy, but she didn't know what it was. Perhaps it was her refined, ladylike manners. It didn't matter that the girl was dressed in a cheap, ugly gown; she still presented a superior attitude. Her manners were somehow haughty, and for a moment Claudia felt the same inadequacy she had always felt around Joanna. She reminded herself that she was the mistress of the house and this chit would be working for her. As Claudia looked into the girl's strange, golden-colored eyes, she had a feeling she had seen her somewhere.

"Is it possible that you and I have met before?" Claudia questioned.

"I suppose it might be possible," Alexandria said cautiously. "Have you ever been to Valley Forge, Mrs. Landon?"

"Heaven forbid! What would I possibly find to do in Valley Forge?"

"Will I be meeting Mr. Landon today, Mrs. Landon?" Alexandria asked, changing the subject quickly.

"Yes, I'll have Mrs. Dodson, the housekeeper, show you upstairs. What did you say your name was?" Claudia asked, looking at the paper as if she were reading.

"I am called Alexandria Bradford," Alexandria

said, standing up as a maid entered the room. Claudia indicated that she should follow the maid, dismissing her with bored indifference.

Once out in the hall, Alexandria breathed a sigh of relief. She would make sure Claudia and her husband were satisfied with her work. No matter how difficult Mr. Landon turned out to be, Alexandria was determined to make him like her. She had to keep this position.

Tag unsaddled Navaron and threw the saddle over the stall door. He was bone weary from trying to find Alexandria. He had just ridden in from Valley Forge where he had gone to her Meadowlake to make inquiries about her whereabouts. No one at the farm had seen Alexandria in months. He could find no trace of her and knew he should give up trying to find her. It was as if she had been swallowed up, never to be heard from again.

His black boots made a clipping sound as he walked up the stone walk toward the house.

Tag was so lost in thought, he didn't notice the sailor who ducked behind the stables and watched until he disappeared into the house.

The sailor pulled his cap down lower over his forehead and faded into the shadows. The man had an old debt to settle, and he wouldn't rest until he had seen his goals accomplished!

Chapter Twenty

Alexandria had unpacked her meager belongings and placed them in the oak chest at the foot of the bed. Her room was on the third floor, and she was surprised to find it cheerful and bright.

There was a tap on the door and Alexandria found Mrs. Dodson in the hallway, ready to take her to see Mr. Landon. She followed the housekeeper down the stairs to the second floor, where Mr. Landon's room was located.

Alexandria had the feeling she was in a frightening, alien world. She knew the first and most important thing to do would be to make friends with the servants. It had always been her experience that servants talked and gossiped among themselves, so perhaps she could learn something that would help Falcon.

"Well, miss, I feel pity for you—you have a job on your hand that no one else would take. Mr. Landon has a powerful temper and can raise the roof if he's a mind to," the housekeeper, who was called Mrs. Dodson, informed Alexandria.

"I had the impression he couldn't talk, Mrs. Dodson."

"Oh, he can make himself understood, all right. He has very little trouble getting his point across, as you will soon find out. He can talk, if you call the gibberish that comes out of his mouth talking. I can tell you right now, if you want to keep the job, you must report everything of importance to Mrs. Landon."

"Why is that?"

"Because she rules the roost around here. All your predecessors kept her well informed. You must do it in such a way that Mr. Landon won't be suspicious. If he finds out you are running to his wife with tales, he will send you packing. That's what happened to all the others. He's a mean one, I can tell you."

By now, they had reached the top of the landing, and Mrs. Dodson led Alexandria down the hallway to a massive, hand-carved door that she knew would lead to the master bedroom. She was feeling nervous at the thought of meeting the formidable Mr. Landon.

Mrs. Dodson's knock was answered by the tallest man Alexandria had ever seen. She was sure he must be at least seven feet tall, and he had broad shoulders and muscled arms, as well. Although the man didn't appear to be more than thirty years of age, his hair was snow white. A long scar ran down his cheek and across his lip, giving him a menacing appearance.

"This is Barlow. He looks after Mr. Landon, and you will be spending a great deal of time with him. Barlow, this is the new girl who has been hired to look after Mr. Landon. Her name is Alexandria."

The giant man looked Alexandria over with what she was sure was a frown of disapproval. His only sound was a grunt as he pushed past them and walked into the hall.

"Don't mind Barlow," Mrs. Dodson said, lowering her voice. "He is loyal to Mr. Landon, and he's resentful of anyone he thinks might be taking over."

"He is a bit frightening," Alexandria said, as her eyes went past Mrs. Dodson. The room they were now in appeared to be a sitting room, and she saw the connecting door that led to what she knew would be Mr. Landon's bedroom.

"Just don't cross Barlow, and you shouldn't have anything to worry about. Come with me, and I'll take you in to Mr. Landon's room."

Alexandria followed closely on Mrs. Dodson's heels. When they entered the bedroom, her eyes went immediately to the man who lay on the giant four poster bed. He was propped up on pillows, and Alexandria noticed that his face was thin and sunken, and his pallor was ashen. She thought that at one time he might have been a big man, but now he was no more than a mere shell of a man. His eyes seemed to bore into hers, as if he were trying to stare her down, but Alexandria's eyes never wavered.

"Mr. Landon, this is Alexandria Bradford. She will be replacing Miss Wilson."

Howard Landon's eyes swept the young girl's face. The moment he saw her she reminded him of Joanna. It wasn't that they looked anything alike—it was more the proud carriage of the head and the way she walked. He wanted to hear her voice and hoped that it, too, would remind him of Joanna.

It was as if this young girl had brought a breath of springtime into his drab existence. In the past, all the women that Claudia had assigned to his care had run to her with every little thing, and that was the reason he had insisted they be dismissed. He hoped this girl would be different.

Alexandria moved forward, feeling pity for this man, who was almost as helpless as a baby. She knew she should hate him for what he had done to Falcon. But he was so pathetic she couldn't find it in her heart to hate him. She fluffed up his pillow and pulled the covers across his chest.

"I'm glad to be working for you, Mr. Landon. I will try to carry out all your wishes. I am told that you like to have someone read to you. I enjoy reading very much, and perhaps you would allow me to choose some books that I have enjoyed in the past."

Howard closed his eyes, listening to the sound of her voice. Since Joanna had come over from England, their accents were different, but the voice tones were the same—clear, soft, and soothing.

Alexandria wasn't aware that Mrs. Dodson had left the room, and she thought Mr. Landon had fallen asleep since he was so still and his eyes were closed. She walked softly across the room and stood staring out the window. It was hard for her to realize that this was the house were Falcon had lived as a boy. It was even harder to grasp the fact that the sick old man who occupied this room had stolen this house from Falcon and his sister.

Hearing a funny grunting sound, Alexandria spun around and found Mr. Landon watching her. He was motioning to the night stand that stood beside his bed, and she finally realized he must want a drink of water.

Lifting the water pitcher, she poured some of the

liquid into a glass and held it to his mouth. Since one side of his face was paralyzed, much of the water spilled out of his mouth and ran onto his nightshirt. Howard Landon watched Alexandria to see what her reaction would be to the spilled water. The other women who had taken care of him had all panicked at this point. He watched as her mouth eased into a smile.

"I will have to be more careful in the future, Mr. Landon. I believe I filled your glass too full," she said, dabbing at his nightshirt with a white napkin.

Howard felt joy in his heart. She was neither afraid of him nor did she seem to be disgusted by his awkwardness.

"It is a bit stuffy in here, Mr. Landon. I believe I will open the window and let in a breath of fresh air," she said in a cheerful voice.

Howard's eyes followed her across the room. Her hips swayed gently as she walked. It felt good having a young girl to look after him instead of the older women who jumped out of their skin every time they came near him. He was glad Alexandria didn't fear him, and for the first time in many years, he felt almost lighthearted.

Tag removed his hat and tossed it onto the window seat. Sitting down in a chair, he propped his dusty boots on the foot rest. He had ridden to Front Street in the hopes of finding Alexandria there, but he had found no sign of her anywhere. With each passing day he missed her more and more. He was backed against a wall. He couldn't go to the authorities and ask them to help him find Alexandria, since her stepmother already had them looking for her.

He swore under his breath. Damn it, didn't she know he would never have betrayed her to her stepmother?

Mrs. Green had handed him a letter when he first entered the room, and he opened it absent-mindedly. Seeing it was an invitation from Claudia to come to tea on the next Thursday, he smiled. That was one invitation he would gladly accept. Time was slipping away, and he hadn't yet decided what would be the best way to go about seeking his revenge.

Tag stood up and walked into the study with the intention of answering the invitation, but when he passed the double doors that led out into the garden, he walked outside. He remembered how Alexandria had loved tending the garden. He felt a deep ache in his heart, and he knew without a doubt that he loved her. What he felt for her was as different from what he had felt for Morning Song as day from night. Morning Song had been the sweet love of his childhood . . . Alexandria was the love of his manhood. As deeply as he had felt for Morning Song, he knew it in no way compared with the all-consuming love that raged out of control within his body for Alexandria.

Tag was finding out that there were many different kinds of love. None before had been as deep and lasting as the emotions Alexandria had now awakened in him. What he felt toward her was what Windhawk and Joanna shared—a true, deeply lasting love. Tag shook his head sadly, thinking of Morning Song. He now realized that she had been more of a friend than a lover to him. And he knew in his heart that Morning Song had realized that fact long before he had.

Tag paused on the stone walkway and touched the petal of a red rose that reminded him of Alexandria. He knew if he didn't find her, he would spend the rest of his life seeking her. He wanted her not only as a woman but as . . . what? . . . his wife?

Hearing a rustling in the bushes at the back of the garden, Tag turned around just in time to see the man dressed as a sailor disappear out the back gate. He knew the man had too much of a head start for him to try and overtake him. He thought of what Farley had told him about the man. It was really irritating him now that the stranger seemed to be watching his every move. He decided the time had come to find out who the man was. Surely if he and Farley were to carefully lay a trap for the man, they could catch him.

He turned his footsteps back to the house, thinking that he would answer Claudia's note.

Alexandria had been working for Howard Landon almost a week. Against her will, she found herself liking the old man. It was hard to associate him with the man she knew he had been in the past. He was kind and considerate to her, and she like doing things for him to make his life a little easier.

One of the first things she had done was to have his bed moved to the window so he could look down on the garden. Today, she had replaced the drab brown curtains at his window with cheery yellow ones that she had made in her spare time, and that seemed to please him. She was learning what foods he liked and had even experimented with new dishes to please him.

Yesterday Alexandria had sent Barlow into town to purchase a wheelchair so she could take Mr. Landon for walks in the garden. She had been appalled to find he never got out in the fresh air. In fact, she was going to talk to him about moving his bedroom downstairs so he would have easier access to the garden.

Alexandria tiptoed across the room and saw that Mr. Landon was sleeping. Not wanting to disturb him, she moved quietly to a chair and sat down waiting for him to wake. The new wheelchair had been delivered today, and if he was feeling up to it, she wanted to take him into the garden.

Alexandria's eyes traveled up to the mantel to the portrait that hung there. She knew without being told that it was a portrait of Falcon and his family. It was easy to recognize him as the small boy in the painting. She looked at the beautiful young girl with the red-gold hair and knew that it had to be his sister, Joanna. She was puzzled as to why the portrait hung in Mr. Landon's bedroom and why he insisted she dust it every day. It certainly didn't seem to her to be the act of a man who hated the James family.

Alexandria's eyes traced the outline of young Tag's face. It was easy to see the man in the boy of the picture, even though the boy's hair had been more of a red-gold when the painting was done, and it was now golden. Although the eyes were now colder, they were still the same deep violet-blue as when the artist had captured the boy's image.

Alexandria brushed a tear from her cheek and turned away. It was painful for her to gaze upon Tag's face. It was strange, but since being in this house, she had now begun to think of Falcon as Taggart James. She loved him terribly, but she knew she had been nothing more to him than a slight distraction. It didn't matter how he felt about her; she would still help him in any way she could.

Seeing that Mr. Landon still slept, she tiptoed out of the room. So far, she hadn't been able to hear anything that would help Tag, but she intended to keep her ears and eyes open, and to be ever watchful.

When Alexandria reached the hallway, she almost bumped into Mrs. Dodson, who seemed very agitated about something. When Alexandria would have gone around the woman, Mrs. Dodson stopped her.

"Mrs. Landon will be wanting to see you in the sitting room right away. You'd best make haste and not keep her waiting."

"Do you have any notion what she wants to see me about?" Alexandria asked, dreading the thought of facing Claudia Landon again so soon.

"It's not for me to ask or you to know," Mrs. Dodson said, looking down her nose at Alexandria with a superior air. "You will find that you will last longer around here if you answer questions, not ask them."

Alexandria pushed past the housekeeper and made her way downstairs. She hoped that Claudia wasn't displeased with her work. If she were to dismiss her, she wouldn't be able to help Tag.

She found the sitting room door open and entered with her head held high. She saw Claudia standing in front of the window. The room was stifling hot and reeked of Claudia's perfume. Alexandria felt a sense of uneasiness when Claudia turned around with a frown on her face.

"How is my husband feeling today?"

"He seems to be in good spirits and is now resting."

Claudia motioned for Alexandria to be seated. "Starting today, I want you to report to me each morning about all that happens with my husband during the previous day. I want to know everything that he is thinking and doing. No detail is to be overlooked. Is that clear?"

"I will be glad to report to you how Mr. Landon's health is each day, but I will never become a snoop and tell you everything that he is doing," Alexandria said, feeling very indignant that this woman expected her to spy on Mr. Landon and report to her. She saw Claudia's face flame and knew she had caused her to lose her temper. She would probably be out of a job, but she had no intention of doing what Mrs. Landon asked.

"You forget yourself, young lady!" Claudia said in a harsh voice. "You work for me, and you will do as you are told. Do I make myself clear?"

Alexandria stood up. "I understand you all right, Mrs. Landon. You want me to spy on your husband. It is against my principles to stoop to spying. If that is what you expect out of me, then I am wasting your time and mine!"

Claudia gritted her teeth in anger. This young girl was being insulting, and she didn't intend to keep her under her roof a moment longer than it would take for her to pack her belongings. Again she thought how much Alexandria reminded her of Joanna.

"How dare you speak to me in such a manner? You forget your place. Go upstairs at once and pack your things—you are leaving this house! I will not have anyone as impertinent as you staying under my roof!"

Out of the corner of her eye, Claudia saw a shadow

fall across the open doorway and knew Barlow had been spying on her. She swore under her breath, knowing the man would report everything that had taken place to Howard. She had tried many times to get Barlow to do just what she had asked Alexandria to do, but he had always refused. Now the man was barely civil to her, and she knew Howard would never allow her to be rid of him, though she had tried often enough.

Turning back to Alexandria, her eyes showed her anger. "Well, what are you waiting for? Did I not dismiss you?"

Alexandria looked right into Claudia's eyes and had the satisfaction of watching the older woman lower her eyes first. "I am going, Mrs. Landon, but I doubt that you will find very many people to work for you who will be willing to do as you asked."

"Leave this room at once!" Claudia ordered in a loud voice, and the frown that passed over her face seemed to twist her features into distortion.

Without a word, Alexandria swept out of the room, thinking she couldn't leave soon enough to please herself. On her way upstairs, she brushed against Mrs. Dodson, but didn't stop to talk to the woman. It wasn't until she reached her own small room on the third floor that she realized she had spoiled any chance she might have to help Tag. Not only that, she would be out in the cold again with no place to go. She doubted that Claudia would pay her the wages she had earned, and she didn't have any money. Once again she was faced with the problem of not having a shelter over her head.

She felt miserable as she gathered up her few

belongings and neatly tied them into a bundle. Looking about the small room for the first time, she walked to the door. Her hand was on the doorknob when a loud knock startled her. Opening the door, she found Barlow standing in the hallway.

"You are not to leave this house. Mr. Landon wants you to stay," he said, looking at the bundle she carried in her arms.

"I cannot do as he asks. Mrs. Landon dismissed me," Alexandria said, thinking this was the first time Barlow had ever spoken directly to her.

Barlow took the bundle from Alexandria and tossed it on the bed. "Mr. Landon says you stay. His wife will not bother you again," the huge man said, turning away and walking back down the hallway.

Alexandria stared after him in amazement. Closing the door, she sat on the bed. It seemed that she wasn't unemployed after all. She sighed in relief and began putting away her clothing. She wondered what Claudia would say when she found out her husband had countermanded her orders. Apparently Mr. Landon was satisfied with the work she was doing.

Alexandria knew she had made a powerful enemy in Claudia Landon, and that one day she might very well have to face the consequences!

Claudia was alone in the sitting room, and she paced back and forth. She ranted and raved, and her voice carried as far as the kitchen.

The servants all went about their duties, talking in hushed tones. They had often seen Mrs. Landon in her present state of mind. They had learned that when she was having one of her tantrums, it was

269

better just to leave her alone until the storm blew over.

"How dare, Howard belittle me like this?" Claudia raged. "He's done this to get back at me! I'm his wife, and he shames me before the whole world!"

Claudia's face was red and her eyes had a wild look. "I will see you pay, Howard. Mark my words, before long that girl will leave this house." Her voice droned on and on. The servants knew it would be hours before the mistress of the house calmed down.

Chapter Twenty-one

Alexandria was now better able to understand Howard Landon when he spoke to her. Although his speech was garbled, if she listened very carefully she had little trouble understanding what he was trying to convey to her. She was finding out that he had a sense of humor, and one thing he was particularly amused by was the fact that he had countermanded Claudia's orders to dismiss her. He seemed to delight in anything that would cause Claudia distress.

In some odd way, Alexandria had come to like Mr. Landon. She felt pity for him because of the limited life he lived, confined to his room. It was difficult to associate him with the man who had caused Tag and his sister to flee from their home. How could this sick old man be the monster Falcon had told her about? She couldn't see him conspiring with Claudia to have Tag and Joanna killed. Tag had to be wrong— Howard Landon just couldn't be responsible for Morning Song's death.

She noticed he was unusually jovial this afternoon because Barlow was going to carry him down to the garden, where Alexandria would read to him in the summerhouse. She was anxious to see if Mr. Landon would enjoy a daily outing in the garden. It was almost inhuman the way Claudia had kept him shut up in his bedroom.

As Alexandria patted her hair into place, she looked at her reflection in the cracked mirror that hung on the wall of her bedroom. Her hair had grown longer, she noticed. As she stared into the amber-colored eyes that were reflected in the mirror, she wondered why she had been cursed with such unusual eyes. If only they were a pretty blue . . . or even a brown. She sighed wistfully. There was nothing she could do about her eye color, or even her appearance, she thought.

Her two gowns were not of a very good quality— they had been washed several times and were beginning to fade. What did it matter about her appearance anyway? She wasn't going to see anyone of importance in the garden, and besides, she was only a servant in this house. Certainly no one would expect her to dress other than in the sober gowns she wore. Still, there was a part of her that wanted to be presentable. She had been brought up always to look her best.

Alexandria thought of her stepmother and shuddered, wondering what Falcon had told Barbara about her. Shrugging her shoulders, she left her room, glad for the opportunity to be out in the fresh air.

Claudia sat beside Falcon Knight and felt her heart flutter. Never had she been so deeply affected by a man before! She had thought herself in love several times in the past, but those had been puny feelings compared to what she was now experiencing. As she looked into Falcon's ice-blue eyes, she could feel the tenseness in him, and she wondered if he were feeling the same wild attraction she was experiencing. Claudia realized that Falcon Knight was years younger than she, but that didn't bother her. Her hungry eyes ran over the breadth of his wide shoulders, taking in the way his blue coat fit snugly across his chest. His long legs drew her attention next. His gray trousers were molded to his thighs and tucked into a pair of polished back boots. He was everything a man should be, she thought, thinking that she couldn't wait to invite him into her bed.

Glancing up into his face, she saw that he was watching her closely. Thinking he might be able to read her thoughts, Claudia suddenly felt tongue-tied and searched for something to say to him.

"I . . . how is Alex, your ward?" she asked, voicing the first thing that popped into her head.

"As boys go, he is a handful," Tag answered in a cool voice. He felt a strong aversion being so near Claudia. All he could think of at the moment was that it was she who had been responsible for Morning Song's death.

"How is your husband?" he asked, trying to cover up his dislike of her.

"Poor Howard isn't good. I feel so sorry for him being confined to his room all the time."

"I was wondering if it would be possible to meet him?" Tag asked, watching Claudia's eyes closely.

"I'm sorry, but as I told you before, my husband doesn't see anyone. This is very difficult for me to say, but poor Howard isn't quite right in the head."

"I wasn't aware that Mr. Landon was suffering

from a brain disorder. How long has he been this way?"

Claudia dabbed at her eyes and gave Tag a sad smile. He could tell she was acting the roll of the grieved wife. He knew her too well to believe she had any genuine feeling for his Uncle Howard.

"My husband was stricken just a short time after our wedding. I have lived a very lonely life as the wife of a cripple," she said suggestively.

"Were you and Mr. Landon married here in Philadelphia?" Tag asked, wondering how far Claudia would take her lie.

"No, as a matter of fact, we were married at Fort Union in Indian territory."

Tag glanced down at the tip of his shiny black boot. "That seems a long way from home. Surely, you weren't traveling for the fun of it."

"No, I met Howard while he was searching for his niece and nephew. Two more ungrateful people you will never find. If you can believe this, they ran away from Howard and were living with the Indians somewhere out West."

"That is hard to believe. Why would they live with the Indians when they could enjoy the comfort and luxury of this house?"

"It was all Joanna's fault. She has no conception of how to live. I suppose she enjoys living among those savages. She is a horrid girl—defiant and rebellious. My husband and I have tried everything possible to get Joanna and her brother to return here, but with no results."

"Tell me about her brother. Did you say he also lives with the Indians, Claudia?"

274

"Yes, his name is Taggart—a most unlikable young boy. He would do anything his sister asked of him. It's possible that Howard and I could have convinced the boy to return here with us had it not been for his sister."

Tag noticed the undisguised hatred in Claudia's eyes when she spoke of Joanna, and he knew she was still blaming Joanna for everything that had ever gone wrong in her life. "How old is the boy now?"

Claudia looked thoughtful for a moment. "I don't know. Perhaps he is in his teens . . . I can't be sure . . . perhaps he's older." Her eyes searched his face. "Why are you so interested in Joanna and Tag?"

"Merely curiosity. I wonder what would cause them to prefer living with the Indians when they could live here." He made a wide swing with his hand. "Surely, they would prefer all this to an Indian tipi. How could they not want to return when they would have an aunt such as you concerned about their welfare?" he asked sarcastically.

Claudia's eyes sparkled, missing his point. "I once saw the Indian Joanna is living with. He was positively fierce-looking. He's the reason my husband had a stroke. We had managed to capture Joanna, and Windhawk followed and took her away from us."

Claudia's eyes swept past Tag to the open door that led to the garden. "It's much too nice a day to speak of such things. Let's go for a walk in the garden."

Tag stood up and nodded. "It would be my pleasure to escort you," he said, holding out his arm. Claudia had told him nothing he didn't already know. He would have to find another way to gain information from her. He saw the way she looked at him, and he shuddered inwardly. Tag wasn't sure he could give her what she was clearly wanting from him. He felt degraded at the thought of even touching her.

Alexandria closed the book she had been reading and smiled at Howard Landon. "I want to thank you for allowing me to stay on in your employment, Mr. Landon. I really do enjoy reading to you."

Howard smiled at the lovely young girl. She had such a soothing effect on him. He could listen to her for hours as she read to him. Her golden eyes sparkled with life and enthusiasm. It made him feel good just to be near her. He knew that he was using her as a substitute for Joanna. Howard had never been able to get close to Joanna. He wanted to give Alexandria all the things that young girls wanted, in order to make her happy. He was determined to dress her in lovely gowns and watch her bloom and grow.

"We . . . put . . . one over on my wife," he said in his slurred manner of speaking. His smile was distorted because one side of his face was paralyzed, but Alexandria could tell he was pleased.

"You shouldn't be so pleased with yourself," she said in mock reprimand. "What a way for a man to behave toward his own wife."

Howard's eyes danced merrily. "She is a wind . . . bag."

Alexandria couldn't stop the smile that caused her dimples to dance across her cheeks. Standing up, she tucked the covers about Howard's legs and pushed the wheelchair down the garden path. "It will soon be time for your afternoon nap. I must get you back into the house."

"I . . . want to stay," Howard protested.

"No. We shall do this again tomorrow, but not if you become overtired," she told him firmly.

Howard gave in gracefully, feeling good that Alexandria seemed truly to care about him. When Barlow had told him about the conversation between her and Claudia, Howard had immediately sent for his wife. Claudia had ranted and raved at his decision to keep Alexandria on against her wishes, but in the end she had relented, knowing he always had the last say.

It had warmed his heart to discover that Alexandria had refused to go behind his back and report to Claudia. There had been many women who had been hired to look after him before Alexandria. The others had been only too happy to comply with Claudia's wishes. That was the reason none of them had lasted very long.

Howard might be a cripple, but he was still in command, up to a point. Claudia had often defied him, but she stopped just short of disobeying his direct orders. He knew she was too afraid she might find herself out on her ear if she pushed him too far. He was disgusted by the show of affection Claudia always demonstrated toward him when anyone was around. He knew that she hated him every bit as strongly as he hated her.

Claudia was holding on to Tag's arm as they walked up the pathway. She was talking to him about the masquerade ball she was giving the next week and didn't see Alexandria as she wheeled Howard toward them.

Tag heard the squeaking of the wheels and looked

277

up. In spite of the fact that time hadn't been kind to Howard Landon, Tag had no trouble recognizing him immediately. His hair was now completely white, and he had a pale, unhealthy pallor, but there was no mistaking the man Tag had hated for so many years. He wondered if Howard Landon would recognize him and prepared himself for whatever was to come. If his Uncle Howard recognized him, then he could lay everything open. He would have preferred to be better prepared before meeting his uncle, but it was too late to turn back now. If Howard were mentally unstable, as Claudia had said, Tag thought there would be no danger of his knowing who he was.

Alexandria saw Falcon and drew in her breath. Was he crazed to come here and take a chance on being seen by his uncle? Surely Mr. Landon would have no trouble recognizing him, since he stared at the portrait of the James family all day. She felt fear and uncertainty as she considered whether to turn the wheelchair around and go in another direction—but it was too late now, Falcon and Claudia had both seen them. She gave no thought to the fact that Falcon would probably recognize her. All she was concerned with at the moment was his safety.

It was apparent that Claudia was very displeased, by the frown on her face. Tag walked toward them, never taking his eyes off his Uncle Howard. He watched for any sign that would show his uncle might recognize him.

"Well, it seems you will be meeting my husband after all, Falcon. Although what he is doing out in the garden, I'll never know," Claudia said, as her eyes bored into Alexandria's.

The sunlight was glaring in Howard's eyes, and he squinted against the glare to see who was walking beside Claudia. When they had drawn even with them, Howard thought there was something vaguely familiar about the man. He waited for Claudia to introduce them, knowing she had no choice.

"Howard, I would like you to meet a friend of mine, Falcon Knight, from England," she introduced them grudgingly. "Falcon, my husband, Howard Landon."

Tag inclined his head as his eyes locked with the man he had traveled so far to confront. It made him angry that his old enemy was no more than a shadow of his former self. How could he gain satisfaction in besting a sick old man? A mask fell into place as Tag hid his true feelings. He smiled slightly.

"I am pleased to make your acquaintance, Mr. Landon," he said in a cold voice.

Howard's eyes narrowed, and his heart skipped a beat. There could be no mistake! This man who called himself Falcon Knight was none other than Taggart James! Howard's eyes ran over Tag's face, and he felt his heart leap with joy. He had waited for this moment for many years. Had he not known all along that Tag would one day return? He shifted his eyes to his wife and saw the way she was hanging on to Tag's arm. He realized she had not the slightest knowledge who he was. The foolish woman really believed that he was Falcon Knight from England.

Everyone was startled when a horrible sound issued from Howard's lips. At first, they all thought he was having an attack, until Alexandria realized he was laughing. The sound was most unpleasant, and the side of his face that was paralyzed seemed to curl up to reveal his teeth.

Claudia looked from her husband to Alexandria. "You'll take him to his room at once!" she demanded angrily. "In the future, you will not bring my husband downstairs without my permission, Alexandria. Is that clearly understood?"

Tag's head shot up, and for the first time he noticed the young woman who stood behind Howard. As he looked into golden eyes, he read the pleading in the shimmering depths. She was mentally asking him to not give her away. His anger knew no bounds as he thought of all the torture she had put him through by running away. He had the strongest urge to shake her until she begged his forgiveness. Seeing a tear slide down her cheek, he relaxed. It would serve no purpose to acknowledge that he knew her.

"I will take him to his room, but only if he wants to go," Alexandria said, looking at Claudia with defiance written all over her face.

Claudia's face flushed, and she reached out and grabbed Alexandria by the arm. "You will do as I say this instant!" she screamed harshly.

Before Claudia knew what was happening, Howard picked up his cane, which was lying across his lap, and waved it in her face, uttering unintelligible sounds. Claudia had seen her husband angry often enough to know he was in no mood to be trifled with. Taking a step backwards, she grabbed hold of Tag's arm.

"I told you he was crazed!" Claudia yelled. "He tried to hit me!"

Tag looked into Howard Landon's eyes and saw they were alive with intelligence. He knew immediately

280

that he was as sane as anyone. He also saw recognition in the old man's eyes and wondered how long it would be before his uncle would tell Claudia his true identity.

"No, your husband isn't crazed, Mrs. Landon. He knows exactly what he's doing," Tag said in a harsh voice.

Howard began babbling something again, and Alexandria bent forward to catch his words. After he finished speaking, she looked at Tag. "Mr. Landon wants me to tell you he is pleased to meet you and wants you to know you are welcome in this house anytime. He wonders if you will come to his room around seven this evening?"

The look that passed between Alexandria and Tag went unobserved by Claudia. Her mouth was gaping open in amazement as she looked at her husband. "How can a little chit who has only been in my employment for several weeks know what you are saying when I can never understand you, Howard?" Her voice sounded resentful as she raised her head and glared at Alexandria.

"It's not difficult to understand Mr. Landon when one takes the trouble to listen, Mrs. Landon. If you will excuse me, I believe he wants to go to his room now. Will you be coming to Mr. Landon's room later, Mr. Knight?" she asked, hoping he would refuse.

Tag bowed slightly. "I wouldn't miss the chance to have a private conversation with you, Mr. Landon," he said, glancing back at his uncle. He wondered what Howard wanted to see him about. Even if he knew his uncle were laying a trap for him, still Tag would go to his room. He was surprised when the old man held out his hand to him. When Tag touched his Uncle Howard's hand, it felt cold and clammy. He was surprised, however, at the strength in the old man's handshake.

He stood silently as Alexandria wheeled his uncle up by the garden path. Tonight he would also see Alexandria alone. There were many things they had to discuss. He wanted to know what she was doing in this house. He wanted some answers, and damn it, he would get them before the night was over.

Claudia bit her lip. "That was a most unpleasant experience. I'm sorry that you had to be subjected to such a crude scene, Falcon."

"Not at all, Claudia. I found nothing unpleasant in your husband's attitude toward me."

Claudia shook her head. "It certainly seemed strange to me. My husband has never before issued anyone an invitation to his room. He doesn't even like it very much when I invade his sanctuary."

"Why is that?"

"He has this fantasy. It's hard to understand. You see, he has this obsession with his niece, Joanna. In fact, there is a portrait of her and her family that hangs in Howard's bedroom. He has insisted that her bedroom stay the way she left it, and sometimes he has Barlow carry him into that room, where he spends hours." She shrugged her shoulders, "I told you he had lost his mind."

"Who was the girl with him? Is she a relative?"

"Heavens, no! She is some girl I hired to look after my husband. It was a sorry day indeed when I took her into my home and gave her the position as my husband's companion. I believe in some way she reminds him of Joanna." Claudia looked up at Tag and smiled. "Let's not talk about them. I was wondering if you would stay to dinner?"

Her eyes held an invitation to more than dinner, and Tag wanted to shove the hand away that she placed on his arm. "I am afraid I must decline tonight. I have a previous engagement. I would, however, like to return around seven, if you have no objections. I would like very much to accept your husband's invitation."

Claudia's mouth formed into a pout. "You will accept my husband's offer, but not mine?"

Tag pushed his dislike for her aside. He knew he must placate Claudia for the time being. With a swift motion, he pulled her into his arms, and his mouth came down on hers, grinding her lips against her teeth. He felt only revulsion at the touch of her hot, moist lips, and he quickly broke off the kiss, feeling sick inside. He knew he had to pacify Claudia for the moment—he must try to cover up the distaste he felt for her.

"Does that seem like I am uninterested in your invitation? You will have to give me my way in time. The day will come when I will ask something of you. Will you give it to me when I do?"

Claudia's head seemed to be swimming, and she was sure her heart would burst from her body at any moment. "I will give you anything you want, Falcon. You have only to ask. Will I see you tonight when you come to visit my husband?"

"No," Tag said, as he moved her aside and walked away without looking back. He knew when he returned tonight he might be facing death, but he would come anyway. Somehow, he got the impression that his Uncle Howard never confided in Claudia. He wasn't sure what kind of game his uncle was playing, but he would soon find out. As for Alexandria, he would force her to leave with him tonight. She would have to answer for running away from him!

Tag mounted his horse, wondering obsessively what in the hell Alexandria was doing in this house? Didn't she know that when he faced his uncle for the final showdown, she would be in danger?

Today, for the first time, he had seen her dressed as a woman. She had looked like a delicate flower, and her beauty had reached out to him. In spite of the fact that he had been angry with her, he had still wanted to take her in his arms and make her understand that he hadn't betrayed her.

Alexandria was by far too stubborn and willful for her own good, he thought angrily. Morning Song would never have defied him as she had. But then Morning Song had never been alone and had to depend on her wits for her very survival. Tag couldn't help smiling. No one, including himself, would be able to push Alexandria around. She would fight for what she believed in, and he pitied the poor devil who got in her way.

Suddenly Tag's heart felt lighter. At least now he knew where to find Alexandria. He no longer had to spend sleepless nights wondering where she was and if she were safe!

Chapter Twenty-two

Alexandria removed the tray from Howard's lap and gave him a bright smile. "You didn't eat all your meat, Mr. Landon. I prepared it just the way you like it."

He caught her hand, forcing her to look at him. "You . . . know about Taggart . . . don't . . . you?" he said, in a much clearer voice. By now Alexandria was able to understand him better, and she could see a marked improvement in his speech and attributed it to the fact that she had encouraged him to talk more. However, she knew he always played a game with Claudia, because when his wife was around he slipped back into his garbled speech.

The color drained from Alexandria's face, and she avoided looking into his eyes, fearing he would read too much from her expression. Turning aside, she placed the tray down on a chair and began to straighten his bed.

"I'm sure I don't know what you are talking about, Mr. Landon," she told him, tucking in the bedsheet at the foot of the bed.

"You know," he wheezed. "The moment . . . I saw the two of you . . . together, I knew you weren't . . .

strangers."

"You shouldn't be talking—it would be best if you saved your strength."

"Alexandria, you . . . won't believe this, but today is one of the happiest . . . days of my . . . life. I was glad to see . . . Tag! I have been . . . waiting for . . . this day for a . . . very long time."

Alexandria looked at him doubtfully. "Did your wife not introduce the man in the garden as Falcon Knight? Who is this Tag of whom you are speaking?" She hoped her voice sounded convincing, since she had never felt comfortable when speaking an untruth.

"You play . . . games with me, Alexandria," he wheezed. "No matter, it will all come . . . out soon." He turned his head to the portrait, and his eyes rested on Joanna's face. "Soon . . . very soon . . . I will know about . . . Joanna."

Alexandria wiped Howard's face with a damp cloth. "Tell me about Joanna, Mr. Landon. What was she like?" she asked, trying to turn the tide of conversation.

His eyes never left the portrait as he began to speak. "I will never forget . . . the first day I saw . . . her. She was the loveliest young woman . . . I had ever laid eyes on. It was . . . like a breath of springtime . . . just to gaze at her face. She had courage and daring. I have . . . never known anyone . . . like her." His eyes went to Alexandria. "You . . . remind me a little of her."

"Nonsense! The girl in that portrait is far more beautiful than I," she said, smiling.

"Will he come, do . . . you think?" Howard's eyes kept going to the door, as if he were expecting someone.

"Will who come?" Alexandria asked.

"Still you play your . . . little game, Alexandria. I know Tag will come. Come hell . . . or high water, he'll be . . . here."

Alexandria looked at the clock on the bedside table and saw it was nearing the seventh hour. In a panic, she realized that Falcon would be here at any moment. She decided she would meet him in the hallway and prevent him from coming into the room.

"Why don't you rest now? You have had a very tiring day, Mr. Landon," she urged.

"I can . . . rest later. For the first . . . time in a long while, I feel . . . alive!"

Alexandria picked up the tray and started for the door. When she had almost reached it, the door was opened and she stood face-to-face with Falcon. His eyes bored into hers, and she found herself wanting to look away. She had to prevent him from seeing Mr. Landon!

"You must leave immediately," she said lowering her voice. "Mr. Landon knows who you are! Go quickly, before it's too late!" she whispered hurriedly.

"I will not leave, Alexandria, Alex, or whatever you are now calling yourself. I have come to see Howard Landon, and I will see him!" Tag demanded in a cold voice, before he brushed past her and entered the bedroom.

Alexandria felt her face flush with shame as she realized that Falcon knew how she had tricked him. She pushed her shame to the back of her mind as she rushed after him. She placed the tray down on a chair and watched Falcon move across the room.

Alexandria found when she reached Mr. Landon's bedside that her legs were trembling. She couldn't understand what was going on. If Mr. Landon was the monster Falcon claimed he was, wouldn't he have prepared some sort of trap for him? Wouldn't he have alerted Claudia that Falcon's true identity was Taggart James?

She watched Falcon's face and knew he was angrier than she had ever seen him. By now she had worked herself into a frenzy. What should she do? She shivered when his cold, ice-blue eyes rested on her face. Alexandria felt such overwhelming shame that she couldn't bring herself to look into his eyes any longer.

Folding her hands together, she clutched them tightly. She lowered her eyes, remembering how shamelessly she had gone to Falcon at night, pretending to be Xandria. She hoped that Falcon wouldn't realize she had not only pretended to be the boy, Alex, but Xandria, as well. Please let him think Xandria is my sister, she prayed silently, remembering she had once told him that Xandria *was* her sister.

Tag looked past Alexandria and walked to the bed where his Uncle Howard lay. He noticed that the old man's eyes were closed and he appeared to be sleeping. Tag looked at the frail hands that rested on the outside of the covers, remembering a time when there was strength in those hands. His eyes moved up to Howard Landon's face, remembering when his uncle had been cruel and unfeeling to Joanna and himself. He reminded himself that he had every reason to hate this man, but now he could only find it within himself to feel pity for him.

Howard's eyes opened slowly, and he stared at Tag. His eyes locked with violet-blue eyes that were the same shade as Joanna's.

"So, the . . . boy has become a . . . man," Howard said in a raspy voice.

"You know who I am," Tag stated flatly.

"Yes, I . . . always knew . . . you would come back. I have looked forward . . . to this . . . day."

Tag was having difficulty understanding his uncle, so he motioned for Alexandria to translate for him, since she had seemed to be able to comprehend what he had said earlier in the garden.

"I came back to kill you, but I see you are worse than dead," Tag said, as his eyes blazed with anger.

Howard started babbling rapidly, and Alexandria had to translate for Tag.

"Mr. Landon says he wishes you would kill him."

Tag's piercing eyes locked with the old man's. "Why shouldn't I kill you? You are responsible for the death of my wife, Morning Song."

Again Howard spoke, and Alexandria translated. "He says he doesn't know what you are talking about. He didn't even know you were married."

"Like hell he didn't! It seems he and Claudia were aware of everything Joanna and I were doing." He stepped closer to the bed, and Alexandria could see the muscles in his neck standing out. "I could understand if you wanted to kill me, Uncle Howard—but why Morning Song? She had never harmed anyone. The two men you sent to kill me shot her instead. Did you know before she died she gave birth to my daughter?"

Alexandria saw Tag clench his fists and felt tears in

289

her eyes. Dear God! she thought, Tag had every right to hate Mr. Landon. She felt sorrow in her heart that his life had been touched by so much tragedy.

Howard seemed to be struggling to sit up, and he was jabbering so fast Alexandria had to ask him to slow down so she could understand him. When he regained his composure, she turned to Tag. "Mr. Landon said that he never sent anyone to kill you. This is the first he's heard of it!"

Tag bent over and grabbed Howard by the shirt-front. "You lie! I overheard the men talking, and they said . . . Claudia sent them! I have learned that you had my father killed, also. Just try and deny that!"

Alexandria pried Tag's hands loose and pushed him away. "Can you not see that he is an old man? I don't think he would conspire with his wife for any reason. They hate each other! If this thing was done, you are accusing the wrong person. I believe Mr. Landon."

Tag's eyes went back to Howard. "Tell her, Uncle. You didn't even know Claudia when my father was killed." He turned to Alexandria. "My father had been in Oregon country and was recuperating from a broken back. I was told by a very reliable source that he lay helpless while someone smothered him with a pillow! Ask my uncle if he knows anything about that?"

As Howard answered, tears ran freely down his face. He seemed so excited that Alexandria feared he would have another attack. As she listened carefully to his words, she was horrified by his confession.

"He . . . he says it's true that he sent a man to Oregon to kill your father. He . . . even confesses he shoved your Aunt Margaret down the stairs, but he had nothing to do with your wife's death." Alexandria tried to keep the horror from her voice. She couldn't associate this tired, sick old man who had been so kind to her with the unbelievable deeds to which he had just confessed.

"Is there any reason I shouldn't kill you?" Tag said in a deadly calm voice.

By now, tears were streaming down Alexandria's cheeks. "He . . . says he wishes you would end his life, since he is living in hell."

Tag walked over to the window and threw the curtain aside. "This was once my mother and father's bedroom. I cannot rest easy knowing the man who killed my father and took all that belongs to me and Joanna lives in this house." He turned to face his uncle once more. "I want you and Claudia out of this house! If you are innocent of killing Morning Song, then the blame rests on Claudia's shoulders. I will see her punished for the deed. The day will come when she will beg for mercy." Tag's threat hung heavy in the silence until Howard started speaking.

"Mr. Landon says he wants nothing more than to see Claudia pay for what she has done. He wants me to warn you that she is very dangerous. Right now, she doesn't know who you are, but the moment she finds out, you will be in danger."

"Does he intend to tell her about me?"

"No, he says he will not betray you to her. He says to remind you that Claudia wouldn't suffer under the law for having an Indian killed. If she is to be punished, it will have to come from you."

Tag walked slowly back to the bed and stared down at the frail old man. For some reason, he believed

291

him. "You have my word that Claudia will suffer before I'm through with her, but, so help me God, I'll bring you down with her! You have much to answer for yourself. While the law won't touch Claudia for having Morning Song killed, they sure as hell will hang you for having my father killed. Joanna and I will not be at peace until you are both dead!"

Alexandria shivered. She had never seen a man so eaten up with hatred and revenge. This wasn't the Falcon Knight she knew. This was a man who was dangerous and would sweep anyone out of his path to get what he wanted. She knew he had every right to hate Mr. Landon and his wife, but she shuddered inwardly, thinking how cold and unfeeling he was at the moment.

Howard started babbling again, and Alexandria had to ask him to repeat what he had said before she could tell Tag. "Mr. Landon asked if you would tell him about Joanna," she said at last.

Tag's eyes went to the portrait over the mantel, and he smiled. "You obsession for my sister was your downfall, Uncle. I wonder what she would do if she could see you now? I believe she would spit in your face!"

Howard seemed to wince visibly as Tag continued. "Joanna, as you know, is married to Windhawk, chief of the Blood Blackfoot. She has two children, a son and a daughter, and is extremely happy. I don't believe she will ever want to return to Philadelphia, even after I have settled with you and Claudia."

The old man closed his eyes, and Alexandria looked at Tag pleadingly. "He is exhausted, Falcon—please allow him to rest now."

Tag looked into her eyes. "Before long he will have a long, peaceful rest."

Alexandria wanted to plead with him to rid himself of his bitterness. "You could go to the authorities and let justice be served, Falcon. Don't take this into your own hands!"

"You heard my uncle. The authorities will not care that Claudia paid two men to slay an Indian. I will see that she suffers before I'm through." Tag looked down at Howard Landon, who was now sleeping. "As for him, I believe he is already paying. I couldn't have come up with anything that would have been more appropriate. It must be pure hell being bedridden and having Claudia for his wife."

"I never knew anyone could hate so deeply, Falcon. I find I don't know you at all."

He glanced at her, and she saw unleashed anger in his eyes. "I'm not sure I know you, either," he said sarcastically. "Who am I addressing . . . Alex, Alexandria, or Xandria?" He clamped his mouth together tightly and took her by the wrist, pulling her into the outer room. He tightened his grip and stared into her golden eyes.

"I think I much prefer you as Xandria. You did give me some degree of pleasure as her."

Alexandria tried to spin away from him as his insult struck home. Was she to be spared no shame? Falcon had guessed that she was also Xandria! "Let me go!" she demanded, raising her head and looking into his eyes daringly.

"What did you do, Alexandria, go over to my enemy? Did you tell my uncle about me?"

"No! No, I would *never* do such a thing!" She

293

knew it would be useless to tell him that she had taken this position in hopes of helping him. "You are the one who betrayed me, Falcon. I learned from Farley that you went to see my stepmother behind my back."

He smiled without humor. "Ah, yes, I see. It might interest you to learn that I went to see your stepmother, but I didn't betray you, Alexandria. I wanted to find out if your stepbrother was dead. You might be interested to learn that he is very much alive!"

"I . . . he is?"

"Yes, very much so. I also learned that the authorities are still searching for you. I would take care not to be recognized, if I were you," he said, releasing her hand and walking to the door.

Alexandria watched him leave, feeling somehow abandoned. She wanted to rush after him and pour out the love she felt for him, but she dared not. Falcon was so eaten up with hatred and bitterness that he had no love to give anyone, except his dead wife and his sister, Joanna. Alexandria buried her face in her hands and cried out her misery. The way Falcon was acting must mean that he had added her to his list of enemies. She should have known he wouldn't betray her to Barbara. She knew that she should feel grateful that Rodney was still alive, but at the moment Alexandria was too miserable to feel anything but pain.

Alexandria dried her eyes and walked out of the room and down the hallway. Today had been the most emotionally draining day she had ever lived through. She was finding out that it was very painful loving a man who didn't love her in return. She realized that she had half-hoped Falcon would insist that she leave with him, but he hadn't.

Alexandria walked down the backstairs and out into the garden. As she breathed in the sweet fragrance of the roses, which were in full bloom, she tried to visualize Falcon as a young boy running and playing in this lovely garden. It was hard to think of him as other than the angry man she had encountered today.

Tonight he had made it plain he didn't want anything more to do with her. She looked up at the night skies and wished she could bring Falcon comfort in his torment. She could see no easy way for him to reclaim his inheritance, unless he allowed Mr. Landon to help him. But Falcon wanted more than his inheritance back—he wanted revenge!

Chapter Twenty-three

As the days passed, Alexandria's life settled into a routine. Each day she would have Barlow carry Mr. Landon downstairs so she could wheel him into the garden. The two of them hadn't discussed Falcon's visit, but Alexandria could see a change in Mr. Landon. He seemed to grow weaker with each passing day; however, she could sense that a feeling of peace seemed to have settled over him. Once in a while, she would see a smile playing on his lips, and she knew he was pleased about something. It was as if he were waiting with impatience for something to happen.

Alexandria was sure that Mr. Landon had said nothing to his wife about what had occurred between him and Falcon. On one occasion, Claudia had summoned Alexandria to her bedroom and had grilled her about the meeting. Claudia had wanted to know what Mr. Landon and Falcon had talked about, and how long Falcon had remained in her husband's bedroom. Alexandria had told Claudia very little, which didn't seem to please her in the least.

Alexandria could feel Claudia's animosity toward her, but it didn't bother her overmuch. She herself had no love for the woman who had committed such unspeakable deeds. It was hard for her to conceive anyone's deliberately setting out to harm another human being, much less trying to have someone killed. Alexandria's apprehension came from the fear that Claudia might find out Falcon's true identity.

There was to be a masquerade ball, which Alexandria knew Falcon would be attending. She could see that Claudia was attracted to him, and she was finding she felt bitterly jealous toward the older woman. It was common knowledge in the household that Claudia had plans for Falcon Knight. The servants were gossiping among themselves and even laying bets that the mistress of the house would lure the handsome young man into her bedroom before the night was over.

Alexandria rapped softly on Mr. Landon's bedroom door, wondering why he had sent for her during his nap period. The door was immediately opened by Barlow, who nodded for her to enter.

When she approached the bed, she saw that Mr. Landon was propped up on several pillows and there was a glowing smile on his face.

"I feared you might be ill when you sent for me. Are you feeling all right, Mr. Landon?"

"Never . . . better," he said, with a surprising amount of volume. "I have . . . a surprise . . . for you. Look in those . . . boxes that are stacked on the . . . chair," he told her.

"What is in them?" she asked curiously.

"Now, you will . . . just have . . . to open them to find out, won't you?" he beamed.

Alexandria lifted the lid to the first box and caught her breath as she gazed at the lovely gown she found inside. As she lifted it from the box and held it in front of her, she found it was made of a soft white gauzelike material. There was a golden clip at one shoulder, and a shimmering gold belt. She turned to face Mr. Landon with a question in her eyes.

"Who . . . what . . . ?"

"I had . . . it made for you . . . so you could attend the masked ball tonight. I took . . . the liberty . . . of having Barlow take one of your gowns . . . and a pair of your shoes . . . to the seamstress for sizing. Don't you . . . recognize the style? You will be going to the masked ball . . . as an Egyptian . . . princess."

"Oh, no, Mr. Landon, I could never attend the ball! As a servant, I haven't been invited."

"I won't take . . . no for an answer. Since I can't go . . . myself, you will attend for me . . . and tell me all about it . . . tomorrow," he replied, watching her golden eyes light up wistfully.

"It wouldn't be at all seemly for me to attend the ball. Besides I don't think Mrs. Landon would approve."

"No one will know . . . who you are. You are young, and I . . . want to see you . . . have a good . . . time. Would you . . . disappoint an old . . . man?"

"No, of course not, but . . ."

"I will hear . . . no more . . . about this. Take those . . . boxes to your room. The only thing I . . . ask of you . . . is that you come back here before you go to . . . the ball. I want to see . . . how you look in all your . . . finery."

Alexandria felt misty-eyed. "I don't know what to say, Mr. Landon. You are much too kind to me." She clutched the filmy gown to her. "Thank you, thank you so much!"

"I don't want your . . . thanks, Alexandria. Just go and enjoy yourself . . . tonight. That will be my . . . thanks."

Howard's eyes went to the portrait, and Alexandria knew he was thinking about the beautiful Joanna once more. As always, when he stared at the portrait, he shut everything else out of his mind. Alexandria gathered up the boxes and left the room quietly. Her heart was stirring with excitement. She had never owned such a beautiful gown. She wanted with all her heart to go to the ball. Just this once, she wanted Falcon to see her in a lovely gown.

It was well after sundown, and already Alexandria could hear the music drifting up the stairs, and she knew the ball was in progress. Viewing herself in the cracked mirror that hung on the wall, she was unable to see below her waist. The soft material draped across one shoulder and molded her young body. There were tiny golden sandals on her feet, and a black wig topped her head encircled with a blue-and-gold-colored double serpent's crown.

Alexandria blinked in astonishment, wondering if her eyes were deceiving her. The image in the mirror was of a beautiful young girl with creamy skin and bright amber-colored eyes. She had never thought of herself as beautiful, but she felt that she might be tonight. She picked up the gold satin mask that would conceal her identity, and tied it about her head with the long silken ribbons that were attached. Suddenly she lost her nervousness. It was as if having her identity a secret helped to remove her inhibitions. She wished that Falcon could see her now. Would he think her pretty?

With one last glance at the mirror, she left her bedroom and made her way down to the second floor to show Mr. Landon her costume.

Tag watched the dancing couples whirl past him and couldn't help curling his lip in distaste. He had been with the Indians so long that this kind of showy party didn't set well with him. How shallow he was finding the white world. It seemed that most of the people he had met since coming here had very low values. As the music blared loudly in his ears, Tag longed for the mountains with their tall pine trees and the winding Milk River he'd left behind.

As he stood in the shadows, he had no trouble recognizing Claudia. She was the one with the most elaborate gown. She was dressed to look like Marie Antoinette, with a white powdered wig resting on the top of her head. Her laughter and good humor could be heard even above the loud music.

Tag smiled as he looked down at his moccasined feet, thinking he was the only one who wasn't really in costume. He had merely worn the buckskins he was accustomed to wearing. Farley had cut him a leather mask out of one of his old, worn buckskin shirts. He hoped his identity wouldn't be discovered for some time. He was content to walk around and observe without being observed.

"La, sir, are we to be scalped?" a woman wearing a bright red gown from the Napoleonic era declared, tapping Tag on the shoulder with her fan.

"I may very well drag you off to my wigwam,

300

madam," Tag replied, without humor.

The woman responded with high-pealed laughter. "I can't say that I'd put up much of a fight. I wouldn't say no if you were to ask me to dance," she offered.

He bowed elegantly. "You will forgive me if I pass this time. I'm waiting for someone."

"Oh, well," she said, looking at the width of his broad shoulders. "She must be a fortunate lady. I suppose it's my loss." With another peal of laughter, she sauntered off to find herself a more accessible dancing partner.

Alexandria made her way slowly down the stairs. She gazed over the banister at the sea of faces and could hear the loud laughter of the merrymakers. Everyone was obviously in high spirits. She had no desire to join in the frivolities—it would be enough just being an observer. She felt young and light-hearted when a man dressed in a Renaissance costume grabbed her and whirled her around the dance floor. When she finally managed to get away from him, she made her way outside to the garden.

The full moon seemed to hang in the sky like a giant yellow ball. Its bright glow, with the help of several Chinese lanterns, lit the garden.

Alexandria walked down the path, feeling a cool breeze through her thin costume. The music had stopped, and she knew that the merrymakers had gone into the dining room for dinner. She was glad to have the garden to herself. It somehow had a mystical atmosphere. She loved this house and garden because they belonged to Tag.

It was funny, she thought, lately she had begun to

think of Falcon as Taggart James more and more often. Perhaps it was because, in this house, he *was* Taggart James. She was finding out that loving him was the most painful experience she had ever lived through. Perhaps it was because he would never return her love. She thought of Morning Song and wondered what she might have been like. It was hard to think of Tag having a daughter. Would the child look like him . . . or would she resemble her Indian mother? Alexandria found herself wanting to know Tag's sister, Joanna. What was there about her that would cause Mr. Landon to worship her image in the portrait, and her brother to speak of her with such love and respect?

Alexandria moved out of the shadow of light and walked to the small pond that was nestled in a secluded part of the garden. As she watched the moon shimmering on the pond, she reflected on Tag's plight. It was true he had a mountain of troubles facing him, but so did she. The difference between her and him was that he had the love of his sister to sustain him, while she had no one. Never in her life had she felt so alone. There was no one to whom she could turn.

Alexandria looked down at her costume and wondered if the Egyptian Cleopatra had ever felt this alone and hopeless. Raising her arms over her head, she turned her face up to the moon.

"Yellow moon, sister to the sun god Ra, send someone to walk in my aloneness with me," she said softly, half serious, half in jest.

"Take my hand, Alexandria. I will see that you are never lonely again." A deep voice spoke up from the

302

shadows.

Alexandria spun around and almost bumped into a tall figure dressed in Indian buckskins. Even though his face was masked, she knew at once it was Tag. Her heart began to beat wildly, and she didn't know whether to stand there or run.

"How did you know it was me?" she asked, as his hand drifted across her arm.

"Oh, I know you well, little Egyptian princess. Were you not named for the ancient Egyptian city of Alexandria?" He drew her into his arms, and she rested her face against his soft buckskin shirt. "You are never alone, Alexandria. I thought you knew I would always look after you."

She raised her face to him and saw the smile playing on his lips. "You have your own troubles, Tag. You don't need mine added to them."

He touched her cheek. "Your problems have become mine. I think perhaps I inherited them the night I rescued a scrawny, ragged lad from a burly old sailor who wanted to shanghai him to sea."

Tag, I . . ."

"I don't think it would be a good idea for you to call me by my name. We are hardly in what you would term a friendly territory." His words were laced with amusement.

"I am sorry, Falcon—I suppose I wasn't thinking. You have my word I'll be more careful in the future." She was horrified that she had carelessly spoken his name. If they had been overheard, it would have put Tag in very grave danger.

Neither Alexandria or Tag saw the man dressed as a sailor who observed them from behind the willow tree

303

that grew beside the pond. A smile creased the man's face. He had overheard the conversation and now had the proof he had been searching for. The man who called himself Falcon Knight was none other than Taggart James!

"Let's leave the party now, Alexandria. Come home with me," Tag said, brushing his lips against hers and sending shivers of delight down her spine.

"No, I cannot. I must stay here and keep an eye on Claudia. You know she isn't to be trusted," Alexandria said, wishing with all her heart that she could go home with Tag. She had decided that when his problems had all been solved, she would just disappear from his life forever. Alexandria knew if she ever allowed him to make love to her again, she would weaken. She must never given in to the call of her heart. Tag would never love her . . . and she would never stop loving him.

"Would you have me believe that you are staying here only to help me, Alexandria?"

"You can believe what you wish. I will help you if I can, beyond that, I promise nothing."

"I never asked you for help, Alexandria. What you are doing is dangerous."

"I am not afraid. Claudia will never connect me with you."

She could hear the smile in his voice when he spoke. "Are you sure you won't come home with me?" he asked, allowing his hand to drift down her arm.

"No," she replied, pushing his hand away.

"Do you mean no, you won't go with me . . . or no, you are not sure?"

"No, I will not go home with you," she said in a

perplexed voice.

"In that case I had better get back to the ball and make it easy for Claudia to find me."

"Falcon, don't you think it was foolish and dangerous for you to come dressed as an Indian? What if Claudia were to discover who you really are?"

"Would you care so much?" he asked softly.

"Of course I would care. How can you even ask?"

"Look at me, Alexandria. This is the way I have dressed since I was twelve years old. The clothing of the white man does not rest well on my body. For all intents and purpose, I am an Indian! Does that disturb you?"

She looked him over and knew he was right. He did seem to belong in the Indian attire he wore. It was hard for her to fathom his living with the Indians; his manners were so correct, and when it suited him, he could act the perfect gentleman. One wouldn't expect such behavior from a man who had been raised by the Indians.

"Falcon, you also seem to fit well into the white man's world. I cannot believe you learned all your fine manners from the Indians."

He laughed softly. "In truth, I owe my manners to my sister, Joanna. I can see, however, you are going to have to be reeducated about what Indians are really like. They may not have the pretty manners you spoke of, but they are far above us in how they treat their fellow man. One day, when I have more time, I will tell you more about the Blood Blackfoot and their chief, Windhawk."

"Be that as it may, Falcon, you were foolish to come to Claudia's ball dressed as an Indian. She is on the

305

lookout for anything that will tip her off to who you are!"

"Don't you see, little Egyptian princess, the last one in the world Claudia would suspect would be me. When she sees me tonight, it will scare the hell out of her at first. I want her to know she is being watched. I want her to be unable to sleep at night. Let her wonder when and where I will strike. She will reach the depths of hell before I finally bring her down."

The man who had been observing Tag and Alexandria faded into the shadows. He had already found out all he needed to know! There was no doubt in his mind that Falcon Knight was Taggart James!

Tag drew Alexandria into his arms and tilted her face up to his. "Allow me to taste your lips once more, Xandria. I find myself reliving our nights together over and over," he whispered.

She parted her lips in anticipation. When he brushed her mouth and then touched the lobe of her ear with his lips, she shivered. She hadn't realized until this moment how much she had missed his touch. Her shame over her wanton behavior had enabled her to close her mind to the feeling he had awakened in her body as Xandria.

"No, please don't! I made myself a promise I wouldn't allow you to . . . touch me again," she whispered.

He rested his face against hers and smiled. "Did you, Xandria? It has been my experience that the promises one makes to oneself are often broken. Perhaps had I come as Mark Antony you would have been more willing."

It took all Alexandria's willpower to move away

from him. "I don't want you to call me Xandria again," she whispered. "I want to forget she ever existed."

"Why is that? I became very fond of you as . . ."

Alexandria placed her hands over her ears. "Do not speak it!" she cried. "I am ashamed of what I did and don't want to be reminded of my behavior." At that moment, she wanted nothing more than to be in his arms where she would feel safe and secure.

Because of the mask he wore, Alexandria couldn't see the pain that danced fleetingly across Tag's face. "You should never be ashamed of what happened between us, Alexandria."

"You make me feel ashamed when you refer to me as Xandria. I just want to forget all about what she . . . I did."

There was a tense silence between them, and finally Alexandria could stand it no longer. "I must be getting back to the party, Falcon. The music has started again, and soon the people will be coming into the garden."

Tag didn't try to stop her as she turned and rushed toward the house. He watched her until she was out of sight. Staring down into the pool, he saw his image ripple on the surface of the water. He knew what he had to do tonight, and it left a strong taste of bitterness in his mouth. It was time for him to play adoring lover to Morning Song's murderess.

He walked silently toward the house, dreading what must be done to accomplish his goals.

Claudia was in a unusually joyful state of mind. She was the belle of the ball and enjoying every moment of it. She was experiencing the same wild abandonment

307

as had the queen of France whom she portrayed tonight. She had received more than her share of passionate kisses and caresses from the masked gentlemen who were present, but she kept searching for the one she knew could take her to the heights of passion. Falcon Knight had assured her he would come tonight, but thus far she hadn't seen him.

Claudia walked out onto the second-floor balcony, wondering what it was about Falcon that seemed to draw her to him. It was more than the fact that he was so male. Her body seemed to react to everything about him, the deep sound of his voice, the proud way he walked, even the cruel twist to his lips when he was having his own private thoughts. She rubbed her fingertips across her lips, feeling as if her body were on fire just thinking about him.

"Does a penny still purchase a woman's thoughts?" A man spoke just behind her.

Claudia whirled around, and her heart seemed to leap out of her body when she saw the man, who was dressed as an Indian! He was standing in the shadows, and she couldn't tell if his hair had a reddish cast to it, as Taggart James's had when she last saw the boy. Claudia's first reaction was fear, thinking Tag had come at last. She wanted to call out for help, but her voice seemed to stick in her throat. The balcony was deserted and there was nowhere to run. She considered that it might be better to leap over the banister to her death than to face Tag.

"Wait . . . I . . . can explain everything, Tag," she said in a trembling voice, and she backed against the railing.

"Now you have made me jealous, Madame Marie

Antoinette. Who is this Tag of whom you speak?" the man said, reaching out for her hand and raising it to his lips.

"Falcon?" she asked, as relief washed over her.

"It is indeed I, madam. Were you expecting someone else, perhaps?"

"No, of course not," she said, linking her arm through his. I have been waiting for only you."

" 'Twas not my name you called a moment ago. Should I be jealous of this Tag?"

Claudia raised her face to him. "You shouldn't ever be jealous of anyone, if you but knew it."

"Tell me, was I mistaken or where you frightened a moment ago, Claudia?"

"Perhaps, Falcon. One doesn't reach my position without making enemies. Let me tell you, there are those who would like to see me dead."

"Surely, you jest. Who would wish to harm such a charming and lovely lady as yourself?"

"I suppose I'm just jittery. There has been a strange man dressed as a sailor hanging about lately. I don't know who he is or why he would want to spy on me."

"If you feel yourself in danger, you must come to me," he said, raising her hand to his lips once again.

Claudia felt a shiver of delight race through her body and knew she would be safe with this man. She had never found it easy to put her faith in anyone, but with Falcon Knight it was different. She almost felt as if she could confide everything to him and he would understand. So far, he had shown only a mild interest in her, but she hoped that would change before the night was over.

"Come downstairs and dance with me," she said, pulling him by the hand and leading him toward the dance floor.

Alexandria danced with a gentleman dressed as a court jester from the fourteenth century until he became too forward. After she escaped from him, several gentlemen asked her to dance, but she always politely refused. She no longer wanted to be a participant at the ball. She had learned quickly that much of the laughter she was hearing came from the amount of spirits that had been consumed by many of the gentlemen, rather than from any joy they were experiencing.

Alexandria had all but decided to go to her room when her glance was drawn to Claudia. Her heart seemed to plummet when she saw the man who was holding Claudia in his arms. It was obvious to anyone who took the trouble to look that Claudia and her dancing partner were enjoying themselves. Alexandria knew why Tag was playing up to Claudia, but still it was like a knife in her heart to watch them together. She remembered that it had been she herself who had taught him to dance.

Unable to watch any longer, Alexandria moved away from the dance floor to the study, where she could be alone for awhile. Dropping down on a window seat, she gazed out the window. Never had she been so confused and unsure of her own feelings. She knew Tag had every right to lure Claudia into a trap, but she wasn't sure she approved of his methods.

When the door opened, she pressed herself back behind the curtains, not wanting to be discovered by anyone.

"You told me before that you didn't like to dance. You are a marvelous dancer, Falcon."

When Alexandria heard Claudia's voice, she feared being discovered. She knew she should make her presence known, but she didn't. Glancing around the heavy curtain, she saw Tag draw Claudia into his arms and lower his head to kiss her. Clasping a hand over her mouth, Alexandria dared not cry out. How could he do such a thing? she wondered. She felt as if he were betraying her, and it hurt her deeply.

"You are more of a man than anyone I have met in a long time," Claudia said in a husky voice.

"How many men have you known, Claudia?"

"Too many, Falcon, but none of them meant anything to me."

"Not even your husband?"

"Especially not my husband. It's different with you, though. I don't think it comes as any great surprise to you that I want you," she said, pulling his head down to her.

Alexandria watched with tears in her eyes as Tag crossed the room and picked up a bottle of brandy and two glasses from the side table and took Claudia's arm.

"It has never been my habit to keep a woman waiting," he said lazily. "Lead the way to your bedroom, Madame Antoinette. I know of no woman from history whom I would rather make love to tonight, unless it would be Cleopatra, should she be hiding in the shadows . . . but she already turned me down."

Alexandria pulled back, knowing Tag had seen her. She didn't know whether to laugh or cry at his cruel jest. Her mind wouldn't accept the fact that the man she loved would stoop so low as to make love to a woman he detested. Did he want revenge at the price of honor? Was not honor more important than revenge?

Alexandria waited until she was sure they would be safely upstairs before she went to her room. Her face was wet with tears as she pictured in her mind what was going on in Claudia's bedroom at that very moment. Removing the wig and gown, she placed them back in the box. Tonight had been very educational for her. She had found out how far a man would go to get what he wanted. She wondered if the love she had felt for Tag would wither and die now that she no longer respected him.

She lay down on her bed and allowed the tears to fall. No, it hadn't died. If it had, she wouldn't be feeling so miserable. In her mind she could almost see Tag holding Claudia in his arms and whispering passionate words in her ear. She cursed herself for being a fool and believing in Tag—she cursed him for making her love him!

Chapter Twenty-four

Tag uncorked the bottle of brandy and poured some of the liquid into each glass. He knew he would need the artificial stimulant if he were going to be able to give Claudia what she wanted from him tonight. He watched out of the corner of his eye as she slipped out of her gown and petticoats. She removed the powered wig and dropped it on the floor. Raising one of the glasses to his lips, he took a deep drink.

Claudia walked slowly over to him, swinging her hips enticingly. She licked her lips and took her glass. "I doubt that I will need this. I have never been one to drink very much—I find drinking dulls the senses."

She was completely naked, and Tag's eyes roved over her body with complete indifference. Her body couldn't compare with Alexandria's slim loveliness. Claudia's breasts were overdeveloped, her waist was thick, and her hips were wide. Some of the powder from her wig had run down her face, giving her the appearance of a painted clown.

"You will have to indulge me, Claudia. I like to drink and get acquainted before I make love to a woman."

She reached up and removed the leather headband

from his head. "What an exciting thought. No man has ever wanted to know what went on in my mind before. All they ever wanted was to get me into bed." She could hardly contain her excitement as his eyes roamed over her breasts, then down to her hips. She felt she would die if he didn't take her in his arms. Claudia knew Falcon would be the most exciting lover she had ever been with, and her whole body seemed to burn with a slow fire.

Tag watched Claudia lift her glass to her lips and drain the contents. Reaching for the bottle, he filled her glass once more. Setting the bottle on a night table, he began slowly to remove his clothing, while Claudia watched him with hungry eyes.

She could feel the blood beating in her temples as she looked at his magnificent body. She followed him with her eyes as he picked up the bottle and sat down in the middle of the bed. Her whole body seemed to come alive, and she felt an ache deep inside when he motioned for her to join him there.

When Claudia sat down beside Falcon, he tipped his glass to hers. "To a night to remember, Claudia," he whispered, indicating she should finish her drink. "I have waited a long time for this moment."

"Have you, Falcon?" she asked in a breathless voice. "I can never tell what you feel about anything. You are always so secretive."

By now, Claudia's head was spinning, and she didn't know if it was from the brandy or from Falcon's nearness. She emptied her glass, and again he refilled it.

She didn't know how many glasses she had consumed when he finally pulled her back on the bed and pressed his body against hers. She felt a warmth spread over her as his hands ran up and down her back in the most sensuous way.

"Tell me what you fear most in the world, Claudia," he whispered against her ear.

Claudia's head was reeling, and she couldn't understand why Falcon was asking such a question, so she said the first thing that popped into her head. "I fear a young boy who has by now grown to manhood," she answered in a passion-laced voice. "He is out there somewhere watching me, and one day he will try to take my life."

"Who do you hate most in the world, Claudia?" he asked, pulling her even closer and breathing hotly against her arched neck.

"I hate a woman named Joanna—I once told you about her. She is everything I ever wanted to be. I tried to destroy her, only to find she was indestructible."

"We are none of us indestructible, Claudia. Each of us has our vulnerable spot, and I believe I have found yours," he said harshly.

Claudia didn't know what he meant—all she knew was that his wonderful hands were rendering her senseless. All at once, Claudia's eyes closed, and she drifted off to sleep. The liquor she had consumed at the party, along with what Tag had given her, had had the effect he had hoped it would.

Tag stood up and pulled on his trousers and shirt. Standing over Claudia's sleeping form, he stared at her with distaste. She had passed out cold, and he was grateful, knowing he would never have been able to make love to her. He shuddered in disgust when she

315

moaned in her sleep. He doubted she would remember much about tonight when she awoke in the morning.

Tag ran his hand through his hair, feeling as if he were soiled and dirty from being in such close proximity with her. He left the room and climbed up the backstairs to the third floor. Since he had spent much of his boyhood in this house, he knew that the servants' quarters were there. He needed to be with Alexandria tonight as he had never needed anyone before in his life. He wanted to breath in her clean sweetness and feel her soft, silky skin. Knowing how she would feel about his going to Claudia's bedroom, he hoped he could make her understand that he had only done what had been necessary. He had found Claudia's weak points and her fears . . . now he could work on them!

There were three bedrooms on the third floor, but Tag already knew which was Alexandria's since she had mentioned that her room faced the garden. He turned the handle, and the door swung open soundlessly. The bright moonlight was streaming in through the window, and he could see Alexandria curled up on the bed. Kneeling down beside her, he gathered her into his arms and kissed her soft cheek.

Alexandria awoke with a start. Her eyes fastened on the dark outline of a man's face. Before she could cry out in fear, he spoke.

"It's me, Alexandria. Don't be afraid."

She pushed him away and sat up, pulling the covers up to her neck. "What are you doing here, Tag? Get out of my room this instant, before I scream and bring the whole house in to investigate," she whispered.

Alexandria could clearly see the smile playing on Tag's lips as he sat down on the bed beside her.

"I was afraid you would be angry with me. I knew when I saw you hiding in the study that you would believe the worst of me tonight."

"I wasn't hiding, and it isn't any of my business what you and Claudia do in her bedroom," she said, not realizing that the hurt she felt could be heard in her voice.

Tag reached out and touched her cheek softly. "Don't think too badly of me, sweet, sweet Xandria. If you are thinking that I was intimate with Claudia tonight, you would be only half right."

"I don't know what you mean. How can you halfway make love to a woman?"

Tag leaned forward and untied the ribbon of her nightgown and slid his hand across her breasts. "Like this, Alexandria," he said, leaning forward and capturing her lips in a burning kiss.

Alexandria could taste the brandy on his lips and smell the perfume that Claudia always wore, and she began to struggle. She wanted to hit out at him in her pain. He released her, and she drew back, not wanting him to kiss her after he had been with Claudia.

"Don't ever touch me again!" she whispered through tight lips. "As long as you live, never come near me again! I don't like what you have become."

His eyes looked deeply into hers. "Don't say this to me, Alexandria. I need you tonight." His voice was pleading, but she felt no weakening in her feelings toward him.

"Well, I don't need you anymore! If I never see you again, it will be too soon for me!" she cried, getting out of bed to put some distance between them. She was afraid she would weaken if he touched her again.

"You don't mean that, Alexandria. You're just angry with me. Let me hold you for a moment. I promise I will ask nothing more of you."

"No! You are drunk, and I want you out of my room right now."

Tag leaped across the bed and grabbed Alexandria by the shoulders. "I'm not drunk, except from your nearness, Alexandria. Don't you remember how good it was between us? Forget about Claudia and kiss me," he said with urgency.

His mouth settled on hers, and she tried to struggle at first, but soon her lips parted, and she felt him drawing her against him. He was holding her so tightly she thought her lungs would burst from want of air. When he raised his head, he sprinkled kisses over her face.

"You are my only salvation, Alexandria. When I am with you, I can forget about all the ugliness," he breathed hotly in her ear.

"Is that all I am to you, Tag—someone to keep the ugliness out of your life? Do you come to me when you can no longer stand to live with yourself?"

He looked at her with a piercing gaze. "I don't know, Alexandria, perhaps I do."

"I'm not your mother, Tag, and I'm not Morning Song. If you need someone to fill either of those roles, you have come to the wrong person. Because I feel that I owe you something, I will do all I can to help you, but I will no longer play your lover."

"Like hell," he whispered harshly. "You don't owe me a damned thing. I always thought there was more

318

to our relationship than owing, Alexandria. I suppose I was wrong."

"Yes, you were. Now, it's late, and if you don't need your sleep, I do."

Tag stared down at her. He had expected her to be angry, but he hadn't expected her coldness. Morning Song would have forgiven him anything, and he had thought that Alexandria would be the same. But then, Alexandria was nothing like Morning Song. Each day his life seemed to become more and more entangled with hers. His body seemed to have a hunger for hers that would never be satisfied. He was troubled and confused by these feelings that tormented him.

"I'm leaving, Alexandria, but I hate to leave with this misunderstanding between us. I thought you and I always understood each other."

"You were wrong, Tag. I don't understand you at all. We both have our troubles, but I don't solve mine by jumping into bed with someone I don't love."

"You jumped into bed with me, Alexandria—does that mean that you love me?"

His eyes were searching as she looked into their shimmering depth. "Right now, I don't even like you, Tag," was all she could bring herself to reply.

Tag knew he should leave, but something kept holding him there. He took Alexandria's hand, and even though she didn't pull away, her golden eyes seemed to gleam defiantly in the bright moonlight. In that moment he felt pride in her courage. She would always stand up for what she believed in. She would never allow anyone to push her into anything. He knew he loved her more than he had ever loved Morning Song. He could feel her pulling away from him, and he feared he had spoiled any chance he might have had to win her heart. Tag knew that after tonight she wouldn't have a very high opinion of him, and he wanted her respect almost as much as he wanted her love.

"Alexandria, try to understand that I did what I had to tonight. Claudia doesn't have the slightest notion who I am, and I have to get to her the only way I can."

"Doesn't it bother you that that sick old man is her husband? Don't you have any qualms about bedding another man's wife?" she asked, stepping back a pace.

He reached out and grabbed her, slamming her body into his with force. "Hell, no it doesn't bother me—why should it? I feel no guilt where Claudia and my uncle are concerned."

He felt Alexandria shudder and knew she believed he had made love to Claudia. It became important to him that she know he couldn't complete the act. Cupping her face in his hands, he raised it up to his.

"Alexandria, I never completed the act with Claudia. I didn't make love to her. I couldn't."

She looked into his eyes, wanting to believe him. It hurt her so deeply to think that he had been with Claudia.

"You went to her bedroom?"

"Yes, I went to her room with the intention of doing whatever I had to to make her talk. I didn't find it necessary to make love to her. She told me all I needed to know anyway."

"You kissed her."

"Yes, I admit that."

"I don't like what's going on, Falcon. This is a dirty business and I wish I'd never become mixed up in it."

He studied her face closely and wished the ugliness hadn't touched her life. He wanted to shield her from anything that was soiled and dirty. He wished she would come home with him now, but he knew she wouldn't. "We are a pair, aren't we, Alexandria? You don't know whether to call me Falcon Knight or Taggart James. I don't know whether to call you Xandria, Alex, or Alexandria."

She threw back her head and looked at him with her golden eyes sparking fire. "As far as I'm concerned, you may call me Miss Bradford."

He reached out and touched her cheek softly. "Don't say things in anger that you will regret later, Alexandria. Don't tear my heart apart."

She batted his hand away. "I mean every word I said to you tonight, Tag. Go away and leave me alone."

"Alexandria, if you never want to see me again I'll understand. The only reason I can give you for not turning your back on me is that I . . . need you in my life."

She moved away from him and he could see the tears glistening on her cheeks. "You talk about your needs, Tag—what about my needs?"

He clasped her head in his hands and gently raised her up on her tiptoes and laid his face against hers. He breathed in her clean, fresh smell and felt his senses reel. "I will give you anything you want, Alexandria. Just don't abandon me now," he whispered softly.

Alexandria closed her eyes and her hands moved around his waist. She raised her head and saw the sincerity in Tag's eyes. He was tugging at her heart strings, and she felt her anger melt away.

"I could never turn my back on you, Tag. I will always want to be your friend."

He laughed softly and hugged her tightly. His heart felt lighter now that she was no longer angry with him. "Friendship isn't what I want from you, but it will suffice for now. When this is all over, I will ask more of you."

Alexandria started to ask him what he meant, when his head dipped down and his lips brushed against hers, causing tiny shivers of delight to flow through her body like a restless river.

Tag could feel her melting against him and knew she had forgiven him for tonight. He lifted her in his arms with the intention of placing her in bed and leaving, but when he laid her down she locked her arms about his neck. He could see that her eyes were fever-bright, and he felt his body awaken with the raging passion that she always seemed to evoke in him.

He sat down on the bed and touched her lips. "If I stay, Alexandria, it will have to be because you want me to. Say the word and I'll leave now."

Suddenly, the age-old battle raged inside of Alexandria. She wanted him to make love to her, and yet she knew it was wrong. She could see him tensely waiting for her reply. She reached for his hand and placed it on her breasts.

The groan that issued from his lips was smothered when his lips covered hers in a mind-destroying kiss.

Tag could feel the burning need deep inside him as he broke off the kiss and slipped her nightgown off her shoulders and down past her hips. Alexandria raised her hips and he removed the nightgown and tossed it to the floor.

He allowed his eyes to move over her body, and he drew in his breath at how lovely she was. Before, when he had made love to her, it had been dark, and he hadn't realized how perfect she was. As his eyes examined every inch of her, his hands followed the same course.

Alexandria could see the admiration in Tag's eyes, and she shivered with delight as his hands moved up her legs, across her rib cage, and then circled one of her breasts.

When his head dipped down to explore her breasts, he circled each nipple with his tongue and felt them harden to rosebud tips. There was an urgency about him as he stood and stripped off his clothing. When he returned to Alexandria, she stretched out her arms to him and he pulled her tightly to him. "I need you tonight sweet, sweet, Alexandria," he breathed hotly in her ear.

For a long moment Tag just held her to him, loving the way she fit so perfectly against his body. Neither of them spoke as he stroked her softly. His mind was swirling and he felt a whirlwind of feelings when he turned her to her back and knelt over her. He could see that her amber eyes were glowing as he slowly moved forward and entered her body.

At first he went slowly, wanting to give her pleasure, but soon the tide of passion clutched them both in its grip and they moved together in frenzied lovemaking.

323

Alexandria threw her head back as Tag's lips moved down her throat to encircle her breast. This couldn't be wrong, she told herself. Nothing that felt so right and beautiful could be considered wrong. The love she felt for him seemed to spill over her like a volcano erupting.

"Tag, Tag," she murmured softly, as he took her body higher then she had ever flown before.

Tag tore his lips from her breast and groaned when he returned to bruise her lips with a savage kiss.

They were both swept into a world of touching and feeling. Their senses were heightened by the fact that this time they could watch each other's face. Tag thrust forward and saw Alexandria's golden eyes glaze with passion. Suddenly he knew what was different when he made love to Alexandria. With Morning Song, he had always felt somehow unfulfilled—but with Alexandria he found total satisfaction.

Alexandria turned her head, arched her hips, and they both felt their bodies explode in a red-hot blaze of sensuous feeling. They clutched each other tightly until the tremors that shook them ceased.

Alexandria closed her eyes, feeling as if she had been born for this moment. It was as if their hearts had been twined together and no one could ever break them apart. She wanted to give voice to the love that seemed to swell in her heart, wondering if Tag felt it also, but she kept her silence. If she ever admitted she loved him, he might resent her tender feelings for him. She must never allow herself to forget that he had once told her he had loved but one woman and would never love again.

Tag pulled Alexandria's head to rest against his

chest. He had the feeling that he wanted to absorb her into his body and make her a part of him. When this long ordeal with Claudia was over and he had seen it to its conclusion, he wanted to ask ... no, *beg* Alexandria to be his wife. He wanted to tell her of his deep feelings for her, but for some reason he couldn't seem to find the right words. He had transmitted his love to her when he took her body. Every move he had made—every kiss he had given her had told her of his love.

Tag kissed her on the forehead and sat up reluctantly. "I must go now. It wouldn't be wise for me to be found in your room when morning comes. I do want to ask something of you, Alexandria, and I hope you will think hard before giving me your answer."

"What?"

"Come home with me now. I don't want you to stay in this house for another day. I worry about you."

"I cannot come with you now, Tag. When this is all over I will leave, but it will not be with you. After tonight I just want you to leave me alone."

He looked at her long and hard. When he stood up and moved away Alexandria wanted to call him back, but she clamped her lips tightly together. She watched silently as he dressed and walked to the door.

Without another word, he opened the door. When he left she wanted to call him back. She bit her lip so she wouldn't cry out for him not to leave. How empty the room seemed when he had gone. How void her life would be without him. If only she had somewhere to go, she would leave and close this chapter of her life forever. Ever since she had met Tag, it had been a little like living on the edge of a volcano and never knowing when trouble would erupt. She didn't know how much longer she could go on this way.

She turned her face into the pillow, feeling her heartache like a knife in her heart. She loved Tag, and she would love him until she died. She would never be able to put him out of her thoughts. He would always live in her heart.

Claudia awoke and leisurely stretched her arms upward. Her head was pounding, and she felt as if the inside of her mouth were filled with cotton. She sat up and smiled, remembering the night before. Most of it was no more than a foggy dream, and she didn't know for sure where her memory left off and her fantasy took over. All she knew for sure was that she had never spent the night in such complete bliss. She could hardly wait to see Falcon again!

The door was opened, and the housekeeper, Mrs. Dodson, bustled in carrying a breakfast tray, which she placed on Claudia's lap.

"It'll take a week for me to get this place cleaned up after last night, with the help being what it is, Mrs. Landon. There isn't a good day's work between the lot of them—I can tell you that."

Claudia smiled in unusual good humor. "I trust you can handle it, Dodson. Have I had any messages?" she asked, hoping there would be some word from Falcon, since she had been asleep when he left.

"As it happens, cook says this letter came by messenger this morning," Mrs. Dodson said, handing the letter to Claudia, then turning away to straighten the room.

Claudia took the envelope and stared at the bold

handwriting, hoping it would be from Falcon. "You know very well I can't read, Dodson. Send that girl Alexandria to me immediately, and hurry."

Claudia could hardly contain her excitement as she waited for Alexandria to come. She broke the seal and held the letter up to the light. She just knew it would be from Falcon . . . who else could it be from?

Alexandria entered Claudia's bedroom reluctantly. She tried whenever possible to avoid the woman, but she could hardly ignore a direct order.

Claudia was propped up in bed, eating a hearty breakfast. She frowned at Alexandria and motioned for her to be seated beside her.

"Read this to me," she mumbled, with her mouth full of food. "Who does it say it's from?"

Alexandria turned the envelope over. "It merely says your name on the front."

"Well, read the letter to me, you foolish girl, and don't dawdle! What does it say?"

Alexandria scanned the page quickly and drew in her breath. "I . . . think this must be some kind of cruel jest," she said. Scanning to the bottom of the letter, she saw Tag's signature and drew in her breath.

"What does it say?" Claudia demanded.

Alexandria's heart was thundering in her breast, and her hands began to tremble. Tag had started his campaign against Claudia! She cleared her throat and began to read:

Claudia,

I know you have been expecting to hear from me. Never fear, I am always watching your every move. I know everything you do. I even know you entertained a certain gentleman in your

327

bedroom last night by the name of Falcon Knight. We have an old score to settle—you and I. I know you are the one who had my wife killed. How frightening it must be for you to have a faceless enemy. Do you sleep well at night, Claudia? Do you ever go out of the house alone? I look forward to meeting you again after all these years.

Taggart James

Alexandria was unprepared for the woman's reaction. Claudia bounced out of bed and raced down the hallway screaming at the top of her lungs.

"He's here, he's going to kill me!"

Alexandria tossed the letter on the bed and ran after Claudia. Seeing that the distraught woman had dashed into Mr. Landon's room, Alexandria followed her, but she remained in the outer room where she could hear what was being said without being seen.

"Howard, you've got to do something! Tag is here, and he had made threats to me. Help me, please help me! You've got to tell him that it was you who had his wife killed. He won't hurt you, Howard. Tell him you are responsible for his wife's death!"

Alexandria heard Mr. Landon's laughter. "I . . . knew he was back, Claudia. I think . . . he will deal with you . . . soon. Why . . . did you have . . . his wife killed?

Alexandria could hear the humor in Mr. Landon's voice and realized he was enjoying his wife's anguish; he was even adding fuel to the flames.

"How could you know he was back?" Claudia's voice was bordering on hysteria.

"Never mind. . . how I know."

"Tell me what he looks like so I'll know him when I see him," she cried.

Howard's hideous laughter rang out. "How . . . should I know . . . what he looks like?"

Claudia glared at her husband. "I'm not alone in this, Howard. It was you who stole the James fortune and had Tag and Joanna's father murdered. When I go down, I'll take you with me," Claudia threatened.

"What more . . . can be done to . . . me, Claudia? Have I not suffered all these years . . . having you . . . as my wife? If Tag killed me, it would . . . be a blessing."

"You are a monster!" Claudia raged. "How can you make light of this?" Claudia was so distraught, it didn't even occur to her that she was understanding Howard's speech. She didn't realize that when he wanted to, he could speak well enough.

"I don't, my . . . dear. You see, I . . . enjoy a good joke, even if it is on . . . me, and especially . . . if it's on you."

"I will go to the authorities and demand that they do something. Surely there is a law about threatening people's lives," Claudia said, wringing her hands.

"You do . . . that, Claudia, and when . . . they ask you who this person is that . . . threatened you, tell them that he's the person whose home . . . you treat as your own . . . and whose wife was killed by the men you . . . hired to kill . . . him."

Claudia's face became distorted with anger. "All you care about is lying in your bed and staring at that damned picture of Joanna. Do you think I don't know why you keep Alexandria around? I'm also aware of

329

her resemblance to Joanna. Enjoy her while you can, because I'll yet find a way to be rid of her—just mark my words, Howard."

Alexandria stayed to hear no more. She slipped out of the room and up the stairs to her own room. She wanted to send Tag word about what Claudia's reaction had been to his letter. She felt strongly that things would soon come to a conclusion, now that Tag had decided to make his move. Surely, it wouldn't be too long until the whole thing would blow up!

Tag read the note Mrs. Green handed him in silence, while Farley looked on.

"What does Alex have to say? I miss her 'round here—when's she coming home?" the old trapper wanted to know.

"She doesn't say here, Farley. She says only that Claudia received my letter, and it had the desired effect."

"I don't like that little lady being mixed up in this nasty business. I wish she were safely out of it. All hell's gonna break loose in the next few days, and she'll be caught right in the middle of it," Farley stated.

"There isn't anything I can do, Farley. As I said before, she has a mind of her own and I damned sure can't change it for her." Tag remembered the night before when he had held Alexandria warm and yielding in his arms. She had given him all he had asked of her. Today her letter had been cold and impersonal, and he felt confused.

"Ain't a woman always saying opposite of what she's thinking? What you should have done was to bring her back here with or without her permission."

"Not likely. She is as stubborn and bullheaded as Joanna. When she gets a notion in her head, no one can change it."

"I don't think you are feeling brotherly toward our little lady. To my way of thinking, you are having too much thought 'bout her lately."

"You want to know the trouble with you, Farley? You think too damn much," Tag said, stalking out of the room.

The old man's face crinkled as his laughter followed Tag up the stairs. "I figure you got it bad for her," he called out, slapping his legs with mirth.

Chapter Twenty-five

It was two days after the masquerade ball, and Claudia now very rarely came out of her room. Her curtains were drawn, and Alexandria had heard from Mrs. Dodson that she was nervous and jumped at every noise. Mrs. Dodson declared she was not too happy about going into Claudia's room. The housekeeper complained that Mrs. Landon kept a gun under her pillow and aimed it at her every time she entered her bedroom, claiming someone was trying to kill her.

Alexandria had noticed that Claudia's lawyer had come to the house several times, but she had no notion as to what the two of them had discussed.

Mr. Landon was growing steadily weaker, and this seemed to cause Claudia much distress. Alexandria knew Claudia feared that if he died she would be turned out of the house.

The doctor had been sent for, and he informed Alexandria that Mr. Landon was failing rapidly. He cautioned her to keep him as quiet as possible and allow no one to upset him.

As she sat beside Mr. Landon's bed reading his favorite book aloud, Alexandria noticed that his eyes kept wondering to the portrait of Joanna.

"If only . . . Joanna had come," he said in a strangled voice. "If only . . . I could . . . look upon . . . her face once . . . more before I die."

Alexandria closed the book and patted his hand. "You shouldn't talk such nonsense, Mr. Landon. Nothing is going to happen to you."

He smiled as his eyes lighted on her curly head. "You can't . . . fool . . . an old trickster, Alexandria. We both know . . . it's just a . . . matter of time . . . for me."

She stood up and opened the window so the morning breeze would penetrate the room. "I won't listen to such talk! You and I will prove the doctor wrong," she said, thinking that she had grown very fond of the sick old man.

He motioned for her to come closer. "I . . . believe . . . you really mean that, Alexandria. I can't tell . . . you what a joy you have been . . . to me. You have . . . brought a . . . ray of sunshine into my drab . . . existence."

She sat down once more and held on to his hand. "You have also brought some substance to my life. I have enjoyed the times we have shared, Mr. Landon."

"If you . . . consider me your . . . friend, Alexandria, tell me what . . . is bothering you. Sometimes . . . I can tell you are troubled about . . . something. I am not without . . . influence, if you are in some kind of . . . trouble . . . I can . . . help you."

"I don't want to talk about me. Besides, the doctor said he didn't want you upset, remember?

"I will be upset . . . if you don't . . . tell me . . . what you fear," he said, looking deeply into her amber

333

eyes.

"I . . . it's hard to talk about."

"Try."

For some reason, Alexandria had the feeling she could trust Howard Landon. After all, he hadn't betrayed Tag to Claudia. He might have done some bad things in the past, but she felt he had changed. Perhaps she could end her dependency on Tag if she were to talk to Mr. Landon about her problems, she thought.

"I am afraid you may not think very highly of me when you learn what I have done."

"Tell . . . me, and let me judge . . . for myself, Alexandria."

She took a deep breath, not knowing where to begin. "I was born and raised on a large farm in Valley Forge. My mother died when I was quite young, and my father remarried. My stepmother, Barbara, has a son named Rodney who is some ten years older than I. When my father died, she found out the farm had been left to me by my mother's father. Barbara must have decided that if she were going to keep control of Meadowlake, she would have to force me to marry my stepbrother, Rodney."

Alexandria's voice faltered, and Howard could tell she was having trouble reliving what had happened to her. He patted her hand comfortingly. "Go on, Alexandria . . . what happened next?" he urged.

"Barbara and Rodney forced me to come here to Philadelphia, where her sister lives. They found a parson who was willing to marry me to Rodney without my consent. You can imagine how horrified I was! There was no one to whom I could turn for help.

The night before the wedding was to take place, Rodney came to my bedroom and tried to . . . he was . . ."

"I know what . . . you are trying . . . to say, Alexandria. Go on from . . . there."

"I tried to get away from Rodney, but he was very strong. I picked up a lamp and threw it at him, and he was engulfed in flames! Barbara had me locked in the basement, and I thought I had killed Rodney. She threatened to have me committed to an asylum for the insane, and I didn't know where to turn. With the help of one who will remain nameless, I was able to escape. I have since learned that my stepbrother didn't die, but the authorities are still searching for me."

Howard was quiet for a moment. "How . . . did you meet . . . our friend?"

"I cannot tell you, since that has no bearing on my situation. You know about my past. Do you still want me to stay?"

His eyes held a light of kindness as he squeezed her hand. "I not only . . . want you to stay, but . . . I am going to help . . . you get out of this . . . situation. Tomorrow morning . . . I will have Barlow go . . . to Mr. Hammond's office . . . and tell him . . . I want to speak to . . . him. He is a man with great . . . power. I can assure you that soon . . . you will be able to go on with your . . . life, with no fear of your . . . stepmother and . . . stepbrother. What they tried to force you to do . . . was criminal, and I will see that they are . . . punished."

"Mr. Landon, I'm frightened—suppose I am arrested?"

"That will not happen . . . you have my . . . word. By this time tomorrow . . . you will be free of your stepmother!"

Tears ran freely down Alexandria's face. "Oh, Mr. Landon, if only it were true! You cannot know what it's been like living with this hanging over my head."

Howard's eyes went to the portrait. "Perhaps in doing this for you . . . I can somehow make up . . . for the wrongs . . . I have done. I believe . . . Joanna would like that."

He closed his eyes, and Alexandria knew he had drifted off to sleep. She somehow felt better after having told Mr. Landon about herself. She didn't know if Mr. Landon could help her or not, but she was weary of hiding and was ready to face whatever it took to see this thing to the end.

Alexandria had no idea that her conversation with Mr. Landon had been overheard. Claudia smiled to herself as she quietly left the outer room. It would be easy enough to find out from the authorities if they were searching for a young girl by the name of Alexandria Bradford! Claudia hurried down the stairs, to set in motion the means that would rid her of Alexandria Bradford once and for all!

It was the cool of the evening just before sunset, and Alexandria was walking in the garden. She was excited, and was looking forward to the next morning when Mr. Landon would try and clear her name. When she was cleared, she would be free to return to the farm and the life she had loved since childhood. The love of the land had been born and bred into her. She missed the fresh scent of the country air and being able to watch things grow.

As she made her way down to the pond, her mind was far away, and she didn't see the shadow that fell across her path. The man spoke her name before she realized he was there. Alexandria whirled around to see a stranger step into the path just behind her.

"Alexandria, I want to speak to you. I'm sorry to have to address you by your given name, but you see, I do not know your surname."

Alexandria saw the man was dressed as a sailor, and she knew he must be the one who had been watching Tag for some time. She felt afraid of him and drew back a step, ready to flee back to the house.

"No, don't go!" the man called out. "I mean you no harm—I want to talk to you about Tag."

"I know of no one by that name, sir, you are mistaken," she said, taking another step backwards.

"I have seen the two of you together many times, so you don't need to try and protect him from me. I would be the last one in the world who would wish the boy harm."

"Who are you?" she asked, losing some of her apprehension and becoming curious.

"Walk with me to the pond where we will be out of sight of the house, and we can talk unobserved," he said, stepping aside so she could pass in front of him.

Alexandria's fear returned at the thought of being alone with this stranger. Even though he had said he wouldn't harm Tag, it could be that he was only trying to pacify her so he could lure her away from the house.

"How do I know I can trust you?" she asked, taking another step backwards.

The man glanced toward the house and then back

to her. "Look at me, Alexandria. Do I remind you of anyone?" he asked. "Have you ever seen me before?"

She searched his face, thinking he did indeed look familiar to her. "Who are you?"

"Someone who wishes only to help Tag. Please talk with me," he urged.

Alexandria hesitated for only a moment before she preceded him down the path to the pond. The stranger stayed a short distance from her as she waited for him to speak. "We are totally alone now. Say what you came to say and then leave," she told him, with more courage than she actually felt.

"Look at my eyes, Alexandria," the man said, smiling slightly. "Where have you seen eyes the color of mine before?"

It was hard to determine the color of his eyes without getting closer to him, and she was still too frightened to get too near. "I cannot see your eyes," she told him.

The stranger took several steps in her direction and came up beside her. "Where have you seen eyes the color of mine, Alexandria?" he repeated.

Alexandria gasped as she stared into violet-blue eyes so like Tag's that it astounded her. The man removed his cap, and she saw his reddish-gold hair blowing in the evening breeze. Suddenly she knew who the man was! Had she not many times seen his likeness in the portrait that hung over the mantel in Mr. Landon's bedroom?

"How can it be? You are Mr. James! I was told you were dead!" she blurted out.

"As you can see, I am very much alive. I have been watching the boy for some time, but I wasn't sure he

338

was my son until two nights ago, when the two of you were here at the pond and you called him by name."

"The night of the masquerade ball? Why haven't you gone to him and told him who you are? Dear Lord, he thinks you are dead!"

"I haven't gone to Tag because I thought I could watch over him and keep him from harm if he didn't know who I was. As for being alive, there were times in the past when I wished I had died."

Alexandria reached out and touched his arm in her excitement. "Mr. James, do you have any idea how happy Tag will be to see you?" Tears blinded her, and she was so happy she had the strongest urge to hug this man who was Tag's father.

"When the time is right, I'll go to the boy, but I must not do so now. He is in grave danger, as you are already aware. I knew when I heard the two of you talking the other night that you cared about my son. That is why I have decided to reveal myself to you now. You must promise me that you will not tell Taggart about me. Do I have your word on that?"

Alexandria nodded. "Yes, but it would make him so happy if he knew you were still alive."

"There will be time for happiness later. Right now, all I'm concerned about is my son's safety. You have been living here," he said, nodding in the direction of the house. "Tell me what has been going on."

Alexandria sat down on the grass, and he joined her there. She told him all she knew about Claudia and Mr. Landon. The sun went down and the dinner hour came and went, and still they talked. She found Russell James so easy to talk to that she even ended up by telling him about her troubles with Barbara and

Rodney, and how Tag had come to her rescue at the tavern after she had run away. She didn't realize it was so late until he stood up and helped her to her feet.

"It grows late, and you should be in bed, Alexandria. I want to thank you for talking to me and telling me about my son. I can see why he loves you. You are such a lovely young lady."

"Tag isn't in love with me, Mr. James. I am no more than a friend to him."

"As you say, Alexandria, but I think I saw more than friendship pass between the two of you the other night."

On impulse, she stood on her tiptoes and kissed his cheek. "I am so glad you are alive. I have grown to know your family quite well through Tag."

"If that's the case, can you tell me about my daughter Joanna?"

"I would rather Tag tell you about her. I *will* put your mind at rest by telling you she is alive, and from what Tag says, very happy."

"I like the loyalty you have shown my son, Alexandria, so I will not press you further about Joanna. Run along now, and I'll see you again soon.

As Alexandria made her way back toward the house, her heart felt lighter than it had in months. It seemed everything was beginning to fall into place. Perhaps now that Tag's father was here, the long ordeal would soon be over.

When Alexandria reached the house, she noticed there were two carriages at the front, so she walked around to the back entrance. When she entered the kitchen, she was met by an angry Mrs. Dodson.

"Where have you been? The entire household has

been searching for you, Alexandria!"

"Has Mr. Landon taken a turn for the worse?" Alexandria asked apprehensively.

"Not so far as I know, but Mrs. Landon wants to see you in the parlor at once!"

Alexandria nodded, and hurried to the parlor, fearing that something might have happened to Mr. Landon and Mrs. Dodson just wasn't telling her. She heard the murmur of voices coming from behind the door and rapped softly. The door was opened by Claudia, and when she saw Alexandria, a spiteful look came over her face.

"Come in, won't you? There are some people here who are very anxious to see you," Claudia told her in a honey-sweet voice. Taking Alexandria by the arm, she practically dragged her into the room.

Alexandria felt her knees go weak, and she grabbed her throat in horror as she recognized Barbara and Rodney waiting inside for her!

"You will have your just reward now," Claudia hissed in her ear. "No one ever crosses me and gets by with it," she whispered so no one could hear but Alexandria.

The last thing Alexandria remembered was the room spinning around; then everything seemed to go black, and she had the sensation of falling! She wasn't aware that Rodney picked her up in his arms and placed her on the couch, while Claudia looked on with satisfaction.

"What will you do with the girl?" Claudia asked, her eyes gleaming brightly. "Will you have her locked away for her crimes?"

Barbara smiled slightly. "No, Mrs. Landon, I

think we will take her back to the farm where she belongs. I want to thank you for getting in touch with us so promptly. When the authorities came to us and told us Alexandria had been found, you can't imagine how it gladdened our hearts—isn't that so, Rodney?"

Claudia looked down her nose at Barbara Bradford. She could well imagine what they had in mind for poor Alexandria. She imagined that the previously planned wedding would now take place. Glancing at Rodney—who would have been hideous to her even without the burn scars on his face—Claudia shivered. Better Alexandria than herself, she thought.

As Rodney picked Alexandria up in his arms, she moaned softly but didn't regain consciousness. He stared down at her beautiful face and smiled, thinking that this time she wouldn't escape him. He placed her in the hired coach and rubbed his hand over his scarred cheek. Alexandria would pay for what she had done to him, he thought bitterly.

After watching the carriage pull out of sight, Claudia went upstairs to Howard's room. When she entered, she found him staring at the portrait of Joanna.

"We have quite a lot of excitement here tonight. Too bad you missed it, Howard."

He didn't even look at her, and, as always, he managed to shut her voice out.

"Yes, you should have seen Alexandria; she just swooned away," Claudia taunted.

That got Howard's attention. "You better . . . not have . . . harmed the girl," he said, turning purple in the face and gasping for breath.

"Me? No, not me! She was carried away by her

342

stepmother and stepbrother. Poor Alexandria, I think she will soon be the wife of her hideous-looking stepbrother," she continued, trying to bait her husband.

Claudia watched as Howard tried to rise. He started coughing and gasping for breath. She had only meant to torment him; the last thing in the world she wanted to do was cause him to have another attack.

"Howard, hold on, don't move—I'll send for the doctor immediately!" she said, running out of the room and calling for Mrs. Dodson. By the time she returned to the room, Howard was white as a ghost, and Claudia knew he was dead! His eyes seemed to be bulging out of the sockets, and it was as if, in death, he were still staring at the portrait of Joanna.

"Howard, no! You can't die on me now! Not now!" Claudia screamed at the top of her voice. "She grabbed Howard's shoulders and began shaking him violently, while his head lolled from side to side. "Damn you, Howard, I didn't mean this to happen. I'm lost—I'm lost!"

When the doctor and Mrs. Dodson returned, Claudia was wringing her hands and raving like a madwoman.

"I didn't know that sending the girl away would kill you, Howard! Come back—come back! All that money . . . this house . . . everything gone . . . gone!"

The doctor gave Claudia a strong dose of laudanum, which seemed to calm her after awhile. He then helped her to bed, thinking she had lost her mind.

Claudia's dreams that night turned into nightmares, and she could see Howard's bulging eyes staring at her accusingly. At times in her dreams she would escape from Howard, only to have a faceless Tag chasing after her. She moaned and twisted in her sleep, seeking release from her nightmares.

Chapter Twenty-six

Alexandria regained consciousness slowly. She realized, from the swaying motion that rocked her back and forth, that she was riding in a coach. She held her hand over her mouth, thinking she was going to be sick, as her stomach seemed to churn with each movement of the coach.

Barbara jerked Alexandria's head up. "Well, well, we have had a bit of trouble finding you. We shall just see that you don't get away again."

Rodney rubbed his scarred face with the back of his hand. "You've got a lot to answer for, Alexandria. As my wife, you will know what it feels like to be scarred. I think I'll just take a hot iron to your pretty face."

"Don't talk such nonsense, Rodney. Didn't I always try to teach you to be kind to those that do you harm?" his mother scolded.

"I don't recall your ever saying that to me, Mother. If you'll forgive me, I don't feel too kindly toward Alexandria at the moment."

Alexandria leaned her head back against the coach and willed herself not to be sick. The nightmare was starting all over again. Was she never to know any peace and contentment in her life? She thought of

Tag, and her heart sent him a silent message to find her. She prayed he would learn what had happened and come to rescue her. He was her only hope. She knew that if he didn't come soon, she would never see him again.

"We have a little party waiting for you back at my aunt's house. She will have the parson waiting for you and me, and we'll be joined as man and wife tonight. There won't ever be any question of your leaving me again, Alexandria," Rodney said coldly.

"I will never marry you! You are no better than an animal," she spat out.

His fist swung out, catching her squarely on the jaw. Alexandria grabbed her head and slumped forward in pain.

"Now look what you have done, Rodney! Why can't you control that temper of yours until you have at least wed the girl? We don't want the parson seeing her all bruised up, now do we?"

Alexandria closed her mind to the pain. She could endure anything but Rodney's putting his hands on her. Please, Tag, she prayed silently, come and save me!

Tag and Farley were just finishing a late dinner, when Mrs. Green came hurrying into the room, looking distressed about something.

"There's a man at the front door who says he wants to see you right away, Mr. James. He says it's urgent. I tried to tell him you were dining, but he was most insistent that he speak with you."

"Did he say what his name was?" Tag wanted to know.

"No, but he's dressed as a seaman, and I think he might be the man who's been hanging about lately," Mrs. Green stated flatly.

Tag tossed his napkin on the table and walked hurriedly toward the front door, flanked by Farley. Tag threw open the door and came face to face with the man.

"I'm Falcon Knight. I'm told you wanted to see me," he said, looking the man over closely.

"If you have a care about Alexandria Bradford, you had better come with me in a hurry. I saw her being carried off tonight by her stepmother and step-brother."

"How do you know this?" Tag asked, eyeing the man suspiciously.

"I know because Alexandria told me that her stepbrother was scarred, and the man I saw lifting her into the carriage had a scar on his face."

"Don't trust him," Farley said, poking his head around the door. "I seed this man afore. He's the man I had the tiff with . . . the one who's been spying on you."

"Lord, I don't have time to argue with you," the stranger said. "Do you know where they would have taken the girl, or not? I would have followed them myself, but I was on foot and lost them. Tell me where they live, and I'll go get her myself if you aren't going to help me."

"Farley, go saddle three horses and bring them around to the front," Tag said, deciding to trust the stranger. He rushed into the study, grabbed up his gun, and poked it into his belt. By the time he reached the front door, he found that Farley had already saddled the horses and was leading them to the front of the house.

"I don't know who you are, stranger, but if you are telling the truth, I'll have a lot to thank you for before the night is over," Tag said, swinging himself onto his horse.

After Farley and the stranger were mounted, Tag led the way toward Front Street. He didn't know who the man was, or how he knew about Alexandria, but he felt he had no choice but to trust the man. If there was the slightest chance that he was telling the truth, Alexandria might be in grave danger.

Farley rode alongside the stranger and looked at him suspiciously. "Ifen you aren't telling the right of it, I'll pump some lead into you."

The stranger didn't answer. He merely kicked his mount in the flanks and rode up beside Tag.

Russell James was disappointed. He had half-hoped his son would recognize him. But how could Tag be expected to remember him? he asked himself. He had only been a boy the last time they had seen each other—and after all, Tag thought he was dead.

Alexandria stumbled and would have fallen if it hadn't been for the fact that she was being held up by Rodney. By now, she realized that the drink Rodney had given her earlier must have been drugged, because all she wanted to do was lie down somewhere and sleep.

"I always did say you didn't have good sense, Rodney. You gave her too much of the drug," she heard her stepmother say.

Alexandria was aware that there were several people

in the room. She vaguely recognized Johnny, the boy who had helped her escape from the basement. She wondered why he was looking so sad. There was a man dressed in a black suit standing before her and Rodney, but she was sure she hadn't ever seen him before. He was asking her a question. What did he want her to say?

All of a sudden there was a loud crash at the front door, and everyone turned their attention to the three intruders who burst into the room.

Alexandria thought she must be dreaming, because she was sure Tag was standing before her.

"Stand away from Alexandria," Tag ordered, pointing his gun at Rodney.

"What's the meaning of this?" Barbara demanded to know, wondering who the three men were.

"You have something that belongs to me, Mrs. Bradford," Tag said through clenched teeth. "I'm here to collect it."

"If you've come to rob us, we have nothing of value here," Rodney spoke up.

"Ah, but there you are wrong, Rodney. You see, Alexandria belongs to me, and I place a great deal of value on her," Tag said lazily.

"Who are you, and why do you come in here busting up my son's wedding?" Barbara said, glancing at the young man who was aiming a gun at her son.

"Farley, get Alexandria and bring her over here," Tag ordered. "If I find that you have harmed her in any way, you will pay dearly." Tag spoke directly to Rodney.

"You have no right to take Alexandria away from

349

her family," Rodney spoke up.

"Oh, no? We'll just see about that. Preacher, you have come here tonight to perform a wedding, and you damned sure won't be disappointed," Tag said. He removed a gold piece from his coat pocket and tossed it to the man he assumed was the preacher.

"If any one of them moves or looks like they want to interfere," Tag told Farley, "shoot them!"

"Now, that would be a real pleasure," Farley said, aiming his gun at Rodney after handing Alexandria over to Tag.

Russell James rested his gun across his palms and gave Barbara a look that made her shiver. She didn't know who these men were, but she knew she dared not interfere.

Tag raised Alexandria's head and realized immediately that she had been drugged. "Are you willing to have me for your husband, Alexandria?" he asked in a soft voice, noticing she couldn't seem to focus her eyes clearly.

"I . . . want to sleep," she whispered.

"Later, my love. Right now, we are going to be married, so there will never be any question in any of these folks' mind that you belong to me."

The parson wished himself anywhere but where he was at the moment. He had come here tonight to perform what he thought would be a simple wedding ceremony, and it had turned out to be anything but simple.

As he recited the words, Tag shook Alexandria, and her eyes fluttered open. "Say I do, Alexandria," he urged.

All Alexandria wanted to do was lie down, but

someone kept making her stand. If she did as they asked, perhaps they would leave her alone, she thought.

"Say I do," Tag coached again.

"I . . . do . . . what?" she asked.

"That's close enough, parson," Farley spoke up. "You heard her say she does. Get on with it."

The preacher eyed Farley carefully. He wasn't about to argue with the crazy old man who kept waving his gun in everybody's face. "I now pronounce you man and wife. What God has joined together, let no man put asunder," he said hurriedly.

"The marriage isn't legal," Rodney spoke up. "Alexandria isn't your wife."

"Is he right, parson? Do I need a document to prove Alexandria is my legal wife?" Tag asked.

The preacher wasn't about to deny that the ceremony he had just performed was legal. He asked their names and Tag gave him his real name and Alexandria's. The preacher printed them on the wedding document and handed it to Tag. "It's legal. Ain't no court in these United States going to dispute your claim, Mr. James."

"They better not," Farley said, waving his gun in the man's face. "Ifen I was to find out that this here wedding ain't legal and binding, it won't bother me one little bit to shoot me a preacher."

Tag lifted Alexandria up into his arms and carried her toward the door. Then he turned back and gave Rodney a penetrating gaze. "I would advise you and your mother never to set foot on my wife's farm again. If you do, I will leave orders that you are to be shot!"

"You can't do this," Barbara spoke up. "I'll have

351

the law on you."

"With what charge, Mrs. Bradford?" Tag asked.
"I . . ."

"Exactly, Mrs. Bradford. You are the ones who will
be arrested when and if I ever decide to talk to the law.
I'm sure there are laws against trying to force a young
girl to marry against her will."

"If there are laws, perhaps you will be the one who
will be arrested. Alexandria wasn't in her right mind
when you married her tonight," Barbara stated.

"I think when she is herself, she would tell you that
she likes being my wife. No lawmaker in his right
mind would deny a woman the right to marry the man
of her choice. I think Alexandria prefers me to your
son any day."

Barbara looked at the handsome young man and
knew that he spoke the truth. "Rodney and I have
some things that belong to us at Meadowlake. You
aren't going to keep us from getting them, are you?"

"Not at all. Farley will be going to the farm bright
and early in the morning to take my housekeeper so
she can set the place in order. He will see that your
belongings are sent on to you."

Barbara and Rodney had no more to say as the
three men left. The parson made a speedy retreat
shortly thereafter, and soon the house on Front Street
became quiet.

"If they hadn't had guns, I would have stood up to
them," Rodney said sourly.

"Oh, shut up, Rodney," his mother said. "I don't
trust that man not to sic the authorities onto us. I
think it might be best if we go and stay with my Aunt
Sarah in Marysville. It doesn't seem too wise to press

Mr. James. I could tell by his speech that he's a well-fixed gentleman and not without influence."

Barbara's sister Annabelle had been cowering in a corner and now spoke up for the first time. "I been studying on who that man is. I had the feeling I'd met him before. He was the same gentleman who I told you about who called himself Falcon Knight. You know, the one I told you who came here asking to buy Meadowlake. Tonight he told the preacher his name was Taggart James."

"Well, that settles the mystery, doesn't it? He married Alexandria so he could get his hands on Meadowlake. We came close to getting our hands on Meadowlake ourselves," Barbara stated regretfully.

"I am never going to find a wife as pretty and well-off as Alexandria," Rodney said, sitting down and clasping his head in his hands.

Barbara looked at her son in disgust. Since the accident, he had become a whining, complaining annoyance. She truly thought that he was becoming sick in the mind. She knew the best thing for her to do was put as much distance as she could between herself and Philadelphia. There was no telling if Mr. James might not decide to have her and her son locked up.

When Tag reached the house, he dismounted and carried Alexandria up to his bedroom. Laying his new bride down on the bed, he undressed her and pulled the covers up over her. She hadn't moved since he had carried her to his horse. Leaning over her, he placed his hand against her chest to reassure himself that her heart was beating steadily.

He shuddered, thinking what might have happened

353

to her had he not arrived in time to save her from becoming Rodney's wife.

Tag touched her face softly, and he felt his heart swell with love for her. He now knew without a doubt that she was the one true love of his life. What he had shared with Morning Song had been beautiful, but that was in the past, and it didn't compare with how he felt about Alexandria. He didn't know how she felt about him, and he wasn't sure how she would react when she awoke in the morning and found herself to be his wife. At least she would know she was safe from her stepmother and stepbrother.

Tag lightly touched his lips to hers, thanking God that she was safely back with him. He didn't know what he would have done if he had lost her. Not only was she beautiful beyond compare, but she was courageous and loyal as well—the two virtues he admired most in a woman. Tag thought he might have been drawn to her at first because she reminded him of Joanna, but that wasn't why he had fallen in love with her. He loved her because she had beauty in her heart.

What if she didn't love him? he wondered. He remembered the last time he had gone to her she had asked him to leave her alone.

Tag reached into his pocket and withdrew Alexandria's mother's cameo necklace and clasped it about her neck. He hadn't been able to give her a ring tonight, but perhaps the necklace would signify his love for her. Later, if she would allow it, he would give her a ring.

"Sleep well, my little love," he whispered. "You are safe with me. No one will ever harm you again."

Tag went downstairs, expecting to find the stranger

who had helped him rescue Alexandria. He had many questions to ask the man, and he intended to have his answers tonight.

He found only Farley waiting for him in the parlor. The old man was stretched out in a chair, his feet propped up and his eyes closed.

"That there stranger done lit out. When I went to stable the horses, he just clean went and disappeared."

"Damn it, Farley! You knew I wanted to talk to him. You should have kept your eye on him."

"That one's a slippery one. I don't know who he is, but you oughta be mighty beholden to him after tonight."

Tag sat down and leaned his head back against the chair, feeling the weariness creep into his body. "I suppose, but I damn sure would like to know who he is and why he keeps turning up everywhere I go."

"There's lots of things that don't make no sense to me. What kind of folks would drug a young girl like our Alexandria, and try to force her to wed?" Farley asked.

"I don't know, Farley. It seems to me that everywhere we turn since we came to Philadelphia, we have run into some shady characters. I have a fear that the whole damned white world is corrupt."

"You have better things to worry 'bout tonight besides the sins of the world," Farley said, crinkling up his face into a grin. "It just don't hardly seem right to me that a strapping young man like you would spend his wedding night with the likes of me."

"You know it wasn't really a proper wedding, Farley. I had to marry her so that damned rabble would stop hounding her."

"You heard the man say the wedding were legal and binding. She's your true and lawful wife."

"I don't want to talk about it anymore tonight. I'm going to bed," Tag said, standing up and moving toward the door. He turned back to Farley. "I will be sleeping in the front bedroom," he said, to clarify his meaning.

Farley's laughter followed him out into the hallway and up the stairs.

Chapter Twenty-seven

When Alexandria awoke, the afternoon sun was streaming through the bedroom window. She sat up quickly, looking about her in total confusion. She saw a man's gray coat thrown carelessly across the back of a chair and a pair of black boots setting on the floor. It took her only a moment to realize she was in Tag's bedroom!

What was she doing here? She tried to remember, but her mind was so fuzzy, and her head was hurting something fierce. She searched the deep recesses of her mind, and in a flash she remembered some of the events of the previous evening. Barbara and Rodney had taken her back to the house on Front Street! She couldn't seem to remember anything past the time Rodney had given her a drink, which she now knew had been drugged. Everything else was a hazy nightmare, and she didn't know what had happened to her.

Feeling something warm resting against her breast, she looked down and discovered she was wearing her mother's cameo necklace. Her face flamed red when she realized the necklace was all she had on.

Alexandria moved off the bed and tried to stand up. When she attempted to take a step, she felt the room whirling and caught onto the bedpost to steady herself. After several attempts, she managed to put her gown on and fasten it up the front.

"Dear Lord, what has happened to me?" she whimpered. "What am I doing in Tag's bedroom?" she cried aloud.

As hard as she tried to remember the events of the previous night, she could remember no more than vague shadows and dark illusions.

The door opened softly, and Alexándria whirled around to see Mrs. Green enter the room carrying a tray of food.

"My poor little dear," the older woman said as she laid the tray aside and helped Alexandria back to bed. "You had an awful experience last night, but you are safe now, the saints be praised."

Alexandria lay back against the oak headboard, her confusion reflected in her golden eyes. "Can you tell me what happened, Mrs. Green? I don't seem to remember."

"Don't you worry your pretty head about anything. I have instructions that you are to do nothing but rest for today." Mrs. Green touched her forehead to see if she was feverish but found it cool to the touch. "I was the most surprised woman alive when Farley told me that you were a girl instead of the boy I thought you to be."

Alexandria looked into the kind, soft eyes of the housekeeper, feeling guilty that she had deceived her. "I'm sorry, Mrs. Green," was all she could manage to say.

The housekeeper's eyes were dancing merrily. "Nonsense! You have no reason to feel sorry. You just

358

eat the food on your tray and try to get your strength back."

When the housekeeper placed the tray on Alexandria's lap and handed her a napkin, the girl caught her by the hand. "Please tell me what happened to me, Mrs. Green. How did I come to be in this bedroom?"

"All I know is that the strange seaman that's been hanging around here spying on Mr. James came bursting in last night insisting you had been carried off by your stepmother and stepbrother. Mr. James and Farley left here with the man, and when they returned, you were with them."

Alexandria stared at Mrs. Green. The housekeeper had called Tag by his right name. That would mean that she knew about Tag's past. "I . . . wish I could remember what happened," she said, placing her hand over her eyes.

"Don't trouble your head about such things. I'm quite sure when Mr. James returns he will explain everything to you. Right now, you should eat a good meal and then do nothing but rest for the remainder of the day."

Tag had seen Farley off to Valley Forge, where he would have to ask directions to Meadowlake, with instructions to make sure Alexandria's stepmother and stepbrother didn't return to her farm. Alexandria had once told Tag that all the servants at the farm were loyal to Barbara, so Mrs. Green and several of the other servants were to follow Farley the next day, to set the place in order and hire new help. If Alexandria decided she wanted to return to her farm, he didn't want her to have to worry about anything.

Tag pulled his horse up and dismounted. He had decided to pay a visit to Claudia to see what was happening with her. He suspected she was somehow involved in Alexandria's abduction. If it were true, that would be one more sin he would lay at Claudia's door. The chips were rapidly stacking against her, and the time was drawing near when Tag would call on her to cash them in.

Before he could knock on the door it swung open, and Mrs. Dodson faced him. "Mrs. Landon isn't receiving visitors today, Mr. Knight. The house is in mourning. You see, Mr. Landon passed away last night."

Tag's eyes narrowed, and Mrs. Dodson shivered at the coldness in the blue depths. "Tell Mrs. Landon I am here. I think she will want to see me."

In no time at all, Mrs. Dodson returned and led Tag upstairs. She left him in front of Claudia's bedroom door with a disapproving frown on her face.

Not bothering to knock, Tag pushed the door open and entered the darkened room. It took him a moment to see Claudia huddled in a chair near the window. Her hair was tangled and hung lankly about her ghostly-white face. As Tag approached her, he could see that her eyes were wild with terror.

He towered above Claudia and looked down at her, unable to hide his look of contempt. "I understand condolences are in order, Claudia." he said in a cold voice.

Her head snapped up, and she stared at Tag as if she didn't really see him. "He's gone. Howard's dead. and it's my fault. I didn't know he would have such a

360

violent reaction when I sent Alexandria away. I'm lost and have nowhere to go. I will be put out in the cold."

Tag knelt down and grabbed her arm. "Don't crack up on me now, Claudia. I want your mind to be clear when we have our little talk."

She grasped his shirtfront and leaned her head against his shoulder. "You have to help me, Falcon. I'm surrounded by enemies. Everyone wants to see me dead!"

He dislodged her hands and forced her to look at him. "Not everyone, Claudia. I don't want you to die. I want you to live to be a very old woman."

"You're the only one who I can turn to, Falcon. When it's learned that Howard is dead, I'll be asked to leave this house. What shall I do?"

"Do nothing for now. Just try to pull yourself together. The harder ordeal is ahead of you, Claudia. Prepare yourself for a battle you will never forget."

Claudia looked at him in confusion. "I don't know what you mean, Falcon."

He stood up. "No matter—in time everything will be made clear to you."

Tag left the room and stepped out into the hallway. He went to the bedroom that Howard had occupied, opened the door, and walked to the portrait that hung over the mantel. As his gaze swept each member of his family, his thoughts were in a turmoil. One of the enemy was dead and the other was very close to losing her mind. He wanted Claudia to be in full possession of her faculties before he moved in for the final blow. Deep inside Tag, there was a strong bitterness that his hadn't been the hand that had ended the life of his father's murderer. His eyes traced Joanna's face, and he remembered the anguish his sister had suffered because of Howard Landon. He could now close that chapter of his life and concentrate his efforts on Claudia. In a way, he supposed there was some kind of justice in Howard's death, after all. Somehow he found satisfaction in the fact that one of the enemies was responsible for the death of the other. He knew that Joanna had long ago put her bitterness aside. It was he who had been eaten up with hatred for all these years. He still had one more debt to settle before he could be at peace with himself.

When Alexandria stepped out of the bathing tub, she was feeling much better. She dried herself off, then combed the tangles from her wet hair. The gown she had worn the day before had been washed and pressed by Mrs. Green, and Alexandria slipped it over her head and buttoned it up the front.

It was late in the day when she finally made her way downstairs. Mrs. Green had told her that neither Tag nor Farley were at home, and she felt restless. There were so many things she wanted to know . . . so much that she didn't remember. She watched the clock on the mantel tick the minutes away, thinking that if someone didn't tell her what was going on, she would explode!

Alexandria was sitting down to a solitary dinner when Tag finally came home. He entered the dining room and sat down beside her, looking at her inquiringly.

"I have been waiting for you to come home all day," she said accusingly. "Please tell me what has been going on. Mrs. Green has been close-mouthed and refuses to tell me anything."

Tag looked away from her and waited for Mrs. Green to place a plate of food in front of him and leave the room before he replied. "Tell me, how much do you remember about last night, Alexandria?"

"I remember nothing much past Rodney's giving me some kind of drink. I believe he drugged me."

"Yes, I'm sure of it. You were in no condition to know what was going on last night."

Alexandria pushed a piece of meat around her plate with her fork. "Yes. I just can't remember what happened." She lifted her eyes to his. "Tag, tell me before I lose my mind. Was . . . did . . . I . . . was I married last night?"

He smiled slightly. "Oh, yes, most assuredly you were married last night. I myself was a witness to the ceremony."

Alexandria lowered her head. "I cannot stand the thought of being married to that odious man. I will never live with him as his wife, and no one can make me!" she cried, burying her face in her hands.

Tag's good humor startled her. His laughter caused her head to snap up. "I have been called many things in my life, Alexandria, but never odious. As for living with me as my wife, that will be your choice."

"I don't understand . . . you just said that . . ."

"I said, my dear wife, that I was a witness to your marriage. I didn't tell you that I was also the groom."

Alexandria's amber eyes widened in shock. She didn't know whether to laugh or cry. She had thought he was implying she had married Rodney, but had he not called her *his* wife? "I'm confused. What are you saying?"

Tag took a bite of the meat on his plate, chewed it up and swallowed before he answered. Alexandria watched him expectantly.

He watched the different emotions play across her lovely face while he told her all that had occurred the evening before. When he finished talking, Alexandria pushed her plate back and stared into his eyes in total confusion.

"Forgive me, Tag. It seems I have caused you nothing but problems since the first night we met. I'm sorry you were forced to marry me. That must be the last thing you wanted to do."

Her amber eyes were wet with tears, and he wanted to tell her that he didn't mind being her husband in the least. In fact, he had been anxious and unsure as to how she would take the news of being his wife. Many times that day he had wanted to return home so he could tell her of the love in his heart. The fact that he didn't know how she felt about him halted his confession.

"I admit you have been trouble for me, but there was never anything I couldn't handle."

"I won't hold you to the marriage, Tag," she said, looking at him with earnest eyes. "I know what your feelings were for Morning Song. If I am free to go, as you say, I will be returning to the farm as soon as possible," she said, giving him an easy way out of their situation.

"Why don't we wait a few days for you to make that decision. I'm afraid I have some news that's going to upset you."

"It's Mr. Landon, isn't it?" she stated, with uncanny insight. "He's dead."

"I'm afraid so, Alexandria."

She stood up and walked to the window. "I know you hated him, Tag, and with every reason . . . but I grew to care for him. At the end, he was nothing more than a sick old man wanting to make amends for all he had done to you and your sister."

Tag walked over to her and turned her to face him. "Don't ask me to feel sorry that he's dead. I will always remember that he was responsible for the death of my father. You might have felt pity for him, but I can never forget how he treated me and my sister."

Alexandria thought about her meeting with Tag's father. It was true that Mr. Landon had committed many sins in the past, but he hadn't killed Russell James as Tag thought. She did not voice her thoughts, however, since Mr. James had asked her to not to say anything to Tag. "Time has a way of taking care of the ills of the world in one way or another, Tag."

He raised her chin and brushed the tears from her cheeks, smiling down at her. "So young, and yet so wise. I believe that you have touched my life as no other person ever has, Alexandria." He brushed her forehead with his lips.

Alexandria closed her eyes, knowing that though the man she loved was her husband, they would never be as one. Too much stood between them. Morning Song would always be there in his mind. Alexandria knew Tag had only married her to save her from Rodney and Barbara, not because he desired her as his wife.

"Tag, I just want to say again how grateful I am to you. I wish you hadn't found it necessary to marry me

365

last night. I give you my word, when I return to Meadowlake, I will never trouble you again."

His grip tightened on her shoulders, and he pushed her away. "I suppose now that you are cleared of all charges against you, you will be happy to pick up your old life. I am not so fortunate; there is still much to do before I can pick up my life again."

"I will stay and help you, if you wish, Tag," she said, hoping against hope he would ask her to stay.

"Do as you will," he said, moving past her and walking out of the room.

Alexandria placed her hands up to her face, feeling more confused than ever. What did he want her to do. Go . . . or stay? There was no way she would ever understand Tag. He just wouldn't allow her to get too close to him. How she envied his dead wife, Morning Song. She had died having known great love. Just once, Alexandria wished Tag's eyes would soften when he looked at her the way they always did when he spoke of Morning Song.

Claudia had managed to pull herself together after Falcon's visit. She had sent for her lawyer, Melvin Garner, and they had been discussing what they should do now that Howard was dead and Taggart James had returned.

"I can't see how you are going to be able to hang on to this house much longer, Claudia. The time will come when Taggart James will come out in the open, and you, my dear, will be in a lot of trouble."

"Is there nothing I can do?"

"Oh, yes, there is quite a lot you can do. I suggest you start accumulating all the cash you can—discreetly, of course. There are three ships in drydock at the James Shipyard that are ready to launch. I believe I can find a buyer for them, and they should bring a tidy sum. There are some very expensive pieces of furniture and paintings in this house that you could sell. If we are careful, we could come out of this in good condition."

"What do you mean *we* . . . Melvin?"

"Just what I implied, Claudia. *We* are in this together all the way. I am the only one who understands you. I know you have been panting after that Falcon Knight, but you don't really think he will marry you, do you?"

Claudia's eyes blazed. "He cares about me—I know he does. Did he not come to me when he heard about Howard's death? That is more than I can say for any of my other so-called friends. They are all like a bunch of rats deserting a sinking ship."

"You and I are the rats, Claudia. We are two of a kind. I'm afraid you are stuck with me whether you like it or not. I'm your only true friend."

"You're only sticking around because you smell money! You would leave me like all the rest of them if you thought I was penniless."

"Just as long as we understand one another, my dear," he said, removing a cheroot from his vest pocket and lighting it.

Mrs. Dodson came into the room and leaned close to Claudia's ear. "There's a gentleman at the front door who says his name is Rodney Wilson. Do you want to see him or shall I send him away? He says it's urgent."

"Tell him to go away," Claudia said, not wanting to

speak to the man.

"I told him you were in mourning, but he insists you'll want to hear what happened to Alexandria."

"Oh, very well, show him in," Claudia said ungraciously.

"Who is this Rodney Wilson?" Melvin asked with interest.

"No one—just a nuisance."

Rodney entered the room, nervously twisting his cap in his hand. The scar on his face seemed redder than it had the night before. "Mrs. Landon, thank you for seeing me. I knew you would want to know what's happened to Alexandria."

"What's the matter—did the chit run away again?" she asked, with little interest. "Don't expect me to help you find her again."

"No, ma'am, she didn't run away. Three men came bursting into my aunt's house just as I was about to marry her. They held a gun on me, while one of the gentlemen forced the parson to marry him to Alexandria."

"What's this?" Claudia said, her interest piqued at last. "What man?"

"I never saw him before in my life. He told the parson his name was Taggart James!"

Claudia gasped, and her eyes became wild with fear. "What are you saying?" she cried. "Why would Tag want to marry Alexandria? It makes no sense!"

"I don't know if that's his real name. My aunt told us he once came to the house using another name."

Melvin spoke up. "What name?"

"I can't recall; something like a bird, I think."

"Was the name Falcon Knight?" Melvin asked,

with a sneer on his face.

"Yes, that's it . . . Falcon Knight!" Rodney said, nodding his head in agreement.

A loud, piercing scream issued from Claudia's lips, and she flew across the room and threw herself at Rodney. Before Melvin could drag her away, she was pounding against the man's chest.

"You lie! You lie! Falcon Knight could *never* be Taggart James! Falcon cares about me. Why are you saying these lies to me?"

It took all Melvin's strength to keep Claudia away from Rodney Wilson. "I think you had better leave now," Melvin told the badly shaken Rodney, who was only too happy to make a speedy retreat.

When Claudia and Melvin were alone, he shook her hard, trying to calm her down. When that didn't bring the desired results, he slapped her several times, and she collapsed against him. Helping her to the couch, he sat down beside her.

"Well, one thing has come from all this, Claudia. We now know who the enemy is!"

"No, it can't be true—I don't want to believe it. Not Falcon!" she cried.

"I'm afraid your Falcon Knight was only using you to gain information. You know he's Taggart James!"

"But I loved him," she cried, trying to associate the handsome, golden-haired man with the twelve-year-old boy she had hated so avidly!

"If you will stop and think, Claudia, you will see the advantage we now have. Taggart James doesn't know we are on to him. The possibilities are limitless, if we put our heads together and plan."

Suddenly, Claudia started laughing hysterically.

Once again, she had come up the loser, just as she always had with Joanna. Alexandria had ended up with the man Claudia loved, and she would make them both pay! Falcon had made a fool of her, and she intended to see him dead. She hadn't even been aware that Falcon . . . no, Tag . . . *knew* Alexandria.

"Tell me what we should do, Melvin," she said, as her eyes sparkled with renewed life. Claudia always seemed to thrive on hatred.

Her eyes clouded as she remembered the day Alexandria had wheeled Howard into the garden and Falcon had been there. The two of them must have contrived the meeting. Her mouth flew open and a strangled cry issued from her throat. Howard had known who Falcon was all the time! That was why he invited him to come to his bedroom that night.

"They were all in this together!" she screamed. "I will see Tag and Alexandria in their graves! He deceived me by making me love him. You will pay, Taggart James—you will pay with your life!" Claudia screamed.

Chapter Twenty-eight

A week had passed since the night Tag and Alexandria had been married. The house was silent, and Alexandria found that time lay heavily on her hands. She had spent the morning in the garden weeding the flower beds, and later in the day she ate a solitary lunch.

Tag was very rarely at home, and Farley was still at Meadowlake. Since Mrs. Green was also at the farm, and the two remaining servants were busy trying to keep the big house running smoothly, there was no one for Alexandria to talk to, and she was feeling neglected.

Alexandria made her way to the stable, thinking she would take a ride on one of Tag's horses. Perhaps it would help her clear her mind and give her a fresh outlook. After Tom, the man who tended the stables, had saddled a gray mare, Alexandria mounted and rode away at a steady pace. The estate wasn't very extensive, and she soon felt the longing to ride in open country. Tag had cautioned her about leaving the grounds, but she saw no harm in riding past the gate. She would just ride a ways down the hill and then return to the house.

As the hooves of the big gray beat out a rhythmic sound on the road and the wind ruffled Alexandria's hair, she began to feel more lighthearted. She was from the country and was becoming stifled by living in town.

She had been married to the man she loved for over a week, but not once in that time had he came near her bedroom, nor had he given the slightest hint that she would be welcome in his. Knowing he had married her only to protect her, Alexandria realized theirs would always be a marriage in name only. She couldn't understand why Tag had wanted to make love to her before they had been married, but didn't come near her now that she was his wife.

Even though Tag hadn't confided in Alexandria, she knew he was spending his days planning how to recover his estates and shipyards from Claudia. It was as though they were all waiting for the final chapter in a book. No one knew how the book would read between now and the end.

Alexandria couldn't help feeling sad over the death of Mr. Landon. No matter what he had done in the past, she would always remember him for his kindness to her. She doubted that anyone besides herself would mourn his passing.

Alexandria knew that she should be feeling relieved now that the threat of Barbara and Rodney was no longer hanging over her head, but she wasn't. She was for frightened for Tag. Soon he would reveal his true identity to Claudia. When that day came, he would be in real danger. She wished Farley would return—she felt better with the old trapper around to keep an eye on Tag.

Alexandria hadn't seen Russell James since that night in the garden, but she knew he would be around somewhere, watching over his son. She was grateful to him for the part he had played in her daring rescue, and she wished she could see him to tell him so.

Alexandria could see a coach approaching from the opposite direction and she moved out of the road to allow it to pass. She paid little attention to the people who occupied the coach as the flying dust from its wheels stung her face.

She often wondered what Tag would do when he found out his father was alive. Surely he would be overjoyed, and perhaps it would erase some of the bitterness he carried around in his heart. She tried to imagine what he must have been like before Morning Song had been killed. Had he laughed a lot? Had his days been filled with happiness? Her mind shied away from thinking what his nights had been like.

Alexandria had been so deep in thought that she hadn't realized she had ridden so far from the house. Turning the gray homeward, she allowed the animal to gallop at top speed.

As Alexandria rode along, she wondered about Tag's baby daughter. He never mentioned the child, and she had never even heard him call her by name. She wished with all her heart that he would give her a chance to raise his daughter. Legally, she was the child's stepmother. She made herself a promise that if she were ever allowed to care for the child, she would love her as if she were her very own. But Alexandria doubted she would ever get that chance. Tag hadn't actually said anything, but she suspected that when this ordeal was over he would be returning to the

373

Blackfoot tribe, and she doubted that he would ask her to accompany him.

Just ahead of her, Alexandria saw the coach that had passed her earlier. It had pulled over to the side of the road. Thinking they might be having trouble, she halted the horse to see if she could offer them some assistance. Seeing no one about, she started to ride on when she heard a woman's voice call out for help from the other side of the coach. Without thinking, Alexandria dismounted and ran around the coach. She had no time to react as a hand reached from behind her and clamped over her mouth. She kicked and struggled, trying to get loose, but the man who held her was much too strong. When she saw a woman come from behind the bushes that grew beside the road, Alexandria recognized Claudia.

"Hurry up and put her in the coach, Melvin, before we're seen," Claudia said, watching the roadway nervously.

Alexandria renewed her struggle, but she soon found it was useless to fight. What a fool she had been to disobey Tag when he told her not to leave the grounds. She didn't have the slightest notion what Claudia and Melvin wanted with her, but she knew that whatever it was, it wouldn't be anything pleasant. As Melvin tossed her into the coach, she could see the house only a short distance away. She realized that if she hadn't been so foolish, she would have been safely back at the stables by now.

Claudia climbed into the seat opposite her while Melvin seated himself beside Alexandria, keeping a firm grip on her arm so she wouldn't try to escape. A coachman seemed to appear from out of nowhere, and

374

the coach lurched forward.

"Why are you doing this, Claudia?" Alexandria demanded to know. "What right have you got to force me into this coach? You had better let me out right now!"

"Shut up!" Claudia hissed, swinging her hand wide and catching Alexandria a stunning blow across the face.

Alexandria's temper flared, and she struggled to get at Claudia but Melvin Garner held her firm.

"You shouldn't strike such a lovely flower, Claudia," Melvin said in a silky voice. The man looked at Alexandria with appreciation in his eyes. "I had no idea that she was such a comely young lady."

"I won't hear this from you, Melvin. Is beauty all you men ever have on your mind? I see nothing unusual about Alexandria."

His eyes drifted across Alexandria's face, and he looked into her golden eyes, eyes that at the moment were hostile and defiant. "If you were a man, Claudia, you would appreciate what a rare jewel our little captive is," he said in a caressing voice. His hand slid up Alexandria's arm, and she shuddered.

"Take your hands off me!" Alexandria demanded. "I insist you stop this coach right now and let me out!"

"I'm afraid that won't be possible, my dear. You see, you will be the lovely bait Claudia and I will use to snare your husband, Taggart James!"

Alexandria looked quickly at Claudia and saw the satisfied smile on her face. "I . . . don't know what you are talking about. I know no one by the name of Taggart James."

"How prettily she lies to protect her husband," Melvin taunted. "Would you do as much for me, Claudia?"

"If you were standing on the gallows, Melvin, I would be the one to pull the platform from under you," Claudia said spitefully.

"Tut, tut, do you want our guest to think we don't hold each other in high regard?"

Claudia turned her attention to Alexandria. The hatred she had once directed at Joanna had been transferred to the small, golden-eyed girl. She saw the red handprint on the girl's white cheek where she had struck her, and she wished she could scratch her eyes out.

"Why are you doing this, Claudia?" Alexandria asked, fearing that through her these two might find a way to harm Tag.

"Melvin already told you—we are going to use you to lure Tag into a trap. How will you like being the cause of his death, Alexandria?"

"I told you I don't know anyone by the name of Tag. Why don't you just admit you made a mistake, and let me go?"

Claudia turned her gaze out the window of the coach, and Melvin chuckled to himself. Alexandria wondered how Claudia had found out about Tag. She struggled, trying to reach the door, but was pulled back, only to land hard against Melvin.

"Do that again, Alexandria. I like to feel you in my arms," Melvin said caressingly.

Alexandria moved as far away as she could from the odious Melvin. She closed her eyes and prayed for Tag's safety. She wouldn't be able to live with herself

376

if anything should happen to him because of her carelessness!

They had been traveling for some time, and it was now almost sundown. Alexandria looked out the coach window and saw that they were at some kind of shipping yard. She assumed it would be the shipbuilding firm that belonged to Tag and the James family.

When the coach came to a halt, Melvin opened the door and pulled Alexandria out of the coach. She saw the shipyard was deserted. It was late in the day; all the workers had gone home for the day. For the first time since she had been captured, Alexandria began to feel fear for herself. She was being led toward the water's edge to a big ship that was riding high in the water. As she was led up the gangplank, she tried to pull back, but Melvin lifted her into his arms and carried her on board.

He carried her down the companionway and into the deep hold of the ship. The only light they had was a lantern that Claudia carried to light their path. When they reached what Alexandria was sure was the very bowels of the ship, Melvin placed her on her feet.

"Surely you aren't going to leave me here," she said in a shaky voice.

"Alas, I fear we must, pretty lady, but have no fear—there is water to drink, and you will have this lantern until it runs out of fuel."

Claudia looked about the dank, dark hull and shivered. "Never fear, your husband will soon be joining you, Alexandria. This is the last sight you and Tag will ever see before you die."

Claudia set the lantern down, and then she and Melvin left, bolting the door behind them.

Alexandria clamped her hand over her mouth to keep from crying out. Terror such as she had never known encased her mind. Her legs were shaking so badly she sank down to her knees. She was in a circle of light, and the rest of the big ship was in total darkness.

"Dear God," she prayed aloud, "don't let me die like this." She thought of Tag and how much she loved him. As much as she hated being here alone, she prayed that Tag wouldn't suffer the same fate. "Oh, Tag, don't do anything foolish!" she cried, and her voice echoed and reechoed throughout the darkened hull of the ship.

Alexandria was overcome by a feeling of utter desertion. She knew that the next day was Sunday and the men who worked at the shipyard wouldn't be coming to work. As the ship swayed up and down with the restless motion of the water, she reached over and turned down the wick of the lantern, wanting to conserve the fuel as long as possible. She had a horror of the lantern's going out, of being left in total darkness. As the flame became smaller, so did the circle of light that surrounded her.

Alexandria's body trembled with pent-up emotion, and loud sobs broke from her lips.

"Tag, Tag, my dearest love!" she cried, pounding against the unyielding door with her fists. "I don't want you to be here with me, but I do wish I could see you just once more if I'm going to die!"

Tag ran through the house, calling Alexandria's name even though he knew she wouldn't answer. Tom, the stableman, had told him that the gray Alexandria had been riding earlier had returned over two hours ago. Tom and two of the stableboys had searched for Alexandria until dark without finding any trace of her.

It was Tag's hope that she had been thrown and had made her way back to the house on foot, but there was no answer from Alexandria, and none of the servants had seen her.

After riding out himself without finding any trace of her, Tag returned to the house, not knowing what to do next. His first thought had been that her stepmother was somehow involved in Alexandria's disappearance. Before returning to the house, he had ridden by Annabelle Norris's house, only to find that the place was boarded up. On inquiring about Barbara's whereabouts from the neighbors, Tag had been told that she and her family had left several days earlier.

Tag paced back and forth, waiting for any news of Alexandria. He felt helpless, not knowing where to look. He had visions of her lying injured somewhere, even though every inch of the surrounding countryside had been searched thoroughly.

When a knock sounded on the front door, he rushed forward to answer it, hoping there would be some news of Alexandria. The small boy who stood outside handed Tag a letter and darted off into the night without saying a word.

Tag rushed back inside, broke open the letter, and began to read:

Tag, it is known who you are. That which you hold most dear is in my hands. If you want her back unharmed, you must come to the James shipyard on the stroke of midnight and we will talk over the terms of her release. You are being watched, so tell no one where you are going, and come alone if you want your wife back unharmed.

The letter was unsigned, but Tag knew it would be from Melvin Garner. Since Claudia could neither read nor write, he knew Mr. Garner was in on Alexandria's abduction with Claudia.

Glancing at the clock on the wall, he saw it was now ten-thirty. He raced to the study to get his guns and made sure they were loaded before pushing them down into his belt.

He bounded onto his horse and quickly galloped off into the night. He wished that Farley were with him. What he must do now, he would do alone. He would trust to his instincts and his Indian training to get Alexandria back.

His mind was tortured about Alexandria's safety. What if they had already harmed her? He knew what Claudia was capable of when she was crossed, and he could only imagine her anger now, since she obviously knew he had posed as Falcon Knight to get close to her.

Even though Tag was anxious to reach the shipyard, he chose the longer route, which skirted the town. His Indian training alerted him to the fact that he was being followed. In the dim light of the crescent moon, Tag planned how he would outsmart whoever was closing in behind him.

When he rounded a bend in the road, he grabbed onto a low-hanging branch, swinging himself skillfully up into the tree. His Indian pony, Navaron, had

380

been trained well, and when Tag left the animal's back, the horse didn't even break his stride but kept racing down the road.

In no time at all, a lone rider rounded the bend, and when the man passed beneath the tree, Tag leaped down upon him, knocking him off his horse. The two men rolled over and over down a steep embankment and ended up with Tag on top. With very little trouble, Tag subdued the man. Even in the pale moonlight, Tag could tell he had never seen the man before. Doubling up his fists, he struck him across the jaw and felt the man go limp beneath him.

Tag quickly gained his feet and raced back up the embankment. He gave a loud whistle and was soon rewarded by the sound of Navaron's thundering hooves coming toward him. He swung into the saddle and galloped away, heading for the shipyards.

Claudia watched Melvin's face as he blew out the lamp in the shack where the shipbuilding tools were kept. She was angry with him because he had just taken over without consulting her. She would much rather have lured Tag into a different kind of trap. Her pride still stung from the way he had trapped her into loving him, and she knew she wouldn't be satisfied until she made him crawl.

Melvin led Claudia out of the shed and steered her toward the ship where Alexandria was being held. "We'll stand on the deck and wait for your man to come," he said, helping her up the gangplank.

She turned to him when they reached the deck of the ship. "Are the men in place?"

"Yes, they are standing by at the gates. Don't

worry, Claudia, Taggart James will be surrounded the moment he comes into the shipyard."

"I wish there was a full moon tonight—I can't see anything," Claudia said, straining her eyes in the near darkness.

Melvin laughed. "Before the night is over, you will have seen all that's important to see. If things go as I planned, by this time tomorrow night you will be a very wealthy woman, and Tag and his lady will be carried out to sea where their bodies will become bait for the fish."

Claudia shivered. She had never liked the sea, and as a child had often had nightmares about drowning. "I'll be glad when it's all over," she said, more to herself than to Melvin.

Melvin's arm went about her waist. "We are going to be wealthy, Claudia. We can get married, and you can have all the things you ever wanted. How will you like that?"

She felt his thick lips on her neck and had the urge to push him away. How dare he think he could run her life! For the time being, though, she needed his help. After this was all over she would rid herself of him for good!

"Claudia, what if Taggart James doesn't come?"

Her eyes pierced the darkness. "He'll come . . . oh, yes, he'll come. Nothing can keep him away. I just hope we haven't underestimated him."

Tag had seen the dozen or so men who were hiding near the front entrance of the shipping yard. He smiled to himself as he dismounted and slipped over the back fence to fade into the shadows. He knew the shipyards very well, since his father had often brought him here as a child. He had overheard the men talking and had gathered from their conversation that Alexandria was being held on board one of the two new ships that were at anchor in the water.

Keeping well into the shadows, he made his way silently down to the water's edge.

Alexandria huddled against the wall of the ship, shivering. The lantern had gone out some time ago, and she was now in total darkness. She suppressed a sob and closed her eyes. She had never been in such total darkness before, and she felt as if she were in a tomb in the bottom of the ship. Having no way of knowing how much time had passed since she had been locked in, she didn't know if it was day or night.

Alexandria wished someone would come. Anyone! She longed to hear another human's voice.

She tried to think about the times she had ridden across the pastures at Meadowlake with the sun beaming down on her face. What she wouldn't give to see the sun right now!

Alexandria's throat felt parched and dry, and she wished she knew where to find the water container to quench the burning in her throat. She didn't dare move from the wall of the ship because it was too dark and she had the feeling she would wander around for eternity in this living hell.

She tried to force herself to think of something pleasant, but her mind seemed always to center on Tag and the danger he might be in at this very moment. She knew he would come, because he was fearless and never seemed to stop and measure the danger of a situation. She remembered the night in the tavern when he had come to her rescue against the huge, burly sailor and knew he wouldn't hesitate to come to the shipyard to face Claudia. Surely Tag would realize that Claudia and Melvin Garner had set a trap for him.

Alexandria felt the cold dampness seep into her bones and knew the feeling of utter hopelessness. As frightened as she was, she knew she would rather die here alone in the darkness than have Tag share her fate.

The shipyard, with its dark shadows and eerie silence, seemed like something out of a nightmare to Claudia. She stepped closer to Melvin, trying to draw comfort from his nearness. She thought of Alexandria in the bottom of the ship and found malicious pleasure in knowing the girl was now paying for what Claudia considered crimes against her. In punishing Alexandria, it was almost as if she were striking a blow against Joanna. Even with everything that was at stake here tonight, Claudia's main thoughts were still of Joanna. Her hatred for her had grown and festered all these years, and her one regret tonight was that Joanna wouldn't be here to witness her brother's death. Claudia had always been a little in awe of the love the brother and sister had shown for each other. She would make sure that Joanna heard of her brother's death; then perhaps Joanna herself would come to Philadelphia and Claudia could have her final victory!

"Don't turn around or cry out, either of you," a menacing voice said from the shadows behind Claudia and Melvin.

In spite of the warning, Claudia turned to see Tag step up beside her.

"Take me to my wife," he demanded in a voice that was cold and threatening. "If either one of you makes a wrong move, it will be your last," he said, pointing the guns he held in his hands at Claudia and Melvin.

Chapter Twenty-nine

The sound of footsteps atop ship caught Alexandria's attention over the shifting and groaning of the ship riding on the water. She listened carefully, hoping her ears weren't playing tricks on her. She was sure of it now—someone was on board, and they were making their way down to her!

Standing up, she found her legs stiff and cramped, so she had to hold on to the wall of the ship to keep her balance.

Thinking it might be Claudia and Melvin Garner returning, she felt around in the darkness until she found the lantern. Flattening herself against the wall, she lifted it up over her head so she could use it as a weapon against them in hopes of making her escape.

Hearing a grating sound just outside, Alexandria waited for the door to open. When it swung wide, she had to close her eyes against the blinding light from the lantern. When she opened her eyes again, she saw it was indeed Claudia and Melvin. By now, she realized she had lost her advantage, for they were blocking the doorway.

Alexandria's eyes still hadn't become accustomed to the light, and she hadn't seen the man who stood just behind Claudia and Melvin.

"Alexandria!" The voice she loved so well, called out her name with obvious concern. Tag's voice seemed to echo around the empty hull of the ship, gladdening Alexandria's heart. "Are you unharmed?"

"Tag!" she cried, standing as if rooted to the spot. "You came!"

Tag shoved Claudia and Melvin through the entrance and moved to Alexandria's side while keeping the guns trained on the other two. "Are you all right?" he asked again. "Have they hurt you in any way?" He allowed his eyes to roam fleetingly across her face, just long enough to see that she was all right.

"I am unhurt," she said, moving closer to him. "I was frightened," she admitted.

Tag's eyes went to the woman who was responsible for abducting his wife, and Claudia could feel the chill of those eyes even in the half-light.

"You have a lot to answer for, Claudia," he said in a cold voice that sent shivers down her spine.

"It wasn't my idea to take Alexandria, Tag. Melvin was the instigator. Please believe me!" she pleaded, feeling the hand of death closing in all around her.

Tag stared at Claudia's companion with contempt. "Melvin Garner is nothing but your pawn, Claudia. He is someone you keep around to do your dirty work. I could easily crush him like a bug."

Melvin took a step forward, but the look Tag gave him made him reconsider.

"Tag, listen to me," Claudia pleaded, holding her hands out to him. "I didn't intend for your Indian wife to be killed. I only wanted to . . ."

"Shut up, Claudia," Melvin broke in. "He can't

prove a thing against either one of us."

Tag motioned for Claudia and Melvin to move away from the door, and he pushed Alexandria toward the exit. "I think the two of you will find it quite comfortable down here . . . at least, as comfortable as Alexandria found it."

"No, Tag, don't do this!" Claudia screamed. "I can't stand to be in darkness!"

"I doubt that it was all that much fun for my wife either, Claudia. You had no thought of Alexandria when you locked her down here."

"For God's sake, at least leave us a lantern," Melvin said, adding his plea to Claudia's.

"I don't think so. You see, it has always been my contention that one can think better in the darkness. You both have a lot to think about, do you not?"

Alexandria tugged at his sleeve, and he glanced down at her dear little face. "Tag, couldn't we leave the lantern with them?"

His eyes shifted back to Claudia. "You see how it is? My wife has a kind heart and, unlike you, doesn't like to see anyone suffer unduly. Because it is her wish, and for no other reason, I will leave you the lantern."

Tag pushed Alexandria out the door and turned to keep his guns trained on Claudia and Melvin. He didn't see the man who came up from behind him and clamped his hand around Alexandria's mouth, muffling her cry—nor did he hear the man who brought the heavy object down upon the back of his head, rendering him unconscious.

Again Alexandria was locked in the darkness of the

ship's hull, but this time, Tag suffered her same fate. She was sitting on the floor with his head resting on her lap. As her hand moved over his face, she could feel his steady breathing and was hopeful that he was merely unconscious.

Evidently some of Claudia's men had grown suspicious of the long delay and had come to investigate, thus catching Tag and her unawares. If only Tag would wake up, she thought, cradling his head against her breast and kissing his mouth. "Tag, I love you so much—wake up," she pleaded. She could feel his warm breath fan her cheek and knew he was still alive.

Claudia had said she would be returning shortly, and Alexandria knew she was only giving Tag time to regain consciousness before she finished with them.

Alexandria heard Tag groan, and she touched his cheek softly. "Tag, try not to move—you may have been injured."

"What happened?" he asked, sitting up slowly and staring into the darkness.

"Some men came up behind us, and Claudia had us locked in the ship. Are you all right, Tag?"

"I'm fine," he said, standing up slowly. "I don't suppose there is a way out of here."

"No, the only way out is the way we came in, and I heard some men talking beyond the door. I suppose they are guarding it. It doesn't seem Claudia is taking any chances that we might escape.

"I was a fool not to anticipate this happening, Alexandria. Windhawk taught me always to cover my back."

"You shouldn't have come at all, Tag. Didn't you

know they were only using me to get to you?"

He felt for her hand and pulled her up beside him. "They had something that belonged to me, and I had to get it back," he said, placing his cheek against hers.

"Me, Tag?"

"What else."

"I don't really belong to you, Tag. You were forced to make me your wife."

He closed his eyes. "Be that as it may, you are my wife until one of us decides differently. Until that day, it is my duty to protect you."

Alexandria had no time to reply because at that moment the door swung open, and Claudia and Melvin entered.

Tag pushed Alexandria behind him as he watched them advance on him.

"Well, well, it seems you are awake, and we have quite a little party prepared for you, Tag," Claudia taunted him.

"I never cared much for your little parties, Claudia. They were a bore," Tag responded sarcastically.

Claudia's eyes blazed with anger as she stepped in front of Tag and slapped him hard across the face. She expected anything from him but the laughter that issued from his lips.

"Thus speaks the scorned woman," he said in an amused voice.

"You will pay, Taggart James! No one makes a fool out of me and gets by with it," she hissed.

"I remember that Joanna always pitied you, Claudia. Myself . . . I never even liked you. I think you are the one who is paying," Tag said, knowing just how to bait Claudia. For some reason, Joanna had always been the object of her hatred, and he knew she wouldn't want to think Joanna pitied her.

A loud cry came from Claudia's lips. "How dare Joanna pity me! She is nothing—nothing!"

"Not so, Claudia—my sister is everything that you will never be."

Claudia whirled away and grabbed Melvin's arm, rambling like a madwoman. "Kill them—kill them both!"

"All in due time," Melvin said, moving to stand beside Tag. "Before you die, I have drawn up a document I would like you to sign. It merely states that you are leaving all your worldly goods to Claudia with me as the executor."

Tag smiled coldly. "Now why should I want to sign something like that?"

"Because you'll have no choice."

"You are a fool if you think there is anything you can do that will make me sign those papers. I have no fear of you or Claudia."

"No?" Melvin said, smiling slightly. "Take him men," Melvin ordered. "Hold him tight and don't allow him to get away."

Tag was immediately surrounded on all sides as six men grabbed him and held him fast.

"You will never make me relent, Garner. I would go to my death before I would leave to Claudia what belongs to me and my sister."

"Take the girl," Melvin called out, and before Alexandria could move, she was grabbed by two men who held her in a tight grip.

Tag struggled against the men who held him, but he knew it was useless. "If you harm my wife, I'll kill you if it's the last thing I ever do," he called out. For the first time he felt fear, not for himself, but for the woman he loved.

"You are in no position to harm anyone, Tag," Claudia said, grabbing a handful of mink-colored curls and jerking Alexandria's head backwards. Again her hatred for Joanna seemed to focus on this girl. One of the men who held Alexandria had a knife shoved into his belt, and Claudia grabbed it, holding the blade to Alexandria's throat.

"Will you sign or shall I slice her throat?"

"No, Tag, don't do it," Alexandria cried. "They will kill us anyway! Don't listen to them!" Alexandria didn't know from where her courage came. She only knew that if Tag could meet death bravely, then she would draw strength from him and do the same.

Tag strained against the men once more, but with very little effect. He blamed himself, knowing he should have kept a closer watch over Alexandria. He had known what Claudia was capable of doing. Why hadn't he given Alexandria better protection?

Melvin could see indecision in Tag's face, and he grabbed the knife from Claudia. "I once watched a man suffer unspeakable agony as his fingers were lobbed off one joint at a time. Do you think Alexandria would scream out for mercy if she were to suffer the same fate, Tag? Why don't we test her and find out?" Melvin grabbed Alexandria's hand and raised the knife.

Tag could see the horror in Alexandria's golden eyes as she looked at him. She was frightened, but no sound issued from her lips. In that moment, he felt pride in the tiny girl who had been called upon to face so many dangers since he had known her. Yes, he was proud of her, but he knew he could never allow Melvin to hurt her if he had the power to prevent it.

"You win. I'll sign whatever you want," he said, knowing he faced defeat.

"Now, you're making sense," Melvin said, tossing the knife on the floor and walking over to Tag. "Release him men, but keep a gun trained on the girl. If he makes a wrong move, shoot her!"

Claudia held the lantern up so the light fell onto the paper Melvin handed Tag. Tag didn't bother to read the document as he took the quill and signed his name across the bottom.

At that moment, there came the sound of gunfire from above, and all the men reached for their weapons. In the confusion, Tag leaped forward and grabbed Alexandria, pushing her against the wall and shielding her with his body.

Suddenly, twenty men came swarming through the door, and in no time at all the newcomers had subdued Claudia's men and held them at gunpoint. Claudia and Melvin were quickly tied up, and as silence fell across the room, a lone figure came through the door.

Alexandria exchanged glances with Tag as she recognized Russell James.

No one spoke as the tall red-headed man gazed across the room to make sure Tag and Alexandria were unharmed, nor was the silence broken as he moved over and picked up the piece of paper from the floor and studied it.

"This isn't legal," he said in a humorous voice. "It would never have stood up in court."

"Who are you?" Claudia asked. "Those men with you work in my shipping yard. Not one of you will retain your position if you don't help me!" she cried out.

Russell James looked at Claudia, a smile playing on his lips. "You are wrong, Mrs. Landon. These men work for me and have for years."

He walked over to Tag and Alexandria and smiled at the lovely young girl. "So we meet again, Alexandria. You keep turning up in the strangest places."

She smiled brightly. "And you keep coming to my rescue."

Russell James bowed slightly and gave her a roguish grin. "Someone has to keep an eye on you and this young man." He turned to his son and blue eyes locked with blue eyes. "As I stated before, this paper would never hold up in court."

Tag smiled, wondering who the hell this man was and who had appointed him his guardian. Whoever he was, Tag was damned glad he had shown up when he did.

"Why do you say that?" Tag asked, a slow grin spreading over his face.

"Because neither the house, nor the shipping yard belongs to you . . . not yet, anyway," Russell James stated.

"I'm not following you, unless you, like Claudia, want what belongs to me and my sister, Joanna."

"It's been a long time, Tag, but I had hoped you would know me anyway."

"I have never seen you before I returned to Philadelphia," Tag said, looking the man over carefully.

Russell James laughed again. "Will you tell this

young pup who I am, Alexandria? You see, Tag, our little girl here had seen me only in a portrait, and yet she still knew who I was right away. Go ahead . . . I give you leave to tell him, Alexandria."

Alexandria put her hand on Tag's shoulder. "Tag . . . this is Russell James . . . your father!"

Tag shook his head in disbelief as he stared at the big red-headed man. "What trick do you play? You cannot be my father—my father is dead!"

"No, I'm not dead, Tag, but there were times in the past that I wished I were. I'll tell you all about that later—right now, we have some business to finish."

Tag looked down at Alexandria, and she nodded and smiled. He couldn't understand what was happening, but he felt joy in his heart. He was afraid to believe that this man was really his father, and yet, some vague boyhood memory suddenly sparked to life within Tag. He was older than Tag remembered, but yes, he was his father.

"Father," he whispered, and the two men embraced. Tag felt a tightening in his throat, and Russell James felt tears wet his cheeks. Alexandria covered her face as tears flowed from her eyes. She was so happy that Tag and his father had at last been reunited.

There was no more time to talk as several uniformed authorities swarmed onto the ship to take the prisoners away. Claudia was led away struggling and screaming, carrying on like the madwoman she was.

Alexandria stepped up on deck, breathing in the fresh, clean morning air, thinking how good it was to be alive. She waited for Tag and his father to join her as she watched Claudia being taken away.

All at once, Claudia broke away from her captor and ran down the deck of the ship. Before anyone could stop her, she quickly climbed up on the railing and jumped overboard.

Alexandria ran to the railing and stared down into the water. She could see the waves rippling against the ship and strained her eyes to find Claudia. Suddenly Claudia surfaced and cried out as she struggled to stay afloat.

"Help me, someone—I can't swim!" Claudia cried.

Several men dived off the railing of the ship and swam toward the drowning woman, but Alexandria knew they wouldn't reach her in time. She watched as Claudia was swept away in the current, soon to be lost from sight.

Alexandria shuddered and closed her eyes as she felt Tag come up beside her. She heard him mutter softly.

"It is ended, Morning Song," he said, not realizing he had spoken aloud. "Your spirit can now be at peace."

Russell James placed his arm around Alexandria's shoulder. "Let's go home, my dear—it's all over," he said in a kind voice, hugging her to him.

Alexandria had bathed, eaten a light supper in her room, and had now fallen into an exhausted sleep. The horrible ordeal of the last two days had taken its toll on her, and her sleep was deep.

Tag and his father sat in the study getting reacquainted over glasses of brandy.

"I suppose you will be wanting to move onto the estate tomorrow," Tag said, still unable to believe his

396

father was actually alive. Now as he gazed at his father's face it stirred many boyhood memories, and he wondered why he hadn't recognized him at once. He supposed it was because he had believed him to be dead.

"No, not until the whole house has been completely redecorated and every stick of furniture replaced. I have an aversion to living in that house until it has been restored to its original beauty," his father told him.

"You've been inside then?"

Russell smiled. "Yes, on several occasions, but unknown to the Landons, of course." He took a sip of his brandy and set the glass down. "You have grown into a fine young man, Tag. Tell me . . . where is Joanna?"

Tag leaned back, knowing the rest of the night would be spent in recalling the past and telling his father about Joanna and Windhawk and Morning Song—about their life and the Blackfoot Indians.

Russell listened to his son speak, interrupting him every so often to ask a question. It was hard for him to visualize his daughter married to an Indian, but when Tag told him how Windhawk had saved his and Joanna's life, the objections he felt seemed to diminish. He could hear the love and respect in his son's voice when he spoke of Windhawk.

Tag told his father of his own marriage to Morning Song and about her tragic death.

After he had finished speaking, both men lapsed into silence for a long time. Finally Russell spoke. "I can hardly imagine being a grandfather. I hope you will understand that I am a bit horrified by the fact that my daughter is married to an Indian and my grandchildren are all half-breeds. I suppose at one time in my life I would have strongly objected, but I have lived a lifetime and have seen many things. Hopefully learned a few things."

"I think you will like Windhawk, Father. He is like no man I have ever known, whether he be white or Indian."

"Well, I'm sure as hell going to find out. I have every intention of seeing your sister. I will expect you to take me to her."

Tag smiled. "I thought you might feel that way."

"We will leave as soon as I put things in order here. Will we take Alexandria with us?" Russell asked, watching his son's face closely.

"I . . . don't know, Father. She may not want to go."

"Why don't you ask her and find out?"

"I think because I'm afraid she will say no."

"She is quite a lady, this wife of yours. If I were you, I wouldn't let her slip away."

Tag looked at the ceiling for a moment and then back to his father. "Tell me, what have you been doing all these years? We thought you were dead," he said, in an obvious attempt to change the subject.

"For the most part, I have sailed the seven seas. I don't know if you are aware of it, but Howard Landon hired a man to come to Oregon to kill me."

"Simon suspected as much, but we thought the man had succeeded, and so did Howard Landon— what happened?"

"You may well ask. As it happened, the man did smother a friend of mine to death, thinking it was me.

As you will remember, I sent word that you and your sister were to take a ship and come to me in Oregon. When the *Althea* docked, and you and Joanna weren't on board, I boarded her, heading back to Philadelphia to find out what had happened to the two of you. There was a fierce storm, which blew us off course in the Atlantic, and the *Althea* went aground somewhere off the coast of Florida. Many of the passengers and crew were shanghaiied by a Russian merchant ship—and I didn't get free until a year ago."

"We James's are not known for living simple, quiet lives, are we?" Tag asked, smiling.

Russell picked up his glass and held it out to his son in a salute. "No, but we sure as hell are survivors."

"Joanna is going to be overjoyed when she learns that you are alive, Father."

"Do you think there is any chance she will come back to Philadelphia with us?"

"No; she would never leave Windhawk, nor would he allow her to go. She's happy, and that's all anyone can ask out of life."

"I suppose so, son. What about you—will you return to Philadelphia with me?"

"I don't know. Much of my future plans will depend on Alexandria."

"I hope you will come back with me, Tag. I always had the dream that you would one day grow up and I could rename the business James and Son."

Tag was thoughtful for a moment. "I find myself torn, Father. I have lived as an Indian since I was twelve. Mine was a peaceful and rewarding existence. When I returned to Philadelphia, I found an artificial world that I didn't belong in and didn't understand."

"What about Alexandria? Surely you don't find her artificial, son?"

Tag gazed deep into his father's eyes. "No, she is the most real thing that has ever happened to me."

"You said that you loved Morning Song. Does her ghost stand between you and Alexandria?"

"No. I have loved two unique and wonderful women. Morning Song belongs to the past . . . without Alexandria, I have no future."

"She must love you. I feel sure she does."

"I don't know. I suppose I'm afraid to ask her for fear of what she may say."

"You can't know until you ask."

"How soon do you think we can leave?" Tag asked, changing the subject again.

Russell James drained his glass and stood up. "We should be ready to leave in about a month."

"You understand that more than likely we will have to winter with the Blackfoot—since it is almost summer now. Winter comes early to Blackfoot country."

"Will I be welcome in the Indian village, do you think?"

Tag smiled. "You will be astounded by the welcome you will receive by Windhawk and his Blood Blackfoot. Joanna is very important to the tribe—as her father, I expect you'll be offered a rousing welcome!"

Chapter Thirty

Alexandria awoke the next morning, feeling stiff and sore all over. She turned toward the window and thought about the events of the previous two days. It was hard to realize that Claudia was dead, and Melvin and her other accomplices were locked away, awaiting justice.

Alexandria had never known anyone who was so evil. Barbara and Rodney were not unlike Claudia in some respects, but although they had schemed and plotted to take Meadowlake away from her, she doubted that they would ever plan to kill anyone.

Spring was over, and so was a chapter of Alexandria's life. She watched the cool summer breeze stir the curtains at the windows. Tag had helped her overcome all her difficulties, and she could now return to Meadowlake with no fear of her stepmother and Rodney.

It was wonderful that Tag and his father had been reunited. Now perhaps Tag could put the bitterness out of his heart and look forward to a bright future. Alexandria knew she wouldn't be a part of that future. It was very painful thinking about leaving Tag, but she had decided it was time for her to go home to

Meadowlake. It didn't matter that, according to the law, she was Tag's wife. As painful as it was to admit, Alexandria knew Tag still had deep feelings for Morning Song. She herself needed some time to be alone at Meadowlake, so she could reflect on her future.

How different her life was now. At one time, all she had wanted was to live at Meadowlake in peace and contentment, without Barbara's constant badgering and Rodney's leering glances. Now she knew that wouldn't be enough. Alexandria had found a true and lasting love, and she would never love another man as deeply as she did Tag.

What Alexandria really wanted to do was to tell Tag of her love and beg him to allow her to stay with him. But she knew she had been little more than a nuisance to him—it was past time for her to leave. She had worn out her welcome, and she knew it would be best if she were gone when Tag and his father returned in the afternoon.

Alexandria jumped out of bed and hurriedly put on her clothing. She had made her decision. She would go home to Meadowlake! It was past the planting season, but if she worked very hard, she could still put in some crops for this year's harvest. Again she reminded herself that she was her mother's daughter. She would be strong and face whatever the future had in store for her.

When she reached the dining room, she found Farley eating his breakfast, so she sat down beside him.

"I'm glad to see you back, Farley. We missed you around here."

He shoveled a hot biscuit into his mouth, and

grinned. "I heard you had some excitement while I was gone. Sorry I missed it."

Alexandria smiled at the old man who had become so dear to her. "We could have used you. Tell me, what do you think of Meadowlake?"

Farley shook his fork at her. "I like your farm better than this here place, but it's still a tad too civilized to suit me. I was glad when Tag told me this morning that we was going home."

"You . . . and Tag are returning to the Blackfoot village?" she asked, as her heart seemed to break into a thousand tiny pieces.

"Yep, as soon as things get cleared up here. I surely was surprised to learn that stranger was Tag and Joanna's pa, weren't you?"

"No, I have known for some time who he was."

"Well, why didn't you say so, then?" Farley asked pointedly, giving her an amazed glance.

"Mr. James asked me not to tell anyone."

"Well, I'll be a lop-eared jackrabbit. I found me another woman who can keep her mouth shut. I was beginning to think Joanna was the only woman I know who could keep a secret."

"I suppose I will be returning to Meadowlake," Alexandria said, hoping Farley would tell her that Tag wanted her to go with him instead.

"I 'spect so. Mrs. Green stayed behind to wait for you. She sent all them servants packing and got the place running right nicely. I guess you'll want to see to the planting and all."

Alexandria stood up. "Yes, I suppose I will. Do you know when Tag will return?"

"Nope. Him and his pa went riding out bright and

early this morning. They didn't say when they'd be back."

"Do you think Tom would mind driving me to Meadowlake today, Farley?"

"I can't see why he would. You go put your things together, and I'll see to the hitching of the buggy."

Alexandria left quickly, hoping Farley wouldn't see the tears in her eyes. As the old man watched her leave the room, a smile covered his face. Alexandria would have been surprised if she had known how well he understood her feelings. He scratched his grizzly white beard and ambled outside. He thought it would be a good idea if Alexandria was gone before Tag returned. It wouldn't hurt the young pup to have to go after her. Farley knew that the two young people loved each other, but they were too foolish to admit it. He reckoned that some time apart would do them both good. He didn't have the slightest doubt that when they left Pennsylvania, Alexandria would be with them. Maybe, if Tag thought he had lost Alexandria, he would do something about their situation.

Tag and his father had a busy day. The first thing they did was go to their house and dismiss all the people who had worked for Claudia and Howard Landon. They then went into town and hired new servants, laborers, and decorators to redecorate the house. By midafternoon they ended up at the shipyard. Russell had found his old bookkeeper and had put him in charge of straightening out the finances. It was long past the dinner hour when they finally returned home.

Farley came ambling in as Tag and his father were eating a late dinner, and the old man sat down to have a second helping of dessert.

"Where is Alexandria?" Russell asked. "Has she already gone to bed?"

"Nope, she lit out for her farm early this morning. She told me to tell you both that she didn't like good-byes, and she wished you both good fortune. Said if you was ever out her way you was to drop by."

Tag stood up and threw his napkin on the table. "The hell she did! What right has she got to go anywhere without consulting me? Why did you allow her to leave?"

Russell caught Farley's eye, and he saw the twinkle dancing there. That wily old fox, Russell thought, he knew exactly what he was doing. Russell James smiled to himself. The old man had realized that Tag would never allow Alexandria to go without at least an explanation—they both knew he would go after her.

"I didn't see no sense in holding her here. It's past planting time on her farm. I 'spect she's got her work cut out for her."

"Well, that's gratitude for you. She forgets all we went through together and just runs off without a by-your-leave," Tag said, stomping out of the room.

Farley leaned back in his chair and suppressed his laughter. "You're his pa—how long you 'spect it'll take him to go after her?"

"Well, I would say he will be angry for about a week—then he will begin to be angry with himself for caring. By the third week, I would estimate he would be ready to knock anyone out of his way that tried to keep him from her."

* * *

Alexandria had always loved Meadowlake in the summer. The land seemed to reflect every shade of green known to man. She had found that keeping busy gave her little time to dwell on her heartache. It wasn't until late at night, when she lay in bed listening to the sound of the wind in the trees and the night birds singing to their mates, that she would feel lonely. At those times she would often cry herself to sleep.

If she closed her eyes and concentrated very hard, she could remember what it had felt like to have Tag take her in his arms and make love to her. Many times Alexandria had resisted the urge to go to him and tell him how much she loved him. She thought about how Tag had come into her life at the time when she had needed him most. He had stood by her and helped her through every difficulty. She tried to imagine what Morning Song had looked like and what there had been about her that had inspired the undying love of a man like Tag.

She wondered if Tag and Farley had started back to the Blackfoot country. How empty her life was now that she knew she would never see Tag again. All she had to look forward to was growing old alone. No matter that their wedding had been held under the most adverse circumstances, she knew she would always think of herself as Tag's wife.

Alexandria rolled over on her back and closed her eyes, praying for a reprieve from her misery. Would it not have been better if she had never met Tag? She turned to her side and stared at the shadows dancing on the wall as the breeze blew the branches of the trees. No, how could it be better never to have known love?

She closed her eyes tightly, wishing for the sleep that eluded her. Wasn't love supposed to be beautiful? It wasn't supposed to leave an empty void in one's heart.

Alexandria pulled her mount up beside the stream. Dismounting, she bent down and cupped her hands, taking a deep, cooling drink of water. The day was hot and cloudless, and the sky was a hazy blue. She turned her head to the sun and closed her eyes, feeling its warmth on her face. She could smell the fresh, clean aroma of the damp earth, which had been left behind by an early morning shower. She was almost contented as her eyes moved over Meadowlake, knowing that as far as the eye could see, the land belonged to her.

Tag dismounted at the hitching post in front of the big stone farmhouse, while his father and Farley watched the uncertainty in his eyes. Mrs. Green had been watching out the front window, and she rushed out to the front porch to greet them with a welcoming smile.

"I was wondering when you would be calling on us," she said warmly.

"Where is Alexandria?" Tag asked, wondering why she hadn't come out of the house to greet him.

"I saw her riding toward the stream just a short time ago. I imagine she's still there. It's just over that hill, if you want to follow her. You won't need your horse; it's but a short distance."

* * *

Hearing a rider in the distance, Alexandria place her hand above her eyes to shade them from th glaring sun so she could see who her visitor was. On good thing she had found since she returned t Meadowlake was that her neighbors had welcome her back wholeheartedly. Once they had learned th Barbara and Rodney weren't coming back, many them had offered to help her in any way they coul She was finding out, from the comments many them made, just how much they had disliked h stepmother and Rodney.

When the rider drew near, Alexandria saw that was Bart Lewis, whose farm bordered Meadowlake the east. He had been very helpful to her since h return. He had even sent some of his workers to he her plant the corn and potatoes. Alexandria's hea went out to Bart, because his wife had died thr years back, leaving him with three small children raise.

"You are looking lovely today, Alexandria," he sai dismounting and removing his wide-brimmed hat.

She looked up at him, thinking he was a nic looking man, with his sandy-colored hair and de brown eyes. She was grateful to him for his kindnes and it showed in the bright smile she gave him. must warn you, I am a fool for pretty words," s laughed, feeling flirtatious.

"I passed by your cornfield, and even though y planted late, if the weather holds I believe you w have a good crop this year."

"I couldn't have done it without you, Bart. I ho the time will come when I can repay you for all yo kindness."

"When I help a pretty woman, I don't want thanks, but you could do me a favor."

"You name it."

"I was kind of wondering if you will be going to the Hamiltons' barn raising this Saturday week?"

"No, I wasn't planning on going. There is so much to do around Meadowlake, I don't feel I can spare the time. If you would like me to keep the children while you go, however, I would be delighted to accommodate you."

"No, that wasn't what I was asking." His eyes shifted down to study the toe of his boot. "I was wondering if you might like to go with me?"

"The lady won't be going anywhere with you. Hasn't she told you she has a husband?"

Alexandria spun around to face Tag. She could tell by the coldness in his blue eyes that he was angry. "Tag, when did you come?" she cried, wishing she dared throw herself into his arms. Her heart seemed to soar with happiness because he had come to see her! She noticed he was once again dressed in buckskin. Could this mean he was going back to the Blackfoot village?

His eyes moved past her to stare at the man who was looking from Tag to Alexandria in confusion. "I asked you a question—did Alexandria tell you she had a husband?"

"No . . . I never . . . she didn't tell me," Bart stammered.

"Tag, I would like you to meet Bart Lewis, my friend and neighbor. Bart, this is my husband, Taggart James," Alexandria said, trying to cover up for

409

Tag's rudeness.

"Just how good a friend are you to my wife, Mr. Lewis?" Tag asked angrily.

Bart looked at Alexandria. "I see that the two of you have things to discuss. I'll just be going on home now." He swung into the saddle and looked back at Alexandria. "If you need me, you have only to . . ."

"She won't be needing you," Tag said, pulling Alexandria close to him possessively and giving Bart a murderous look.

As Bart rode off, Alexandria moved away from Tag. She couldn't understand why he was behaving in such a rude manner. "You could have been a little nicer to Bart. He has been a good neighbor to me."

"I didn't ride all this way to watch some neighbor fawning over my wife."

"Bart is not like that—he is a gentleman, and besides, I don't know what business it is of yours."

Tag looked as though he would like to say more, but he clamped his jaw together tightly. He was still angry, but he decided not to pursue the matter. He didn't quite know how to deal with his jealousy, since he had never before experienced this strange, troubling emotion.

"I'm sure if you come up to the house, Mrs. Green will have a good meal ready for you," Alexandria said, still confused by Tag's strange attitude.

"My father and Farley are with me," he mumbled, not yet ready to forgive Alexandria for being with another man when he had been unable to get her off his mind.

Alexandria gathered up her horse's reins and started walking in the direction of the house while Tag caught up with her. "I wasn't sure if you were still here or if you had gone to see your sister."

"I'm on my way there now." His voice still sounded strained and angry.

"I'm delighted you decided to come by and see me before you left," she said, covering up the agony she felt at the thought that he was leaving. She realized she might never get to see him again.

"Why didn't you say good-bye to me before you left Philadelphia, Alexandria? One would have thought you might at least have left a note or something."

She glanced up and saw he was watching her closely. "I told Farley that I always hated good-byes."

"So he said."

"How long will you be staying at Meadowlake, Tag?"

"We want to get started as soon as possible." He stopped and caught her hand. "I was wondering if you might not like to go with us?"

Alexandria couldn't believe she had heard correctly, and she couldn't contain her joy. She hadn't expected him to want her to go to see his sister with him. Suddenly her face fell. "I can't just leave. There is no one to look after the farm."

"I anticipated that. My father knows this man who has agreed to run Meadowlake for you until you return. He is completely trustworthy and will be satisfied to take ten percent of this year's profits."

"I . . . don't know. I just hadn't thought. . . ."

"Come with me," he urged, raising her hand to his lips. "Even though the journey is long and hard, I want you to meet Joanna, and I want her to come to know you as I do. You are my wife."

411

Alexandria felt her joy spill over. After what he had just said, there was nothing that would stop her from going with Tag. He might not love her, but she had the feeling that he needed her. She knew that she must not put too much emphasis on his invitation. She was sure he had only come for her because he felt duty bound to. Whatever the reason, she would jump at the opportunity to be with Tag, even though she was sure it would end in heartbreak for her.

"I would like very much to meet your daughter and your sister, Joanna, Tag," she said, turning away so he wouldn't see the tears in her eyes. She had been so afraid she would never see him again. Now, he was asking her to go with him. No matter what the hardships were, she would endure them just to be near Tag.

The mild days of early summer were over, and a hot July sun beat down on Alexandria as she left Meadowlake behind. She rode beside Russell James, while Tag and Farley led the way.

Alexandria admitted to herself that she was frightened at the prospect of facing a whole Indian tribe. Farley and Tag had assured her that she would be safer among the Blackfoot than in her own bed, but still the apprehension wouldn't go away.

The first week they covered many miles each day. They were traveling at a fast pace that Alexandria was sure she would never be able to keep up. It wasn't until the third week that she felt they were leaving civilization, as she knew it, far behind. The land they were traveling through was covered by dense forests and they only saw an occasional farmhouse.

Tag had ignored her for the most part, leaving Farley and Russell to look after her comfort. Alexandria had begun to wonder why Tag had asked her to accompany him. She knew it wasn't out of any love he felt for her. Perhaps he felt he should take her to meet his sister, since she was his wife.

As they rode across a small stream and up a steep embankment, Alexandria noticed that Tag seemed withdrawn and unapproachable. This mood seemed worse than it had when he been eaten up with hatred for Claudia and Mr. Landon. What was tormenting him now, she wondered.

She noticed the way he held his head high and proud, seeming to stare straight ahead. As if he felt her eyes on him, Tag turned and glanced back at her. She couldn't read the expression on his face, but she could feel the chill of his blue gaze even from a distance.

Alexandria began to wish she hadn't consented to make this journey. She had no way of knowing what would be the end result.

"It will be all right, Alexandria," Tag's father encouraged her as he rode up beside her. "Give him time to sort out his feelings."

Alexandria gave Tag's father a weak smile, but said nothing. She had come to believe that not even time would bring her and Tag together.

Chapter Thirty-one

Alexandria lay on a blanket, feeling the hard ground beneath her. As she ran her hands along her legs she could feel the taut muscles that had formed from riding every day from dawn to dusk. She remembered the way her body had ached for the first two weeks of the journey, but after that she had become accustomed to the rigorous pace Tag had set for them to follow. It was as if he were so anxious to reach the Blackfoot village that he pushed them almost beyond endurance. His father and Farley seemed to have no trouble keeping up, but there had been times when Alexandria felt she couldn't go another mile. She was very careful not to complain, however, for fear Tag would think her weak in comparison with Morning Song.

As they traveled across the vast wilderness, Alexandria saw country she had never dreamed existed. She was overwhelmed by its untouched beauty, certain that some of the sights Farley showed her had been seen by very few white men.

Tag still ignored her, and she felt an ache deep inside, knowing that he must regret bringing her along. He was more like the cold, polite stranger than

414

a man who had once held her in his arms and whispered passionate words to her.

Alexandria didn't know this man. He was different from Taggart James or Falcon Knight. Farley had told her he was now Night Falcon, the Indian. It seemed the farther they got from civilization the more primitive Tag became. Dressed in his buckskin clothing and moccasins, he seemed more Indian than white to her. She knew that if it weren't for his father and Farley, she would feel very much alone—the two men made an effort to include her in everything.

Tag and his father had ridden away from camp before sundown. It was dark now, and they still hadn't returned. Alexandria sat up and looked across the campfire where Farley was turning a rabbit on a spit that extended across the glowing coals. Smelling the food, Alexandria felt her stomach churn and was afraid she was going to be sick. She had known for several weeks now that she was carrying Tag's baby. She had tried to hide that fact from Tag, not knowing what his reaction would be.

Farley ambled over to her and sat down, offering her a plate of roasted rabbit and beans. Alexandria could feel the bile rising in her throat, and she quickly turned away. She clamped her hand over her mouth, praying she wouldn't be sick.

Farley laid the tin plate aside and turned Alexandria around to face him. She looked up slowly into his face and realized, from the twinkle reflected in his dancing eyes, that he knew about the baby she was carrying.

"Why haven't you told Tag 'bout the baby?" he asked, as his mouth eased into a grin.

"I . . . don't know what you are talking about, Farley." She stood up and turned her back to him.

The old trapper watched her walk toward the fire, thinking she was the sweetest, loveliest lady he had ever seen, with the exception of Joanna. No, maybe she occupied an equally large share of his heart, along with Joanna. He wondered how Tag could be so blind to the change in Alexandria. How could her own husband not know that she was with child when it was so obvious to him?

When Alexandria turned back to Farley, the look on her face reminded him of the time in the tavern when Tag had rescued her from the sailor—lost and forlorn.

"You won't say anything to Tag, will you, Farley?" she asked in a soft voice.

He ambled over to her and pulled her into his arms, feeling very protective toward her. "Don't you fret none—I know when to keep my mouth shut." He wanted to assure her that Tag loved her and would take care of her, but he didn't know if that was any longer true. Tag had been acting very strange since they had started on the journey home. He spent most of his time with his father, and he seemed to be shutting Alexandria out. The old man knew Alexandria was feeling the effects of Tag's neglect, and he wanted to shake some sense into Tag's head.

"I wish I had never come, Farley. I believe that Tag regrets that he asked me along. Morning Song is dead, but he will never let her go in his heart."

"Come on back to your blanket and eat something," Farley urged, wanting to change the subject because he had no words of comfort to give her.

Alexandria allowed him to help her back to her

416

bedroll and she sat down, but she refused the offered food—her stomach still felt too unsettled to eat anything at the moment, and she feared she would be sick.

"Farley, tell me about Morning Song—what was she really like?"

The old man leaned back against the trunk of a tree and was quiet for a long moment. He could feel Alexandria's need to know about Tag's dead wife. "She were a pretty little thing," he reflected. "She were soft-spoken, and her whole world was Tag."

"Was she very beautiful?"

"I have to tell you that after Joanna and yourself, she were probably the purdiest female that ever walked this earth," he admitted reluctantly.

Alexandria couldn't help but smile at his compliment. "Joanna always comes first with you, doesn't she, Farley? She is very fortunate to have a friend like you."

The old man gave her an answering smile. "I'm the lucky one. Joanna and Tag are the family I ain't never had. I'd do anything for them, the same as I would for you."

Alexandria realized that Joanna must love this old man, for she herself adored him, and she believed him when he said he liked her also. "Tell me about Joanna, Farley."

He raised his head and looked at the twinkling stars through the branches of the tall pine tree. "Joanna is like the music to a song. She be as graceful as the bird that wings its way through the sky. When she smiles at you—you feel kinda like you been blessed in some way."

417

Alexandria felt a chill pass over her. How would she ever be able to compete with Tag's dead wife, let alone his sister, Joanna? The baby she carried would never mean as much to him as the daughter Morning Song had given him. She began to feel as if she were an intruder in his life, and she wished there were some way she could return to Meadowlake.

"I am a bit apprehensive about meeting Joanna. What if she doesn't like me?" she asked, voicing her uncertainty.

The old man laughed. "She'll like you all right—you needn't worry 'bout that."

"What makes you think so? You can't be sure," Alexandria said, knowing it was important that Joanna like her.

Farley grinned broadly. "When Joanna hears how you helped her brother, you don't have to fear, she'll take you right to her heart," he said with assurance.

"Were Joanna and Morning Song close, Farley?"

"I'll be straight with you—they was as close as any sisters coulda been."

Suddenly, Alexandria didn't want to hear anymore about Morning Song or Joanna. She knew she would never measure up to either one of them in Tag's eyes. In coming with him, she had asked to be hurt. She tried to think of something to talk about that would take her mind off Tag. She had often wondered how a lady like Joanna could be content to live in an Indian village and forsake the life of comfort and wealth she had been accustomed to as a girl.

"What is Windhawk like, Farley? He sounds so awesome to me."

"There ain't never been no one like Windhawk, and

I don't think there ever will be again. His people, the Blood Blackfoot, follow him with blind obedience. His enemies fear the mere mention of his name, and with good cause. Windhawk is . . . Windhawk!''

Alexandria could hear the respect in Farley's voice as she tried to picture the chief of the Blackfoot in her mind. "I confess I am a bit frightened at the prospect of going among the Indians. Are you sure it is safe, Farley?"

"Like I done told you, you'll be safer in the village than you was walking the streets of that Philadelphia. No one will harm you. There's just one person I want to warn you 'bout and that's Sun Woman, Windhawk and Morning Song's mother. She ain't going to take too kindly to you being Tag's wife at first. You just give her time, and she'll come 'round."

Alexandria laid her head against her knees and closed her eyes. "When will Tag and his father return to camp, Farley?"

"Like as not, they'll be back afore long. We ain't no more than a day from the Blackfoot village, and I 'spect they are doing some scouting. We've been watched ever since afore sundown."

Alexandria looked up quickly, and her eyes scanned the darkened shadows, searching for any signs of Indians. She felt fear in the very depth of her being, thinking they were watched by hostile eyes. "Who is watching us, Farley?" she asked, moving closer to the old man.

"No need to fret . . . it's just some of Windhawk's Bloods. They'll show themselves afore too long."

Alexandria caught Farley's arm. "Do you mean that they will come into camp?"

419

"Yep, but you ain't in no danger. Just stay close to me, and don't act scairt—Indians don't cotton to anyone that shows fear," the old man cautioned.

Alexandria swallowed past the lump of fear that seemed momentarily to have closed off her breathing. How could she not show fear when her heart was beating so loudly and she felt so shaken? She wished fervently that Tag would return. She knew that with him beside her it would be much easier to put on a brave front.

All at once, as if one of the dark shadows detached itself, an Indian stepped into the firelight, his dark eyes boring into Alexandria. She could feel the chill of his glance, and her spine seemed to tingle. She was unaware that Farley had helped her to stand as the Indian moved slowly toward them. The campfire seemed to glisten off the man's bronze chest, and Alexandria clamped her mouth shut trying to keep from crying out in fear.

The man wore nothing but a leather breechcloth, and Alexandria felt her face flame with color. When the Indian spoke to Farley, Alexandria didn't understand the words, since he spoke in the language of the Blackfoot.

"Much time has gone by since I have seen you, old man," the Indian said. "Many have waited for you and Night Falcon's return."

"It is good to see you, Gray Fox. Yes, Night Falcon is with me, but he is away from camp now. He will return shortly," Farley answered in perfect Blackfoot.

"He will not be coming tonight. He sent me to tell you that he will ride on to the village. Night Falcon has asked me and my warriors to watch over the white woman. We will camp nearby tonight," Gray Fox said, nodding at the white girl. "I was told that the white girl is Night Falcon's wife."

Farley took Alexandria's hand and squeezed it reassuringly. "Yes, this woman is Night Falcon's wife. She will be treated with the respect you would show a brother's wife."

As Gray Fox glanced at the white girl, he was astounded to discover she had golden-colored eyes. Her beauty became apparent when he stepped closer. "It is good that you are Night Falcon's woman," he said, astonishing Alexandria by speaking in English.

Alexandria couldn't find her voice, so she merely nodded.

"You will be welcome in the Blackfoot village," he told her, turning away. Without another word, he seemed to fade into the shadows he had come from only moments before.

"I . . . who was that?" Alexandria asked, feeling her knees go weak.

"That was Gray Fox. He is a powerful war chief and friend to Windhawk. Tag has sent him to tell us that he has ridden on to the village."

Alexandria was still staring at the spot where the Indian had disappeared. "Tag won't be with us when we enter the village tomorrow?" she asked, trying to mask her disappointment.

"No, but you ain't to worry. You'll be watched over tonight by the Blackfoot warriors. They will make camp nearby—nothing will harm you," the old man said, helping her to sit down.

Alexandria wanted to ask him who would protect her from the Indians, but she didn't voice her concern since he seemed to think she had nothing to fear.

As she lay o her bedroll, she wondered what Tag was doing at that moment. She wished with all her heart that he had stayed with her so she wouldn't be entering the village with just Farley at her side.

Closing her eyes, she tried to will herself to sleep, knowing she would need all her strength and courage the next day. The wind in the tall pine trees made a strange howling sound, and she felt herself quake in fear. Dear Lord, what was she doing here? She didn't belong—why had she come to this land that would forever steal Tag away from her?

It was at the first light of dawn that Tag and his father crossed the Milk River at its shallow point and rode into the Blackfoot village. Tag felt a lightness in his heart that he hadn't felt in many months. It was strange . . . he had thought it would be like coming home, but it wasn't. His happiness came from knowing he would soon see his daughter and his sister. He thought how joyful Joanna would be when she learned their father was still alive!

Glancing sideways at his father, he saw an answering happiness on his face. Tag's eyes went to the spot where his and Morning Song's tipi had once stood, and he felt a pang of regret. It would be hard to face the fact that he would never see Morning Song again. Alexandria's face flashed through his mind, and he suddenly wished he had brought her to the village with him. He somehow needed the comfort that only she could bring him. It was hard for him to realize that she had become such an important part of his life. He would always remember Morning Song . . .

as a dear childhood friend with whom he had shared many dreams and fathered a daughter. Alexandria was his future, just as Morning Song was his past. At the moment, he couldn't seem to separate the two of them in his heart.

Joanna had just placed Tag's sleeping daughter in the cradle when she heard the camp dogs barking, followed by the sound of a loud commotion from the women and children. She watched as Windhawk picked up the spear that he kept by the opening of their lodge and stepped outside. She smiled down at Tag's daughter, who had become as dear to her as her own daughter. Many times during Tag's long absence she had worried about his safety. She knew that without Windhawk's strength she would never have been able to endure not knowing what was happening to her brother. Each day she went to the river and searched the horizon, looking for any sign of Tag's return.

Windhawk watched the two riders as they approached his lodge. Many of his people were following beside them, and he knew immediately that one of the horsemen was Tag. He felt his heart gladden that Joanna's brother had returned safely. His eyes moved briefly from Tag to the white man who rode beside him, then back to Tag.

By now Tag and his father had drawn even with Windhawk. Tag smiled as he gazed down at his brother-in-law, reading the joy in Windhawk's dark eyes.

He leaped from his mount and embraced Windhawk. "All is well, Windhawk. I have returned!" he said in the language of the Blackfoot.

Windhawk's dark eyes were shining as he nodded. "It is good. You have been missed, little brother. Your sister has been concerned for your safety." Windhawk's eyes moved to the other white man, who by now had dismounted, thinking there was something vaguely familiar about him.

"Windhawk, I would like you to meet my father, Russell James," Tag said in English, and Windhawk could hear the pride in his voice. "Father, this is Joanna's husband, Windhawk."

"How can this be?" Windhawk asked in astonishment. "Your father is dead!"

"We were misinformed about his death—I will tell you about it later."

Russell James looked into the Indian's dark, searching eyes, wondering what there was about this man that would cause his daughter to abandon her own way of life to live in an Indian village. He could see that the chief was a handsome man, but there would have to be more to him than just handsomeness to make Joanna love him.

"You are welcome in my village, father of my wife," Windhawk said in halting English. "Come inside; I know there will be much joy when Joanna sees you and your son." Windhawk swept the lodge flap aside, and Tag entered first.

Joanna glanced up, expecting to see Windhawk, and she seemed to freeze for a moment. She couldn't believe her eyes. Then her feet seemed to fly across the room as she ran into her brother's open arms.

"Tag, Tag, you have come home!" she cried. Tears of joy streamed down her cheeks as she sprinkled kisses over his face.

Tag hugged her tightly, laughing at the way she kept touching his face to make sure he was really there and not just a figment of her imagination.

"Are you well? Did you come to any harm?" she asked, looking him over carefully.

"I am fine, Joanna," he assured her laughingly.

"Tell me everything," she said, leaning her head against his broad shoulder. "I want to hear all that has happened to you since the day you left."

"Slow down," he chuckled. "One thing at a time. First, I have a surprise for you that will please you very much."

"I don't care about anything you would bring me but yourself, Tag. I am just glad to have you back safe and sound."

Tag turned around and called over his shoulder. "Father, I guess Joanna doesn't want to see you."

"I . . . what did you say?" she asked, standing on her tiptoes and gazing over Tag's shoulder. A sob broke from her throat when she saw her father. He was older than she remembered, but she knew him in an instant. Somehow she untangled herself from Tag and found herself being crushed in her father's arms. She wasn't aware that Tag had moved over to the cradle to stare down at his baby daughter. She only knew that she was sobbing happily as her father ran a soothing hand up and down her back.

"Papa . . . how can it be?" she asked, slipping back into the name she had called him as a child. I thought . . . we all thought you were dead." She raised her face to him, and he cupped it in his huge hands.

"Your eyes aren't deceiving you, my dear, sweet little girl. I am very much alive!"

"Oh, Papa," she said, touching his face softly. "I . . . love you so much!"

Russell James hugged her to him and buried his face in her hair. He could feel tears in his eyes, as he thought how much she looked like his dead wife. Silence descended on the lodge as the two of them wept openly.

Windhawk caught Joanna's eye, and he sent her a smile. His heart was overflowing with joy because of her happiness.

Joanna took her father's hand and led him over to Windhawk. "Papa, I want you to know Windhawk. Please accept the man I love."

Russell James and Windhawk stood eye-to-eye as they assessed each other. Windhawk was more than willing to accept the man who had given life to the woman he loved, but he waited for some sign that the man would be willing to meet him halfway. When Russell James smiled and held his hand out to Windhawk, the chief of the Blackfoot, he began to relax.

"I can say in all honesty that I owe you a great debt, Windhawk. My son has told me about how you have taken care of him and my daughter. You would have to be an exceptional man to have won Joanna's heart. As her father, I offer you my gratitude and my respect."

Windhawk clasped Russell's hand and smiled. "As the father of my wife, you will also be my father," he said, deeply moved.

Russell James could feel the pull of Windhawk's powerful personality and knew that his daughter had found an exceptional man. Both men could read mutual respect and acceptance in the other's eyes.

Happiness followed as Russell James was introduced to Joanna's son, Little Hawk, and her daughter, Sky Dancer. He then was handed Tag's daughter and told she went by the name of Little Princess. Russell had thought it would be hard to accept his grandchildren, knowing they would be half-Indian. But as he held Tag's daughter in his arms and Little Hawk sat at his feet, asking all kinds of questions in perfect English, he felt his heart melt. His two granddaughters looked so much alike that they appeared to be twins. They were both light-skinned, with long black hair. He was astonished to find that they both had blue eyes. Little Hawk was dark-skinned like his father and had dancing ebony eyes that sparkled when he looked at his grandfather.

When the excitement died down, Joanna watched as Tag lifted his daughter in his arms and left the lodge. She realized he needed to be alone for a while.

Windhawk had discreetly left Joanna and her father alone to get reacquainted. Russell James told his daughter all that had happened to him and Tag in Philadelphia. She shed no tears when she heard of Claudia's death, nor did she feel regret at Howard Landon's passing. Joanna now knew she could put the past out of her mind and look to a bright new future with no dark clouds hanging over her. She hoped that Tag would now be able to put the bitterness and hatred behind him and get on with his life. She looked forward to meeting Alexandria, knowing the girl had helped Tag find himself.

The night had turned quite cool, and Joanna and

her father sat beside the fire. "What do you think of Alexandria, Papa? What is she like? Do you think Tag loves her?" Joanna wanted to know.

"As to what she is like, you can judge for yourself. I find I'm very fond of her. The rest you will have to ask Tag himself."

"I cannot wait to see her. I am grateful that she helped Tag when he needed it."

"That son of mine seems to have picked up several champions along the way."

"How is Farley?" Joanna asked with a smile, knowing her father was referring to the old trapper.

"He seems to be in good health and spirits," her father assured her.

"I can't wait to see him—are you sure he is all right?"

Russell laughed. "I never met anyone who was more all right than that old trapper. I'll always be grateful to him for standing by Tag."

"Yes, he is wonderful," Joanna agreed, linking her arm through her father's. "I cannot tell you how wonderful it is to see you, Papa. You can't know how devastated Tag and I were when we heard you were dead. It's like a miracle having you back with us."

Russell searched his daughter's lovely face. She had been only a young girl the last time he had seen her—now she was a woman who seemed to be blooming with happiness. "Are you truly happy, Joanna? Is Windhawk good to you?"

"Papa, I could have searched the whole world over and never have found anyone as right for me as Windhawk. He is the kindest, most considerate man. You will realize this when you come to know him. I want you to like him. If you will only meet him halfway, you will like him, Papa."

Russell kissed her pert little nose. "With such a strong recommendation, how can I not?"

Soon Windhawk returned, and he sat beside Joanna and talked to her father. It didn't take long for Russell to recognize Windhawk's intelligence, and he began to see why his son and daughter admired and respected the young chief of the Blackfoot tribe.

Tag pulled the blanket over his daughter's head. His heart was at peace as he walked beside the river. The people of the Blackfoot tribe respected his need to be alone—for although they would have liked to welcome him back among them, they left it until another day.

Tag closed his eyes, and he could almost hear Morning Song's voice whispering to him. The tiny bit of humanity he held in his arms was a part of Morning Song . . . just as she was a part of him.

"Please understand, Morning Song," he whispered aloud. "I don't love you any less because I took another wife. What you and I had was beautiful, but I love Alexandria."

"My daughter cannot hear you, Tag. She is dead," Sun Woman said from behind him.

Tag turned around to face Morning Song's mother. He had dreaded facing her, fearing she wouldn't understand about Alexandria. "It is good to see you, my mother," he told her, bending to kiss her cheek.

"Word has already reached me that you brought a white wife with you. Will this woman be good to you and my dead daughter's baby?"

"She has a kind heart, my mother. I believe she will treat the child as her own."

"Will you be returning to the white world, my son?"

"Yes, but when I leave, I will leave a part of myself behind, my mother."

Sun Woman touched his face. "I have always known the time would come for you to leave us. I think Morning Song knew it also. It is good that you filled her life with happiness before she died."

"I . . . does it bother you that I now have another wife?"

"Do you love this woman?"

"Yes, very much."

"How, then, can I object? I am pleased to see the sadness gone from your eyes. Morning Song would be happy also. I do not want to see this woman for a time, but I will come to accept her, if it is your wish."

Tag looked into the face that had become so dear to him over the years. He would miss many things and people when he returned to Philadelphia. Sun Woman would be one of those he would miss.

"I will see to it that my daughter visits you when she is older. I will always tell her about her mother and the Blackfoot people. She will grow up being proud of her Indian blood. This I promise you!"

"It is good, my son. I am content. Will you give this daughter a name? You failed to do so before you left. We were forced to call her Little Princess."

"I have been thinking about that. I have decided to call her after my French grandmother—her name will be Danielle!"

"It is a strange-sounding name, but if it is after your grandmother, it is good," Sun Woman said, leaning forward and placing her cheek against Tag's.

"Has my daughter's death been avenged, my son?" she asked softly.

"Yes, my mother. Morning Song can now rest in peace. . . ."

Chapter Thirty-two

Alexandria rode beside Farley, not daring to look back at the six Blackfoot warriors who were following closely behind. Her heart was in her mouth as they crossed the river and rode up the bank toward the Blackfoot village.

Alexandria glanced at the numerous women and children who rushed forward to greet Farley as they entered the village. Their dark eyes stared at her curiously, and she had the feeling she had just entered an alien world. The horses moved past the throng of people, and she kept hoping to see Tag. Farley gave her a reassuring smile as they reached the center of the village, and he halted his mount before a huge lodge.

Farley dismounted and helped her down. "Where is Tag?" she asked, looking about her and seeing that the Indian women and children had gone on about their business, seeming to ignore her and Farley.

"I 'spect he's inside," he said, pushing the lodge flap aside and yelling at the top of his voice. "Joanna, it's me, Farley . . . I'm home!"

Farley pulled Alexandria into the lodge behind him, and her eyes hadn't yet become accustomed to the darkness when she heard a soft voice she knew could only belong to Tag's sister, Joanna.

"Farley, I have missed you! Things just haven't been the same around here without you."

Alexandria hadn't yet been able to get a close look at the woman who was crushed in a bear hug by the old trapper. She saw only a woman dressed in fringed buckskin and knee-high moccasins, with red-gold hair that hung down her back to her waist.

Alexandria had always dreaded this moment. She so desperately wanted Joanna to like her. She wasn't prepared for the bright smile or the heartfelt welcome in the violet-blue eyes that sought hers.

"Alexandria, my dear. I feel as if I know you already," Joanna said, taking the young girl's hand. "You are every bit as lovely as Tag and my father said you were." Joanna slid a comforting arm about Alexandria's waist, remembering how frightened she had been when Windhawk had first brought her to the Blackfoot village. "You must be very tired from such a long journey."

Each woman looked into the other's eyes, and each formed her own opinion. Alexandria thought that nothing she had heard about Joanna had done her real justice. Surely there was no more beautiful woman anywhere in the world. Her face was perfectly shaped, and her smile was genuine, as was the softness in her eyes. Joanna caught the anxious light in the golden-colored eyes and she wanted to assure Alexandria that she need not worry. The young girl's skin was smooth and ivory-colored, and Joanna could see how Tag would be drawn to her. Although Joanna

433

was a head taller than Alexandria, she could see that the girl carried herself straight and proud.

"I . . . have been looking forward to meeting you, Joanna. Tag has told me so much about you."

Joanna's laughter was infectious, and Alexandria felt her heart lighten. "You are not to believe everything that my brother tells you about me, Alexandria—he tends to exaggerate where I am concerned."

"I think he was being truthful. You are very lovely."

Joanna smiled and her violet eyes twinkled with mirth. "I think I'm going to like you, Alexandria James."

"I think I liked you before I met you, Joanna," Alexandria said, her amber eyes glowing earnestly.

Farley ambled over to the two cradles and looked down at the sleeping babies. He had known Joanna would put Alexandria at ease. Maybe she could help the two young people find their way to each other, he thought, touching the dark head of Tag's baby daughter.

"Tag and my father rode out with Windhawk this morning—they should be home for lunch," Joanna said, voicing Alexandria's unasked question. "Would you like to see the children?" Joanna asked.

"Yes, very much."

Joanna led Alexandria first to her own daughter's cradle. "Little Hawk, our eldest, is with his grandmother this morning—you will see him later."

Alexandria looked down on the sleeping baby, amazed by her shock of ebony hair. The child looked so angelic in sleep that Alexandria couldn't help but touch her soft cheek. "She is lovely, Joanna. I can see that you would be proud of her."

"Indeed I am," Joanna said, moving Alexandria to the cradle where Tag's child lay. She watched Tag's new wife's face for her reaction to the child. "This is Danielle, Tag's daughter," Joanna told her.

There could be no mistaking the mist in the amber eyes as Alexandria reached out her hand and touched the head that was covered with black downy hair and was so soft to the touch. The child opened her eyes, and Alexandria saw that they were startlingly blue, in deep contrast to her golden-colored skin. When the child began to gurgle and laugh, Alexandria felt a tug at her heart.

"Oh, she is so lovely! May I hold her?"

"Of course, you can. By Indian custom, Danielle is now your daughter." Again Joanna watched Alexandria's face carefully, to see if she would accept the child that Tag had fathered by another woman.

Alexandria lifted the child in her arms and held her close to her heart. The tears that ran from her eyes fell onto the child's face.

"I didn't know how I would feel about this child, but I believe I love her already," Alexandria said, kissing the smooth cheek.

Joanna felt relief wash over her. Tag's daughter was so dear to her, she was glad to see that she would be loved by Alexandria. It tore at her heart to know that Tag would be taking Danielle away from her when he returned to Philadelphia, but she could see that the child would be in loving hands. Joanna would take comfort from the fact that Danielle would have Alexandria for her mother.

435

The two girls hadn't noticed that Farley had left them alone. When the lodge flap was thrown aside, both of them looked up.

Joanna had been dreading the moment Sun Woman would confront Alexandria. Her mother-in-law stared at Alexandria long and hard before she crossed the lodge.

"Have courage. This is the baby's grandmother, Sun Woman," Joanna whispered quickly, trying to prepare Alexandria for what was to come.

Alexandria stared into hostile dark eyes. She was certain Morning Song's mother, if she were of a mind to, had the capacity to rip a person to shreds.

Sun Woman looked down at her granddaughter, then back at Alexandria. Morning Song's mother didn't say a word, but Alexandria could read her thoughts and handed the baby to her. Sun Woman took the baby and walked out of the lodge without a word.

"I . . . do not understand," Alexandria said, looking to Joanna for an answer to the woman's strange behavior.

"First, let me tell you that Sun Woman loves her granddaughter very much. Danielle has become a substitute for her dead daughter, Morning Song. She knows that you and Tag will be taking the child away when you leave, and she has to deal with that fact in her own way. Be patient with her, and she will come around before you leave," Joanna assured her.

Suddenly Alexandria realized why Tag had asked her to come with him. He wanted her to look after his daughter until they got back to Philadelphia. She felt

436

her heart sink, along with her last hope of winning Tag's love. She was nothing more to him than just someone to care for Danielle. She knew in that moment that he wouldn't be happy about the baby she was carrying. Knowing she must hide her disappointment from Joanna, Alexandria gave her a weak smile.

"I must convince Sun Woman, for Tag's sake, that the baby will be in good hands—mustn't I?" Alexandria asked softly.

Joanna hadn't missed the sparkle of tears in Alexandria's eyes, and she understood better than Alexandria realized. Joanna was beginning to see that Morning Song's ghost stood between Tag and his young wife. She knew she might have to take a hand, if Tag didn't come to his senses before too long. Surely her brother wasn't aware of the fact that he was hurting this lovely young girl.

"I hear riders coming into camp—it might be your husband and mine," Joanna said, taking Alexandria's hand and leading her outside.

Alexandria watched as Tag and his father dismounted in a cloud of dust. She knew without being told that the tall, handsome Indian who took Joanna's hand would be the legendary Windhawk. She looked at Tag shyly, thinking he had never looked more unapproachable. He wore nothing but a leather breechcloth. Alexandria couldn't help but notice the way his firm, hard body rippled with muscles. She quickly looked up at his hair and focused her eyes on the leather band about his golden hair. He was laughing at something his father had said and hadn't even noticed her. She had never felt more like an intruder than she did at that moment.

"Alexandria, I would like you to meet my husband, Windhawk," Joanna said, pulling her attention away from Tag.

When Alexandria looked into Windhawk's dark eyes, at first she felt a prickle of fear. He was so different from any man she had ever seen. He was no ordinary Indian—one look told her that he was a man of great strength and character. His eyes were kind as they rested on her.

"I welcome you to my village, Alexandria," he said, nodding his head slightly. "I hope you will feel that our home is yours," he added.

"I . . . thank you," she said, meeting his dark gaze.

Windhawk turned to Joanna and said something that made Joanna laugh. "My husband has told me he has never seen eyes the color of the golden falcon's wing. He thinks they are most wondrous to behold."

Tag moved forward to join in the conversation. "I thought they were a most unusual color myself when I first gazed upon them, but then at the time, I had no way of knowing just how unusual they were," he said, smiling at Alexandria. She knew he was reminding her that at that time he had thought her to be a young boy.

Russell James draped his arm about Alexandria's shoulder. "I think Alexandria is as lovely and unusual as the color of her eyes. I find myself feeling privileged that she has come to me as a daughter."

Alexandria cast Tag's father a grateful look. She felt closer to him than she did to the others—he, more than anyone else, seemed to sense what she was feeling.

As they entered the lodge, Alexandria found that Tag wasn't with them. She knew he had gone to see Sun Woman, who had his daughter.

Later, as she helped Joanna serve the lunch of deer meat and berry cakes, she wished she could be alone to cry out her misery. She didn't belong with these people, and she didn't belong to Tag. They were a family, and she felt left out of the love they had for one another.

Alexandria knew she must tell Tag that she wouldn't live with him as the mother of his child. He had the money to hire a woman who would perform that service. All she wanted was to return to Meadowlake and heal her broken heart. How easy it would be to love and be a mother to Tag's daughter—how great was the temptation to give in just so she could be near Tag. No, her pride wouldn't allow her to bask in what crumbs he wished to toss her way. She would return to Meadowlake and have her baby. When she and Tag were alone, she would tell him she wished to leave as soon as possible.

A short time later Tag joined them, and they all had lunch. Tag noticed that Alexandria was unusually quiet. He knew how difficult it must be for her being in an alien world that she couldn't possibly understand. He blamed himself for not spending more time with her. For some reason he was at a loss as to how to approach her. He had so many things to say to her, and he didn't know how to say them. Perhaps he would take her for a walk tonight and explain some of

439

his feelings to her at that time.

Joanna watched Tag and Alexandria, knowing there was something very wrong between them. They certainly didn't act like two people who had only been married a short time. She caught Windhawk's eye and knew he realized it also. Happiness was such a fleeting thing, and Joanna knew how precious it was, since she had come close to losing it herself at one time. She didn't want the same thing to happen to Tag and Alexandria.

After lunch, the men rode away from the village once more. Alexandria and Joanna cleared the dishes away and then played with Joanna's children. Alexandria wished that Sun Woman would bring Danielle back so she could get to know her better, but she didn't suggest it to Joanna.

That afternoon she laid down to rest for a while, claiming that the heat and the long journey had sapped her strength, which wasn't far from the truth. She could have told Joanna that she was feeling sick to her stomach, but she didn't. She would hide her secret about the baby as long as she could. Perhaps she could return to Meadowlake right away, and Tag would never have to know about the baby.

That evening Tag surprised Alexandria by suggesting they go for a walk. As they walked beside the river, Tag reached for her hand. A bright moon shone down upon them, casting a silvery light over the river.

"I can see why you love it so much here, Tag. It's so peaceful and serene. I suppose I never gave much thought to how the Indians live. I am surprised to find they have a very fine life."

"Alexandria, most people would be surprised to find the Indian lives no differently than the white man did hundreds of years ago. The difference is that the white man has forgotten what's important in life, while the Indian has never lost sight of what's important. The white man is driven by the need to acquire more land and more money, while the Indian is satisfied to take what God placed on earth for his needs. Greed is almost unknown to the Indian. He is always willing to share what he has with his neighbors in their time of want."

"I hadn't thought of that."

"You have a wonderful opportunity, Alexandria. Look around and observe while you are here. You will find a whole new world at your fingertips."

"I . . . was wondering if you were going to return here to live after you take me back home?" She was finally able to voice her thoughts.

Tag turned to her and studied her uplifted face. "No, there is nothing for me here now. There was a time when I thought of this as my home, but I realize that is no longer true."

"I'm sorry, Tag," was all she could think of to say.

"Are you?" he asked in a deep voice.

"Yes," she whispered.

"I wish I knew what you thought about many things, Alexandria. I have known you for what seems like a lifetime, and yet, I find I don't really know you at all."

"I am not complicated, Tag. You are the one who keeps his thoughts to himself."

"I suppose that is true. Tell me what would you like to know, and I'll try to explain it to you."

"I'm . . . not sure. How do you feel about your daughter?"

"That is the easiest of all to answer. I want to take her back to Philadelphia with me and raise her to the best of my ability. I want her to grow up being proud of who her mother was."

"Yes, I can see that Danielle will have much to be proud of when she grows to be a young lady."

"What's your next question, Alexandria?" he asked, moving closer to her.

Alexandria could feel the warmth of his body, and she wished her thoughts weren't so jumbled. Even now, his thoughts were of his dead wife. Alexandria found she didn't want to compete with a ghost. "I wonder if you would mind very much if I were to ask you to send me back home to Meadowlake as soon as possible?" Say you *would* mind, her heart silently cried. Tell me that you need me to be with you, she thought to herself.

He reached out and brushed a lock of hair from her face. "What if I said I needed you with me, Alexandria?" he asked, hardly above a whisper.

"I would ask you in what capacity."

"Danielle needs a mother," he said, watching her face closely.

"You can easily find someone to take care of your daughter, Tag. You don't need me for that."

"What would you say if I told you I need you as Xandria?" he asked, still watching her closely.

"Then I would say to you there are dozens of

442

Xandrias in Philadelphia. Xandria was no better than Molly, the girl at the tavern who threw herself at you. After all, did I not come to your bedroom many nights, Tag? Someone with your experience with women will have not trouble finding many Xandrias."

Suddenly his hands went out to grip her by the shoulders. He pulled her tightly against him and muffled her cry as his mouth ground against hers. It was pain, and it was bliss, as his hands ran over her back, pulling her even tighter against his hard body. When he released her, she stepped back a pace, touching her bruised lips.

"I can find another Xandria, but what will you do?" he asked insultingly. "Will you seek out another man and sneak into his bedroom at night to give him what you gave so freely to me in the past?"

Alexandria gasped at his cruel words. "I have never given you any reason to say these things to me! You should know you are the only man who I have ever . . . who has ever . . ."

"Forgive me," he said, turning his back and staring across the wide Milk River. His thoughts were in a turmoil. Why had he insulted her when all he wanted was to tell her that he loved her? How would he be able to go on without her? She had become so much a part of him, he couldn't imagine what his life would be like without her. When he was near her, his body ached to possess her. At night, he often awoke after dreaming about her, and then he had trouble going back to sleep. He had purposely stayed away from her, hoping she would be content to remain his wife if he didn't place any demands on her.

443

"If it is your desire to return to Meadowlake, I will take you in another week," he said at last. "I would consider it a favor if you would help me with Danielle until we reach Philadelphia. I know nothing about tending to a child."

Alexandria felt her temper rising. If all he wanted was a nurse for his daughter, then that's exactly what he would get! "I will help you with your daughter. I feel I owe you that much," she agreed angrily.

He spun around to face her. "You owe me nothing! If anyone is owing, it's I who owe you."

"Let us say, then," Alexandria told him, "that neither of us is owing the other. When we return home, we will each go our separate ways."

"I will ask you one question, and I expect you to answer it truthfully. Do you resent my daughter because she is half-Indian?"

"NO! How can you ask me such a thing? I think your daughter is lovely. How can I hold her parentage against her? I am not the bigot you seem to think I am."

"Why did you agree to come with me, Alexandria?" he asked.

"I don't know. I wish I hadn't," she declared through trembling lips. "I wish I had never met you, Taggart James!"

"I cannot find it within my heart to wish I had never met you, Alexandria. I can only remember the intimate times we have shared. You gave me pleasure, but I know I also fulfilled a need in you."

"I was being ungrateful just now, and I spoke without thinking. I will always be indebted to you for

444

helping me get free of Barbara and Rodney, Tag. Beyond that, don't ask anything else of me!"

"Let us just say anything you feel you owe me is canceled by what I owe you, and let it go at that. I would ask you to do me one other favor, however, if you don't find it too tiresome."

Her eyes gleamed, and she cast him a scolding glance. "You may ask. . . ." she said, throwing back her head and causing her hair to swirl out about her.

Tag caught his breath as he looked into her beautiful face and felt his heart race. The many things he had wanted to say to her tonight would now never be voiced. He had hoped that Alexandria might love him, but he saw no evidence of love in the depths of her amber-colored eyes.

"My sister and Windhawk won't understand if we don't act as a married couple. Sun Woman would be very distressed if she thought there was trouble between us. You see, she and I had a long talk today, and she wants Danielle to be brought up in a happy environment."

Alexandria began to see what he was trying to say to her. "If it is your wish, I will play your devoted wife until such time as we leave this village. It shouldn't be *too* much of a hardship on me," she replied in a heated voice, still too angry to feel hurt. "In return, all I ask is that you see I get back to Meadowlake."

"Agreed," he said, taking her arm and leading her back toward the village.

Alexandria felt tears in her eyes and fought to keep them from falling. What she really wanted to do was throw herself into Tag's arms and beg him to love her.

She had too much pride for her own good, and she knew she would never allow Tag to see how much she loved him—she prayed he would never find out about the child she carried. Knowing the kind of man he was, she realized he would insist on taking care of her should he learn of the baby.

Chapter Thirty-three

Alexandria lay on the soft blanket in Joanna and Windhawk's lodge. She felt tense and restless, unable to relax because Tag lay beside her. How strange it was to be considered his wife by everyone else when she didn't really feel like his wife at all. Even though Joanna had hung a blanket to offer her and Tag more privacy, she still felt embarrassed to be lying beside Tag.

Alexandria became more and more aware of Tag's presence. She closed her eyes tightly, wishing she could fall asleep, but knowing she couldn't.

"Alexandria, you need not feel ashamed to lie beside me. I am your husband, you know. I can assure you no one thinks anything about our sleeping together," Tag whispered near her ear. As his breath fanned her hair, Alexandria squeezed her eyes even more, willing her body to stop trembling, but it didn't help.

"Are you cold?" Tag asked, reaching out in the darkness to feel her hand.

"No . . . I . . . yes, perhaps a little."

He laughed softly. "What's a husband for if he can't keep his woman warm." Before she could object,

447

he pulled her into his arms.

Although Alexandria wore a high-necked white nightgown, she could feel the heat of Tag's body and knew he wore only a breechcloth. She feared what she would do if he continued to hold her, so she tried to move away.

"Lie still, I'm not going to bite you," he whispered, amusement in his voice. Suddenly, Tag became aware of the soft curves that seemed to fit so perfectly against his body. Her hair smelled of some sweet herb and filled his senses. Without his realizing it, his hands moved from her arm up to tangle in her hair. He heard her gasp when his lips moved over her face, seeking, and then finding her mouth.

Alexandria wanted to push him away, fearing the others would hear, but instead her lips opened beneath his probing tongue. It seemed as if an explosion erupted inside her body as he pulled her tightly against him. She could feel his swollen manhood pressed against her thigh, and she melted against him.

"Xandria, Xandria," he muttered hotly in her ear, as his hands worked her nightgown up to her waist. "I have missed this," he told her in a deep, husky voice.

"No, Tag, don't do this. The others will hear!" she protested weakly.

"They won't hear if you don't fight me," he whispered, moving his hand down her thigh, finding the core of her womanhood and massaging it with a soft, caressing motion.

By now Alexandria was past protesting when his lips dipped down to nudge her gown apart before they moved over her swollen breasts.

"Tag, please," she whispered faintly. "I don't want this. I'm not Xandria!"

"Yes, you are. You are the same woman who drove me out of my mind with her wildly enticing body. Don't turn away from me, Alexandria! Give yourself to me now, heart and soul. I want all of you."

His voice was soft and pleading, but there was also an urgency in the way he spoke. She had never seen him like this before, and she couldn't find it within her to deny him anything. If she gave him her body now, what would she have to lose?

"The others will hear," she said, in her last hope of saving herself.

"Not if you keep quiet," he smiled against her cheek. His hands knew just where to touch her to make her mindless while his lips played with her breasts, raising the tips into swollen peaks as he circled them with his tongue.

"Xandria, my love. No one has ever made me feel the way you do," he breathed against her lips.

She could feel a groan rising in her throat and clamped her lips tightly together. Could he have meant to call her his love, or had he just been overcome in a moment of passion? Suddenly Alexandria knew that he wanted more from her than she was willing to give. She didn't know what it was that he was demanding, but she felt frightened. "Tag, I cannot allow you to do this," she said softly against his ear. "Please don't!"

He was quiet for a long moment and he drew away from her. "I will take you to a place I know where we can talk. I think the time has come for you and me to speak our minds," he said, pulling her gown down and lifting her into his arms.

"Tag, what are you doing?" she asked as quietly as she could, so she wouldn't disturb the others.

He didn't reply, but merely wrapped the blanket about her and carried her around the curtained-off area that had served as their bedroom. Alexandria knew if Tag could see her face, it would be stained with color, since Windhawk and Joanna were most probably not asleep and would know what Tag had on his mind. She couldn't voice her objections, however, since it would only make the situation worse. She was grateful that at least his father was staying in Farley's tipi, sparing her *that* humiliation.

When they were outside, Tag found one of Windhawk's horses grazing nearby, and he placed Alexandria on the animal's bare back. He then climbed on behind her, and guided the animal forward.

Once they were away from the village, she turned her head to voice her objection, but he caught her lips with his and smothered her protest. Tag pulled her tightly against him, and his hands moved up and down her leg. Alexandria was no more capable of objecting than she was of speech at that moment. Her body seemed to be in torment to feel the oneness they had once shared. She didn't know where they were going nor did she care. She was vaguely aware that they were riding in the woods, but it didn't matter . . . nothing mattered but the feel of Tag's lips, and the way his hands moved sensuously across her body.

Alexandria realized that they had stopped when

Tag lifted her to the ground. When she would have moved away from him, Tag pulled her to him, holding her tightly.

"What will the others think?" was the weak protest she made.

"They won't think anything, Alexandria," he whispered raggedly. "The Indian doesn't look at love the same way a white man does. To him, it is merely a part of life, which he accepts without shame and embarrassment. You are my wife now, Alexandria. You shouldn't feel shame because I want you."

"I don't feel like your wife, Tag," she admitted.

He laced his hands through her hair and tilted her face up to him. "By the law you are my wife. No one is more married than you and I. If it would make you feel more married, we could have another ceremony. Fort Union is no more than a three-day ride from here. I'm sure we could find someone there who would join us together for a second time."

"No, I don't want that. It's hard to explain how I feel."

"Try, Alexandria. You will find me very willing to listen to you."

"Sometimes, like now, I feel the same shame I did when I came to you as Xandria," she told him, burying her face against his shoulder.

"Alexandria, you must put that out of your mind. You should never feel shame because you want to be with me. You came to me at a time in my life when I needed you. What you gave me lent me the strength and courage to do what I had to do. I needed you when you were Xandria. I drew strength from you

451

when you were Alex . . . but most of all, my little love, I need you as *Alexandria* . . . for in her, I found the perfect combination of all three."

Her head snapped up, and she studied his face in the bright moonlight. Was he admitting that he loved her? "You need me?" she asked in an uneven voice.

He laughed softly, watching the shadows from the trees play across her face. "Yes, my foolish, foolish love. I need you and only you!"

"You are not saying that just so you will have someone to look after your daughter?" she asked, still too afraid to reach out and take what he was offering her.

Tag hugged her tightly, while his body shook with laughter. "As you so aptly pointed out to me, I could easily find someone to take care of Danielle. I believe you also pointed out that I could find someone who could take the place of Xandria, but what you don't understand is that when you came to me as Xandria you got into my bloodstream by way of my heart. I cannot replace you, my love. Whatever your name is and whoever you are called, I need all of you, Alexandria."

Alexandria thought her heart would burst because it was so full of happiness, but still she was afraid to hope. Perhaps even now she had misunderstood Tag's meaning. "Are you saying you love me?" she asked in a painful whisper.

Tag lifted her up and sat down on a fallen log with her on his lap. There was no laughter in the blue eyes that looked deeply into her amber ones now. "Oh, yes, Alexandria! I am laying myself open—in case you don't feel the same about me. I am admitting that I love you . . . if you don't love me, what shall I do?"

Tears of happiness spilled down her cheeks as she threw her arms around him. "I think I have loved you since the night you came rushing into my life at the Fox and Hound Tavern! I just never thought you would return my love."

"I think the first time I realized that I loved you, Alexandria, was when you ran away. I was frantic trying to find you! You had complicated my life, and I didn't *want* to love you, but I was helpless against your charms."

"You didn't want to love me because of the way you felt about Morning Song?"

"I suppose that must be true."

"I can understand the way you felt about her. I will never try to take her place. I realize there will always be a part of you that I will have to share with her memory."

Tag rested his face against her cool cheek. "I think it's time for me to put your fears at rest, my love. What I had with Morning Song in no way compares with how I feel for you. Her ghost no longer haunts me. Because of the kind of person Morning Song was, when she was dying she set me free. When I avenged her death, it released my heart, Alexandria."

"I'm not sure I understand."

"Alexandria, I now know that what I felt for Morning Song was what one would feel for a dear friend. Her memory will always be sweet to me, but I can admit that I didn't love her with the all-consuming love that I feel for you. I think *she* always knew that we weren't right for each other. Had she lived, I would soon have realized it also."

By now, tears blinded Alexandria, and she wiped them away with the back of her hand. She had never thought she could compete with Tag's memory of his dead wife. He was telling her now that she didn't have to compete. How was it possible that he loved her?

"Alexandria, you have become my life. I don't think I could go on if you didn't love me. Walk beside me as my friend, Alex . . . stay beside me as my wife, Alexandria . . . come to my bed as my love, Xandria. I desperately need all three of you, my little wife."

Alexandria reached up and touched his face. Her heart was too full of happiness to speak. She thought of the baby she carried and knew Tag would share her happiness when he learned she was with child. "I will always walk beside you, Tag. No man has ever been loved the way I love you. I love you so much that if you wish to stay here with the Blackfoot, I will make my home here with you. I will do anything that will make you happy."

She looked at Tag's face and saw what appeared to be tears in his eyes. Surely she was mistaken—a man with Tag's strength would never cry. Her hand moved up to his cheek and touched the wetness there, and she felt the answering tears in her own eyes.

"My love," he whispered, as he crushed her in his arms. "Because of you, I am a whole man. By loving me in return, you have set me free. I am touched by your devotion, but I will not ask you to live in the Blackfoot village. We will return to Philadelphia and make our life together there."

454

"Are you quite sure, Tag?"

"Yes, although I will want to return to the Blackfoot village sometimes . . . will you come with me?"

"Yes! Oh, yes, Tag!" she cried.

He brushed the tumbled curls out of her face and smiled down at her. "You have put me through hell, and you have also led me out of my hell, Alexandria. With you, I have found the true meaning of happiness. What more can a man ask for out of life?"

"Tag, I will be a good wife to you, and a good mother to Danielle. You have my word that I will treat her as my own daughter. I will love her as much as the baby I now carry."

Tag looked at her quickly, and she saw joy spread over his face. "You are with child?"

"Yes. Do you mind?"

He bent his head and found her lips, giving her a kiss so sweet that it brought renewed tears to her eyes.

Alexandria was vaguely aware that he lifted her into his arms and laid her on the blanket. When he came to her, he lifted her nightgown over her head, and then pulled her against him. She gloried in the feel of his hard body pressed against her soft curves. He seemed in no hurry to make love to her, but was content to kiss and caress her for the moment.

As the wind rustled in the trees and a breeze cooled their overheated bodies, Tag made love to Alexandria slowly and lingeringly.

"Alexandria," he whispered against her lips, as his hands moved across her soft breasts and down over her smooth hips, pulling her closer to him. "You are the most enchanting and exciting woman I have ever

455

known."

Since the ground was hard, and he feared he would be too heavy for her, Tag rolled over and moved her on top of him, whispering her name again and again.

Alexandria could feel the raw strength of his body and she melted against him. She wondered vaguely how such a powerful man could be so gentle, and she marveled that such a strong man could have such a loving heart. No longer did Alexandria envy Morning Song, because she now held Tag as the Indian girl never had.

"I love you, Tag," she whispered, sprinkling kisses over his face.

"Always love me, Alexandria," he groaned, as he plunged deep inside of her, causing her to grab hold of his shoulders. Wave after wave of pleasure rippled through her body as he moved his hips slowly forward and back.

Alexandria felt him move forward and moaned softly. Tonight she had been handed man's greatest gift to a woman . . . Tag had given her his heart!

As Tag experienced the beautiful feelings of being united with the woman he loved, his body began to burn with a slow fire. He could feel the need deep inside building to a feverish pitch as he caressed Alexandria's silken skin. His senses were reeling as he felt the fire within him rising higher and higher. He clasped her tightly to him, murmuring her name. Her silky hair brushed against his lips, and he closed his eyes. Surely this woman had been created just for him. He wanted to explore all of her and know her mind as well as her body.

Alexandria couldn't seem to think clearly as Tag took her to dazzling heights of ecstasy. Her head seemed to be spinning as Tag thrust forward, and her body felt as if it were exploding. As Alexandria felt an answering shudder wrack Tag's body, she knew they had both reached the pinnacle of bodily fulfillment.

Slowly she became aware of the sensation that she was floating in an endless sky. Her whole being seemed to relax as Tag clutched her tightly to him.

"My love, my love," he whispered in a deeply moved voice. "I could not live if you were to take this away from me."

"Never, Tag. I will never leave you," she cried, pressing her face against his shoulder, overcome with feelings that she had never before felt. Alexandria raised her head and caught the soft look in his eyes, and a gasp escaped her lips. Never had she seen such an adoring look in anyone's eyes. The love Tag felt for her was plainly written on his face.

His hand was trembling as he touched her lips. She laid her cheek to his and felt their tears mingle. The two of them had been handed a precious gift, and they were both wise enough to realize it. While a cool breeze stirred the leaves on the tree, they held each other. There were no words spoken between them. They were content merely to touch each other and send the message of love with their eyes.

Alexandria knew she would always look back on this night as her wedding night. She would remember this time as when she and Tag had truly found each other. Her heart was filled with happiness, knowing that this strong, wonderful man loved her. No longer would she feel that Morning Song stood between them. There was nothing between them now, except the special love that would bind them to each other for as long as they both lived.

It was almost daylight when Tag carried Alexandria back to the village. Her eyes fluttered open when he laid her down on the blanket, only to drift sleepily shut again. Tag kissed her soft cheek, thinking that after so many years of seeking who he was, and where he belonged, he had found himself at last. With the help of this one small girl, he was now free. No more would he be haunted by ghosts of the past . . . no longer did anger and revenge burn within his heart. His heart was too filled with love for his amber-eyed wife.

Tag thought of the baby Alexandria carried and suddenly felt impatient to return to Philadelphia. He wanted to help his father rebuild the James empire. It was difficult for him to realize that he had been drifting in his mind for years, searching for where he really belonged. Since he had been a boy, he had not known what he wanted out of life. Tag would always cherish the years he had spent with the Blackfoot, and he knew he would miss Joanna, Windhawk, Farley, and Sun Woman when he returned to Philadelphia, but still he was anxious to get on with his life. Tomorrow he would start making arrangements for the return journey. He wanted his baby to be born in his own home and not here in the Blackfoot village.

Tag thought of Sun Woman and knew she would be hurt when he took Danielle away from her, but his daughter belonged with him. He had no doubt that

Alexandria would give her the love she needed.

Alexandria sighed in her sleep, and Tag gathered her close to him. He rested his lips against Alexandria's sweet-smelling hair as his hand drifted down to rest gently against her still firm, flat stomach, and he felt great love for his unborn child.

He closed his eyes, feeling at peace with himself.

Joanna and Windhawk walked beside the river in silent companionship. Windhawk realized that Joanna was feeling sad because her brother would soon be leaving, and he wished he could bring her comfort.

"Joanna, will it not help to think of your brother being happy? I see in him a man who knows what he wants out of life. He has a fine woman to walk beside him and make his days happy. He has told me that he will come back to see you often."

Joanna looked up at her tall husband and tried to smile. "I know what you say is true, but I cannot help but be sad. I always knew that one day Tag would leave me—I suppose I should have prepared myself for this day." She turned away to stare across the river. "Not only will I miss my brother, but it's hard to let my father go, as well. I admit it tears at my heart to know I won't see Danielle for many years. I have come to think of her as my own child."

Windhawk took her hand and turned her to face him. "When you love someone, you never have to let them go, Joanna. You can keep an image of them in your heart and the sound of their voice in your ears."

Tears moistened her eyes as she looked up at him.

Windhawk was her life. She drew strength from him as a flower draws strength from its roots. "You are very wise, my husband. I know it is as you say. You have my word that I will not cry when they leave, if you will stand beside me."

"It will do no harm if you cry with me, Joanna. I have wiped away your tears before."

She closed her eyes, feeling his presence through every pore of her skin. "Yes, you have often dried the tears of this foolish woman, Windhawk."

He drew her face up to his, this woman who was his whole world. "Do you wish you could go with them, Joanna?" he asked, almost afraid to hear her reply.

She took his hand and raised it to her face. "I will never want to leave you, Windhawk. I couldn't exist without you beside me. The two of us have proven that one can reach across the world and find love."

"The time will come, Joanna, when your world and mine will collide. Will you stand beside me when that day comes? Will you not turn back to the white world then?"

"I will always stand beside you, because your world has become mine. I am more Indian than white."

He chuckled as he lifted her into his arms. "Strange, you don't look anything like my people to me."

Joanna's laughter joined his, and she realized that Windhawk, with his vast knowledge of human nature, had erased the sadness from her heart. How she loved this man who had the wisdom to understand a woman's heart!

Joanna looked out over the land that was her home.

460

She hadn't been born into this world, but she felt like its daughter, all the same. She loved this land of Windhawk's birth, for here she had been reborn.

Yes, she would miss Tag when he left, but she could take comfort in the fact that he had found love and happiness with the small, amber-eyed Alexandria. Joanna knew if it were possible for Morning Song to look down on Tag at this moment, she, too, would rejoice in his happiness!

Chapter Thirty-four

Alexandria made her way to Sun Woman's tipi, knowing she had to face the woman for Tag's sake. She was nervous and a bit frightened as she called out to be admitted into Sun Woman's tipi. Almost immediately, the tipi flap was thrown aside, and Alexandria stood face-to-face with the formidable Indian woman, and she almost balked. She had to remind herself that she was doing this for Tag, and that seemed to give her the courage she needed. Sun Woman looked at Alexandria with dark, hostile eyes and showed no sign that she was welcome in her tipi.

Joanna had told Alexandria that she had taught Sun Woman to speak English, and she had agreed that the time had come for the two of them to reach an understanding.

"May I enter?" Alexandria asked, speaking slowly and distinctly so she could be understood.

Sun Woman merely nodded and moved aside.

"I want to talk to you about Danielle," Alexandria said, entering the darkened tipi. As her eyes slowly became accustomed to the dim light, she saw that the small tipi was neat and clean. Danielle was lying on a buffalo robe, cooing and gurgling happily. Alexandria moved across the tipi and bent down, lifting the child in her arms.

Sun Woman stood unmoving, her arms folded across her chest, giving Alexandria a defiant look.

"I want you to know that I will love your granddaughter as if she were my own. You have my word that she will never be second to any children Tag and I might have."

"Why do you tell me this?" Sun Woman said, advancing closer and looking into the strange, golden-colored eyes.

"I tell you this so your mind will be at rest. I know how much Tag loves you, and neither he nor I want to see you suffer. I understand how you feel about this child and how you will miss her. I just wanted you to know she will have a good life."

Sun Woman seemed to lose some of her hostility, and suddenly she appeared to be a tired old woman who had suffered much in her life. She sank down on the buffalo robe and motioned for Alexandria to sit beside her.

"I can see that you love Tag, and this is a good thing, since he is like a son to me. But how will I know my granddaughter is happy? How will I know if she is being taught her Indian heritage if I do not see her grow with my own eyes?"

Alexandria's eyes widened in surprise. Was Sun Woman saying she wanted to go with her and Tag to Philadelphia, or was she merely hoping they would leave the child with her? "I think you know Tag well enough to be sure he would never leave this child behind when we leave."

"This is true."

"Are you thinking . . . would you consider going with us when we leave?"

Sun Woman's eyes seemed to light up as they rested on Alexandria's face. "I am told by everyone who knows you that you are a good woman. If this is so, would you allow an old woman to live with you for a time, so she could see the daughter of her daughter settled in her new home?" Sun Woman seemed to be holding her breath, waiting for Alexandria's reaction to her request.

"I think I can speak for Tag when I say you will always be welcome in our home, but you will find everything different in the white world. Will you not miss your home and family here?"

"I have found that when one loses one of one's children, it is a very sad thing. Children are supposed to outlive their parents. I made a promise to my dead daughter that I would watch over her child for as long as I live. How can I keep that promise if you do not allow me to be with her sometimes? I will not want to stay away from my people for very long. I want only to see where you are taking my granddaughter, and the kind of home in which she will be living."

Alexandria could feel the old woman's pain as if it were her own. She placed Danielle in Sun Woman's arms and, on impulse, kissed the wrinkled, bronze cheek. "I would love to have you come with us, Sun Woman. You see, you have lost your daughter, and when I was a child, I lost my mother. Perhaps we can both help each other."

Sun Woman's eyes were shining with tears as she

looked on the face of the young girl. She hadn't wanted to like Tag's wife. She had wanted to resent her for taking her daughter's place and then taking her granddaughter from her, but she felt a tug at her heart.

"Perhaps it is so, golden-eyes. I will go with you to this white world. I will endure the loneliness and the strange ways of the white man, because I must. You are kind to consider an old woman's wishes."

Alexandria smiled. It was hard to think of Sun Woman as elderly. She was handsome of face and carried herself straight and tall. "I would like to be your friend, if you will allow it, Sun Woman."

"Being friends is a good thing. It is often that friendship turns into love. Perhaps you will allow me to stand in the place of your mother?"

"Perhaps . . . if you will allow me to stand in the place of your daughter," Alexandria agreed, watching Sun Woman's face closely.

"It is good . . . it is good," Sun Woman said softly, nodding her head.

It was a clear, crisp morning when Tag walked out of Windhawk's lodge to join Alexandria, who was saying good-bye to Joanna.

The pack horses had been loaded, and Sun Woman was already mounted on a horse, with her granddaughter, Danielle, strapped to her back.

"I will miss you, Alexandria," Joanna said, hugging her tightly. "Send me word when the baby comes."

465

"Yes, I will do that." Alexandria noticed the way Joanna's eyes kept going to Sun Woman, and she knew she was concerned about Windhawk's mother. "Joanna, I know that you are thinking Sun Woman is going into a world she doesn't understand, but you have my word, I will take care of her and make her feel welcome in our home. You know Tag will look after her."

"Please take special care of her. She is a wonderful woman and will be very loving, if you will allow her to be."

"I know she is. Try not to worry."

Joanna smiled. "I'm glad my brother has you. I find great comfort in knowing you love him."

"Tag has said we will return soon, and I confess I'm already looking forward to it."

"Don't forget to write me by way of Fort Union," Joanna reminded her. "I want to hear everything about Danielle."

Alexandria saw the tears sparkling in Joanna's eyes, and she thought how like Tag's those eyes were. She knew that it had been hard for Joanna to let Danielle go after having tended her from since birth. Finding no words to comfort Joanna, Alexandria merely nodded and kissed Joanna on the cheek. She then mounted her horse so Joanna could talk to her brother alone.

"It seems we are always saying good-bye lately, Tag," Joanna said, going into Tag's outstretched arms.

"Between you and me there is never a good-bye. I always keep a picture of you in my heart."

Joanna had promised Windhawk she wouldn't cry, but she couldn't hide the tears from Tag. "I will miss you, my brother. Take the greatest care of yourself."

They embraced, and Tag turned quickly away and mounted his horse.

Windhawk rode up beside her, and when Joanna looked into his eyes he sent her a silent message of love. Even now, he was lending her his strength to get through this ordeal.

Joanna watched until they were out of sight of the village; then she entered the lodge. Windhawk, her father, and several of his warriors were riding with them for a week, but Joanna had been surprised and delighted that her father wanted to spend the winter with her and Windhawk. She knew she would miss Sun Woman, but they would see each other before too long.

The loneliness seemed to be closing in about her, until she heard a dear, beloved voice call out.

"Joanna, you wanna talk?"

She turned around and smiled at Farley. "Yes, my friend, I need to talk."

The old man sat down cross-legged and grinned broadly. "I 'spect Windhawk and your pa will be home afore you have time to miss um."

Joanna began folding freshly washed baby clothes and placing them in a basket. "I suppose you are right, Farley."

"You know, I been thinking . . . how would you like to go for a ride today? I figger White Dove wouldn't mind keeping an eye on the younguns for you."

"I think that's an excellent idea, Farley," she answered, knowing the dear old man was trying to distract her from her sadness.

As Joanna and Farley rode across the river, she could feel the warm breeze stirring her red-gold hair, and her heart became lighter. She was grateful for many things. She had a kind, loving husband, two wonderful children, a family that loved her, and friends like Farley. Suddenly, it was as if her heart were singing with joy. Joanna lifted her face to the heavens and silently thanked God for blessing her life!

As Tag rode beside Windhawk and his father, he felt momentary sadness in his heart. He had lived with the Blackfoot since he had been twelve years old. No one had touched his life in quite the same way Windhawk had, not even his own father. Farley had become such a part of his life that it had been very difficult to say good-bye to the old trapper. Most of all, he would miss Joanna. In the past she had always been his port in the storm. He was a man now though, and he must not think about the past.

Tag turned and looked behind him, catching Alexandria's eye. He was reassured by the understanding reflected in her golden glance. He was closing one chapter of his life and entering into another. The past would always occupy a small corner of his life, but it was the future that beckoned to him now. He was no longer that lost twelve-year-old boy, but a man who knew where he was going and how to get there. With

Alexandria by his side, there was nothing he couldn't accomplish!

Tag nudged his horse on to a faster pace, anxious to get home. After so many years of searching within himself, he now knew where he belonged. He would build a good life for Alexandria and the children.

He slowed his horse and dropped back to ride beside Alexandria. Up until now, there hadn't been much of a chance for them to be alone. When he smiled at his tiny golden-eyed wife his eyes spoke of many wonderful things to come.

Epilogue

Valley Forge, Pennsylvania

Tag walked in the twilight, allowing his gaze to wander over the hills and valleys of Meadowlake farm. The air was cold and crisp, and he thought it might snow before morning.

They had been staying at Meadowlake for the last three months, while the house in Philadelphia was being redecorated. Last night Alexandria had given birth to his baby, and Tag was bursting with pride over his new son.

Hearing footsteps behind him, he turned to see Sun Woman approach. "It will snow before morning," she said, coming up beside him.

"I was just thinking the same thing myself. Are the children settled for the night?" Tag couldn't get over the sight of Sun Woman dressed in the white woman's clothing. She wore a green print skirt and a white blouse. The only things Alexandria couldn't convince her to part with were her moccasins. She stubbornly argued that the leather shoes Alexandria had given her pinched her toes.

"Yes, my son, and Alexandria is resting, as well."

"Are you happy here, Sun Woman?" Tag asked softly.

"I am not unhappy, even though many of the ways are new to me. I like many of the white man's comforts, such as the soft beds and the padded chairs. As soon as the cold season passes, I will return to my village."

"I'm glad you came with us, my mother, and I know Alexandria shares my feelings. I also know you must leave when spring comes. You will be missed when you go."

"It is good here on this farm, but I do not like it in that place you call a town. I will miss many things when I return home. You, my son, have granted me peace of mind. I can leave knowing my granddaughter has a good life."

"Are you sure you want to return to the Blackfoot village? You will always be welcome here with us."

"Yes, I am sure. I would like to think of my granddaughter being here at Meadowlake. I do not like to think of her in that big town."

Tag laughed. "Alexandria shares your views on Philadelphia. I have a feeling this will become our permanent home."

"I have come to love your golden-eyed wife. She is good to you and my granddaughter. When I do leave, I will know that all is well with you and Danielle."

Tag kissed Sun Woman on the cheek and walked toward the farmhouse. Living in the white world had been a hard adjustment for Morning Song's mother to make, but she was a strong, stubborn woman, and when she made her mind up about something, she usually obtained her goal. Next spring they would all return to the Blackfoot village, and then his father would come back to Philadelphia with them. Perhaps he could even convince Farley to come back, if he assured him he could stay at Meadowlake.

When Tag entered the house, he climbed the stairs quietly. Entering his bedroom, he tiptoed over to the bed, thinking Alexandria was sleeping. Her mink-colored hair was fanned out on the pillow, and she looked so beautiful he felt his heart swell. Her eyelashes fluttered open, and he looked into her golden eyes.

"How do you feel?" he asked, kneeling down beside her.

"I feel wonderful. How is our son?"

"He is sleeping."

"How is Danielle? You don't think she will be jealous of the new baby, do you?"

"I have it on good authority that she is delighted with her new baby brother."

"Don't forget to pay special attention to her. I wouldn't want her to think she has been replaced."

Tag smiled and kissed Alexandria's cheek. "You are a wonderful mother to both our children. It isn't likely that either one of them will suffer from lack of love."

Alexandria smiled weakly, and her eyes drifted shut again. She was just too weary to stay awake.

Tag rose and crossed the room quietly, standing for a moment to look down at his sleeping son. The baby's hair was golden in color, in startling contrast to his sister, whose hair was black as midnight.

Tag left the room and a moment later entered his daughter's nursery. How angelic Danielle looked, with her dark hair spilled over the white pillowcase. She was a lovely child, and she had such a happy disposition.

As if the child sensed her father's presence, her eyes opened, and she favored him with a smile. He knelt down beside her and gathered her close to him.

"Baby?" she questioned in her childlike language.

"Your baby brother's sleeping, just like you should be."

Danielle put her chubby arms about her father's neck and laid her face against his. "Mama?" she asked sleepily.

"Your mama is sleeping. You can see her tomorrow. Close your eyes and sleep," he said, kissing her smooth cheek.

As Tag held his sleeping daughter in his arms, he was overcome with many emotions. He wanted her life to be filled with happiness.

He touched her silken hair and felt a lump in his throat. Her skin took on a soft golden glow in the dimly lit room, and Tag knew she would always look different from the other children in the neighborhood, because her mother had been an Indian.

He realized the time would come when Danielle would have to face who she was, but not for a long while. He knew how cruel the white world could be to those who were the least bit different from them.

In that moment, he decided that Danielle would be educated in only the finest schools, where she would be taught to be a lady. He would lavish money on her clothing and lift her so high that no one would dare look down on her. He would arm her against whatever came, hoping to give her confidence and pride in both her white and Indian heritage.

Until the day when Danielle had to deal with who she was, he and Alexandria would protect her from as much hurt as they could.

Tag blew out the lamp and moved silently across the room to the door, closing it softly behind him.

Danielle sighed in her sleep, not knowing of the concern her father had for her future. She was past her first birthday and had never known anything but love in her life. She was too young to know that one day her strength and courage would be tested—that one day she would have to stand with her feet in both the white and the Indian worlds!

Blackfoot Territory

Many miles away from Valley Forge, in the Blackfoot village, there dwelt another half-Indian, half-white baby girl.

It was early evening. Joanna held her sleeping daughter in her arms, wondering what the future held for her child.

The child was fair of skin and looked enough like Danielle to be her twin sister.

Joanna couldn't help being concerned about her daughter, since she looked more white than Indian. When Sky Dancer had been born, her eyes had been a nondescript color, but now that she was older they were a bright violet-blue, like her mother's.

Joanna didn't worry about her son, Little Hawk—he was a small replica of his father and looked every bit an Indian. He would be groomed to take his father's place one day.

Sky Dancer smiled in her sleep, and Joanna remembered her mother's once telling her that when a baby smiled in its sleep, it was seeing angels. She pushed the ebony hair away from her daughter's face and hugged her tightly.

After much discussion, Windhawk had agreed to allow Sky Dancer to go to Philadelphia when she was older. She would stay with Tag and Alexandria and be educated in the ways of a proper young lady. Joanna wanted her to know both the white and the Indian world.

Joanna hadn't noticed that Windhawk had come up behind her. She watched as Sky Dancer slowly opened her eyes and smiled. Windhawk lifted his daughter into his arms and she giggled with delight. When he looked into Sky Dancer's eyes he couldn't help but smile. His heart seemed to contract when she threw her arms about his neck and kissed him on the cheek.

Little Hawk ran up to his father and grabbed him around the legs. Windhawk bent down and lifted his son in his arms, as well.

They left the lodge for a walk by the river. The sun was going down, painting the countryside with a soft, rosy hue.

Joanna glanced across the Milk River and sighed contentedly. She had never imagined it was possible to attain such complete happiness. She often missed Tag and Danielle, but they would be coming to visit before long. She felt Windhawk's eyes on her and glanced at him. His eyes spoke of the deep love he had for her, and she leaned her head against his shoulder.

Life was good here in Blackfoot country. With

Windhawk beside her, she would teach their children the important things in life.

Joanna's son held his arms out to her, and she lifted the child into her arms.

As the first stars twinkled in the ebony sky, Windhawk and Joanna walked back toward their lodge. Their love was so strong, it had reached across the gap that had separated their two worlds. Joanna had no desire to ever leave this land. She would be content to remain beside her tall, dark husband until the end of time!

CAPTIVATING ROMANCE FROM ZEBRA

MIDNIGHT DESIRE   (1573, $3.50)
by Linda Benjamin

Looking into the handsome gunslinger's blazing blue eyes, innocent Kate felt dizzy. His husky voice, so warm and inviting, sent a river of fire cascading through her flesh. But she knew she'd never willingly give her heart to the arrogant rogue!

PASSION'S GAMBLE   (1477, $3.50)
by Linda Benjamin

Jade-eyed Jessica was too shocked to protest when the riverboat cardsharp offered *her* as the stakes in a poker game. Then she met the smouldering glance of his opponent as he stared at her satiny cheeks and the tantalizing fullness of her bodice—and she found herself hoping he would hold the winning hand!

FORBIDDEN FIRES   (1295, $3.50)
by Bobbi Smith

When Ellyn Douglas rescued the handsome Union officer from the raging river, she had no choice but to surrender to the sensuous stranger as he pulled her against his hard muscular body. Forgetting they were enemies in a senseless war, they were destined to share a life of unbridled ecstasy and glorious love!

WANTON SPLENDOR   (1461, $3.50)
by Bobbi Smith

Kathleen had every intention of keeping her distance from Christopher Fletcher. But in the midst of a devastating hurricane, she crept into his arms. As she felt the heat of his lean body pressed against hers, she wondered breathlessly what it would be like to kiss those cynical lips—to turn that cool arrogance to fiery passion!

Available wherever paperbacks are sold, or order direct from the Publisher. Send cover price plus 50¢ per copy for mailing and handling to Zebra Books, Dept. 1715, 475 Park Avenue South, New York, N.Y. 10016. DO NOT SEND CASH.